CAFÉ CÉLESTE

Françoise Mallet-Joris

CAFÉ CÉLESTE

TRANSLATED FROM THE FRENCH BY
Herma Briffault

FARRAR, STRAUS AND CUDAHY

NEW YORK

Part I: SPRING

MARTINE had asked more than once to be transferred to another department. She would have liked to be in Stationery or Haberdashery, perhaps. But all they offered her by way of exchange was Ladies' Wear. And that, no, she would not accept, for it would mean having to contend with those dreadful females, smelly and corpulent, impudently trying to get on the good side of the shop-assistant by appealing to her feelings and humanity. "I want your advice; do tell me how I look in this frock?" Rather than be obliged to answer such questions, Martine preferred to remain in Foods. But it was quite a trial to have to watch them prodding the Camembert, sniffing the fruit, exhibiting their indecent appetites—or rather, their gluttony. It made her quite sick, every day.

A far cry, this, from the work she had dreamed of doing! She had always fancied herself in an office doing some kind of clean, neat, impersonal work, handling nothing but papers, expressing herself only in administrative formulas, knowing people only through their classifications in the files. The bankruptcy of her father had ended all her dreams. He had been a chemist in the rue de Rennes and, having unsuccessfully tried to cheat the tax-collector, he had died of shame—whether over his dishonesty or his lack of skill was never quite clear. Very soon at odds with her mother, Martine, although she had a small settled income of her own, had wanted to earn her living. Well, she was earning it, but in what a way! She who would have liked to shut herself off behind a glass panel from everything, avoiding all human contacts, she who could not endure the spectacle of the streets, a picture show, the noise of the radio, now found herself in the very centre of this offensive crowd, packed into it and unable to forget it for a moment.

Articles of clothing, of multicoloured plastics, cheap jewellery, soaps odorous with synthetic scents, variegated shampoos swelling transparent little bladders that looked like delicately coloured small balloons, boots smelling of cheap leather or hot rubber, enormous piles of "Special Bargain" sweet biscuits, women's "Latest Novelty" underwear ornamented with pastel ribbons: none of humanity's most vulgar desires was left unsatisfied in this so-called one-price store, the Prisunic, to which swarmed that humanity Martine so detested. From the minute the doors opened in the mornings, the various departments became crowded with customers, mostly women, all of them taking their time, visibly enjoying a moment of luxury and relaxation, their eyes devouring forms and colours, rapturously examining the merchandise, discussing prices, bragging about their children's appetites, their husbands' tastes, their boy-friends' preferences, and all of them, even the smug, level-headed old women with humble shopping bags, were burdened with cares, preoccupations, and even sorrows, but burdened as if by a wealth they flaunted with ostentation, or so it seemed to Martine.

And Fate, with supreme mockery, pinned her there in the centre of a world of which she could never be a part, of which, she told herself, she did not want to be a part, and, adding insult to injury, Fate had assigned her to the food department. She was a captive here beneath the pitiless tubes of fluorescent light, behind this counter brimming with the provender of earth and its smells. It was hell. There were days when it almost seemed to her that these edibles had faces, faces which she loathed, each in a special way. She hated those fat red Dutch cheeses for their roundness, their insolent weight; the pale cream, unctuous and sweetish, which she had to spoon into cartons; the milk which still had the very smell of the cow from which it had come, and her stomach turned when she thought of those smelly udders, and the cow's bristling hairs; she hated the Gruyère, sharp, sourish, that she had to slice; she more than hated the Camemberts, stinking as flagrantly as old tramps and still bearing the imprint of the thumbs that had prodded them.

Thank God, Claudette took charge of the dairy products section half the time, leaving to Martine the fruit, the inoffensive tinned goods, the cellophane-wrapped vegetables ready for the stew; but also there was the meat counter, with those red triangles streaked with yellow fat and garnished with sprigs of parsley, not to mention the pasties and sausages redolent of garlic. And even the preserves, harmless enough in appearance, had a way of turning into something revoltingly palpable, cloying and sticky, when a housewife hesitated too long over them. "No more blackcurrant syrup? What a shame! You can't think how fond my husband is of it! And you should see my youngsters lick it off their fingers! Even the littlest one. . . ."

Martine looked away, gazing with feigned indifference at the other departments, the children's red and green pinafores, the brown imitation-leather suitcases, and when all else failed, the big square clock on the wall. And the customer would move away, shrugging with a disdain that hurt her, despite everything. Oh, those stupid, ill-dressed, ill-fed women, crammed with cheap literature and meat, subsisting on the cheap cuts of life, and satisfied with their lot! But it was not so much their poverty that she detested (although these families were, Heaven knows, unattractive enough, all of them eating the same tinned foods, the same selected cheap quality meat, all of them wearing the same checked jumpers splitting at the seams, the same loud coloured jerseys which were no protection from the cold), it was not their poverty that she held against them, but their vulgar and violent zest for life that persisted in spite of everything.

"Poverty is a virtue in itself," Stéphane was always saying, "we ought to thank Heaven that we live in a poor neighbourhood, in the midst of the poor, my dear Martine." But Stéphane, sitting at the piano on the orchestra stand at the Brasserie Dorée, could have no idea what it was like. Anyway, as Martine sometimes remarked, he had a positive talent for not knowing what was going on around him. "Work", "poverty"—he had a gift for talking about these things as venerable abstractions, as concepts, as rules of life. And of course he was right, she always thought so when she was with him. But when she was again here behind her counter, she told herself that this poverty had no relation to the austere and self-abstaining poverty he talked about. On the contrary. What exasperated

Martine was the appetite of these people—ever since she was in Foods she could only think in terms of food. That they could afford only the poorest substitutes for food, clothing, reading matter, and yet could pounce upon them so voraciously! The rush of the housewives in the morning, their excitement over managing to snap up the freshest meat, the quickest selling bargain! The Saturday rush of undernourished and over-painted girls, hurrying from their factories and offices to spend their money on gimcrack jewellery! And even the prostitutes were there, choosing a scent, yes, with sudden gravity, or pressing a chipped red lacquered thumbnail into the cheese!

It was because they weren't poor enough, thought Martine, in a kind of rage, they were still not poor enough to be rid of this aggressive zest for living. But who was poor enough? Even the tramps on the quays sucking at their bottles seemed to be endowed, all of them, with what she did not have. Why? What was it that separated her from them? Was it her plainness, or the modicum of sanity she believed she had and which she would gladly have done without? She did not know and did not care to know. For years she had prided herself on possessing nothing, on being not only the plainest of all but also the worst dressed, the most ill-tempered, the least attractive woman in the world.

But she had Stéphane, now. Just when, perhaps, she was on the point of losing her mind in her glacial isolation, she had met Stéphane. At last she possessed something. And slowly, very slowly, that hard and fearful solitude was perhaps beginning to melt, although she was not conscious of it yet.

At the sound of the gong, she untied her apron and with a firm step went towards the cloakroom.

"Mademoiselle! I say, My biscuits!" implored a lady with an armload of parcels. Without a word, Martine stretched out her hand, pointing at the clock.

"But I've been asking for them for the last five minutes!" the lady persisted. Martine disappeared into the cloakroom without a backward glance. She gave her hair a touch with the comb, then unbuttoned her white overall. Her figure was tiny, thin, flat-chested, as devoid of charm, as weak and sickly-looking as her pale, frowning little face with its long, thin nose, and the grey eyes that were usually squinting as if in an effort to see more clearly. She buttoned her coat with the same precise gesture she had used to unbutton the overall, and went out into the street.

This was another thing she detested: this narrow and colourful street that was always congested. She detested everything in it, the passers-by, the costermongers' carts, the prostitutes, the neon lights, the shops and cafés. In this tumult, beneath these lights, hemmed in by this crowd, she walked alone, taking quick little steps, holding herself very stiffly, feeling conspicuous and scorned. The shop windows showed her what she looked like as she passed, a girl with a thin neck and a pale little face above a coat that was much too big. What a mistake that coat was! "It shows you off to advantage," the shop assistant in the rue de la Gaïté had said with a treacherous smile. And she had let herself be trapped into buying it, just like those stupid women who were trapped into buying their clothes at the chain stores. Alice, who was in Millinery, put on a good imitation in the evenings, after work. "Oh, Madam, that hat's absolutely you! It's rather Spanish. . . ."

Yes, she'd let herself be trapped. Martine repeated the words several times, pressing the wound to make it bleed. Secretly she had hoped, no doubt, that Stéphane would remark, as the assistant had said, that the coat showed her off to advantage! She'd had what was coming to her: he hadn't even noticed that she had a new coat. Of course, he never paid attention to such things. If he did, would he bother with her? At any rate it certainly proved that he did not notice her plainness. . . . She walked faster, turned the corner of the boulevard, hurried towards the big café-restaurant, the Brasserie Dorée, and the appeasement that she was beginning urgently to need.

The restaurant was quiet, for it was still no more than six o'clock. At the far end of the room, a weary looking family group surrounded by staved-in suitcases sat on the banquette against the wall on which some pictures were hung—some wretched purple nudes the manager had bought up cheap. Here and there a few buxom matrons sat drinking tea or chocolate, their elbows on the bare wooden tables, half hidden behind bouquets of artificial flowers— the Brasserie Dorée had made no attempt to modernize itself in half a century. Among those women customers one often saw some of the shopkeepers of the quarter (today, there was Stéphane's dairywoman, "Madame La Crémière", as he always called her; she often came to gaze upon Stéphane); in the past eight years he had acquired some renown in the rue d'Odessa. Martine took no offence: it was so unlike the real Stéphane, the one she knew. That he should be the idol of his milk-dealer, that she herself should stand behind a counter of the Prisunic—they had been brought together, she reflected, by such ironies of Fate.

She sat down directly facing the orchestra platform, which was covered with worn red carpeting. She, who never set foot in other cafés, always feeling that she was being noticed and stared at, felt no embarrassment here in the Brasserie Dorée. Here, she had the comfortable feeling that Stéphane's presence, his handsome profile as he sat there at the piano, protected her, in some mysterious way. And she particularly liked to arrive too soon, so she could gaze upon him unawares. When they were together, she never dared to look at him as much as she liked. His hair that was still dark and thick, the ironic lines at the sides of his mouth, his full lips, his chin, a proud chin she thought it, his wide, light blue eyes fringed with long dark lashes, everything that remained intact in this forty-six-year-old man who had once been a paragon of masculine beauty, fascinated and at the same time frightened her. And to reassure herself she had to think of his age, of the wrinkles, of the secret sorrows, and even of that fatigue which sometimes made him, short of breath, lean upon her for support.

The three-piece orchestra was finishing a number, and the evening customers were beginning to arrive, a different species from the afternoon crowd. The women who came here in the evenings were younger, wore more make-up, and were accompanied by male escorts, lovers or husbands. Besides these couples, there were the usual travellers with suitcases at their feet and sandwiches in front of them. Within an hour the café would be full, the dinner tables would be laid, and the Morani Trio would step down to make way for the "regional orchestra" and the "special entertainers" who justified the management in doubling the prices of drinks. The manager was strolling about: a big man, sad and pale, of uncertain nationality, but whose big, vague eyes that now looked as if swimming in a yellow liquid, had given him an exotic aspect in his youth when the Brasserie Dorée was a place of splendour.

There was a brief silence and some faint applause.

"Oh, if only we played on into the evening!" muttered Bruno, ritually depositing his violin upon the piano.

"Let's play the *White Horse Inn* selection," murmured Stéphane, cracking his knuckles. "Hullo! There's Martine."

From afar, he honoured her with a slightly ironic smile.

"What are we playing?" asked Marcel, leaning forward.

"*White Horse Inn.*"

"Oh! Good."

Marcel played the 'cello or the guitar indifferently; Bruno played the violin or sang or shook the maracas, with the resignation of a café musician who knows that any day he may have to change his job. But Marcel was not resigned. This was the last year he intended to go on playing in this dingy old-fashioned place where the pay was bad. He wouldn't have kept on here this long if his wife hadn't been pregnant, for he was worth more than this. A café-restaurant musician! Good enough for the other two, who couldn't hope at their age to find anything better.

"Ready? Go."

And off they went, lackadaisically. No one listened to them, anyhow. There had always been an orchestra playing in the afternoon which no one listened to, except the rapturous old ladies in the first row.

"The usual beer, Mademoiselle?" asked Toni, the waitress, with a knowing smile. She would soon go off duty: her day also ended at seven o'clock. She liked to show Martine that she recognized her, knew who she was, why she was there.

"Yes, please," said Martine frostily.

To be treated like one of those stout females up there drooling with sentimentality! To be in a class with "Madame La Crémière"! When Stéphane went to get his quart of milk, the woman told him, "I'll come early so I can have you all to myself," and he was even able to laugh at this!

"One beer, one," sang out the waitress.

A big-bosomed girl, she slept with the manager, but she, too, admired Stéphane, and to spite Martine, she sidled up to the piano.

"How about a cup of coffee?" she suggested to Stéphane.

"No thanks, I'll soon be finished. . . ."

Wagging her hips, she drifted off, mourning over him. "Such a handsome man to go out with that little fright!" The manager wasn't handsome either, but she didn't mind.

At last, Martine noted with relief, the Morani Trio was standing up, taking their bows. Two or three women, at Stéphane's feet, were applauding with all their might, and he went on smiling. "Always those smiles! For Toni, for those old bags. . . ." Bitterness welled up in her, but it vanished as he came towards her between the tables, bowing to left and right, tall, slender, the man who confided his secret thoughts to her alone.

He sat down facing her and she immediately saw how tired he was. He was panting slightly, seemed depressed, and for a minute his fine long hand rested on her hand as he remained silent, his eyes half-closed. How defenceless he was! she thought, with a pang of joy. How exhausted, how disarmed! How much he belonged to her! But he opened his eyes all too quickly and began to laugh.

"Well, how was I today? Quite in the mood, the spirit? Good old *White Horse Inn*! That arrangement is my own, you know: an arrangement for cheap orchestras. Did you see how I clowned it, gave it gipsy rhythm? And how they loved it? Especially the three fat little women in the front row. Post-office clerks, I bet. The kind you read about in the little classified advertisements: 'Respectable forty-year-old woman desires to get in touch with, etcetera . . . object, matrimony!' They go into raptures, they coo like pigeons, it's extraordinary how popular I am with middle-aged women! I wouldn't be surprised if one of these days they climbed right up on the stand and raped me!"

Beneath his apparent irony one could detect a real gaiety. Secretly
flattered, perhaps. His smile was absolutely charming. But, feeling
Martine's gaze upon him, he hurriedly recovered himself, and spoke
with a sudden gravity that instantly transformed his face—his high
forehead and aquiline profile predisposed it to noble expressions; he
would have made a good tragic actor, playing the rôle of the
"confidant", a Horatio to Hamlet.

"I see you don't understand me, my dear. Do you really think
I'm content with my lot, elated over this kind of third-rate success?
By the way, did you know they're increasing my salary this year?
My poor dear Martine! If you could only imagine what this kind of
success represents for a musician. . . ."

The lines of bitterness instantly deepened at each side of his
beautiful and sensual mouth. In that still handsome face this immedi-
ate correspondence of expression with the spoken word, this
exaggerated miming, was rather embarrassing. He was like a silent
film actor who, having normally to make himself understood without words, finds it difficult to use both forms of expression simultaneously. Stéphane hummed two or three bars; some women
turned round to look, recognized him, and smiled ingratiatingly.

"There!" he went on, the bitter smile persisting, but less forced.
"Do you see? One or two notes, and their powder-base cracks!
How bored they must be!"

He was speaking exuberantly, amused. But a shortness of breath
made him pause and dissipated the slight annoyance Martine always
felt at seeing him in a gay mood.

"Oh, poor Stéphane!" she said, with all the sweetness there was
in her. "Tired?"

"Worn out," he confessed, without miming the words this time.
"I can manage the first two hours, but by the end of the afternoon . . ."

"You ought to stop work for a few days, take a rest."

"If I stopped, I'd never begin again."

The only feeling he ever had which he could not manage in
the least to dramatize was his feeling of fatigue and physical exhaustion. For a moment his face, involuntarily contracted, was pitiable

without any effort on his part. Then he shrugged, flashed her a designedly Satanic smile, and again his face was that of an actor in the silent films.

"To die while playing *Si tu m'aimais*. . . . ! Can you imagine that? Can you imagine what solitude, what . . ."

"But you are not alone, Stéphane!"

Her pity for him surged back upon her, a warm and revivifying flood. Without her, how lost he would be! She laid her thin, grasping little hand upon Stéphane's.

"No, my dear, no. You're quite right, I'm too ungrateful. Destiny, no, I should say Providence, placed you in my path. . . ."

Providence was perhaps a very big word to bestow upon Madame Prêtre, the concierge of the block of co-operative flats where Stéphane and his wife, Louise lived. It was Madame Prêtre who had recommended Martine to the Moranis, as just the person for the maid's room that they wanted to sell. And to tell the truth, when Stéphane had first interviewed this thin and wretched creature who spoke with ridiculous pomposity of the "small capital" left her by her father and of how she wanted to "place" it, he had not immediately recognized her as one chosen by Providence. He had left to Madame Prêtre, who liked to put her nose into everything, and to Monsieur Ducas, the agent for the tenant-owners of the building, the business of settling all the formalities.

He clearly recalled (despite his efforts to banish it from his memory) the conversation he had had with Louise on the subject. "The girl who has taken the maid's room is no recruit for your music-hall," he had told his wife, and she had replied, "If she'd been that type, I hate to think what you'd have done with her, after the way you let that poor little Sylvia who's in love with you drift away without lifting a finger. . . ." He had ended the conversation with: "I abominate this sort of silly talk, Louise." Anyway, he had been wrong to drop the attitude of reserve he generally maintained with his wife. In every respect he had been wrong, as was proved by the intelligence and understanding shown him by this girl whom he called, in his intimate diary, "my little Antigone."

Martine disclaimed the compliment with a modest wave of the

hand. "You exaggerate, Stéphane. You have friends. Think of those Monday reunions. . . ."

"Merely business meetings, my dear. It's true I somehow managed to transform them into a kind of literary circle, small and unpretentious. Besides, the other co-ops of the building are delightful people. . . . But a world away from the deep understanding you have shown me, a world away."

Oh, what marvellous peace after her horrible day! And it was always like this. She left the inferno to enter a miraculous world in which she almost could not believe. She was needed. He needed her. But for the pleasure of it, she continued to protest a little.

"You have . . . your wife. . . ."

"And you know what she is, Martine! Yet even you cannot imagine. . . . You are by nature so refined and discriminating, you would instinctively rebel against trying to understand such crudity and coarseness. Just let me give you one example in a thousand. Last night I had difficulty in breathing, and coughed a little. Well, she said to me placidly, yes, placidly, 'You're coughing. That means it's going to rain tomorrow.' What do you say to that? Almost too good to be true, isn't it? And this morning . . ."

She knew how to listen. He had an almost feminine urge to confide in someone, an urge he had never dared to satisfy, secretly afraid of being judged, and with her he unburdened himself. Martine's plainness and lack of charm were his guarantee: she had too much to fear from his judgement ever to become dangerous.

Wildly applauded, the "regional orchestra"—whether Hungarian or Mexican, one was not quite sure—were climbing on to the platform. They were at any rate glittering, lavished with lace at the sleeves, with hybrid head-pieces, half sombrero, half panama, and flashing very white teeth in wide smiles. One of the instrumentalists quickly took down the sign reading "Morani Trio" and carried it to the alcove at the rear which served as a dressing-room.

"You're staying on, Monsieur Morani?" a waiter came to enquire.

The price of drinks doubled with the changing of the orchestras. Stéphane hesitated a second.

"Yes. And bring me a pint. Put it on my account," he managed to add.

It was a useless expense, but fortunately he did have a small sum of money set aside to take care of such impulses. He had not told Louise about his raise.

"Stéphane, I don't want . . ." Martine began.

He raised an imperious hand.

"Martine, let me have the momentary illusion of being a free man, a man who has the right to offer himself a drink before going home, without expecting harsh reproaches . . . a man who, upon his return will find a calm solitude rather than a disrupted home. My dear, these occasions when you and I can be together are oases in our desert. This pure friendship is our refuge. Let us preserve our meetings from anything mean and niggardly. . . ."

The waiter brought the beer.

"I'll put it down," he said, taking a small account-book out of his pocket. "That will be four hundred and thirty, without the tip. Or do I count in the tip?"

"No, no," said Martine, taking the money from her handbag.

Stéphane let her have her way.

"Oh! Without you . . .," he sighed, returning to his grievances.

His face marvellously depicted, by a compression of the lips, his contained emotion; but his handsome light eyes, expressionless as the eyes of a bird, were fixed upon a point well beyond Martine, an invisible point in space.

The rue d'Odessa is a very important thoroughfare, according to those who live in this little corner of Montparnasse. Carefree and gay, vividly coloured with its countless shops that jostle each other in the limited space, the street contains a certain number of sombre retreats, oases of calm and obscurity in the midst of the glitter of modern life which flaunts around them its bright plastic wares, the insolence of its Prisunic store, its drapers' shops, bristling with cotton goods fluttering in the wind like multicoloured and mirthful hanged men, its sumptuous pork-butchers' shops protected from the covetous gaze of the passers-by only by a pane of glass. These dim oases are the cafés that are stamped with the mysterious charm of railway station waiting-rooms—the Montparnasse Station is nearby—and with the antiquated splendours of a glorious past. In the cafés of the rue d'Odessa still reigns the pallid palm tree and the bevelled mirror; installed on the banquettes against the wall are commercial travellers, that most respectable of all human species, and amiable prostitutes, likewise rather obsolete, who pose, in their spare time, for art classes at the Grande Chaumière and talk about Art, still hoping to discover (wandering on the boulevard) some unknown genius who will immortalize them. They talk a great deal about art in these sombre retreats. Merely by frequenting them, our commercial travellers acquire more polish and the prostitutes a greater consciousness of their dignity.

There is no question, in the rue d'Odessa, of bohemianism or drunkenness: Art presides, and Commerce. The cafés where the prostitutes principally hang out are frequented by a few aspiring commercial travellers; the cafés which the commercial travellers use as their headquarters are frequented by a few practical-minded prostitutes. Sometimes Art and Commerce join forces, combining their savings. Then, in their turn, they open a café where the élite of another generation will quench their thirst. In this region between the yellow arrow of the Dupont Café and the flimsy shelters of the covered market upon which the rue d'Odessa emerges, between the glittering Prisunic, Temple of Commerce, and that Temple of Art, the deep and secret music-hall, the haunt of houris, this moral tale has been more than once enacted.

If you reach the end of this attractive little side-street without being seized by one temptation or another—from the simplest, that flashy finery set out in the open air at prices defying competition, to the highest, that studio of André Lhote tucked away among the crowding, respectable, and infinitely humble commercial enterprises; if you can hold out against the neon lights that glare and dazzle and reverberate like electric pin-ball machines, and have a tendency to shoot you out upon the boulevard where you find yourself wearing a purple necktie adorned with the Eiffel Tower (and this inevitably happens if you are a native of Brittany freshly arrived in Paris); if you resist the temptations along the way, the chlorotic palm trees glimpsed in the entrances to the little rooming-houses where the water is always cold, the beds narrow, the counterpanes torn, the knees skinny and the love-making brief; if you are not sucked in by one of those dim and chilly cafés where the customers (and it seems to be the rule that one of them has a wooden leg) are still playing a game of cards begun February 3rd, 1945, and if you avoid that store, the Prisunic, which is to your left as you go towards the Boulevard Edgar-Quinet; if you flee the music-hall (the *Folies-Montparnasse*) to your right, and after that the Turkish baths, with its brass dolphins and jet of water, if you have neither slowed down not hastened your pace, if your eye remains alert and your brain cool on this journey from the Gare Montparnasse to the covered market of the Boulevard Edgar-Quinet, you will finally notice on your left at the end of the street a three-storey building (five if you count the entresol and the attic floor where the servants' rooms are located), which was once, before being converted into co-operative flats, an hotel.

On the ground floor there are still traces of dark-red paint. To the left is a dark hole of a room where a chromium bar glistens. To the right is a carriage-entrance which must have been imposing before the side was cut back to widen the pavement. The two are joined by a kind of beam, roughly nailed in place and also painted dark red, which bears the words: CAFÉ CÉLESTE. A placard, lying askew in the café window, corrects this vaguely Oriental impression: *Cuisine Grec*. But even if this notice, which catches the eye as much by its spelling as by its implications, should lure you into the cool, dim little room you will find no trace of the Parthenon, of Ulysses or of the Delphic Oracle of which, defying the spelling, you had come in search. The walls are not terra cotta after all, but a kind of Chinese red, and are adorned with a frieze of rotund mandarins. Beneath them hangs a calendar that at once attracts attention: a veritable work of art—the perishable part can be replaced, thus making it a perpetual calendar—it bears the picture of a young girl of indisputably Oriental features, holding a bunch of water-lilies (some customers claim the flower is a lotus, but do lotuses grow in China?).

The words COCO-COLA, in marvellously contorted script, in no way dims the charm of that smiling face. Some goldfish, indubitably Chinese, preside in a greenish aquarium at the far end of the room, and above them, perhaps as a concession to the Occident, is hung a canvas on which four silver triangles gleam against a blue background: the people of the quarter, well acquainted with it, will inform you that it is an abstract painting. Finally, set in a niche above the bar, a gilded statue of a god whose name nobody knows, writhes its arms and legs in a dance that is more Hindu than Chinese —but can one ever be sure? In any case, the god is not Greek.

The only vestiges of that noble civilization to be found here are the food prepared in the restaurant kitchen and the lofty name of the proprietor: Socrates. But even the cooking, after long contact with France—and even Socrates himself—are hardly Greek for Socrates inherited this restaurant from an uncle who was a Turk. A Turk! exclaim all the Greeks in indignation. A Greek! exclaim all the Turks in horror. However, leaving this doubtful family question to be solved by others, you may perhaps forsake the Café Céleste, with the idea of crossing the Boulevard Edgar-Quinet in peace, and of course you will be sucked up, like the electric pinball which starts off again, by the rue de la Gaîté where other mysteries await you. Too bad! If this occurs, you will never make the acquaintance of Socrates.

Socrates was alone, that afternoon, with Dimitrios and Constantine and the smiling mandarins.

"Another drink?" he suggested.

Dimitrios and Constantine cried out in protest.

"Come, come, only a drop. An Amer-Picon, you like that. . . . After all, I can afford to offer a Pico to my best friends."

Dimitrios held out his glass without further ado. Constantine, who was a good psychologist and hoped to be asked to stay for dinner, feigned shyness.

"Business good?" he asked.

"Excellent! Excellent! I can say without boasting that I make more money than anyone else in the whole street!"

"Is that a fact?" asked Constantine, cleverly blending credulity and mistrust.

Three days before, Socrates had refused to lend him five thousand francs, with the dignified pretext of being "short of cash". Constantine had decided to have a modest revenge.

"With a little bistro like this?" he murmured.

Socrates flared up. His kinky black hair, his big moustache, his dark complexion, his bulging eyes, gave him at such moments the aspect of a comic-opera bandit. Constantine was conscious of his own more dignified looks: his white hair swept straight back, and his crookedly set eyes predisposed him to play the part of an Iago; he also had a very gentle smile.

"A little bistro? A little bistro? What about the restaurant? What do you think? I know a Swiss, yes, a Swiss, who comes here every summer just for my cooking!"

"Five tables don't make a fortune," said Constantine.

The trouble was that he could never find out if Socrates was merely boasting and was as poor as himself—in which case he would have crushed him with disdain and tried to find another protector—or if he was merely stingy. Stinginess is a respectable thing.

"Yes, exactly, with five tables! It's little restaurants like this that do the best business. I could take a café or restaurant with a hundred tables, I could take something palatial, say, the Dupont, but I wouldn't."

"Well, I never," said Constantine.

Even Dimitrios, staring into his empty glass, seemed surprised. He was younger than the other two, barely thirty. Completely stupid and resembling the Delphic Oracle, he acted as guide to young Englishwomen visiting Paris in the summer. The rest of the time he did nothing at all.

"But the taxes! Oh, my friends, what I save on taxes! On my little bar, here, I don't declare a penny. And it pays! A car, now. I've done without one up to now, because I don't know how to drive, but this year I'm going to get myself one of those leather and chromium affairs. . . . But I'll have to take driving lessons, and that's a nuisance."

His exuberance sounded a bit false, and he became dimly aware
of it. There was no way out, he was going to have to invite them to
dinner. He would have to break the thousand franc note in the cash
box. If only a customer would come in! Or someone from the
house, with whom he could start up a conversation! Say, Doctor
Fisher, who drank so much; or Madame Prêtre, who always liked
to have a chat. Or even an ordinary customer. But, as if on purpose,
no one came.

"It's not very lively at this hour of the evening, in any case,"
muttered Constantine.

And the foolish Dimitrios: "You'll take me for a drive in your
car, won't you, Socrates?"

Socrates observed Constantine's smile. No, he wasn't fooled.
But if only he would get up and go, if only he would drop
in on any other Greek in the neighbourhood, there might be
a way to . . . With desperate cordiality Socrates launched into a
reply.

"Of course I'll take you for a drive, and I'll take Costi, too." He
employed the diminutive form of the name in an effort to soften up
Constantine. "Well, now, of course, the bar . . . it's not the biggest
item. . . ."

Constantine raised his eyes, dubiously.

"No," Socrates went on, feeling he again had the advantage.
"What brings in the money, you know, are certain little
matters. . . ."

He was none too sure what yarn he was going to spin, when
Constantine interrupted with a favourable interpretation.

"Matters better not talked about?" he said.

"Matters better not talked about," Socrates went on, encouraged.
"Contraband, see. Watches from Switzerland, cheese from Holland,
all kinds of things. . . . Oh, there's a good profit in it. Those fellows
deal with me, see. They have a drink, they leave me my profit on
this and that. . . . Oh, I tell you"—the lie was pouring out smoothly,
bountifully, intoxicatingly—"they always bring me a little something on the side, some caviar, say, they get it almost for nothing,
vodka, or brandied fruit, or American cigarettes. You know, I used

to think I'd like to eat caviar every day, for breakfast even, but now I'm sick of it. . . ."

A pleasant warmth suddenly filled him, as if he had been drinking a heady wine. He no longer had to watch them, he felt their belief in what he was saying. Dimitrios was in a state of unreserved admiration, and even the mistrustful Constantine was won over: he had that weakness of some Orientals who, infinitely mistrustful when confronted with a straightforward transaction, become as wide-eyed and convinced as children listening to a tale of Ali Baba in the presence of anything the least bit shady, incredible, impossible, provided it be accompanied by underhand dealings, bargainings, and secrecy.

"I'll have that Amer-Picon," muttered Constantine, quite convinced. Socrates uncorked the bottle.

Greece! Greece that had seen him triumphant, that had seen him lording it over his father's restaurant where someone else did the cooking, while his mother presided at the cashier's desk, covered with jewels, her fingernails black. From childhood he had offered free drinks and free meals to his friends, reigning over a realm of sparkling glasses and silver and white tablecloths, and over the skinny dishwashers who in their time off, sold sponges to the tourists, and over the cooks—all perfectionists—who asked him to taste the sauces (he remembered that the eldest one had a gold tooth). He had reigned over the cold rooms in the basement where, on the marble-topped tables, were set out the skinned lamb which still had its little head and black tail, the duck which still had its gaudy feathers; over the room where the fruit was piled in symmetrical pyramids in wicker-work baskets, and lorded it, finally, over the floor above, over the suddenly quiet apartments of the king and queen, the sumptuous rooms with crocheted lace curtains, bronze chandeliers, and an enormous wireless set enthroned on a table-runner of wine-red silk.

And the statues that were there! A Laocoön of green marble! A Parthenon that seemed to be made out of sugar! And the pictures! Some painters came to the restaurant who were only too glad to have a few free meals. And the enlarged photographs of the grandfathers and grandmothers in carved and gilded plaster frames! And the doilies that were just about everywhere, even on the gigantic and magnificent plush armchairs!

All this had been at his service, unalterably his, from the age of five to that dreadful year in his thirties which had marked the end of his reign. Everything had vanished, the basement with its meats, and the cook with the gold tooth; the sparkling dining-room and the respectful faces of the customers behind the neatly piled fruit; the mother, dignified at the cashier's desk, surrounding herself with a rampart of muttered figures; and even the Laocoön, even—tears still filled Socrates' eyes at the thought—even the wine-red silk table-runner with fringes, under the wireless set. . . . His mother, systematically tearing out her hair, had shrieked that it was all his fault. All those friends he invited to dinner every day, all those free drinks, all those presents (nine pairs of boots in one month given to people they did not know!) and he felt as innocent as a child.

It was not until he had come to France to claim the heritage of the Turkish uncle whom they had always despised that he had felt the extent of his downfall. No one now regarded him with admiration. No one now solicited his bounty. No one depended upon him. Sometimes he doubted his own existence. He was so used to the noise he made that this silence around him gave him the impression of being dead. Socrates, whose name was no longer praised by complacent lips, Socrates who no longer aroused fear or envy, was condemned to exist all by himself! Was this possible?

Then he had met Constantine, who had accepted a drink, had accepted a pair of boots (which Socrates had given him at great personal sacrifice), had accepted a meal. He had come back for more, again and again, with Dimitrios, who was nothing but his witness, the crowd, the Greek chorus. And in a precarious and fugitive way, heavy with liabilities, Socrates had once again become king! Once more he breathed, he existed. In his new life he forgot his old mother who, in Athens, was selling her jewels and making beaded articles while waiting for her son to make a fortune. The uncle's legacy, that slightly Turkish money, ran through Socrates' fingers, forming sand-castles that very soon caved in. The Café Céleste, last vestige of the uncle (who had written in his own hand that notice, "Greek Cuisine"), still existed. But for how long?

Socrates poured out the drinks, not looking into the future, not seeing anything beyond the present moment, feeling nothing but the agreeable elation that had returned, his reconquered royalty, his momentary triumph. However, he preferred to save his ammunition. Would he have to invite them to dinner this evening?

A man came in and leaned against the bar. Socrates was saved.

"What can I give you, Monsieur Morani?"

"A glass of Suze, my dear Socrates."

Constantine and Dimitrios were rather upset. Beaten in the game of innuendo, they now lost confidence in their perseverance. Socrates was capable of staying there, chatting with his customer, for hours, apparently without the least thought of approaching dinner-time.

"How did things go for you this afternoon, Monsieur Morani?"

"Like all the afternoons of my life, Socrates. But there was something of a crowd. I'm wearing myself out, simply wearing myself out. . . ."

"A musician like you, Monsieur Morani! You, who won Second Prize at the Conservatory!"

"Yes, such is life, Socrates. That Second Prize won't prevent me from ending up in a hospital while you enjoy your retirement on the Riviera in the midst of palm trees and millionaires. Well, well, here's the Doctor. . . ."

And Dr. Fisher also came in, not by the glassed door opening from the street but by a little side door which gave upon the inside stairway. He grasped Stéphane's hand in silence.

"A glass of rum," he said briefly.

Socrates poured out the drink for him, smiling at the phantom palm trees and millionaires. Slowly, Constantine and Dimitrios prepared to go.

"See you soon!" Socrates called out to them, gaily.

What did the future matter? He, too, had a generous tot of rum.

"No, no, gentlemen," he protested when Stéphane and Dr. Fisher made a gesture as if to pay. "It's on the house!"

"I'm sure you can permit yourself the luxury," said Stéphane, laughing, "but after all. . . ."

"For the love of art, Monsieur Morani," said Socrates, as always. He had time for a good chat. Morani's politeness did not cost much, fortunately; one need only be polite in return. Oh, if only there were more people like him!

"She's not beautiful! She's certainly not beautiful!"

Martine, her nose pressed to the plate glass window, had turned her back on the counter, the customers, the gaudy animation of the crowd surrounding her, to peer into the street. The counter was at right angles to a window, and it was through some striped cotton curtains and artistically draped fishermen's nets that Martine could glimpse the pavement, the costermongers' barrows, the passers-by who were not hurrying on this already warm spring day.

"Mademoiselle! This is the third time I've asked you for some ham!"

"Ask the other girl," Martine replied crossly, without turning.

She did not wait in vain. Louise Morani was coming down the street with a full shopping-basket, swinging along as completely at ease there as she would have been in her own bedroom. A lock of black hair had come loose from her chignon, and with one hand she pinned it firmly in place. . . . Avidly, avidly, Martine's eyes drank in the least movement. Louise moved about among the costermongers' carts, picked up a fruit, put it back, selected. . . . Watching her, you were sure that no one would sell her an unripe fruit or an already wilted lettuce. You knew that if she protested, an exchange would be made, that if she counted her change it would not be short.

"Well, she's not beautiful! She's certainly not beautiful!"

Avidly, Martine's mind analysed, found fault with the figure that had put on weight, with the languid way Louise had of walking. Why, she walked as if wearing house-slippers! Her chignon had come loose again. . . . She turned her back, arguing with a flower-seller, but without any superfluous gesturing. She deposited a bunch of iris on top of her shopping-basket. . . . "She's common.

She wears an imitation mother-of-pearl comb. She has the voice of a fishwife. She is heavy and slow. She is forty-five years old. She is stupid, badly dressed. . . ."

Then Louise turned, and the fine oval of her face, shining in the sunlight, was as if reduced to its essential features, simplified by harsh shadows: the line of her too-dark eyes thus emphasized gave them a ruthless look, the nose was a little too long, it was a sly animal's nose, thought Martine, and the mouth was set in a hard and tortured line. . . . But her vivid face!

Martine turned abruptly away, as if she had been slapped.

"There's your ham!" she said furiously to the woman who was still despondently waiting to be served by Claudette.

Quelled, the woman drew out her purse, paid, and disappeared without a murmur. But Martine did not look out into the street again.

It was like that every day, or almost. Ever since she had first discovered that Louise Morani did her shopping in the outdoor market directly beneath that window, Martine had not been able to resist the fascination of the street. Yet she could have gone to gaze at Madame Morani as much as she liked at the Café Céleste, where she often dropped in for a drink. Or she could have seen her at home in her flat, on some pretence or other. But what fascinated Martine was to see without being seen, to lie in wait, as if in the hope of surprising some secret. Tell herself as she would that it was ridiculous—and the floor-manager had even scolded her for this habit—she continued to gaze out of the window. It almost seemed to her, so tense did she become, that she could physically feel the moment when Louise was going to pass by, and sometimes she did guess the moment exactly. And the days when she had not caught a glimpse of her, she felt cheated.

Thank Heaven it wasn't jealousy, she told herself. And who, anyway, could imperil that exalted friendship she had with Stéphane, the friendship that had saved her from dull despair? She had at last found a kind of justification for her existence. Not that she shared her friend's beliefs: but she was happy to feel that he was as detached from the things of this earth as she was, finding in this condition a justification. While automatically serving the customers, who were momentarily banished from her mind and inaudible to her, she gradually brought herself into unison with Stéphane while waiting for the hour when they would meet. Yes, his love for her was pure. Yes, the rest did not exist, and they were not outcasts of society, but elevated above it. No, nothing could shake this conviction, not even the insulting radiance of that face. . . .

The sunlight did not penetrate the cramped little room which the proprietor of the Brasserie Dorée pretentiously referred to as "the artists' dressing-room". It was furnished solely with a big cracked mirror, a chair, and a shelf where the make-up pots were aligned. Bruno was there, creaming off the dark tan base that he used in the hope of transforming himself into an exotic type, when Stéphane came in, went over to the closet which could be locked with a key, and hung up his jacket (marked with the initials S.M.).

"Well!" said Bruno, "isn't your girl-friend coming?"

He dipped some cotton-wool into an almond lotion and ran it over his cherubic face. Despite his efforts, that face looked much too jolly to go well with the sentimental songs he played on his violin, crooning snatches of them now and then.

"I'll see her in her room," Stéphane yawned, sinking down on the chair. "Besides, she's not my 'girl-friend', at least not in the way you imply."

"Oh, I've no doubt you could find a better looker to sleep with."

"Bruno!" Stéphane scolded.

But he spoke without harshness, aware of the little violinist's disarming fondness and admiration. After all, they had worked a long time together.

"Madame Bart was here today."

"With her family, unfortunately. Did you see the little boy threatening to climb up on the platform?"

By now they knew almost all the usual customers who came there to relax at less cost than at the music-hall. For the most part, the customers were local tradespeople, with occasionally some railway-station employees.

"Not many people this evening."

"They don't have much of a show, this week," said Bruno with satisfaction.

He was thirty-eight years old, with a round little paunch, a round and good-natured face, and a snub nose; for all that, he aspired to become a sort of Frank Sinatra adored by the masses. He was no more interested in the violin than in the maracas he occasionally shook in a Latin-American rhythm. He had always dreamed of making his name as a singer, and this made him nourish a veritable hatred for the evening performers, the young hopefuls picked up off the street by the manager and paid as little as possible, but who sang whole songs in a blue or pink spotlight, while he had to content himself with crooning a few snatches of song and this in the crude light of day.

"She's not bad looking," said Stéphane indulgently.

"She's just a model! Nothing but a model! And she expects to make a career of singing? Oh, I tell you, the Brasserie Dorée has sunk pretty low!"

"Yes, ourselves and Gloria Grétry, not very glittering. . . . Grétry! But at least, she's quick, she's lively. . . ."

The comparison wounded Bruno.

"You oughtn't to say such a thing, Morani! All the same, you're not going to compare us to that. . . . We're musicians! That counts for something."

The wad of cotton-wool still in his hand, his face three-quarters cleaned of grease paint, with only a few streaks of dark tan still showing, he was flaming with indignation, entirely convinced by his own words. But Stéphane heaved a sigh of discouragement.

"Musicians! Oh, my poor Bruno! We may have been, once upon a time. But now? Old has-beens. Café employees. Unimportant employees, at that. Afternoon instrumentalists, you might say a tea-room orchestra, less than the radio. . . . Musicians for a waiting-room, where we're listened to between trains." He paused, then went on in a more vehement tone, the lines about his mouth sarcastic. "We have our admirers among the ladies: my concierge, my milk-woman, and that good creature, Germaine Lethuit, and

Socrates, who calls me 'Professor' at the drop of a hat. We're celebrities in this part of Paris! What better could we hope for, eh? To be celebrities in one's own neighbourhood! At least our credit's good; if we don't press it too far, of course. We're in the category of circus performers—even though we've sold our stuff for eight years at the same stand. . . ."

He was now pacing the narrow room, under the pale light bulb, striding up and down, breathing deeply, enjoying the silence of Bruno who was listening in awe, as he would have listened to Tino Rossi. In a few minutes he would go out, breathe in the spring air with delight, and go up the boulevard, where he would be hailed at intervals by people who knew him by sight, kindly tradespeople shutting up shop for the night. He would have a drink with Socrates, "on the house", and Socrates would stare at him with great compassion. He would say a few words to Madame Prêtre, the concierge, cast a glance at that little Sylvia (completely stupid, but charming), who was, according to Louise, in love with him. He would perhaps run into one or two of the neighbours who were a part of that little circle that met together every Monday ("We, the Celestials", as Stéphane liked to refer to himself and them, enjoying the pun), the very cultivated Gérard Ducas, or Jean Cadou, the promising abstract painter, or Dr. Fisher, whose door displayed a brass plaque with the initials L.P.R. (League of Political Refugees). All of them respectable people, ready to listen, and all of them considering him, despite his misfortunes, an exceptional person. And when he had arrived (climbing slowly, breathing heavily) at the second floor, if Louise had gone out, he would continue to climb until he reached the fifth floor where he would find Martine, inexhaustible fount of that sympathetic understanding for which he had such an insatiable thirst.

The concierge is one of those people, rare in our time, whose authority is still absolute. You have only to question her subordinates, inferiors, captives, or foster-children—as she variously considers the occupants of "her" building. The horror—or the fervour—with which they stigmatize her vices or glorify her virtues can

only be explained by totemism. Tutelary deity or Fury of the
household, crouched in her inevitable lair, hoarding her thunder-
bolts—she is not quite sure whether they are destined for the enemy
without or the prisoner within—legendary ogress, *Deus ex machina*
of tragi-comedy, Greek chorus perhaps! The concierge, in a
society respectful of myths, should wear an insignia, mantle or
peplum. For lack of one, Madame Prêtre (predestined sacerdotal
name!) heaped upon her vast rheumatic body an immense number
of flannels, sweaters, and, for the upper part, shawls, impressive by
their quantity if not by their quality.

Her physical aspect justified her priestly name: a lace modesty
vest covered the upper portion of her furrowed bosom, a black
ribbon adorned with a cameo held the hanging folds of her neck in
place, and her beaked nose, her full and slightly reddened lips, the
crafty expression in her eyes, all gave her the look of an aged
Talleyrand. In her character there was something of the diplomat
and the pander, two functions, socially useful and morally debat-
able. Madame Prêtre, who held the reins of the Café Céleste
building in her firm hand (adorned with an imitation emerald),
responded perfectly to this dual designation.

At seven o'clock that same evening Madame Prêtre, sitting in a
wicker armchair in *her* doorway, was simultaneously enjoying the
mild evening air and the strategic position. To her left she had a
wide and uninterrupted view of the Boulevard Edgar-Quinet,
including the covered market, the entrance to the metro, the grassy
strip where out-of-work acrobats and fire-eaters often performed,
while on her right, the rue d'Odessa seemed to pour down to her
very feet its colourful confusion. Psychologically, the wicker armchair, exactly filling as it did the small space between the tiny café
terrace and the main entrance, made it impossible for any occupant
of the building to go in or out without being inspected by
Madame Prêtre.

Socrates had more than once invited Madame Prêtre to sit
squarely upon the café terrace. She would be more comfortable
there, he argued, and would even be useful, acting, as it were, the
part of a customer, setting an example that eventual customers

might follow. But Madame Prêtre had deemed this intermediary position to be more in conformity with her dignity. And she so enjoyed herself there that whenever there was the least ray of sunlight, the wicker armchair, carried out of the concierge's lodge by a young, slender, and charming girl, was set down between the door and the terrace, to be occupied a few minutes later by Madame Prêtre. Then the young and slender creature, who was no other than the daughter of Madame Prêtre (Sylvia by name, to be precise), went off towards her Destiny, which at the time had a form infinitely less young and slender, bore a famous name, had a bald head, and was of the male sex.

On this fine day in spring, Madame Prêtre sat there from ten in the morning until seven in the evening, leaving the chair only twice: towards noon, she went in to finish the mutton stew of the previous night; then, towards three o'clock, she went in to supervise Dr. Fisher, who was using her telephone—she suspected the Doctor of cheating on his telephone calls. (Madame Prêtre, like many people whose functions accustom them to the sacred and holy, no longer respected anything or anybody, not even a man who had a brass plaque on his door, L.P.R.) That day, then, she had peacefully and comfortably been able to check thoroughly all the comings and goings of the co-operative-owners (and co-ops are a wilder and more elusive game than ordinary tenants). At eight-forty Martine Fortin had had her morning coffee at Socrates' and had arrived at the Prisunic before the doors opened. At ten o'clock, Monsieur Ducas went off to his antique shop in the rue de Rennes.

"Already out-of-doors, Madame Prêtre!" he had said in his twittering voice, raising his hat very politely.

"I like the fresh air, Monsieur. How is Monsieur Cadou this morning?"

"He was out late last night, unfortunately. Impossible to keep these young people in check, Madame! And you know what artists are!"

He was wearing a navy blue cheviot suit; he was a fine gentleman, well-dressed, with a private income, generous as to his tips. Madame Prêtre did not criticize him, despite his rather odd friendship for the young painter. She criticized no one, in fact, but merely observed them with a kind of disinterested amusement. Two strange men (with frayed shirts) had come at eleven o'clock to see Dr. Fisher. Strangers, perhaps foreigners, and not patients, Madame Prêtre had concluded at once. The brass plaque, which made such a good impression in the stairway, was for people like that. Did Dr. Fisher, in the name of those mysterious initials, distribute subsidies? Did he himself receive subsidies? Madame Prêtre would not have been able to say, precisely. However, she was quite sure that his clientèle of young servant girls did not provide enough money to pay for his car and his flat above the Café Céleste. She, too, would like to know some magic initials that would allow her to pamper Sylvia.

Between eleven o'clock and noon, there had been an influx of customers to the bar. Without interest. And Madame Morani had gone out to do her marketing a little earlier than usual. With the pretext that she worked at the music-hall at night (as a dresser, which wasn't anything like being an actress, all the same!), she was rarely up and about before eleven o'clock. She had said good morning to Madame Prêtre and Madame Prêtre had said good morning to her. No one in the house liked Madame Morani, and Madame Prêtre liked her no more than the others. But they respected each other, like fighters resting between rounds, and their mutual respect showed in the way they saluted each other. Return of Monsieur Ducas towards noon, and of Madame Morani, towards a quarter past. Monsieur Cadou had not put in an appearance; he must have had too much to drink the night before. The unknown young man who rented the third floor flat had not gone out at all. Martine Fortin had come back towards six (which meant she had come straight from the Prisunic), and Madame Morani went out again. She must be dining out. Monsieur Morani returned at seven and seemed to be in fine fettle.

"Mademoiselle Fortin is upstairs," said Madame Prêtre.

To herself she repeated, as she often did, "When you think how many pretty girls would ask no better . . . Well, it's his own business!"

There, the day was ending. She felt the air freshening, it was raw cold, penetrating; after all, spring had not yet arrived. Another day had passed during which Madame Morani must have smiled at some man in the street, while Monsieur Morani and Mademoiselle Fortin enjoyed some happy moments in what had been the servant's room, a day when Monsieur Ducas had worried about young Jean Cadou's escapades (yet you couldn't always expect the young fellow to be satisfied with the distractions an old antiquarian could give him), another day when Dr. Fisher had got himself tight; another day when Socrates had filled the little restaurant with the sound of his bragging and boasting; in short, another day when Madame Prêtre had been confirmed in her opinion of the world which was "not much for clean hands and pure hearts", as she always said, with satisfaction. But despite her dim view of the world, she felt not the slightest ill will, her knowledge of life provided her with enough pleasure. And when she calmly disposed of humanity in a few words as "a lot of stinkers", addressing her good friend Mademoiselle Marie, she was quite ready to include herself in the lot.

The sky was darkening, and the neon lights in the street took on importance, seeming to expand. A group of young people arrived and went into the little restaurant across the street. A man and woman, apparently a married couple, went into the Café Céleste and the loud voice of Socrates could be heard, reciting the bill of fare. Dr. Fisher had gone down into the bar and was having a drink, most likely rum. Sylvia had not returned home.

"They must be having dinner in a restaurant," thought Madame Prêtre, "with cocktails, champagne, flowers . . . perhaps photographers, since he's so famous. . . ." These thoughts awakened no voluptuous idea, nor even any hope of gain, at least not at that moment. If she was so anxious for her daughter Sylvia to have those photographs, that champagne, that liaison with a rich old man, it was because, in the opinion of everyone, such a situation was enviable—and why should Madame Prêtre have a different opinion? Yes, she wanted, she demanded, that enviable situation for her daughter! And the fact that others might perhaps have more right to it only strengthened her desire.

The unpretentious little neon sign of the Café Céleste lit up in its turn. Darkness was now almost complete. There were fewer people passing in the street, but the roar of the city remained the same, only more muffled, because it now issued from inside the houses. There was already a queue in front of the music-hall. Madame Morani hurried past on the opposite pavement, on her way to work there. It must be later than eight o'clock. Dr. Fisher was still in the bar, and there were three men standing there and two couples having dinner. Sylvia might not return home before eleven, or perhaps even midnight.

Socrates came out on the terrace for a moment, turning his back on the noise of the dining-room, and stood motionless, staring into the darkness, looking towards the street, the lit signs, the dark sky fretted with chimneys. Presently he looked down at her.

"Still there, Madame Prêtre?"

"As you see, Socrates. . . ."

"How about a nice hot cup of coffee?"

"No, many thanks. It gives me heartburn, palpitations. You see, coffee is, for me . . ."

Around them, the sounds of the street were dying down, and a kind of tame little breeze was starting up.

"It's getting cold. Want me to take in your chair, Madame Prêtre?"

He was always very kind and obliging with her, with everyone, but at the same time constrained, shifty-eyed, as if he were on the point of asking for a loan.

"Perhaps. Well, no. . . . Not yet. . . ."

"Now, no need to worry. She'll not be home before eleven or twelve o'clock. Young girls today . . ."

He meant well, but Madame Prêtre was furious at being seen through.

"Come to think of it, yes, take in my chair, Socrates," she said curtly, getting to her feet with difficulty. "And you'd better keep an eye on your customers. They're capable of slipping off without paying. It's funny what a queer lot of people patronize your place. . . ."

The neon lights vibrated for themselves, exchanging little darting flashes. A muffled ringing of a bell sounded from the music-hall. People were going into the cinema two by two. The tiled façade of the Turkish baths glimmered in the shadows. From time to time an invisible man laughed loudly, and his laughter reached the deserted little terrace. Socrates re-entered the café to enjoy the present moment and the absence of his tormentors.

"A round of drinks on the house!" he called out. The burning warmth that invaded him almost consumed the hard little lump of insecurity in his breast.

Madame Prêtre, back in her lodge, climbed into her baggy flannel nightgown, turned on the radio (a very old-fashioned model), muttered aloud. "The little fool! I'll bet she's ruined everything," she fumed, her heart overflowing with that painful wrath which was her way of expressing her love for her daughter.

The Boulevard Edgar-Quinet was an oasis of shadow and silence, where the metro entrance offered an inviting refuge.

Martine was asleep in her hot room under the eaves—in summer the place was an oven—lying very straight and still, her feet together, her hands folded, and her quieted face displayed the hesitant sweetness, slightly ugly and touching, of the women portrayed by Clouet.

Stéphane, in his bedroom, was writing with childlike contentment, setting down in a fat blue exercise book phrases that contained a great many capitalized words.

At the music-hall, between the scenes of "The Sultan's Favourites" and "The Chorus of the Tulips", Louise Morani was running from one dressing-room to another, hooking young and ill-washed girls into their costumes, tossing back that thick lock of black hair which was always falling over her eyes.

In the little bistros below street-level at least three card-games were in progress, but only one game of billiards.

At the end of the street, where loomed the great dark mass of the railway-station, humming softly, there suddenly arose, as if marking a frontier, the bright yellow arrow of the Dupont Café.

It was spring, and the weather was calm and warm.

The narrow windows were set high, the niggardly light that
filtered down was golden. The room was a long rectangle. The
women moved about from one to another of its three grey marble
platforms. The platform in the centre of the room was almost
square and was surrounded by four short columns; the other two
were ranged along the sides of the room and were divided by thin
marble partitions into three compartments. Through a door at the
far end came the steam, thick, moist, tepid. The room was still not
crowded, for the baths had just opened.

The level slabs of grey marble framed and supported the soft
and naked female bodies that were evenly distributed, three to each
platform. The women, still shivering a little, waited quietly, chin
on knees, for the slow vapour to reach them. When it finally did,
they gave a long sigh of contentment.

The bodies relaxed, sprawled on the marble as if on a butcher's
slab, the plump curves flattened out, the thin angles of elbows and
knees repeating and combining with the ridges and corners of floor
and wall. They seemed to be there for eternity: the white flesh had
been created to contrast with the hard grey marble, the heavy
breasts and thin hips made to complement each other, the one
demanding the other, the curve opposing the angle, the angle
inviting the curve, that deformed body over there conferring upon
the other, nearby body, a function and nobility. Alone, on the
central slab, stretched out at the foot of a column, the perfect body
of a very young girl glowed golden, her rounded arms curved
above an expressionless face, her small round breasts erect, and this
isolated female body held a particular harmony in all its lines and
colourings, down to the rosy heels, an elegant and fragile detail in a
composition of generally strong tonalities.

Louise, on her slab, was watching the new arrivals, leaning on one
elbow and absentmindedly biting her arm, her eyes moving from
one to another of the newcomers—an Armenian woman worn
out by too many pregnancies, an adipose Jewish matron accompany-
ing a bride-to-be, ready for the ritual bath—analysing them without
indulgence but also without displeasure. She loved to look upon
those naked bodies displayed with such careless frankness. It was

life she read there, the normal wear and tear of child-bearing accepted or refused, of misery or prosperity, of rich food or poor food, of exhausting or tender love, the lines left by the passing days, the stamp of that life which was for Louise something warm and hidden, like this room, delightful and terrible, filled with anecdote and drama, but in which she easily made a place for herself, becoming easily and solidly a body among bodies, without judgement or revolt, and almost complacently displaying her still beautiful naked self on the slippery marble.

The warmth increased. A woman was bent over at the copper tap, washing her hair. Louise swung her feet to the already wet floor and went towards the far end of the long room into the sudarium, a little round marble cylinder of a room where forms moved indistinctly in billowing white vapour that rose from a well at its centre. She sat down on the rim of the well, leaning her face towards the burning hot vapour, breathing calmly as drops of sweat beaded her face and dampened her hair. "It's good for the complexion," she thought, and it was her only thought.

"Hello, Lou!" called out one of the indistinct forms.

It was Sarah, the pride of the music-hall of the rue d'Odessa, Sultaness and Tulip, reigning queen of the quarter, a girl waiting for luck to come her way.

"Hello, Sarah! So you come here, too?"

"I simply had to," said the girl, stretching her lovely body as it lay on the marble lip of the well. "I was beginning to put on weight. . . ."

Louise gave the girl a long look.

"You could do with some," she said, pronouncing judgement like an expert.

"It's not the fashion," said Sarah. "And in the bride's boudoirgown this summer they're going to see that I have a bit of a tummy."

The abdomen, with its deep navel, did indeed bulge out in a tender curve.

"Anyway, I hope I'm not going to act in that peep-show much longer," said Sarah, with conscious vulgarity. "There's a fellow . . ."

"The short dark one, very well dressed, the one that brought you the flowers?"

"Right. He was saying, the other day . . ."

She talked, Lou listened, encouraging her with brief questions asked at the right moment, as with an "*Olé!*" called out to a Flamenco singer. The warmth became too intense, they left the sudarium for the long room where, in a corner, they inundated each other with cool water poured from a rusty and handleless saucepan, saying nothing, engrossed for a while in the simple delight of cool water.

The room had become noisier. A shrill, gay chatter arose, small groups of women had formed. Leaning against the columns, stretching their arms or rinsing each other's hair or tinting it with henna, abundant hair, thin hair. . . . They were living intensely again. Three women were grouped round that slender young girl, dragging a secret out of her and sharing it, laughing or groaning with the same vehemence, vigorously slapping their thighs (stout thighs, flabby thighs), entrenched in their fortune or misfortune as in a feudal domain where they were glad to do the honours. They, who had but a short while ago been set down here like objects, were women again and were recalling with rude words of the flesh the children born of their bodies, the men welcomed into their beds, the money counted by their tireless hands. Expressing themselves awkwardly in various accents, they exchanged these memories like things, vaunting them, exhibiting them, and in their talk the beds of love, of childbirth, of death were evaluated in terms of blood and base sufferings. In this conversation, the very festivals and seasons were things to be touched and felt, devoured, summed up in terms of money, unleavened bread, roast lamb; the nations mingled their salt, the truth and the essence of their substance, to satisfy their ravenous appetites. And their lives were there, self-assured, rich even in vice, misery, sickness. *Lives*, in short. Their lives were there, set down like objects.

Lou combed her hair. Sarah, flat on her stomach, hid her impudent face in her muscular arms, the attitude revealing the hidden dignity of her back and shoulders.

"Are you staying on awhile, Louise?"

Sarah always addressed her with a certain ceremony. There was apparently something in Louise's dark eyes, something in the fine oval of her face, that inspired respect and gave the lie to her sensual and almost vulgar mouth, the heavy chin, the deep, warm voice, prompt with whispered advice and hearty invectives.

"Yes, dear. You're leaving?"

"He's been waiting outside for me since five o'clock," said Sarah peaceably. And she sat up, stretched her arms, and calmly walked towards the rest room, setting her feet down firmly, indifferent to her own beauty.

"I was as good as that, or better, at her age," thought Lou, without rancour. "She's as old as I was when I married." Yes, better than that. But she drew no pride from the fact. A painter who was now famous had once done her portrait: he had posed her leaning against the bridge above the railway at Signac. Oh, that little town crowded within its walls like money in a shut purse, like fabric squeezed through a ring! She did not regret having left Signac, but sometimes returned to it in thought. The narrow, cool street, the bedroom with its whitewashed walls, set below street-level. . . . The "Prospect", as they called the Promenade, where she and a girl friend used to walk in the evenings—the girl was always laughing, her face was flat and almost featureless, what was her name? Those were lovely evenings, with the young fellows on bicycles calling out mockingly to them, the dances in the long wooden pavilions, to which the soldiers came, and the little country inns which, thanks to their tiled floors and check curtains, were somehow homely and innocent. . . . Innocent, too, the soldier's képi fallen on the floor, and the new blue satin dress (how awful she must have looked in it!) rumpled by moist hands, and, on leaving the hotel, that yawning sleepiness of early morning, the burning-hot coffee gulped down in haste, the distant bugle, the bicycles skimming past like swallows, and herself hurrying, hurrying in her run-over high-heeled shoes to the box-factory where she worked.

All her childhood and innocence were, for her, in those summer-scented memories. She recalled how completely fresh and restored her body had felt at six o'clock in the morning, the happiness of being alive, the sweetness of being satisfied, like an animal that has fed to repletion, she could recall everything, even to the smell of glue in the ugly box-factory. After that, there had been the period at the Hôtel de la Paix, with breakfasts in bed together, she and the painter. They had had a suite of rooms, the big sitting-room smelling of beeswax, and an uncomfortable bedroom with rose-pink lampshades. What had become of the blue satin dress? And the flat-faced girl who giggled so stupidly? That year (was it even quite a year?) and that moderate prosperity due to the portrait of her at the bridge and to the generosity of the painter, had blemished her reputation more than five years of dancing and all-night carousing would have done. People stared at her dresses when she walked on the Prospect. And she hadn't cared a bit.

She stretched, wondering what time it was. Must she go home to Stéphane? The thought of it shattered her trance of well-being, made her shiver disagreeably, and, by an association of sensations, recalled to mind the overcrowded and chilly suburban trains of the war years, the red-faced farmer from whom she had bought eggs. . . . Stéphane had scolded her a lot over her trips while he was a prisoner! As much as over the long-ago evenings of dancing. But they were certainly not picnics, those train trips, she had angrily protested. She had helped out the whole neighbourhood with the food she had procured. "And bought the flat," he had retorted, "and put money aside." Well, he would have been very upset, wouldn't he, if he'd come back to find her penniless and without a roof over her head? But this was not being entirely honest: after all, she had not utterly hated the bitter struggle for a few eggs, a ham, some butter. Sometimes, even when she was aching, frozen, exhausted, weighed down with her heavy fibre suitcase, she had felt triumphant when she brought back her spoils to the rue d'Odessa.

As for him, he had brought nothing back from the war but his illness, his snivelling fatigue, and one more reason to consider himself her superior, one more reason to complain about her and his life to the residents of the Céleste building and to the people at the Brasserie, another reason for him to pour out his troubles even upon the breast of Martine Fortin.

"I believe he chooses them ugly on purpose," she thought with amusement. For indeed they were numerous, those plain girls, outcasts and introverts, whom Stéphane had raised to the rank of platonic dispensers of solace and consolation, sympathetic echoes. The echo generally disappeared at the end of a few months, condemned as unworthy. After which, with a great show of disenchantment, Stéphane again took refuge in his private diary. Well, one of these days, thought Louise rather maliciously, he would come upon a plain-Jane who would not let herself be liquidated without protest. And Martine Fortin might well be that plain-Jane.

Meanwhile, Louise must go home. Slowly she got up, showered herself with cold water at the tap, and went into the rest room with its faded dark red wall-paper, where some women were dozing on the straw mats scattered on the floor. She would have liked to stretch out there, too, long enough to smoke a cigarette, but then she would not have time to stroll on the boulevard. That evening, she chose the boulevard: she needed a breath of air.

She dressed quickly, and went out. The air was exactly the temperature she liked, tepid, and yet now and then threaded with a fresh breeze, a little wave of wind. She leaned against the walls of the baths a moment, waiting. This was the hour when the lights came on. She knew and loved all the neon signs, but she was waiting for the one she preferred, the gigantic yellow arrow of the Dupont Café, which flashed suddenly, at almost exactly eight o'clock. It was as though her chosen section of the city, her quarter, were signalling to her; it was like the clash of cymbals before the music begins, a blatant and vulgar gong. And blatant it was, as it suddenly flashed there in the sky, spraying down upon the people in the street, spattering them with the bogus gaiety of its light. Simultaneously, on a nearby roof, the red circles of the Martini vermouth sign began to turn giddily, flashing on and off, projecting on the open square below the frantic blinking of its reddish eyes. But the Montparnasse railway-station remained quiet, a mastodon crouching in the shadows, growling a little, with one cold spot of light, its peaceful clock, upon its forehead.

Oh, and after this pleasure, there was the little Jewish milk-bar where she so liked to sit, wedged in among unknown people who were talking with a foreign accent, to eat buttered black bread with cucumbers and sour cream! Or, on the Boulevard Edgar-Quinet, that foreign land, that provincial district, it was good to enjoy the fake luxury of the little so-called hostelry, she liked the rare steak they served there; how good it was, washed down with a bottle of Beaujolais. Oh, and at the Miramar cinema they were advertising a Technicolor super-production with Austrian waltzes, Swedish actors, water-skiers kissing against a background of the Midi that she recognized without nostalgia. . . . And there was that cheap hotel with windowless rooms where rough and humble North Africans rinsed out their mouths before and after the act of love. . . . No, she would not be tempted: such modest pleasures as these were reserved for Monday, her night off, when the music-hall where she worked was closed, when the Café Céleste was closed, and when Stéphane attended his little "reunions" there. She firmly repressed such desires on other days.

Leaving the little square, she walked up the street, continuing to enjoy a few electric signs as she passed, a lit window here and there, a lantern at the end of an alley-way, softly glowing. . . . The world was real, solid, and well-adjusted like herself, full of delightful things within reach. As for the things that had eluded her . . . what did it matter? Since she never left her quarter, she concentrated all her obscure courage upon being satisfied with her surroundings. Yes, she was still full of life, as on those unsullied mornings of her youth, was still endowed with a strength that would serve no other purpose than to live, without thought and without regret: it was quite enough. Walking towards her characterless home, towards a husband, she no longer respected, towards an evening of mediocre and ill-paid tasks, she felt in harmony with the world, a part of the order of things, and she walked triumphant.

Near the Café Céleste, a beggar approached, holding out his hand. She waved him away, back into the greyish shadows of the wall. He, too, had his place in the world as it was: he had only to make the best of it.

The kitchen was small, they were crowded too close together there. Stéphane drew himself up to his full height and frowned, setting his face in an expression of long-suffering patience, exasperated in advance. Louise, on the other hand, hunched herself up in an effort to take up less space, but the effect was to add an all too evident indifference to her massive impenetrability. And each of them assumed that attitude of insulting politeness of people who have often hurt each other.

"Had a good day?" she asked listlessly.

"If you could call it that," he murmured. "I ground out the usual soothing-syrup." (Would she never realize how much this debasement of his ambitious dreams cost him?)

"Many people?" (Complain, complain, he must always complain. Yet he had a part-time job, not too ill-paid, had a rent-free flat, and a wife earning money. . . .)

"Quite a few. I get no percentage, you know." Then he incautiously dropped the sardonic tone to blurt out a naïve remark: "Martine wasn't there."

"But you went up to her room to talk to her." She smiled. "I met her on the stairs just now, and you can bet she didn't need urging to tell me about it."

"What nonsense, Louise. I was preparing our little Monday reunion. Germaine Lethuit, I'd have you know, has produced a masterpiece, she handed it to me to read, and . . ."

"Oh, I'm sure you didn't give Martine any love-talk. And the poor girl's waiting only for that. . . ."

She turned away from him to set a saucepan on the gas stove, so he did not need to conceal an involuntary smile.

"My dear, you imagine a lot."

"Oh, come!" She turned back towards him, an onion in her hand. "As if you didn't know! I'll bet she sleeps with your photo. That's about all she'll ever have to sleep with, poor thing! Still a virgin, at her age!"

"She's twenty-five!"

"Well, that's what I said."

"I don't see anything ridiculous in that," said Stéphane, stiffening.

Every time he forgot himself and joked with her, he immediately
regretted it. What a waste of good intentions! "If Martine prefers
to keep her virginity for a great love . . ."

Lou went over to the meat-safe and took out a beefsteak which
she regarded complacently.

"Don't worry," she chuckled, "she'll have quite a wait! No one's
going to ask her not to keep it!"

Her loud laughter rang out above the sputtering of the meat in
the pan. Stéphane shrugged. Naturally, Louise was incapable of
understanding the beauty of Martine's unyielding pride, incapable
of appreciating the refinement of a girl who refused to allow any
familiarity, any casual affair, anything that would compromise her
in that job which was beneath her. "A real little Anouilh heroine,"
he had once called her, with genuine tenderness. The beauty of
poverty, of abstention. . . . Louise's words offended him all the more
since, at the back of his mind, he had sometimes secretly wished
that the little Anouilh heroine had been a little more generously
blessed by nature. That was what he detested in Louise. She always
managed to stir up in him all the nasty or ignoble thoughts that had
ever flitted through his mind, all the things he had so firmly
repressed. Until, sometimes, such thoughts came to the surface,
ruthlessly, and he suddenly "saw in her true light" some girl or
other, and discarded her utterly.

"Did you remember to buy my special bread?" This was his
implicit revenge on Lou for her jesting.

"Oh! I completely forgot! You should have asked me at once!
Shall I run out and get some?"

"No, my dear, no. It doesn't matter. I can manage quite well."
He had resumed his gentle tone which she loathed, for she was
helpless against that martyr's attitude of his—the attitude of one
who expects the worst and trusts to Heaven.

"Yes, yes, I'll run out. It'll take only a minute."

"The meat will be done, my dear. Give me a piece of ordinary
bread, I don't want to make you late."

She held out the loaf of bread. He took it, and stoically cut a
slice. She served up the steak.

"Did you show Martine the little lampshade I promised to let her have?"

"I gave it to her," he said, in a less restrained tone. The steak was good, and he liked onions. "She'll give it back to you next month, when she hopes to be able to buy another."

"I don't need it, as you know very well."

"That's what I told her, but . . . You see, she's so proud, so scrupulous! A little heroine . . ."

". . . of Anouilh. I know. Nothing but angels in this house."

Stéphane, his mouth full, let out a sigh, which was accomplished with some little difficulty.

"How bitter you are, Louise! How disillusioned! I'm quite aware that this world is imperfect, cruel at times, but isn't it our duty to turn towards the light? To create around us a kind of . . . why not? A kind of transformed world, of . . ."

Louise never listened to such disquisitions. She went on eating. Stéphane continued in another key:

"With that said, my dear, I must admit, while blaming the way in which you acquired this flat, that the other people in this building are absolutely charming. And I regret all the more that you persist in not wanting to take part in our little reunions. . . ."

"It's not my cup of tea," said Louise. "Do you want some cheese? I bought some Brie."

Stéphane permitted the interruption.

"Is it good?"

"See for yourself!"

He hesitated a moment.

"I'm not sure, my stomach's a little upset tonight. Oh, I'll risk it. Give me a small piece. I'm not going to bed straight away. Is there some wine?"

"A little left in the bottle. . . ."

She served him the wine and cheese, but did not sit down again. It was late. Standing in front of the cracked looking-glass, she tidied her hair.

"We really need another mirror. . . ."

"As I've often told you," said Stéphane. "I sometimes regret the way you neglect those little things that make up the charm of everyday life. You should see Martine's room—how impeccably neat it is, in spite of her poverty. She has some very clever ideas too. For instance, she has a kind of collapsible cupboard, I don't know how to explain. . . ."

He gestured vaguely. Lou slipped into her coat. She wished she might afford a new one this year, a soft beige tweed. . . .

"I'm off," she said, breaking into his eulogy of Martine Fortin. "And be on your guard, Stéphane, all the same. Those skinny girls are the worst. They'll gobble up a man before he knows what's happened!"

"Martine's not . . ."

Smiling, substantial, Lou halted in the doorway.

"Martine's an angel, that goes without saying. Only, don't forget, that angel *bought* her room. . . . You'll not be able to get rid of her as easily as you got rid of the others. . . ."

The look of offended dignity that Stéphane put on was wasted: Louise had already gone. And so, with a sigh, he took another piece of cheese.

Stéphane settled down to write. The bedroom in which he sat repeated almost exactly in its bareness the Van Gogh reproduction hung on the white wall: iron bed, solitary chair. . . . The close similarity was rather disturbing; the room suffered from the comparison, lost its power to convince. Was it the real room that added to the picture, or the picture that added to the room an insistent and rather declamatory note, the ostentation of a beggar exhibiting too many sores at a time? Whatever the cause, the duplicity cast a shadow on the picture itself: one had doubts of Van Gogh before doubting Stéphane.

Stéphane was writing in his diary. He wrote as he spoke, with ease and pleasure. His pen ran smoothly, his style was fluent, there were no words crossed out. The words poured out inexhaustibly, his recriminations became amplified, became transformed into noble lamentations, the ill-temper of everyday life became sardonic bitterness, the small grievances became great wrongs. This diary was solemn: the words Resignation and Death often recurred. However, Stéphane's face, as he wrote, reflected nothing but childlike pleasure. As he went on writing, he admired in the mirror of his words the image he called Stéphane, while at the back of his mind a tiny glimmer of consciousness applauded the skill with which he fooled his little world.

Where had it begun, this taste of his for dissembling? Which one of his parents, respectable and kindly middle-class provincials, was to blame, what subtle quality had there been in that peaceful and luminously mediocre atmosphere of his home (that neat kitchen with red-tiled floor, where every object took on strangeness in its beeswaxed banality; that little back-yard garden where a single bent tree flourished; that parlour, with its long sideboard, worn and old, and on it for ornament, an exemplary cat), what heritage or happening had caused the evil seed to sprout in his heart as a child? As secret as fear, dissembling had perhaps been a game to begin with, then it had gradually become deeply rooted, and had finally developed to such an extent that he had almost become unaware of it, as, in the midst of a dream, one is only confusedly aware of exterior reality.

His parents were sensible people, making a religion of orderliness, liking religion because it represented order. They paid great attention to what-would-people-say, the opinion of neighbours. But they loved each other, loved their son, and were happy in their mediocrity. Even so, Madame Morani did have one weakness, which was to regret at times the splendours of her past life, now gone for ever: her father, a ruined man, had once been a prosperous ship-owner. And Monsieur Morani (an English master during Stéphane's childhood) had one vanity, which was to boast to his colleagues of his wife's ancestry. Could these two failings have been the cause of all the evil? Surely not: there was not enough fertility in their combined natures to foster a vice. Madame Morani continually boasted of her father, but she harboured no bitterness, entertained no foolish desires; Monsieur Morani continued to love his wife as much out of vanity as out of any real tenderness (though she was quite pretty), but he indulged in no wild speculations to recoup her wealth. On the contrary, apart from their allusions to the prodigious old grandfather, they lived very unpretentiously, even being inclined to deprive themselves of small pleasures and harmless expenditures, under the pretext that one should keep one's place and that some things weren't "suitable" for people of their "class". Stéphane's persistent tendency to dissimulate could scarcely have had its source in those small defects of his parents. Perhaps, then, one should seek it in their virtues?

But who knows? He may have told his first lie by sheer chance, mere accident; the lie may have been the recourse of a mind humiliated by too much humility, as another mind might have been humiliated by too much pride. Stéphane felt the need to dazzle— and his parents, accustomed to dwell admiringly upon an ancestor (still alive and virtuously deploring his ruin), were ready and willing to be enthralled by a still more inviting illusion. The ease with which he managed to fool them horrified Stéphane, for, though he never showed it, they had convinced him of a secret and almost innate inferiority. Lies gradually became natural to him, were told almost without his intervention; he did not create them, but yielded to them, and each day the burden of lies accumulated, became more cumbersome, like an unwanted guest who settles in and, by force of habit, ends up by being accepted as a friend.

At school he was only a moderately good student. But he made himself noticed by his good behaviour: he soon learned to adopt a pose, and thus had the pleasure of satisfying everyone at little cost to himself. His thirst for praise was stronger than his love of deception, with this strange result: by the age of thirteen or fourteen he was so used to obtaining results by fraud that when he succeeded by other means he was bewildered, doubtful that he deserved it.

He had begun keeping a diary at the age of sixteen, when he entered the Conservatory of Signac. He considered himself at this epoch to be a very alluring personality. Young, handsome (and he was extremely so), he saw ahead of him a glorious future as a great musician, and this gave him a kind of self-respect. However, this consideration remained purely exterior. He respected his rôle of young-man-with-a-future, and yet could never think of himself except as acting the part; he felt only vaguely related to the part he played. The condescending attitudes of his classmates, who were all from a better class of society, had something to do with this. But even more important was the fact that his ingrained habit of dissimulation had confirmed him in his feeling of being cursed with a secret defect. This insecurity, this difficulty of reconciling the image he presented to the world with his secret feeling, was very painful for an adolescent. His pride, his natural mediocrity—mediocrity of character especially, for he was not lacking in talent—impelled him each day to practice paltry frauds, even in his way of executing music. His secret feeling of inferiority fed on this, while he swaggered with pride at every achievement. It would perhaps have been better for Stéphane had there occurred an open conflict: there was none, and he discovered the miraculous expedient of keeping a diary.

Once more, it was a case of pure chance, and of an act quite natural to one of his age. For who has not, at the age Stéphane then was, felt the need to look in a slightly clouded mirror and see himself reflected more fervent or more cynical than life, in conformity to an ideal image of the self which will vanish like smoke at the very first juncture? But if Stéphane had any genius it was his gift for benefiting in a tortuous way from the most ordinary circumstances, and for turning them to unexpected account. By an impulse that was still perhaps natural, he refrained from recounting in his diary, which he kept very faithfully, the humiliating or suspect little events, the minuscule deceptions he practised and from which he could derive no glory. By a kind of magic, these events, these deceptions, once omitted in his record of the day, completely vanished from his memory. Lying acquired a magic value for him, it was the equivalent of a sacrament.

From then on, the character he had assumed became amplified, took on vigour and assurance. Whenever he had doubts as to the origin of an impulse or the reason for such and such an act, or felt the least moral qualm, the diary was there, it remedied all things. He might have had a bent for social-climbing, or have gone in for cynicism, as well, but he had inherited from his parents the taste for virtue. And is not virtue the ideal least subject to dispute? Who can judge of the virtue of a man, if not that man himself? Since he was judge of his own case, priest of his own religion, nothing could any longer really affect Stéphane, he was unassailable.

And now, this evening in his forty-sixth year, he continued to write in his diary. Or rather, a certain Stéphane was writing: a man deceived but loving, a failure but talented, bitter but philanthropic, alluring but virtuous. For, like those mosses that invade a tree, covering it, stifling it, and even after its death continuing to embrace it, what remained of Stéphane himself in this man sitting there, enchanting himself with his own flourishes, his own eloquence? Nothing, unless perhaps, beneath a great deal of feigned bitterness, a little real sadness, an almost childlike feeling of distress and solitude, a fleeting glimmer of anguish, quickly stifled by words and gestures, but which, after all, one must call his soul.

Mademoiselle Germaine Lethuit was the first to arrive. Socrates welcomed her affably. He had already closed the restaurant to ordinary customers by shutting the door and propping a chair against it, and had turned over the "Greek Cuisine" placard to its "Closed Monday" side. Now he arranged some chairs around a table. The remainder of the chairs were stacked at the far end of the room beneath the abstract painting.

"Would you care to have something to drink, while waiting?" asked Socrates.

Demonstrating a virile taste, Germaine Lethuit said she would have a glass of red wine. She was wearing a tailormade suit and a loosely knotted black tie, which must surely impress the inhabitants of the quarter.

"I'm not turning on the lights over the bar," said Socrates. "Maybe that will keep people away. Last Monday they were hammering on the door every five minutes, and the disturbance upset Monsieur Ducas."

The dark red paint of the walls was scaling off in flakes. The young girl with the nenuphars was smiling. Socrates had once thought of replacing her with a Greek warrior, but had never realized the plan, any more than he had realized his idea of repainting the restaurant a brighter red. A rose-shaded lamp had been provided by Madame Prêtre, to give a greater atmosphere of intimacy to these reunions, in which she never failed to participate.

"I was so sorry not to be able to come last Monday," said Germaine, rather nervously. "I so wanted to hear Monsieur Ducas's talk! It must have been quite wonderful."

"Wonderful," said Socrates. "Some time ago I laid in a couple of casks of d'Arbois wine, and I offered them some. Were they pleased! They don't often taste a burgundy like that!"

"Probably not," said Germaine rather stiffly.

"Oh, I'll not deny they're well-bred and well-educated people," Socrates went on, "but despite all that, they don't have the means. Now, when I lived in Greece, I remember meeting Princess Marina once, and, just imagine . . ."

Germaine was not listening. She was shaken by an inner trembling. What? Could Germaine Lethuit, that secular and Republican Amazon, that terror and benefactor of poor families whom she assisted on behalf of the State, that support of an old father and of a sister, Pauline, could she tremble? Any acquaintance of hers would have laughed at such an idea, for it in no way corresponded to her character or appearance. Germaine Lethuit was a smiling little red-haired creature with lively round eyes, energetic movements, and a booming, almost masculine voice, a surprising voice to come from that nervous little body. "She's an apostle!" Stéphane had said of her. And it was true, that, no matter what the cause, provided it were new, Germaine Lethuit embraced it with that ardour of which martyrs are made.

The venerable Socialism generally accepted in her family was not enough for her. She needed constantly to renew her stock of causes; painless childbirth had never had a better propagandist than this woman who was not a mother, Free Love had never been so ardently upheld as by this virgin exempt from any suspect emotion. Nothing could be farther from the austere principles paraded by Stéphane. But the old-fashioned and purely idealistic way in which Germaine Lethuit defended her revolutionary ideals drew them together. Stéphane's stern pronouncements were as foreign to his everyday life as her inflamed theories were to hers. Somehow this fact gave them something in common.

Germaine lived at Meudon in a little house on the Place Jeanne-d'Arc—symbolical!—with an aged father, a retired schoolmaster who, with his big moustaches, was the very image of secular virtues, the type of old gentleman depicted in the advertisements of apéritif wines. Mademoiselle Lethuit's sister Pauline (who had been married but quickly divorced, which restored her to spinsterhood, for which she had a true vocation), gave singing lessons and bred gold-fish. This trio lived in peace and sincere affection, having a naïve and touching faith in the sanctity of compulsory education, the separation of Church and State, and everything that was Good and Beautiful and Secular. In short, theirs was a religion like any other. And these three pious and rather ingenuous inhabitants of the Place Jeanne-d'Arc (Jeanne considered merely as a national heroine, of course) had some inoffensive but ridiculous little manias which were softened by their reckless and total kindliness. If a newspaper opened a campaign for a charity, the trio in the Jeanne-d'Arc villa immediately contributed as far as their very modest means would allow.

The children of the slums, the homeless, the conscientious objectors all benefited from their gifts. Not a week passed without some sniffling little schoolboy coming to sell them stamps in a campaign to raise money for holiday camps—such stamps accumulated in an old box kept for the purpose—and to wait hopefully for a caramel, which was always forthcoming. Even when a Sister of Charity appeared in the little garden which was kept with jealous care, one of the two girls would slip a coin into the outstretched hand, but on the sly, hiding the act from the old man, and with a feeling of committing a sin (a word used with regret, since they had a horror of Christian terminology). The sisters pretended not to notice that their father was deaf; and he pretended to be unaware of the vocal efforts of his daughters. The life they led could well have figured in a Golden Legend.

However, Germaine Lethuit had a weakness, a flaw, one could

not go so far as to call it a blemish, but, shall we say, a slight shadow lay upon her irreproachable virtue. She harboured, in relation to her sister Pauline ("The artist of the family," the old schoolmaster called her) a very slight, almost imperceptible jealousy. Was it the musical gifts of that sister, gifts that are always a little privileged, and the prestige they earned her with the population of Meudon? Was it Pauline's unhappy marriage—her husband, an employee of the Post, Telegraph, and Telephone Department, had run off with a day's receipts and gambled the money away at the races—which surrounded her with a romantic halo?

Whatever the cause, Germaine had always felt, but without bitterness, that she was reduced to a more practical and humdrum rôle. She earned more money, made the decisions as to what should be bought. It was she who had selected the refrigerator, a very modest one of unknown make; it was she who had decided that they should buy the Sunday edition of l'Humanité. In short, she was the Martha to that Mary. But people tire of being ordinary, and it was perhaps this lassitude, this desire to have, in her turn, some artistic prestige—for she held in pious horror anything involving sex, even episodic, even matrimonial—rather than true inspiration which had impelled her one fine morning to take up a pen and write her "Ode to Conscientious Objectors", this being a matter that had always interested her.

And today, at the Café Céleste, she was awaiting in agony the judgement of her friends. What a triumph to take home with her, if the poem were found pleasing! But would it be?

"Oh!" she exclaimed, with feigned sprightliness, "Look who's here! Our darling little Sylvia!"

Sylvia Prêtre was, indeed, coming in, followed by her mother, and carrying the wicker armchair. While Socrates fussed round the concierge, who always listened tolerantly to his talk, Germaine addressed a few affectionate words to Sylvia. Despite Sylvia's pretty face and smart clothes and her affair with "the famous man", she considered the young girl possessed a fine mind which had only lacked education to develop it. And every time she saw her, she tried, as best she could, to sow a few good seeds in that neglected soil.

"But I see no one but women here!" boomed a voice.

It was Stéphane in his Monday guise, white shirt open at the throat—an artist may allow himself such a vagary—a velvet waist-coat, hair slicked back, dazzling smile, close-shaven, rejuvenated. He adored these little Monday night reunions, which he had transformed from dull meetings of the co-proprietors of the building into a little circle of the élite, "the Celestials", as he smilingly called them, in which was resuscitated the subdued, prudent, self-complacent and complaisant atmosphere, made up of harmless jokes and shared manias one finds among people hailing from the same province. Bending his tall figure, he came to kiss the ladies' hands, lingering a little over Sylvia's. Martine had not yet arrived.

"Well, my girl?" With Sylvia, he always adopted a bantering tone. "Still moving in high society? Still kept busy with cocktails, opening nights, photographers, dressmakers?"

Sylvia agreed, with a smile to which her short upper lip lent an innocent grace. She had beautiful dark eyes, so devoid of expression that people sometimes felt uncomfortable in her presence.

"And faithful, despite everything, to our little circle! Now, that's what I call charming in a young lady as socially prominent as you are! Today we have something very special, a very fine piece of writing by Mademoiselle Lethuit—why, yes, Germaine Lethuit is launching out into poetry—and this piece is on a subject that will provide us with an interesting discussion: conscientious objectors. A very great theme!"

"On what?" asked Socrates.

A little excitedly, Germaine set about explaining the piece. Madame Prêtre was observing with annoyance Stéphane's conversation with her daughter. Two years before, she had had to nip in the bud a feeling the eighteen-year-old Sylvia had for Monsieur Morani. True, there had since been another regrettable episode, only the year previously, with a photographer. But now, this year, she had finally achieved her ambition, which had always been to see Sylvia appreciated by some man wealthy enough to "pamper and spoil" her (Madame Prêtre's words), and she was not going to tolerate having that hard-won victory endangered. Thank God,

Sylvia was manageable, and this docility compensated for what Madame Prêtre called, not without a sinking feeling, her "foolishness". Sylvia was manageable; all her mother had had to do was to repeat, from time to time, "He's a failure", in regard to Stéphane, or for the photographer, "He's uncouth", and the young innocent was impressed. The affair with the photographer had been much the more serious of the two. Supreme insult, the young fellow had talked of marriage! But Madame Prêtre trusted no one, and she observed with displeasure that Stéphane was patting Sylvia's peach-bloom cheek.

"Oh, my dear child," he was saying with an ardour kindled by the ingenuous admiration in her dark eyes, "don't let yourself get too swept up in the social whirl. Live, yes of course, enjoy life! I myself have had a taste of that sort of thing." He could easily imagine himself as a man-about-town, dividing his time between the theatre and cocktail parties. "Yes. But don't let yourself lose that little oasis within you, to which it is sometimes good to withdraw and meditate. . . ." She was listening to him open-mouthed, as if listening to music: with thrilled incomprehension. But this in no way embarrassed Stéphane. "Oh! my dear girl, who can praise silence and solitude enough?"

He set himself to do so at great length. Sylvia went on listening. How well he talked! Certainly, Henry ("the famous man") was a great man. The papers said so, the general respect in which he was held also said so, and his luxurious flat, his car, his income largely demonstrated the fact. But all the same, Stéphane . . .

"Well, Sylvia?" her mother interrupted sharply, "Aren't you going to say how do you do to Mademoiselle Fortin?"

Stéphane turned round, rather embarrassed at meeting Martine's eyes. She sometimes had that piercing look which was suddenly bereft of the admiration he so liked. But he usually attached little importance to it; if he noticed it now it was only because of his wife's unpleasant words which came back to him most inopportunely: "Don't forget she's *bought* her room. You'll not be able to get rid of her so easily. . . ." Once more, Louise was spoiling his pleasure. None the less, he gave Martine an affectionate smile. He had no reason to feel guilty over having chatted awhile with that girl Sylvia. Anyway, hadn't his talk been as far as possible removed from gallantries?

"Good evening, my dear. I didn't see you this afternoon. Why was that?"

"Did you need me?" she asked with a kind of irony that he found unpleasant.

Unpleasant, likewise, was the fact that Socrates, Germaine Lethuit, Sylvia, and her mother all moved aside, as if recognizing that Martine had certain rights over him.

"Oh come, Martine, I always need you."

"I was inclined to think that Toni was enough," she said stiffly.

She had got it into her head that the waitress was in love with him! He could not keep back a smile.

"Oh, really, Martine!"

The arrival of the others cut short his words.

"Come in, come in," he called, with relief. "You're none too early, my dear friends."

"Don't complain, Stéphane, you had all these ladies," Monsieur Ducas replied in his fluty voice.

He was a dapper little man, fine featured, rather sad looking, and not without kindliness. Jean Cadou came in at his heels, emitting a kind of grunt by way of greeting. This habit, plus a tousled head of hair, a snub nose, and the sullen look of an untidy undergraduate prevented one from immediately perceiving that he must be thirty-five years old. Dr. Fisher brought up the rear, dignified with his thick white hair, his face with its bright blue eyes still that of a disdainful and handsome young man. Socrates hastened to pour out some rum, which the Doctor immediately drank.

"Well, my dear Mademoiselle Lethuit," Gérard Ducas was saying with great courtesy, "it seems we are to hear a poem of yours read this evening?"

Germaine, blushing, was about to reply, but Stéphane assumed the responsibility.

"The theme is fascinating," he said enthusiastically. "It concerns . . ."

"I could do with a drink," yawned Jean Cadou.

"With pleasure, Monsieur Cadou," said Socrates, who was exerting himself to the utmost. "A glass of white wine, as usual?"

"Right," grunted Cadou, flinging his heavy body into a chair, stretching out his long legs ostentatiously, and leaning an elbow on the table. His resemblance (which Ducas was always pointing out with pleasure) to the portrait of Rimbaud by Fantin Latour seemed to authorize this attitude.

"Jean, my boy," Ducas said reprovingly, but with maternal indulgence. "My poor Jean must be excused, he worked all night long," he added to the others. "He had a few drinks last evening and then, suddenly, at about eleven o'clock, he flung himself upon his canvas with a real fury! Splashing everything, paint everywhere! And I will say he did achieve a harmony in reds! Electric tones, false, vibrating—you see what I mean? All modern life in it, the artifice of modern life, felt by a visionary in a night of revelry. You must really see it, my dear Morani. Everything's in it, your Brasserie, you know, that false, discordant world, your little *ritornellos*, your sufferings, too, everything is there, transposed and sublimated, naturally, but . . ."

"I would be very glad to see it, very glad," said Stéphane, a little primly.

The work of others, especially when as abundantly commented upon as this, did not interest him at all; but a universal complacency was the rule in this little circle.

"Me, I'm crazy about red," said Socrates.

Sylvia let out a rather embarrassed little laugh.

"Modern life? Really?" said Germaine Lethuit, who did not like painting, although she was careful not to confess it. "There are good things about it, sometimes, of course. Take, for instance, social legislation . . . even the extension of culture."

"Certainly," said Ducas, who displayed a great talent for patching together bits of conversation, "certainly, only a hundred years ago much fewer people appreciated painting. But supposing, my dear friend, that we change the subject, since the theme of our little reunion today is the reading of your poem? I must say I'm frightfully curious. I never expected to see you turn into a lyric poet!"

"But above all, please remember that what we are concerned with is a poem of social significance," exclaimed Stéphane, once again cutting short the poetess, who had opened her mouth and was about to speak. "Our friend, Germaine Lethuit, afforded me the pleasure, I should say the honour, of submitting this work to me first. I allowed myself to make a few changes and annotations—oh, minimal, scarcely more than grammatical—a few corrections of detail . . ."

"Oh! Monsieur Stéphane! Are we going to hear some of your own poetry?" cried Sylvia, clapping her hands.

Madame Prêtre frowned. Such baby tricks as clapping her hands were still all right for Sylvia, but what would they be in a few years? And supposing she turned out to be incapable of repressing her impulses, incapable of realizing that she must be quick to take advantage of her beauty and win a position in the world that was secure and permanent, supposing she was incapable. . . . Madame Prêtre's heart sank, under her black shawl.

"My poetry? You exaggerate, my child!" He noticed as he spoke the glum expression on Martine's face. "You will see how very little the poem owes to me."

He drew the poem from his pocket, and everyone moved closer, even Dr. Fisher, holding his glass of rum. He always looked as though he were wondering what he was doing there, but he came regularly.

"You, who have had to flee persecutions, Doctor," Stéphane said amiably, "should be particularly interested in these moral problems."

Dr. Fisher bowed, as if before a just homage, but made no comment. Gérard Ducas smiled. He adored these little reunions, they were so exquisitely old-fashioned. It was an atmosphere he enjoyed: courteous, affectionate (they were all very fond of one another), and just a bit ridiculous. He leaned back on his chair, the better to enjoy and savour the poem.

Stéphane, after a final glance around his little flock—oh, how

annoying Martine was, sulking there in her corner—began reading
in his grave, resonant voice, halting occasionally to catch his breath
and then continuing, the "Ode to Conscientious Objectors".

It was a nice sample of down-to-earth *engagé* literature. In the
first strophe (the Ode was constructed according to all the rules;
Malherbe might have disavowed the subject but not the style)
Germaine Lethuit loudly proclaimed that she excluded no conscientious objector, be he even a Christian or a Communist. In the
second strophe she described the horrors of prison, making an
allusion (which Stéphane had criticized as being biased), to "the
hypocritical chaplain digesting his meal" who lavished upon the
prisoners "homicidal advice". A long discussion had followed his
objection to that passage and Germaine, burning with the desire to
have her piece read at the Monday reunion (but perhaps an indulgent
veil should be drawn over this weakness), knowing that the decision
depended upon Stéphane, betrayed her convictions and the sacred
memory of Émile Combes by altering the phrase "hypocritical
chaplain" to read "hypocritical gaoler", which deprived the piece,
it must be admitted, of much of its revolutionary import.

The third strophe (almost entirely due to Stéphane, and in a more
lyrical style), hymned the prisoner's consolations, "a dancing ray of
sunlight", a pet animal (mouse or spider), indicating the "compassion of Nature" (Stéphane in his turn had made this concession to
secularity), a fraternal glance exchanged between men. This strophe
was greeted by a flattering murmur from the antiquarian.

The fourth and last strophe, in a more socially conscious and more
virile tone, predicted the fall of the government and the advent of a
better world, where the toys given to the children would no longer
be guns and rifles but trowels and sickles—the poet had avoided
"hammers" as too symbolical, but did not stop to think whether
the children of the future might not risk hurting themselves more
gravely with trowels than with wooden rifles. Nor did she evoke
the possibility of trowels made of rubber. But then, Germaine
Lethuit was not a mother.

"Some very nice things in it," said Gérard Ducas, who was
usually not given to so much indulgence, but who for a moment

had imagined himself poetically transformed into a conscientious objector and shaking hands furtively with Jean in a dark corner.

"Yes, you agree with me, don't you?" said Stéphane, who could not forgo all modesty in seeming to compliment Germaine Lethuit. "This strikes a rather new note, doesn't it? I'm not fully in accord with the political ideology expressed, but all the same. . . ."

"Oh, neither am I," said Ducas quickly (despite his liking for avant-garde art, he felt it deliciously paradoxical to be at the same time royalist and clerical), "but there are certain features . . . the ray of sunlight, that mouse—is it a mouse?—that gaoler . . ." He went no further in self-revelation.

"That's real poetry," said Socrates, "but I didn't understand very well why they didn't escape to Switzerland if they didn't want to go to war. In Greece . . ."

"As for me, I call them deserters," said Madame Prêtre. "And anyway, if a man happens to know a doctor, it's easy to get things fixed up. . . ."

"Oh yes?" said Dr. Fisher ironically.

They were the first syllables he had uttered. Madame Prêtre, fearing she had hurt his feelings, eagerly tried to correct the impression. "I didn't mean to say, Doctor, that a medical man would tell a lie, naturally, but if a poor devil of a young man came to ask you to do that for him, frankly . . ."

"Perhaps," said Dr. Fisher, "perhaps." (There had been a young maid-servant that very afternoon. . . . Why did they always come to him? And again, why did he do what they wanted?)

Mademoiselle Lethuit felt a little left out.

"The cause of the conscientious objectors," she said firmly, "is so important! To think that some of those unfortunates, whose sole crime was not to want to shed blood, are still in prison, after more than ten years!"

"Oh, my goodness! Is that possible?" said Sylvia, appalled.

Socrates and Madame Prêtre had drawn near. Stéphane usually interpreted for them when the discussion was over their heads. Jean Cadou was drinking. Ducas had buttonholed Dr. Fisher, for whom he had a certain liking. The Doctor had a kind of allure, with his head of white hair and his face that was simultaneously youthful and ravaged by time. Martine was standing at the end of the room by the window, looking out at the street, while not losing a word spoken by Stéphane. He had never before neglected her so ostensibly, and yet, had he not insisted that she join the little circle? A bitter anger welled up in her.

Sylvia was bewailing the plight of the imprisoned conscientious objectors. She was good hearted: the news of such things, in the papers, always made her shed tears. A crime, a sick child, were enough to spoil half of a dinner in town. The idea never occurred to her, however, that something might be done about it. But she greatly admired people who talked about such things, people like Stéphane and Germaine Lethuit, she even venerated them with all her good child's soul, good child, yes, to whom her First Prize (the fur coat) had given a good conscience.

Germaine Lethuit beheld her work disappearing beneath the torrent of comments, as is the common fate of many of the most respectable authors. In a last effort, she squeezed into the group of people whom Stéphane was catechizing. "The ode," she began courageously, "is a type of . . ."

But Stéphane, caught up in the crowd, abandoned her and re-joined Ducas who was attacking poetry that was socially conscious, while Stéphane was defending it heatedly. Already he had appropriated the theories that had presided at the birth of the ode.

"Surely you'd not make poetry avoid the images of modern life? Surely you'd not keep it from celebrating skyscrapers, locomotives, er . . . Well, then, why not stir up the big problems of our time?"

Ducas had a horror of big problems, of brutality, of a lack of the picturesque. A Louis XV armchair, one of those fake *bergères*, with fake shepherds and fake well-washed sheep would have been part of his favourite interior decoration. (For him, there could be no question of shepherdesses.)

"It seems to me," he said, not without a certain irony, "that you, a devout Christian, should defend the eternal values more warmly than anyone else!"

"Long live abstract poetry!" muttered Jean Cadou.

An artist has no business dealing with the great problems, he thought. Nor even with the little problems. All he asked was for people to leave him in peace and buy his paintings; Gérard Ducas could take care of his laundry and worry over conscientious objectors.

Germaine Lethuit made one more effort to intervene.

"Don't you think that a publication . . ." she murmured.

But Ducas did not even hear her. He was celebrating the eternal values, love, Virgil and his shepherds. Germaine sighed. The aureole of poesy had not consented to crown her brow. The attempt had failed. In the goodness of her soul she held no grudge against Stéphane. Courageous Amazon, she resigned herself to her fate, and undertook to initiate Sylvia into the beauties of Socialism.

Stéphane and Dr. Fisher were among the last to leave. Dr. Fisher liked to be talked to, and Stéphane liked to talk. Neither of them paid much attention to Martine, who seemed to be calmly looking out at the street.

"Will you lock up?" asked Socrates. "I'm leaving you the bottle of rum, Doctor. No, no, it's a pleasure to offer it. . . ."

"Rarely, said Stéphane, "does one find a group of such fine people. Certainly, the intellectual level. . . ."

Dr. Fisher nodded in approval, drank, nodded again. Let him go on talking! This warm feeling of not being alone, yet of being indifferent. . . . He was pondering the problem of whether or not to buy a dog. But a dog doesn't talk. A human being is more amusing. You can't laugh at a dog. . . .

Stéphane finally stopped.

"I believe, my dear Doctor, that I'd better go and lie down. . . . Fatigue. . . . Then," a little tardily perceiving the presence of Martine, "I ought to accompany (if one may apply such a word to climbing the stairs) this charming young lady who is listening to us with such patience. . . ."

Why had she stayed on? He had the disagreeable feeling that she was going to be huffy again. Oh well! He would offer her a drink and be quits. Tomorrow in some bar or other, they could have a longer chat. From his youthful experience when he was irresistibly good looking, he had kept a naïve confidence in the power of a few sweet words, a bouquet of flowers, a smile. He wouldn't go so far as to kiss her, for she might imagine . . . But he felt confident of exercising some of his charm.

"Forward march, to our stairway, my dear," he said graciously. "For me, tired as I am, it's a long enough journey. . . ."

His smile mingled delicate health with gallantry. But Martine still looked glum as she came forward and let him take her arm.

"Go, by all means," said Dr. Fisher. "I'll lock up, don't worry."

They went out by the little side door. Stéphane leaned upon Martine, as much from calculation as from the real fatigue which had suddenly overpowered him. Panting a little, he stopped at the foot of the stairs, to gather his strength.

"Well, my sweet?" he asked, during this halt.

It was the first time he had ever called her that, and he did not intend to make it a habit. But he had rather neglected her this evening.

Whereupon, he had an incredible surprise. Wrenching herself violently away from him, her thin little body shaking with rage, her usually vague and blinking eyes now staring fiercely at him, she spoke in a strange, tense, toneless and pitiless voice, hurling the words into his face:

"I hate you! I hate you!"

"So you've been having a spot of culture?" said Henry, not unkindly.

Sylvia was impervious to irony.

"It was marvellous," she said, with touching enthusiasm. "Germaine Lethuit told me all about conscientious objectors, and that's why I'm late. . . ."

She consulted the wristwatch, gold set with diamonds, a gift from Henry. Madame Prêtre had been very pleased with her daughter when she had seen that watch.

"Did you know, Henry, that they're sometimes kept in prison for ten years?"

"Who?"

"The conscientious objectors."

"You don't say!" said Henry, who was thinking of something quite different.

The afternoon had been bad, he had not been able to work. The Mozart record was on the gramophone, he had played it three times, and had not been able to cast out the demon.

"Yes, and they'd rather stay in prison than shed blood. Isn't that splendid? Germaine Lethuit says it's a grave social problem."

"Oh, clearly, if Germaine Lethuit says so."

Mechanically he caressed the shoulders bared by the light dress. Just as mechanically, Sylvia uttered a flattering sigh. Henry was such a discouraging person! He never wanted to have a serious conversation. So what was the use of having a famous man all to herself!

"And she even wrote a poem on it, a lovely poem, that was read aloud."

"Real poetry?" (The music had had the same effect as ten years ago, he felt the same uneasiness. He would never understand what was at the bottom of that music which seemed to reproach him. No, it was not exactly a reproach.)

"Of course, real poetry," said Sylvia, slightly offended. "An ode."

"An ode on conscientious objectors?" Attentive for a moment, he burst out laughing.

"I see," said Sylvia, with an air of shrewdness, "you're opposed to poetry that has a social content." Henry's hand had slipped down inside her bodice. But, forgetting her duty—what would her mother have said!—Sylvia courageously went on talking. "An abstract painter who was there had the same opinion as you."

"Oh, as for me, Sylvia!" said Henry. "Live and let live, that's my motto. I'd willingly paint a conscientious objector if his face interested me."

The music had depressed him, once again. And what a fool idea this had been, to have the girl come here at this hour! Either she would be tired out or else she would suggest going to a night-club—

he wondered who stuffed her head with such notions—and he detested night-clubs more than anything in the world. But that morning, when he'd telephoned her, he had felt in top form, ready to paint, ready to make love. . . . And what an idea to have confronted himself again with that Mozart record, it was like pressing on a wound already half healed. And so there it was, the pain had returned. Or rather, not the pain, that was too noble a word, too strong. The uneasiness, the nausea, the ignoble doubt, the, why not, the colic. . . . He couldn't find words low enough to qualify these spells of depression.

He remained silent. Sylvia also, with great application, remained silent. ("Inspiration," she told herself sagely. "Inspiration. He's a great man, mustn't forget it.") There the great man was, in the immense studio, where several lamps glowed, sitting on the wide Oriental divan in front of the vast window which was veiled by grey linen draperies—all these details, Sylvia conscientiously told herself, had been photographed for *Paris-Monde*—and he was not at all imposing. Henry was a man of medium height, but his disproportionately wide shoulders made him seem to be short and thick-set. Coarse as to hands, short as to legs; with a slight paunch, nothing shocking since he was, after all, sixty-five; eyes sparkling, often with malice; thin grey hair plastered on a round cranium, the round head of a peasant—that was Henry Stass. A great man! Try as she would to efface Stéphane with that phrase, she felt, despite everything, and not without remorse, that photographs of Stéphane Morani in *Paris-Monde* would have been more impressive. Once more she tried to dispel these wicked thoughts and to carry on the conversation.

"Well, Monsieur Morani is for it."

"For what, my pretty?"

"For poetry that has social significance." And since, at all costs, she wanted to get him interested, she elaborated the thought. "You may have known him once, since at one time you painted in Signac?"

"In Signac I knew a Monsieur Morani who's for socially significant painting?"

"For socially significant poetry," she said patiently. "Is there such a thing as socially significant painting?"

But of course, and as usual, when the conversation became interesting, Henry turned a deaf ear, deep in his own thoughts. Signac! What a shame that such a pretty town bore the name of that hateful painter! (And though people said he was a charming man, Henry had never wanted to meet him, certain that they would not like each other). Signac. That was before the Mozart record, before America even, it had been a period of happiness, strength, repletion. . . . The memory of Signac rendered Sylvia still more insupportable. Why, for heaven's sake, why had he asked her to come? Why was he seeing her almost every day? Why were there some moments when she appeared to him quite simply as a pretty and rather witless girl whom he could easily desire, but at others, almost repulsive, with her thin, underfed body, her ordinary body, which aroused pity? It was then—and this was the surest sign of those morbid states into which he suddenly plunged—he seemed to be able to see through her, glimpse that soul of hers which was also thin and ordinary, submissive, and vain, preening itself, adorning its worthlessness with the most rubbishy trifles.

Oh, Signac! He conjured up its little by-streets, so pleasantly picturesque, its good, solid middle-class streets, swollen with self-importance, the little deserted port, the countryside almost colourless in the sunlight. But no image that he could call up had the vigour and meaning it once had. Love had then been something calm and silent, as nourishing as daily food; money had been something not squandered—he had always had a tendency towards avarice; it had been like a wall against which he could lean—and there had been his uninspired painting, for he loathed inspiration, that Mediterranean bromide! He came from the North, from a town of textile mills, one of the ugliest towns in the world, and he loved it, and his rages against Van Gogh, who had marked and disfigured that southern France to such a point that one suddenly caught oneself painting a Van Gogh, in those contaminated landscapes. . . . All the same, with his stolid patience, his hard, slow toil, his paintings laid down one after another like paving-stones, he had succeeded in marking a few landscapes with *his* character, had succeeded in making certain landscapes his own. And perhaps other painters were today hating him for having manipulated the very matter of their environment, for having marked its contours, reduced its colour to heavy splotches, giving things for ever their full weight, and for having, with what triumphant force, *pinned them down to earth.* Oh, Signac! And that moment (yes, it had been fifteen years ago), when he had known that feeling of plenitude, like the peasant who straightens himself up at last, aching, to survey the harvest around him . . . he had been fifty years old.

"*Are* we going out, Henry?"

He gave a start.

"Would you like to have me pose for you, then?" she asked, accommodatingly.

What she meant was, "Do you want me to undress?", thought Henry. She would do anything he asked her. And not solely for money. That was the worst of it. She was not even mercenary. It must be her mother who goaded her, the same mother who ruled that her daughter should be home before one o'clock in the morning and should have a fur coat (which, moreover, he had bought). But as for the girl, poor little fool, it was worse still, with those cultural evening reunions. (He detested the theatre and regularly slept through performances.) And the night-clubs! ("Seen at the Club de l'Etoile, Henry Stass and a pretty brunette who . . .") And it cost a lot, besides. But she was satisfied. She clapped her hands. This was culture, wasn't it, this was celebrity. . . . And all this without a mean thought, without even the vainglory you might expect, but with a dim awareness of her mediocrity, a desperate need to do what others did, to do the right thing, to *earn* a reward for good behaviour since she could expect it for nothing else. . . . Oh, the humility of fools! And sometimes it happened that he, Henry Stass, the rich man with a pretty young mistress (a situation old as the hills and which, God knew, passed for a simple and natural one), he, Henry Stass, experienced a kind of panic during those moments when he felt the futility and tragic meaning of that dim awareness.

All the same, revolt surged in him. What, even a stupid and

pretty girl now had power over him, devasted him, undid him? He sat up. "After all, why not go out? At the Club de l'Etoile . . . we could have one of those lobsters. . . ."

It meant throwing away at least ten thousand francs. She was very fond of champagne. But he must escape this mood, and she must not be disappointed and in tears. No, not that!

"Oh, yes, yes! How wonderful!" she exclaimed, clapping her hands.

Pretending to look for his coat, Henry turned away, to avoid witnessing such immoderate joy.

Little whore, daughter of a whore, why do you deserve to be pitied? A jewel, a fur coat, an American car, that sums up your dream of beauty, and you wholeheartedly make love to me, or rather the newspaper where you first saw my name. Harmless little whore, why should anyone, for your sake, put everything in question?

For a moment, completely flabbergasted, Stéphane was rooted to the spot, more shaken than if he had received a blow, his heart suspended in the void, and as he stood there, panting, the only thing that kept him from falling in a faint was the realization that a stupendous sacrilege, a monstrous injustice, had just been committed.

"You, Martine! You!" he at last found the strength to utter.

Her face was again sullen, but she was still staring at him with that unbearable look of rage in her eyes!

"Yes, me! Did I ever promise to endure everything from you? Am I your slave? Oh, you certainly deluded me, with your moans and groans, your sick and self-pitying ways! Nothing but a victim, eh? What a fool I've been!"

"Martine! I implore you!"

He could hardly breathe, his head swam beneath this unexpected and sudden shock. He staggered, and leaned against the balustrade. She went up one or two more steps, as if she were going to leave him there, but then she turned back.

"Yes, a fool, a damned fool! I believed in that poor Stéphane, that pitiful creature, so hurt, so misunderstood! I swallowed the whole rigmarole: the poor man, gravely ill, and with a wife who didn't understand him. But that stuff's as old as time! It must have fooled people like me for centuries. I've been fooled like hundreds of others—like others you've taken in by the same tricks, no doubt!"

"Martine! I swear to you . . ."

He climbed the stairs behind her, with great difficulty. He was not too stricken to cling to the idea that only jealousy was behind all this. But he must catch up with her, convince her. That she doubted his good faith! He felt like a hunted animal driven to earth, he was shaken to the innermost centre of his being, hurt in the most secret and hidden corners of his soul. And she, feeling this, became more relentless, filled with that terrible joy of at last having a grip on someone, of finally possessing something, if only someone's hatred. Since her childhood, she had not experienced one of these sudden rages which ended almost in convulsions. She had resigned herself to a life cut off from everything, isolated from everything that was living and warm; almost, she had enjoyed her cold isolation. And he had sought her out there, had implicitly promised her power, had made her believe that he needed her—a girl so wretched that she no longer even felt anger, had made her feel that she still had something to give. Yes, he had promised her all that, but let a pretty girl appear, an idiot, a half-wit, and he was ready to abandon her, ready to thrust her nonchalantly back into her original wretchedness. But she was calm now. She would have to find his sensitive point, must find out exactly what hold she had on him, for she did hold him, she suddenly realized. She went up a few more steps. He followed her, very pale.

"No, Stéphane," she said suddenly with murderous sweetness, "you are not a monster. I was carried away. Forgive me."

He stopped, panting, bewildered, but ready to forget. Oh, yes, to forget as quickly as possible. . . . But she was already speaking again.

"I was foolish. To be treated with contempt, you see. . . . But you didn't mean to hurt me. It's so easy to deceive a poor girl. And perhaps to deceive oneself. . . ."

He flinched, and she realized that she had touched that part of his inmost being, that naked, sensitive point he tried in vain to protect, she had hurt him, she had reached that part which she could not name but which, in a kind of fog, she knew was there.

"Martine, I don't understand. I did not try to . . ."

She continued her climb, and he followed her, out of breath. He passed by his own door without noticing.

"I'd like to believe it, Stéphane, I really would. But it's still true that you've been presenting your feelings, your family life, under the falsest colours."

"My . . . life?"

"Oh, come, Stéphane, be honest! No doubt your wife isn't perfect, but what about your own casual behaviour?"

They were now between the second and third floors. People could overhear them, but this did not occur to Stéphane. Martine was now comparing him with Louise! She had hurt him more deeply than she could imagine, for he himself had tried constantly for years, to make this comparison, without coming to a satisfactory conclusion.

"My dear, how can you?" he murmured, clinging desperately to the balustrade. "You know her, you know what she is. . . . I confided in you. . . ."

"She takes care of you, doesn't she? She takes care of you, and she works outside. Oh, I know very well what one could say . . . after all. . . ."

They had gone beyond the fourth floor. Stéphane was coughing, he was at the end of his strength. She did not turn back. She heard his hoarse breathing behind her, but she knew that he would follow her to the top floor, to her room, to her bed, and that he was following her only because of that secret fear she had not yet discovered. But she did not care. She was beside herself with rage, but a cold, calculating rage. They reached the fifth floor. Behind her, his breathing was almost like a death-rattle. She put the key in the lock. She felt Stéphane's breath on the back of her neck. He was incapable of speaking, and yet, she was sure he would have climbed ten more flights behind her, even if he fell down and died afterwards.

She opened the door, went in, and calmly took off her coat. The springs of the bed squeaked as Stéphane collapsed on it. She hung up her coat, disclosing her thin body, slightly awry, the body of which she was normally ashamed, but not today. She turned and surveyed him coldly, experiencing, even so, that little pang at the heart one has upon cutting the neck of a fowl, when the blood, in regular pulsations, begins to spurt out; she stood there watching his panic, gauging it, with neither pity for him and his shameful need of her, nor for herself and the sudden power that need gave her. His face was white, he was pressing both hands to his heart; he was so undone that she was almost afraid he would escape her. She could go no further without utterly crushing him; and if she crushed him utterly, then she would again find herself alone.

She sat beside him on the bed.

"My poor dear Stéphane," she said affectionately, "perhaps I misunderstood?"

It was enough. The man sitting beside her, broken, vanquished, no longer inspired hatred in her. And even that cold lucidity which had suddenly swept over her, that terrible bright joy, subsided, and in an instant her power fell from her hands. Slowly, she released herself from his embrace, letting him breathe a little more freely. . . .

"Now, lie there and rest, Stéphane, you're exhausted. . . ."

He made no resistance. She lay down beside him, her head resting upon his outstretched arm. He did not move, did not repulse her. The tortured animal was dead, a mere pile of feathers on the ground in the sunlight. But does death exist? Another wave of power welled up in her, but already of shorter duration, less strong. . . . She could restore life to this corpse.

"Dear, be calm, relax . . . I didn't intend to upset you so much. I had no idea. . . ."

She felt his breathing becoming more regular, and she told herself again that she still had power over his life. She held him. He could not escape her. Or could he? But the cold waves subsided, she could barely hear their distant roaring in her ears.

"Tell me what has upset you so. I was wrong, perhaps, to talk about. . . ."

She waited for his reply. She could no longer read his thoughts. Oh, that sudden illumination was far away, Martine was herself again, she was once more this graceless body, this face devoid of sweetness.

"You accused me . . ." he was saying, in a voice that was still faint, but now full of resentment. "You told me that she . . . that she had a right to . . ."

He was barely resuscitated, but instinctively he was orienting the conversation towards Louise, instinctively he was already protecting that weak spot, unknown to himself, where she had touched and hurt him, when she said, "It's so easy to deceive a girl . . . and to deceive oneself, perhaps." And she let herself be drawn.

"I didn't mean to say . . . Certainly, she is to be blamed, but perhaps, she, too, has suffered."

"Suffered? Louise suffered?" His voice was firmer, almost vehement, and his breathing had become easier. Obscurely he felt the danger was receding.

"I know quite well that you cannot expect much appreciation from her. She lacks sensitivity. . . ." She was fumbling, experimenting, and not recovering her power.

"Sensitivity! Why, she's a rock, a stone. A woman who was . . . well, you know what she was: a woman I rescued from the gutter, a woman from whom I've waited in vain for eighteen years to have a sign of gratitude or a spontaneous gesture of affection."

In a desperate effort, she daringly ran her fingers through his hair. "I understand," she murmured. "You, so responsive to the least shade of feeling. . . ."

How promptly he eluded her! The handsome face which showed almost no sign of age was already flooded with life. He propped himself up on one elbow. In a minute he would leave this bed where, all the same, he was still lying beside her. . . .

"Shades of feeling! My dear girl, if I told you . . . But I won't. Better to remain mute on the subject of the life she had led. You are too pure, you wouldn't understand. . . ."

His voice, too, had recovered its resonance, and he was speaking almost with pleasure, his eyes staring vaguely ahead. Cautiously, very cautiously she drew near him, talking, in order to distract his attention.

"But why did you marry her?"

"Why, my dear? That does appear quite illogical, quite mad, doesn't it? And I'm afraid I wouldn't do it again. But perhaps I'd be wrong. Perhaps some day we will see the meaning of all this. I was young, more naïve, perhaps a better person than I am now. I wanted to save her, to elevate her, how can I explain? But you must understand me, you who a little while ago—and in spite of any real evidence or apparent truth—were defending the woman you have every right to detest. . . ."

She was pressed against his side, now she could feel the warmth of his leg. She could no longer speak. In her flat little chest, her heart was beating loudly.

". . . and despite everything, you're the one that's right, Martine, in reminding me of the duty I assumed. . . ." He had become entirely himself again. His arm, while he spoke with increasing warmth, involuntarily pressed her thin shoulders. ". . . In that coarse clay, there must be some light of understanding. We must believe it, in spite of everything, even if we are choked with slime. We must have pity, always more pity! Perhaps we will be laughed at. . . ."

He suddenly checked himself. Her thin body was pressed against him, she was clinging to him, her plain face was quite close to his, her round eyes, wide open, terrible, were like port-holes, she was waiting. Squeezed between her and the wall, he suddenly realized the danger of his situation and was again seized by that terrible repulsion he had never been able to conquer, overwhelmed by a childish terror which could be read on his face, where suddenly, the mask torn off, there appeared a look of uncontrollable disgust.

Again! Again that barrier, that dizzy abyss she had never been able to cross and would never have the courage to plumb. All her power vanished, all her malignity was shattered in an instant, as she beheld that horror-stricken face, felt that sudden tensing of the muscles, as if he were gathering himself for flight. A moment longer she remained pressed against him, her short-sighted eyes intensely fixed upon his face in desperate entreaty. Then, suddenly, she burst into tears.

Stéphane, relieved, breathed freely and propped himself up on his elbow. Thank God, the danger had once more passed. As quickly as she, he banished the memory of his fright, of that involuntary start that had put a distance between them. Seizing upon an inspiration, he caressed the hair of the girl who had hidden her face in her hands.

"Martine, my dearest," he said slowly, his resonant voice filling the room, "see how we are punished for our pride. At the very moment when we are passing judgement, when we are speaking plainly, we are overtaken by temptation. . . . Oh, we are all made of common clay, even the best of us. . . ."

She listened. How could she not listen, not believe? In her turn she had stripped herself naked before him, he had seen her defenceless, disarmed, hurt. She had to believe, had to listen. Can one refrain from breathing even though the air be thin?

"Out of the slime," he went on, "we said out of the slime. But at the same time we realize that we ourselves are nothing but slime."

He was sitting on the edge of the bed, now, apart from her. No, it had not been disgust. He said "we". Can you not believe him, O ill-favoured girl with your plain face hidden behind those trembling hands? Can you refuse to pardon him or give him a reprieve, O condemned face, O cursed body?

"Yes, slime. But along with the humiliation, grace is granted us. We can reject that impulse, we can dominate the flesh. We can free ourselves from it! Martine, can we doubt Providence?"

She who had been so clairvoyant a short while ago, could she now doubt Providence? Vanquished in her turn by this man so oblivious to everything, could she reject salvation, reject the protective shade so comforting to her body and face? Besides, where find truth?

"No, Stéphane," she said humbly. "We cannot doubt."

He must speak the truth, and she must believe him in order to be saved. That was essential.

And now, he was pacing up and down the room, with big strides, as naïvely satisfied as a schoolboy rid of a tiresome schoolmaster, slightly ashamed, perhaps, for feeling suddenly liberated.

"Do you know, Martine, what I intend to do for you?"

"No," she murmured.

"Something I've never done for anyone else. I'm going to lend you my diary.... Yes, my intimate diary, the humble and awkward account of my struggles and hopes, of my failures, too. And so, mentally, we will live in each other, and I will have nothing hidden from you. . . . Oh, you'll never again be able to overwhelm me with those dreadful suspicions. . . ."

He had knelt beside the bed, he was talking in the low and cajoling voice of a child who has something to be forgiven. She opened her reddened eyes, in which a faint hope was stirring. He did not know of what he had been so afraid, just now. This poor little Martine, a bit jealous. . . . And she did not know, now, what she had thought hateful in him. That poor Stéphane, with his rather ridiculous but respectable scruples. . . . What had got into her? She no longer knew. . . .

They looked at each other, and nothing in them was any longer disquieting. What in the world had happened? They had forgotten. They smiled. For a moment they were both serene and immovable in the midst of their insubstantial and illusory happiness.

Part II: SUMMER

THROUGHOUT the summer, the little Montparnasse music-hall put on a strip-tease show for the benefit of a slightly different type of audience. Since the usual show was extremely undressed, the company of actresses remained in general the same, except for the stars, who were taking their summer vacations. The themes themselves remained unchanged: only "The Harem" number was slightly more voluptuous, "The Flower-Bed" slightly less multicoloured as the silks and sequins fell, and "The Bride's Undressing" . . . there was little to change in that number. Sarah took off one more little piece of chiffon, that was all. It was a show for tourists, for tourists a little short of money. However, there were some men of the quarter, young men, who paid to see the summer version, that is, they paid to see that piece of chiffon fall; and the sparkling little triangle that remained, shame's tiny and final refuge, haunted their innocuously vulgar dreams.

These first days of summer were by no means warmer than the last days of spring had been. And even, on this particular afternoon, rain had fallen. You felt the humidity of the dressing-rooms, which were not, properly speaking, a part of the theatre but were situated in a kind of annex at the rear, a badly built structure which quickly became damp or torrid or glacial, according to the season. Here, in the low-ceilinged rooms of the first two floors, and in the narrow passageways painted yellow, and in the tiny dressing-rooms, among the smells of greasepaint and sweat, Louise Morani calmly moved about.

"Lou!" cried one girl.

"Madame!" cried another, who was there only for the summer and did not as yet know the dresser.

Louise ran to hook up a singlet on a brown back, or to stitch on a buckle, or to adjust a skirt that was put on only to be taken off.

She liked this intimacy with young and healthy, if not always strictly well-washed, bodies, the naturalness of the familiar and indifferent contacts; and she was loved by the girls, for she was not young enough to be a rival but was still young enough to be regarded as a friend and not, as an older dresser sometimes is, the ambiguous duenna Goya loved to depict.

She was at ease in this back-stage world, in the glaring lights and the colourful animation which gave a semblance of gaiety, indeed, they were often gay, ill-fed and ill-loved and badly lodged as they were, these stereotyped Sultanesses, these over-painted and synthetically perfumed flowers, these peasant girls dressed in satin, these symbolic brides straight from a dream-book, with butterflies on their breasts and a question mark on the pubis. Louise knew them all, the pretty ones and the less pretty, the starvelings and those (a few) who had a limousine waiting for them outside; the married ones, who had a photograph of their little son stuck in their dressing-room looking-glass, and those who considered themselves to be real actresses because they had once figured in a commercial film advertising a brand of soap. Louise knew the name of the little boy, the address of "the dark-haired fellow who's waiting outside", the telephone number of an accommodating physician; she had seen the gentleman-with-the-carnation take off his Legion of Honour decoration (that one had been Sarah's "protector" for three seasons), and she remembered Consolación, an extraordinarily pretty Spanish girl, who had actually managed to become a star, under another name. She had made their daily preoccupations and their infantile rituals her own, as much her own as the memories of her youth, the lanes of Signac, the Saturday dances, and the cool dawns made hideous by the factory.

"Lou?"

Sarah hurried up, her voluminous bridal attire over her arm, naked, save for the silver-gleaming stockings, the bon-bon pink high-heeled slippers, and the regulation little triangle. This Sarah was much less beautiful than the casually indifferent Sarah at the Turkish baths. She was too beautiful, thought Louise, as she led her into the dressing-room, to have much attraction for the tourists whose preference was for the skinnier girls. In order to please, she had to use an outrageous amount of make-up, and assume vulgar poses. Louise dipped a bath-glove in some eau-de-Cologne and rubbed down the well-muscled back.

"That must be cold," she remarked.

"You've said it!" yawned Sarah. "I'll have my dressing-gown, please. What weather for June! And it's been summer now for three days. At least, he might have waited till the end of the holidays to throw me over. Then I wouldn't be here. After all, you give people time to turn round, don't you?"

"Some American men are out front tonight," Louise said, by way of a suggestion.

"They spend three weeks in France and go to look at the cathedrals! No, I'm looking for someone serious."

"They don't grow on trees," said Louise sententiously.

They had ten minutes: already twelve of the girls, the major part of the company, were on stage doing a line of high kicks in not very perfect unison. Louise brought the bouffant trousers of the Sultaness, the short red jacket and the red triangle—the colours had to be varied.

"Oh, you can talk, you're married," laughed Sarah. "You got your man!"

"In the provinces, nothing's easier," said Louise.

But it was true that Stéphane had for a given moment seemed to her to be "someone serious". And not merely because he had proposed marriage. His way of talking, no doubt, and then, who knows, his profession. A musician had seemed rather wonderful to her. She smiled as she thought, "What a fool I was!" And she had been twenty-seven then! But after all, what would have happened to her had she stayed on in Signac? She would perhaps have married a cattle-dealer, or been the mistress of a haberdasher who, in later life, would have been elected a Deputy; who, in any case, would have boggled at marrying her. Besides, she hadn't reasoned it out. Stéphane was handsome, very handsome. That, at least, was true and had, to a certain extent, remained true. As to serious. . . .

"If you knew," she murmured, hooking up the bouffant pantaloons, "what that can amount to, your serious man . . ."

The bell rang three times in the dressing-room, as it did each
night, and Sarah rushed out, as she did each night, in her Turkish
slippers, and the dressing-room door banged shut. "What crazy
things memories are!" thought Louise. And the imperceptible feeling
of displeasure which had hovered for a moment vanished. She must
hurry to transform the Tulips into Houris, a transformation that
never took place without accident—skin pinched in zippers, hooks
popping off at the last minute, a make-up still to do, two pairs of
stockings torn, and not a pair of the same shade of purple in stock. . . .
She went out to wait for the Tulips who would arrive in the little
iron stairway, turning their ankles and laughing too loudly. But
the end of the passageway was obstructed by a man standing there,
who seemed to be looking for something, and at first she didn't
notice anything about him except the exaggerated breadth of his
shoulders. . . .

. . . Everything that he would paint from then on would exist.
Even if he did not believe in it, there would always be someone to
say, "That belongs to his mechanistic period", or "He's returned to
his old theme of the blue bridge". All that he would ever paint was
already classified, labelled, codified. Even the term "evolution"
would no longer be pronounced; at most they would say it was a
matter of completion, of fulfilment. Or even in the unimportant
little magazines, of repetition. His life was behind him, solid and
compact, as clearly defined as the pavements and the skyscrapers he
had liked for their geometrical mass, their crude colourings reminding him of his machines and his industrial landscapes. There it was,
his life, as he had conceived and constructed it, as he had wanted it
to be in the smallest details of its architecture. A significant, successful life. And he was neither in poor health nor worn out, he could
still walk a dozen kilometres a day across Paris, could still do honour
each day, or almost, to an admiring mistress.

With the tip of his brush he gently stroked the canvas. He was
neither fatigued nor ill nor short of ideas. Only the day before he

had made several preliminary drawings for paintings and those
sketches were balanced, harmonious; they, too, *existed*. All he had
to do was get down to work and paint. All that he would paint
would be good ("Stass is always in top form, what vitality!" one
read in the magazines), good, well composed, and with a vitality
of its own. There were painters who knew the pang of suddenly
feeling that their work no longer clicked, that they were no longer
hitting it off, that no matter how they killed themselves over their
work it was without significance, without life. That was not the
feeling he had. His work lived, it continued to have solidity and
power, continued to assert its own rhythm. But he now felt that it
lived independently of him, beyond and outside him. He was the
one who was not alive.

He stopped stroking the canvas. "I'm not fit for anything today,"
he decided aloud. "I'll not do anything worthwhile today." What
others felt about loss of inspiration, that sudden weariness, that
breakdown, that blank vacancy, was what he felt about his life. It
was only after several days of coddling himself, following one of
these "spells", that life gradually recovered its colours and significance and with relief he found himself on his feet again. Sylvia
shook her stupid little head, supposing she was witnessing an artist
in the throes of creation, imagining she was living a great moment
of happiness, for was it not her rôle to give inspiration to this artist?
Her admiration was more than he could bear, so he sent her packing.

At fifty, life had played a strange trick on Henry Stass: he had
become, it would seem, intelligent, or at least, that is the way he
saw his problem. He was almost on the point of calling himself
an "intellectual". The symptoms? Certain music now touched him;
in the past he had bragged about not recognizing any tune except
the Marseillaise. And the music he now liked was good, was well
known. Then, he found that at last he could look at other painters'
work and understand it! In the past he had always felt that he was
the only painter in the world. So others existed, too? And he set
himself to understand his own paintings, to construct them—not that
the works of his youth were faulty in construction, they were good
compositions, but he had been unaware of it.

"My ideas? I haven't any!" he had once declared to a crowd of admirers, who said of him, "He's one of these stupid geniuses." Stupidity is the mitigating circumstance of genius: it reassures, it emphasizes the irresponsibility of the creative artist, who is thus no longer a superior person but merely a privileged one. A thing that escaped all these partisans of the "stupid genius" theory was that Henry himself took refuge in it.

He had survived his first crisis thanks to a big popular success, something he had hitherto lacked. Since then, the crises or "spells" as he called them had occasionally returned. About every three years, or during a bad case of grippe, a too passionate mistress, a too copious dinner, would bring on one of the spells. He decided that it must be a stomach ailment and had consulted several famous physicians who had smiled indulgently and invited him to dine; their wives or daughters had asked for his autograph (Dared she? Why yes, she dared) or a sketch. Henry paid his bill by tracing a few lines with his heavy hand pressed upon an album which already contained an autograph of Mallarmé. When it came to thanking the physician there had always been a great exchange of formal politeness, and all this had taken place in the very social sphere that he held in horror. But he had no stomach ailment, nor liver ailment. Quite certain? Why, of course, of course! Oh, these artists, all of them so highly strung! And the spells returned, with ever greater frequency. They were now occurring about once a month; once a month he had to endure these anaemic and colourless days. "Like a woman," he had been tempted to say, with amused coarseness. But he was not really amused.

"Are you having one of your spells?" asked Sylvia, with a knowing air. He had tried with such phrases to accommodate himself to it and make it an accepted, well-known thing, devoid of interest. But he feared its recurrence, felt it coming, and when it was quite near, in order to trigger it, he would put a Mozart record on the gramophone. Why Mozart? It had been at a concert that one of the worst "spells" had begun, the longest and most painful, the one that had made him renounce the idea that he had a liver complaint. The liver could not account for everything. The suffering was more . . . intellectual. Disgusting to have to confess that! He, an intellectual! Hadn't Maurras said something on the subject, or someone else of the same type? Something to the effect that intellectuals were the cause of all defeats? (Not that defeats concerned him in the least. He had been in America during the war, and people were always coming up to him, mournfully and sympathetically shaking him by the hand, with the unspoken but understood words, "Poor France. How you must suffer!" Like undertakers at a funeral. Besides, he had fought in the 1914 war and was too old in 1940. Too old! Ridiculous, such norms! He had never felt healthier in his life.)

Intellectual, was it? Very well, but why Mozart? That concert had so roused him that he had bought the record and a gramophone. Then he had bought other records of classical music—Bach, Beethoven, things the fellow in the music shop had recommended. But they had had no effect upon him, none whatever. Bach with his mathematical certitude, his pitiless sweetness, was so far from him, so far—how explain? Parallel. They could never meet. Why, even that portrait he had done of the woman in red on the bridge at Signac was enough to quash Bach, weight for weight, certitude against certitude. And Beethoven, too loud, too emphatic, too disordered with his "Ha! That's true! Ha, so much the worse for you!" And above all, stupid! Repeating the same argument over and over again without stopping, then, all of a sudden, patient and smug. Did he think he was drilling a little boy in a too difficult lesson? And suddenly, boom! a blow on the keyboard: "Why is it true? Because I say so, that's why!" All the same, Henry had a liking for him, the sort of liking one has for a friend who is slightly crazy, a friend whose convictions one doesn't share, but whom one likes nevertheless.

But Mozart. . . . How could one be on guard against a child singing? All at once, while you were listening with pleasure, and almost indulgently, there he was murmuring, "Suppose it's true?" You felt like jumping on him, but before you could make a move he'd begun singing again or making a kind of humming all about the meadows and streams, the beribboned sheep, the delightful derelictions of frail women, the facile charm of melancholy. . . . (The lady who accompanied Henry at that concert had murmured, "It's an early piece, of course. It lacks the tragic power and depth of the *Requiem*. . . ." It had given her intense pleasure to initiate this great man, so deliciously ignorant, into the world of music. She was one of the most ferocious partisans of the "stupid genius" theory.) So you gave yourself up to it, since it was an early piece, an innocuous work, you let yourself be cradled on a familiar flood, unaware that the water was treacherous—for insensibly the melancholy lost its charm, became sadness, became more profound, and suddenly just when you had been brought to a standstill by a melodic passage of incredible rightness, and remained there, panting, disarmed, the child started up his song again and drifted away with an air of innocence. . . .

He had bought the record. There it was, like a talisman. Sometimes for weeks he did not take it out of its sleeve, did not even think about it. But the minute he was on the alert, feeling that something was going to bring on one of those "spells", he set it going. And the fact of being magnetized by the magic object, of detesting the magic object, excused him, in short, from thinking.

"When Henry is depressed," said Sylvia with her nauseating little air of superiority, "nothing but Mozart will set him to rights." She had said it so often and it had such a likely air that a journalist had even put it down in print.

He had had a hard time making his way back-stage.

"Why, sir, if you want to see the young ladies, all you have to do is wait for the intermission."

"To the devil with the young ladies! I want to see the dresser."

"Well, to begin with, there are two of them. Had an accident?"

He had almost lost his temper. An accident!

"It's a personal matter."

"Oh, all right," said the stage-manager, with a shrug, "if you insist."

Henry had paused for a moment in the iron stairway, feeling slightly ridiculous. His conversation with Sylvia, which had impelled him to come here without due reflection, came to mind.

"What? He's from Signac, your Monsieur Morani?"

"He and his wife," she had replied.

She did not like to talk about the people who lived in the house where she lived, no doubt because her mother was the concierge there.

"Well, that's extraordinary!" he had reflected, aloud. "Signac! I remember it so well, and yet it must be fifteen, no, twenty years since I've been there."

"The only period when you did landscapes," Sylvia had said. She had made his career her personal property.

"I didn't paint landscapes exclusively."

"Oh, I know," she had said, in a way that had attracted his attention.

"What do you mean: 'Oh! I know'?"

She had dodged the question, for she had thoughtlessly said something that her mother had forbidden her ever to mention. But she had finally confessed. A woman lived in her house, she happened to be the wife of this Monsieur Morani who . . . a woman who had posed for a painter in the old days, and she imagined that . . . believed she guessed that . . . that Lou . . .

Lou! He had almost burst out laughing. "Yes," Sylvia had admitted, "she's called Louise, and she's a dresser at the Montparnasse music-hall." And she had added disdainfully: "She must have been better looking in the Signac period, for I don't see . . ." Women had never liked Lou. They could never see anything attractive in her. "I don't see what can attract you in that young creature," the wife of the mayor of Signac, to whom he had been obliged to let himself be introduced, had scoffed. "In the Signac period." Why, it was yesterday, it was today! He felt in as good form as he had at forty-five, and he had never been handsome. No hair now, but bah! If he was good enough for Sylvia he must be good enough. . . .

But standing there in the little iron stairway, remembering the expression on the stage-manager's face, he suddenly wondered how

old she was now. . . . The man had seemed to think it so incredible. . . . Dressers are rarely young. It was a fact, the minute one said
"dresser" one generally imagined a faded old woman moving about
among the actresses back-stage. Well, now, when she had posed
for the portrait on the bridge, and for the big blue nude, she had
been quite young. He didn't remember ever having asked her age.
But his mistress, a girl with an amusing little flat face, had been no
more than twenty when he made that series of sketches of her, and
she had always said "Lou is the elder of us two." Supposing, then,
that Lou had been a little over twenty, say twenty-two, or at the
maximum, twenty-five. Then she'd now be . . . forty-two? Perhaps forty-five? What? Lou, glowing with a subdued and sombre
fire in her red dress at the Museum of Modern Art in New York,
Lou was now the age he had been when he had painted that portrait?

Someone bumped into him. It was a beautiful brunette in
bouffant pantaloons. She laughed, and automatically he continued
his climb up the little iron stairway. He had halted in the damp
and narrow passageway that smelled of women and powder and
grease paint, and had thought for a moment of beating a retreat. . . .
The Signac period! . . . Then he saw her. Her warm and steady
gaze had struck him like a whip. The corridor was badly lit.
"What tricks a half-light plays!" he told himself, with a kind of
terror. For it was Lou, all right, the Lou of yesterday who was
coming towards him, he recognized that proud straight nose, that
pensive oval of the face, contradicted by the ardent mouth, and the
voice that spoke was hers, he was hearing that same low, grave
voice murmuring, it seemed, without surprise:

"Henry?"

"Lou!" he said, pretending to be amazed.

For all at once he was seized with panic, he was afraid of seeing
her in the light, afraid of seeing the deterioration of a face which
had belonged to him, and he felt like telling her that he had come
there by chance. Yes, that way, he could escape her if . . . But her
voice was still the same!

"Well, I certainly never expected . . . " that voice was saying,

almost mockingly. "Henry! I would have thought you'd be hanging round places smarter than this, by now. I'll bet you've come for
the Sultaness."

She was apparently so convinced that he had not come for her
that he felt slightly reassured.

"Suppose we go somewhere and have a drink together?" he
suggested, still cautious.

"Presently, and as many drinks as you like, but just now I
haven't a minute, I'm . . ."

Tumultuously he was jostled aside by half a dozen girls, almost
naked or draped in kimonos and all shouting.

"Quick, Lou! My stockings! The peacock costume is torn!"

She had time only to call out, "Wait for me in the downstairs
promenade! I'll come as quickly as I can. . . ."

And he was abandoned, while the doors banged shut on all
sides.

He went down to wait, not too sure what to think. Supposing
she turned out to be a horrible faded old woman, and sentimental,
and capable of saying, "Now isn't this something, fancy meeting
again!" Really, there in the dim passageway, he must have had a
poor glimpse of her. Still, a forty-five-year-old woman was not an
old woman. Some were still desirable, even at that age. Yes, but
they were rich women, for whom make-up and clothes could do
wonders. And she was certainly not rich. . . . Oh, well, he would
wait and see.

In the deserted hallway downstairs, the lighting was also poor.
On the walls, innumerable photographs displayed for the excitement of the passers-by two generations of legs and bosoms. On
any other day, Henry might have enjoyed the indigence of this old
barn of a theatre, the hard seats where you felt the wood through
the worn velvet, the bare ceiling and the discoloured frieze of
cubistic roses. . . . But that night, decidedly, it was not for him.
He crossed the street to have a drink, since he had time. It even
passed through his mind that he might simply disappear. But that
would be a barbarous thing to do. The poor soul must be in such
a state of delight. He waited. Fortunately he had arrived towards

the end of the show, and the crowd was beginning to pour out into the narrow street. He never came to this part of Paris, now. Montparnasse was so old-fashioned, so seedy!

He felt her approaching, as he had used to do, and this, too, frightened him. He did not need to see her or even to hear her to know that she was approaching. Ridiculous, no doubt. But God, how he had liked that girl! He still remembered the day when they had been caught in a thicket by some picnickers. He remembered how she had pulled herself up, still in his arms and without covering her bare legs, to shout: "Can't you have your picnic somewhere else?" with such a furious expression on her face that the group had at once fled in disorder.

"Well, Henry?" she said, at his very side. "Where shall we go?"

He still did not dare to look at her. Not yet.

"Have you any idea, Lou?" He spoke casually, since that was the tone she had adopted. "In Montparnasse, you see, I . . . It's years since I . . ."

But she grabbed his arm and proceeded to scold him.

"Well, really! You might look me in the face when you speak! I'm not yet a complete ruin!"

He admired her for pitching into him without delay, and for having understood so quickly. He looked at her, under the crude neon lights (they were going up the boulevard towards the station).

"You are beautiful," he said sincerely.

And it was true. Not that time had left no mark upon her, quite the contrary. But her eyes, though they held a sadder expression, were still clear and penetrating, her lovely mouth was still lovely, and the face was almost more beautiful, as if ennobled by the scars of time. They had stopped to let a group of girls pass by them. Some of the girls were shivering in shabby coats (a fine rain was falling again), a few of the girls were walking arm in arm with their men, and two or three, better dressed and putting on a show of nonchalance were going towards small cars waiting at the kerb, getting in, banging the doors shut as the cars moved off. But most of the girls walked alone, holding themselves very stiffly and wearing that sad, frowning look of girls with nice figures but plain faces, clicking their heels sharply on the pavement and glancing furtively at passers-by.

A taxi passed slowly. As it almost grazed them, Henry stopped it with a wave of the hand.

"Get in," he said, and then, out of sheer habit, called out to the driver, "To the Étoile Club, Avenue . . ."

"I know the place," said the cabby.

And off they went. Lou had got into the taxi without a word.

"You don't have a car of your own?" she asked presently, with a tinge of disapprobation.

"Yes, an American car. But I came on foot."

"Oh! Good! I was wondering. . . . What make?"

He told her.

"How much did that cost you?"

He told her this as well. And the address of his flat and what it had cost him. And the price his paintings now brought. As much as that? She would never have believed it. And he'd been to America? And had decorated a University there? A great big panel. . . . How big, how much? He mentioned the figures. And did he leave the money there or had he changed it into francs? And was American cooking really as bad as people said?

No conversation could have been more natural, more trivial, even. And yet the warmth of life welled slowly up in him, he felt it almost physically, and wanted to thank her. "Poor little Sylvia," he thought, remembering her *"at that period, evidently"*. Poor Sylvia, with her pretty and insignificant face, her efforts to appear knowledgeable, her conversation that changed whenever she got into the car or entered some supposedly "chic" place, as she would change her clothes.

"Are you married?" asked Louise.

"No."

"Your taxes must be really something," she reflected aloud.

The cab had stopped. Henry paid, feeling uneasy. He had named this club because he always came here with Sylvia. Now he hesitated momentarily before the liveried door-man. She must be rather poorly dressed under her coat. He shrugged. To hell with it, he had the right to bring anyone he liked. A painter was apt to be eccentric, as everyone knew.

"Come," he said to Louise.

They entered.

"Good evening, Monsieur Stass."

He gave his coat to the cloakroom girl, not without his customary feeling of mingled embarrassment, and pride. This type of place always intimidated him, but he was flattered to be recognized here. Besides, once he had formed the habit of going somewhere, he always returned, even if he was none too fond of the place. It was the same with Sylvia; he was used to her, without ever being sure that he really liked her. But she cost money (expenses he would have to begin all over again if he changed mistresses), and then, he didn't like change. . . . He was going to make some changes in his property in the Midi this summer, but as to changing clubs, that he would not do. He had had to take himself by the scruff of the neck to bring himself here the first time, and now he intended to benefit from that exploit. What bothered him most were the big bills that had to be paid every month. Still, after all, there was a kind of pleasure in signing his bill off-handedly.

Lou had taken off her modest gabardine coat, and her dress was of an aggressive red, a glaring gipsy red. He shuddered before such courage.

"Good evening, Monsieur Stass."

Was there a note of surprise in the head waiter's voice?

"Your table is free, Monsieur. This way, Madame."

Calmly, without haste, she crossed the dining-room, indifferent to the glances that followed her. The dress revealed her thickened waist, her matronly hips, her still beautiful breasts. In this tepid atmosphere, in the midst of these murmured comments, all these real young ladies without appetite, dressed with expensive simplicity, all these fake young ladies with slightly mauve hair crowned with daring hats, Lou's passing was sensational. They sat down.

"It's Henry Stass," a lady muttered to her companion. Lou would, he imagined, be taken for one of his models. "She should wear fuller skirts," he reflected. "Her bosom is still beautiful, she could . . ."

Then he thought better of it. No, nothing could be changed in Lou, neither her dress nor her elbow on the table, nor that inhuman serenity with which she bore the stares and ordered *foie gras* and lobster.

"Since you're taking me out for once," she began.

"Since I'm taking you out for once, you're going to have indigestion."

She burst out laughing.

"In all the years since you went away," she said, "and my goodness, it's all of twenty years, I've not had the least ailment, no indigestion, and almost no hangovers! What do you say to that? And you don't look too bad yourself, I must say. Of course, your hair. . . . But all the rest is absolutely in place, eh, Henry?"

And there she was, inspecting *him*, without tenderness but as if with a kind of sportive pride. And, once his first embarrassment had passed (not counting the displeasure he had felt at the thought of how much the *foie gras* and lobster would cost), the feeling of well-being he had experienced in the cab suffused him again, more powerfully. His sombre thoughts, his vague uneasiness, his detachment from the world, all these were receding. He regained the power to raise himself above those grubby, seething thoughts, and to crush them disdainfully. With a great feeling of gratitude towards Louise, he laid his hand on her arm.

"I'm so glad to see you again, Lou. I've so often thought of Signac. . . ."

"I'd never have believed it," she said sincerely. "You didn't stay there so long. . . . Could we have some red wine, burgundy perhaps?"

Champagne had been brought as usual: Sylvia would have felt disgraced if forced to drink anything else. He ordered a burgundy. For himself, he ordered a steak. His appetite was returning.

"Red burgundy with the lobster, sir!"

The inferred disapproval of the head waiter left him totally indifferent, now. Indeed, it rather amused him.

"And the champagne? Shall I take it back?"

Henry had drunk a glass of it without noticing.

"Keep it cold, we'll drink it afterwards."

Yes, his appetite was returning, it was good to see the abundant food before him, good to drink, and, why not? Why not drink too much and perhaps—the feeling was still dim and unconscious in the sharp glad tumult that was rising in him, dim and infinitely discreet like the bass notes in a symphony, yet still the very base and foundation of the fragile edifice—perhaps indulge the grave desire. . . .

"Have you gone back once in a while?" he asked.

"Gone back where?"

Signac called to mind pure colours, strong patterns, pleasures and displeasures accepted without qualms. Lou's whole life must have been like that; what life, painting, love had been for him, in short, until Mozart. His steak was served.

"To Signac," he said.

"No, never. Why?"

Why, indeed. In America he had never thought of Signac, either. She was intact, untouched, marvellously free of everything he had feared.

"And I'll wager you've never thought of me, either," he said daringly, playing with fire. Supposing she replied, as Sylvia would have done, "Henry, I've never forgotten you!"?

"Why yes. Only two months ago I saw your photograph in *Paris-Monde* . . ."

"And you thought of me?"

"Oh, Henry, stop hedging!" she laughed. "What made you think of me was that child Sylvia. She must have told you . . . !"

"Yes. This afternoon."

"And you came at once, that's really nice. But you know, I'd never have thought she'd mention me. Especially on account of her mother, who's so terribly proud of her daughter's famous painter! You should hear her talk. . . ."

They ate, drank, and talked slowly, without haste, without excitement, capable of appreciating every pleasure in its turn, in its time. The bottle of burgundy was empty. With a wave of his hand he signalled the waiter to bring another.

"You might have given me some sign of life, Lou."

"How could I imagine," she said calmly, "that you would want such a thing?"

That was so like her. That dignity of a savage, without humility, without demonstrations, accepting everything as her due but asking for nothing—it was so like her. He recalled the Hôtel de la Paix. He could see again the bedroom with its mahogany furniture, stifling and mysterious with its closed yellow curtains, while outside the heat bore down, dense and humid; the deep bass in the orchestra sounded again, less distant, alternating now with the sharp rustling of white tablecloths, of tinkling glasses, and the voices of the obsequious phantoms who were placing before him a glazed sheet of paper, the bill of fare.

"Will Madame have a dessert?"

And the better to hear that music, he neglected the champagne which was growing tepid, drank some more of the sombre burgundy, whose secret warmth glorified with rubies the bass notes, now stronger and more sustained.

She ordered a dessert. She ate. She was there, at his side, she was all that he had loved, all that he had painted, she was all the indifferent power of the earth. She was there, her face ravaged by time, a little intoxicated, perhaps, with food and wine, now and then pushing back a dark lock of hair from her face. She was there, she belonged to him. The sharp, pretentious, irritating notes which end in an interrogation point, were drowned, now, drowned in the sweet dark flood. Eat, my girl, eat and drink, he thought. She was his, she, Signac, and painting were his. He had found everything again, he possessed everything once more. "My girl, my lovely whore, my wife." He stood up.

"No coffee, Monsieur Stass? No liqueur?"

Silent, she followed him.

"Shall I put it on your bill, Monsieur Stass? I hope everything was quite all right, Monsieur!"

Again people were looking at them, but this time he didn't give a good God damn.

"My coat."

How good to be in the street, in the obscurity of the street! He walked ahead with great strides, paying no attention to her. She followed. They did not have far to go, but he could have walked a long time if need be, ploughing his way through the night as if through a calm and tepid sea. There was no need to hurry. And he knew that she would remain silent to the end.

The light of the hall, the lift going up with its gentle mechanical purring. . . . He felt like putting his hand against the gently vibrating walls. Lou herself was as sure as a machine, silent and sure as a machine. . . . He had a hard time opening the door of the flat, for his hand was trembling. There was a bedroom beyond the big studio, but he hadn't the patience to go that far. There was the wide, low divan. . . .

"Shall we go in there for some sleep?" he muttered, later on.

She shook her head.

"Someone expecting you?" he asked, without much interest. He was already half asleep.

"I'm married, don't you know that?"

He scarcely heard her. He had rolled himself up in the red and black blanket, not worrying about comfort, he was too eager for sleep.

"You'll come tomorrow to pose?" he muttered again.

She put on her clothes quickly, also thinking of sleep, of the humidity that awaited her outside, yet contented. Then, softly, she went out, shutting the doors behind her, not thinking to look back, to cast a glance at the studio, at the canvases standing about, at the sleeping man, rolled in his blanket, and watched over by the ponderous women of his paintings, those heavy earthen vessels, like a medieval saint by his guardian angels.

"Don't let's mince matters, let's have it straight—she's a prostitute." Grandfather's voice was still sharp, but now it grated like a rusty hinge.

Stéphane's mother—"the still beautiful Madame Morani", as the local newspapers always called her when they wrote up the annual charity fête—let out a groan.

The scene was unfolding exactly as Stéphane had imagined it, in the preposterous drawing-room with its dust, its blackened mouldings, its frayed splendours. The old one-eyed grandfather, of whom Stéphane had been so frightened as a child, was sitting in the dark crimson armchair, flanked on either side by Stéphane's parents, stiff in high-backed chairs upholstered in threadbare velvet, heads bowed, like guilty people. Yes, how many times had he imagined this scene and hesitated, waited, put it off. He felt almost relieved, at having spoken at last.

"I will not allow . . ."

"But my dear boy," groaned his mother, "supposing you *are* in love with her: Do you *have* to marry her!" Then, to Stéphane's father: "Georges, tell him. . . ."

"Are you telling us the whole truth, Stéphane?" said his father, carrying on. "Perhaps this girl is . . ."

"Yes, that's all we need," interrupted the grating old voice sarcastically.

"To be burdened with a child who may have been fathered by all the men of Signac. . . ."

Stéphane had forseen all this. Was he afraid, or was he secretly happy to have astonished them at last? Did he pity them? Not sure, he waited.

"Stéphane, my dear boy, think of our sacrifices . . ."

"We expected so much of you . . ."

He was well aware of what his parents had expected. They had told him often enough ever since he was old enough to understand. But there they would stay, in their ruined drawing-room, in their shame and resignation. He would never be able to renew the velvets and regild the mouldings for them. Old One-Eye had simply wasted time examining Stéphane's school reports with such care.

"Save your strength, Georges," the old man said now. "I always knew the boy wouldn't amount to much. He didn't want to go into business because he'd have had to start at the bottom. Although my friends had promised me . . . But never mind that now. He wanted to be a great musician. 'So be one, my boy,' I said. 'Strum the piano, if that's what you want.' Well, now he's twenty-eight. At the Conservatory he won the Second Prize, and what has it all amounted to? He's pianist in the great orchestra of Signac!"

"We've done all we could . . ." That was the gentle, ashamed and humiliated voice of his father. And mechanically, as he always did when embarrassed, George Morani tilted his chair, see-sawing to and fro.

"I don't blame you at all, Georges," the squeaky old voice continued. "In your position, you couldn't have done more. Stop seesawing like that. I've always said to my daughter, 'Estelle, you know I didn't approve of your marriage'—now Georges, don't hold this against me, I know I'm blunt and outspoken, but you can depend on me—I said to her, 'Estelle, I didn't approve of your marriage and I'll never approve of it, but I'm the first to admit that, considering his position, your husband has done all he could.' "

"Thank you, Father."

"There's nothing to thank me for. I'm blunt, I'm outspoken, and I'll say this, Georges, you're a man who carries out his obligations, and I don't hold you responsible for the follies of your son. Thank God, *you've* never indulged in that kind of folly."

"Papa . . ."

"Be quiet, Estelle. As I've always told you, maybe you're to blame, with your idiotic romanticism. . . . But never mind. We were resigned to it. Stéphane was not a success. But at least he had work, he had found honest employment in the municipal orchestra, he was a public servant—don't take this for a dig at you, Georges, some government employees are useful and I respect them, and do stop see-sawing like that, it's nerve-wracking—we could think of him as settled in life, after a fashion, and doing what he wanted. We could have hoped for a marriage of the same sort, nothing better, mind, considering your position, Georges, but that at least we could have hoped for. For God's sake! Stéphane wasn't a bad boy, and not everyone can be an eagle. But now the young gentleman who's never done anything feels like distinguishing himself. And how? By marrying a woman of the town—don't interrupt me, I've made my investigations—a strumpet who lived with what's-his-name; some well-known cubist painter, at the Hôtel de la Paix (for greater discretion, no doubt), and for a whole year and a half . . ."

No, he was not afraid. He would brave Old One-Eye. He would show himself in his true light to these three people who had always failed to appreciate him. At last they would understand what he really was. And if they did not understand, Louise would. And that was enough.

"I know all that, Grandfather," he said confidently.

Two desolate cries issued from the high-backed chairs, and from the armchair, an astonished grunt.

"Yes, I know all that," he went on, even more fervently. "I know the life Louise has led, I know all about her wretched girlhood, the factory, the temptations, her mistakes. She must have a little luxury and ease. You said that everyone in Signac knows this, so how could I help knowing?"

"Yet in spite of all that, Stéphane?" murmured his mother. And his father echoed:

"In spite of that, Stéphane?"

Their desolate voices saddened him. But he felt they must be made to understand, and his own voice became warmer, more vibrant, more persuasive, as he went on.

"Not in spite of all that. *Because* of all that! I am marrying her because of all that; I want to rescue that poor creature who is apparently beyond rescue, I want to restore her to human dignity. . . . *Because* of all that, yes. A prostitute, you called her, Grandfather. Well, yes. Prostituted, humiliated, despised by everybody—that's why I fell in love with her, why I stretched out a helping hand. And if you can't understand, if you disinherit me because of it, if you drive me out, I shall go away with her, I shall spend my life with her, a soul that hungers and whose hunger I can satisfy, a fallen creature, to whom I have held out my hand. . . ."

"This is as good as the Comédie Française!" cackled the old voice sarcastically, but with a slight quaver.

They did not want to understand. To the very end he would remain for them the boy who would never amount to anything, a boy who was not "an eagle". For a second his assurance left him and his blue eyes filled with tears. They did not want to share his emotion, his exaltation. It was the same as when he had talked of going away to sea, at the age of twelve. They had never trusted him.

"Very well," he said, in a choking voice. "I may as well warn you. I'm to be married on Saturday. Then we'll leave for Paris, where I intend to settle."

Then for the last time he had left that drawing-room where he had known so many hours of humiliation. And, in a high state of excitement, he had paced the streets of Signac, until it was time to meet Louise on the railway bridge. He always met her out of doors, nothing must happen between them before their marriage, he wanted to prove to her that he respected her in spite of everything.

Did she appreciate this delicacy on his part? He was none too sure. There was something so natural, so primitive, about her, but that would take care of itself. Thinking of her, he calmed down, forgot "their" injustice. And since he still had a quarter of an hour ahead of him, he went into a church to meditate. He pardoned "them". They were incapable of knowing what true superiority was. All that counted for them was money and social rank. When he returned from Paris, successful, at last, just see whether they'd dare turn their backs on him then!

He felt calmer. He would go to meet Louise. She at least knew what he was, knew his true worth. He imagined her running to meet him, as she always did, throwing herself upon him, holding him in her arms. . . . He could meditate no longer. He had too great a need to see her again, to see her dark eyes shining, the knot of her dark hair coming undone as usual.

He left the church. It was still very light and he could see her coming towards him, on the other side of the bridge, over the tracks.

"Louise!"

She saw him and flung up a bare arm. Louise! Although she was quite near, now, he too began to run, in a great outburst of youthful joy. . . .

It was the first time Stéphane had ever let anyone else into the world in which he had always lived: a world not colourless, as one might imagine, but rather more colourful, more expressive, more significant, and more luminous than the real one around him. It was rather like those artificial peaches and pears one finds displayed in an ornamental fruit bowl, and immediately sees to be false because of the abnormal perfection of their bloom: a world, to borrow the common phrase, "too good to be true". Indeed, the world in which Stéphane and Martine now lived together was very beautiful. And everything now encouraged them, the peace they had made, their easy understanding talks, and even the summer which had suddenly burst forth, very blue and warm, very beautiful, too, with a hint of oppressive humidity, a limp and gigantic web in which they were caught and held, mindlessly, until the evenings. They met at seven o'clock, as before, but were now more relaxed, more conciliating; they needed but an instant to recover the tone, find the door, the lock: whereupon they entered into their domain and moved there with ease.

"I defied my family. No doubt I was wrong to do so. But my offence sprang from my high-mindedness and the simplicity of my soul. You, Martine, would have made the same kind of mistake."

Martine said yes. She tried, by finding an idea or word here and there, to make a place for herself in that unreal world, to forget that it was not really the one she had wanted, but something much more down-to-earth. She tried, she honestly tried. And it was actually the first time in her life—since she had first entered school and people had laughed at her as she went by (why is an ugly little girl funnier than an ugly woman?), and since her mother had said, "What a shame you can't have a college education, seeing that you can't hope to marry." The first time since the school prize-givings, and the dances (she had gone to exactly three at the age of sixteen), the various meetings where people looked at her too much or not enough, where people talked to her without kindness or with too much—yes, this was the first time since she had become rigid and long-suffering like someone wounded, and yet resolved not to utter a groan; the first time she had made a real effort.

She said "yes". The effort was so violent that it was almost like shedding her skin, but she made it. She tried to believe him, to identify herself with him, to transport herself into that region where she could be his equal. It was painful, for she had been rooted, even frozen to the ground for such a long time! But she had taken the step and she had succeeded.

She who had been so silent and glum, was now able to talk. Stéphane marvelled at how well they got along. "What couldn't I have done," he thought, "if I had had a wife to help and understand me like this." A vestige of caution kept him from saying the words aloud, and remorsefully he thrust aside a sudden vivid recollection of Louise, as she had been at Martine's age, but the thought formed, despite himself: "What a difference!"

In the humid warmth of the evening, they went on talking as they sat on the terrace of the Café Dupont. Already some tourists were dozing under the striped parasols. In another week the shops would begin to close, one after another, for the summer holidays, and one would have to walk some distance to buy milk from an unfamiliar dealer. Jean Cadou and Gérard Ducas would be going away to stay with "Jean's family" in Normandy, to gorge themselves on cream and summer showers in that land of rich pastures. Germaine Lethuit, in the company of her father, her sister, the cat in a basket, and laden with folding-chairs and oranges, would take a crowded train to Brittany. Socrates would stay on in town, of course, more melancholy and much more talkative than usual, pinning down the unwary customer to narrate the imaginary glories of his life on the Mediterranean shores in the bygone and prosperous times. (Socrates was, said Stéphane, "a mythomaniac".)

Dr. Fisher, with his tin trunk, would disappear in the direction of the Alps, where he usually spent the summer holidays in "the L.P.R. châlet", a big rickety barn of a place on a mournful mountain, where a kind of maid-of-all-work, very dirty and speaking no French, wandered vaguely about. Stéphane detested both her and the place. But he would go there all the same, in the middle of August, and for a month would rail against the boredom of the châlet, against the utter beauty of the place, and against the company of Dr. Fisher, which had little attraction for him. Dr. Fisher did not stop drinking except to give him conscientious medical care. As if medical care were all he needed! People thought a dose of medicine could cure anything. Whereas, what an invalid needed was . . .

For the moment, Stéphane was feeling rather well.

"What shall I order for you, my dear?" he asked.

"What about you? Not beer, remember, it's sometimes bad for you. Suppose we have some port? It's mild and . . ."

The port they sipped seemed to be in harmony with the weather and their softened mood: luxurious and languid. The people passing by walked as if slowed down by the heat, as if swimming through a heavy sea.

"I don't understand," Martine said all at once, "why you never took steps to get some kind of help from a war veterans' association or from Social Security, or something like that. Then you'd not have to spend your summer holidays in a place for refugees. . . ."

She had found by now that maternal and practical tone which gave her a reason for living, provided her with a function, linked her with Stéphane in a way that was, after all, more carnal, a sort of umbilical cord through which a more generous blood than words could flow. To preoccupy herself with his body was like touching, though furtively, the forbidden earthly possessions; and it appeased the nostalgia she still felt even in the splendid illusory universe into which Stéphane had drawn her. Had he been more alert, he would have sensed a danger in this, would have had a foreboding of that voracious appetite of hers which would not always be satisfied with such unsubstantial fare. But he was completely happy to be enveloped in such tender care.

"I know you don't like Dr. Fisher," he said, soothingly, "but after all, although he hasn't been obliged to do so, he has looked after me, poor lonely fellow that I am, for five years. Do realize, dear Martine, that I don't entirely disagree with you. It's obvious that all those refugees, well . . . and it's possibly true that in his professional duties, he has . . . I've heard quite a lot of things said. And I don't know where the money comes from that finances the

League. . . . But we mustn't judge him rashly. Dr. Fisher's attitude towards me has always been blameless."

"All the same, I'm sure that if you'd gone to the military authorities years ago, you'd have had some compensation. They might even have given you a pension."

She laid her hand on his arm. She laid her hand on his suffering, on his malady, not out of pity (just as it had not been out of desire that she had wanted him to take her the day of their big scene), no, neither out of pity nor out of desire, but as one secretly handles an object one would like to possess, on which one would like to write one's name, for the sole pleasure of at last having something of one's own. He who had nothing tangible to give, nothing but insignificant trifles, he who possessed nothing himself, should have been afraid of this. But he was thinking of Louise and had no fear.

"A pension." Louise had said that, too, speaking from the the vantage point of her triumphant good health (thanks to the black market) at the end of the war. "Perhaps you could still get a pension?" It was true the war had been over for two years then. And he was not absolutely sure he had contracted this "fatigue" (he refused to speak of his disease otherwise) in captivity. But she had persisted. "After all, you fought in the war, you were taken prisoner, they can't discharge you like this. Would you like me to go and see them for you?" And he had felt such a note of disdain and of complicity in her voice that he had been forced, yes, forced, to show indignation. He would never exploit his war record. He had only done his duty and did not expect . . . Oh, very well, she seemed to be saying, as if she had expected him to react in this way. Just as when he had declared that the radio she had bought was not a good one (and he had exaggerated in the hope of upsetting her), she had said, "All right, all right", maintaining that she had expected nothing else. That he was ill, that he did not ask for a pension, that he did not earn as much money as she did, all came to the same thing: it was what she had expected.

She was behaving exactly as Old One-Eye had behaved over the mediocre school reports. Louise had gone over to the side of his enemies: all right, all right, her attitude seemed to say, one couldn't really blame him, it wasn't his fault, the results he obtained were respectable if not brilliant. It was the same resignation, but without kindness. He had come to hold a greater grudge against Louise for this resignation (it complemented her odious character of that of a woman who had good health, thanks to black marketeering) than for the occasional philandering of which he suspected her. However, his war record and his bad health had earned him the respect of the whole neighbourhood, and given him a more solid footing than ever his good record in the Catechism class and Father Mourron's fondness for him had done in his childhood. He lost no chance of using it against Louise, this esteem he enjoyed in the quarter, just as formerly he had used his piety and good conduct prizes against his parents and his condescending old grandfather. But use it in any other way? Never.

"I've never wanted to exploit what was for me a mere duty. There are men who . . ."

"I understand your scruples. But after all, Social Security . . ."

He frowned. Martine was too insistent. Although he talked endlessly of his troubles, he did not like to think about them. He had used them; he had brandished his ailments as, formerly, he had brandished that piety which had conferred upon him a kind of equality with the better-born among his classmates ("those boys you cannot mingle with socially", his mother had always said). And since he used his illness, it became, in his hands, something again that was too highly coloured, like artificial fruit, or a *trompe-l'oeil* picture; it was a reproach to Louise, a proof of her guilt, of the world's guilt, in regard to him, and had no direct connection with that fatigue, those spells of oppressive breathing, those little recurrent fevers which did not worry him. To begin with, accepting a pension or Social Security benefits would have forced him to become actually aware that he was a sick man: and so, he rejected the idea.

"How kind you are, my dear! How good, to preoccupy yourself with such distasteful matters! What good care you do take of me, when everyone else abandons and avoids me! Do you know, even in that stupid Brasserie, doing so many things I hate—carrying my

mediocre cross—I sometimes feel you at my side, a little ghost of
a Good Samaritan!"

Instinctively he suppressed his feeling of revulsion and dodged
anything that might have made him lose his perilous equilibrium.
And, without even being conscious of it, he took Martine by the
hand, turning her aside from the forbidden territory and showing
her again the only treasures allowed her, those which would leave
her secretly starved and at the same time elated. . . .

"Is it true, Stéphane? Is it true?"

She was ready to seize upon anything, to feed on anything, for the
moment. Neither she nor he knew as yet that her hunger would
grow and demand more and more.

"Why yes, my dear Martine. Yes, indeed."

How easy it was, he thought, to satisfy her! A little kindness was
enough. It was the same with everyone except Louise. Well, with
almost everyone.

"Of course, my dear."

The peaceful expression on that ill-favoured face was slightly
embarrassing. Stéphane looked away.

"All the same, I ought to go and see Dr. Fisher," he muttered.

At Dr. Fisher's the spongy heat that came through the small low
window seemed to impregnate the dark green curtains, the mahogany furniture, the beautiful carpet that at once attracted the eye.
But the Doctor, with his impeccable shirt, his steely eyes, his
abrupt movements, was one of those men who always look cool.
This was not the case, however, with the fat woman collapsed
there, white faced, on the chair; her print frock was wet with
sweat.

"Now, Madame, you must think it over," he heard himself
saying in a weary voice, which did not at all go with his neat and
elegant appearance.

She disgusted him. A jelly-fish, a veritable jelly-fish, stranded
there, as if in her natural habitat, invading the room with her fat,
her odour, and altogether less embarrassed than he was.

"It's all been thought over," said the jelly-fish obstinately. "I don't want it. Doctor, I implore you! If it's only a question of money, I'll . . ."

She was really not imploring him at all, for she felt her hold on him and had decided to stay there until he yielded, sickened by her, by her female odour, her female eyes. He went over to the window to be farther away from her, with the disgust of a chaste and well-groomed man, the disgust of everything pure that remained in him.

"You quite see, don't you, that when my husband . . . Oh, and all the gossip . . . the things people will say. . . ."

The gossip of jelly-fish! The morality of invertebrates! Of course he could always throw her out. "Who gave you my address?" he could have asked her, and could have said, "What do you take me for? No physician worthy of the name would . . ." But he no longer had the strength to pronounce those proud, dignified, abstract words. He knew only too well how little help such words were, when the time came, that moment without dignity, sticky with blood and sweat and fear. . . . There had been such a day in his life when, seeing the futility of such words, he had repudiated them once and for all, and all the jelly-fish knew it, felt it, clung to him, with their sure jelly-fish instincts, ready to despise him afterwards if there was an accident. "You know what those refugee doctors are, all of them." He could just hear them say it.

"Well, Doctor?"

His whole face contracted with the effort it cost him to speak, he felt so revolted.

"A human life . . ."

He knew only too well how inane, how profoundly inane those words were. Hidden in a closet, holding his breath lest he be detected, he had seen his wife die, his wife Anna whom he had loved more than anything in the world, had seen that beloved body he had caressed countless times, shuddering and gasping in its last convulsions (fortunately she was unconscious), and while this was happening, his sole thought had been for himself, and the necessity of holding his breath. He had concentrated with terrible calmness and with mathematical precision had applied himself as never before to that simple movement of expanding and contracting the lungs.

And no thought of grief had troubled him, nothing had interrupted his effort. Anna had died for him then at that moment, before she had given her last gasp there on the floor. Would it have been different if she had cried out or spoken his name? He couldn't be sure. Well, then. . . . All he asked for now was peace. The peace of summer.

"Very well, Madame. Come at five o'clock on Tuesday. Are you by yourself, at home? No maid, no charwoman? If something abnormal happens, telephone a hospital, in a panic. Say you do not know what is happening, haven't the least idea. And above all, don't mention my name."

"Why, of course not, Doctor!"

Her tone was almost patronizing. Like all of them, like the poor horse-faced woman who already had six children in two rooms, like the little maid-servant who didn't know how it happened (she had gone dancing and had one drink too many and she'd certainly lose her job), like the man who was quite wild and then suddenly became calm as he said, "Could you let me have some regularly? I have such pains . . . and of course I'd never mention your name." All of them, pitiable though they might be, and quite unaware of it, put on that patronizing air as they said or implied, "We'll not betray you. . . ." He'd had enough of it. He went towards her, determined to throw her out if she did not go of her own accord. He was subject to these sudden fits of exasperation. But she stood up docilely, and rummaged in her handbag.

"If you'll allow me, Doctor, I'll give you the entire sum at once. . . ."

Confident in spite of everything. So sure that he would not betray her either.

"Well then, until Tuesday, Doctor. And thanks again."

"Till Tuesday, Madame."

The child of the jelly-fish was condemned. Even if that child was to have been an Einstein or a Paganini, a Rubens or a Pasteur, Dr. Fisher would have condemned it. He had no more regard for Einstein or Rubens than for the deathly pale woman. They were all jelly-fish. He gave himself three seconds before opening the door to the little waiting-room. The end of the day. Stéphane Morani. At least Morani wouldn't cling. It would only be a question of giving him a few free samples of medicine, a chest examination, just to make a show of doing something . . . the poor fellow would be better off in a sanatorium. The Doctor, with an immense effort, had offered to have him taken in charge by the L.P.R. A refugee relative could surely be found, or something. But Morani hadn't wanted that, and Dr. Fisher had at once given up the idea. It was none of his business, it didn't concern him. He gave the medical samples, he offered the châlet, he did what he could. The consultation would not last long, fortunately. They would go downstairs afterwards for a drink at Socrates' bar. He would drink. He was rather fond of drinking; it was pleasant, clean. So much cleaner than making love. Since Anna's death, he had lived a sexless life. What would his compatriots have said about that, they who, even though they were starving, as soon as they had the little subsidy provided by the L.P.R., dashed off in search of a woman, any woman, in this Paris, "the capital of love", this Paris of their dreams. Oh, quickly, to finish with Morani and be able to go down to the bar and feel the dry, pure alcohol burning his palate. . . .

Socrates would recite his rosary of gloomy complaints. "When I was in Athens, throwing my money about, and on intimate terms with all the great families . . ." And Morani would say in his warm, vibrant voice, "You are a Providence for me, Doctor, and I who am, I dare say it, homeless . . ." They never even noticed that he did not listen to them, so intoxicated were they by their own words. Poor devils, he thought, with a kind of benevolent disdain. But, at any rate, they didn't see through him, and they didn't cling to him.

Yes, poor devils. He had once been like that, intoxicating himself with words and high principles, believing he could wall himself safely in with words . . . the omnipotence of the mind, as they say. But those two were untroubled. Nothing could happen to disturb their maunderings, either in the rue d'Odessa or at the Café Céleste. Nothing could disturb him, either, in his indifference. Everything would be fine. The Café Céleste would sink into the darkness of the night and a peaceful inebriation. The two men would talk, raising their absurd walls of words. And as the hours passed, Dr. Fisher would not even understand why, one day, hiding in a closet from the Gestapo, he had held his breath so intently. Wasn't he already dead? He often asked himself this, leaning against the chromium bar. And the thought would be sweet.

He could hardly wait for that hour, that moment of respite. He went to the door of the waiting-room, as always erect, neat, professional.

"Monsieur Morani?"

The concierge's lodge, which one would expect to be as dingy and malodorous as Madame Prêtre herself, and filled with baleful and filthy objects, was instead a rosy temple of walnut wood and taffeta. It was a temple conceived and built for Sylvia, who, looking like a *bisque* doll in her rose-coloured dressing-gown as she lay on her pink bed, was filling out a quiz in her magazine, headed "Are You a Cultivated Woman?", busily hunting up the Nine Muses and the Seven Wonders of the World in the dictionary.

"What's this?" said Madame Prêtre, surprised and indignant. "Aren't you going out?"

She had reserved for herself a kind of alcove at the back of the lodge, where she slept very uncomfortably, but without suffering from it. Madame Prêtre, although she was unaware of the existence of such a virtue (which she would have ridiculed had she known it), was disinterested. She had a greedy interest in the inhabitants of the house, but she was basically disinterested, for she fed upon their weaknesses without any thought of personal gain. Her love for Sylvia was disinterested: she wanted her to be rich and adulated simply for the pleasure of revenge, for the sheer pleasure of success (as one would be proud of playing a symphony on a defective instrument), for the delight it would give her to crush the neighbours and the world, for the joy of seeing herself justified at last in the tender love she had for her daughter. But she had no idea of deriving any personal benefit, although this fact by no means lessened the energy with which she drove her daughter.

"Well?" she repeated, planting herself at the foot of the pink bed. "You're not going out, dearie?"

Sylvia did not raise her eyes, but went on leafing through the dictionary. Her mother knew her well enough to sense that she was hiding something.

"It's been a week, now, since you last went out, hasn't it?"

"So what?" said Sylvia, pouting. But she blushed.

"Something's happening? He's ill?"

"Yes," said Sylvia.

Madame Prêtre sat down on the bed. Those shifty eyes, that tone . . . her throat was tight with apprehension. Sylvia must have done something foolish again.

"Sylvia, you're lying to me."

Silence. Stretched out on the pink bed, Sylvia appeared to be contemplating herself in the mirror.

"Tell me what's going on, my pet, there's a dear. I won't scold you."

Sylvia remained silent. Even at the age of ten, she had refused to speak at certain moments, and for no apparent reason; and even then Madame Prêtre had felt, confronting that little girl who was too good, too pretty, but who had been very slow in school, the same exasperation mingled with love that she still felt today; it was as painful as a sharp twinge of rheumatism in her sluggish body beneath its many shawls.

"Tell your mother, dearie! It's for your own good. Did you quarrel? When did you see him last?"

"He's very busy just now," said Sylvia hesitatingly.

She never replied directly to questions. Madame Prêtre's throat was so tight it hurt and she was beginning to work herself up into a rage.

"What do you mean, he's busy just now? Wasn't he working a fortnight ago? He doesn't work from morning to night, does he?"

Sylvia's little face blanched slightly. She had a horror of her mother's fits of temper. She took refuge in the language of grown-ups.

"You don't know what it's like," she said, in a small, frightened voice. "Inspiration. Sometimes he needs to be alone for a fortnight or a month. . . ."

"Is that what he told you?"

"Yes," Sylvia replied more firmly. For Henry had told her that.

"And he said it was inspiration?"

"Yes."

Madame Prêtre meditated, with the look of a cat that has smelt something nasty.

"There's something wrong somewhere," she said. "When will you be seeing him again? What date did he fix?"

She already knew, without looking at Sylvia, that no date had been fixed for a rendezvous. After a year of the liaison, she had let herself be dropped like this, without a word, without a tear, perhaps in relief. Oh, but Madame Prêtre would not give way to her anger. Sitting on the bed, beside her daughter, she took her hand.

How many times, sitting on this bed, had she not tried with the same patience, the same burning and contained wrath to make Sylvia see reason. And in some instances it had been relatively easy. The photographer, and then Stéphane Morani. . . . As a matter of fact, it was always possible to prevent Sylvia from doing something. The difficulty was to make her do anything. Yet God knew how Madame Prêtre had expended all the diplomacy, energy and patience of which she was capable! And it always came back to the same point, apparently, to that uncomprehending and pouting little face. which was still the face of the ten-year-old child whose mother had blushed when the school prizes had been handed out. "Oh, if only I had had a quarter of her good looks!" Ugly as she had been, she had managed to marry one of the handsomest boys in the Saint-Antoine quarter, Jules Prêtre, a cabinet-maker with a future. But Madame Prêtre's ingenuity had served only to give her a few weeks of happiness and a pretty girl baby. Jules Prêtre had found a way of contracting pneumonia and of being "carried off in three weeks", before he had even noticed how ugly his wife was.

From her infancy, there had been something in Sylvia that

surprised the other children and their mothers. Perhaps it was only her goodness: she was too good. And yet it sometimes happened that Madame Prêtre, exasperated without knowing why, slapped her daughter. Then, overcome at seeing her in tears, she would fold her in her arms.

"Sylvia, dearie, tell me everything. I suppose you had a quarrel? You said something, he boiled over. . . ."

"No, not at all, Mamma! He's the one who told me . . . who told me . . ." She was close to tears.

"Who told you what, my little bird?"

"Who told me: 'We shan't be seeing each other for a while, I've got a lot of work to do, a new model I want to make good use of. . . .'"

"And you didn't think of asking how long he'd be working with that model?"

"N . . . no. . . . I asked when we'd meet again and he said after the summer holidays."

"After the summer holidays!"

Madame Prêtre raised her eyes to heaven.

"And you didn't ask him where you were going to spend your summer holidays?"

"Aren't we going to Arcachon as we did last year?"

This ingenuous question got the better of Madame Prêtre's patience.

"To Arcachon? And where will we get the money to go to Arcachon, answer me that?"

"Why . . . at the bank . . ." murmured Sylvia.

"Do you know what I've put in the bank for you these two years you've been going with that famous man and his 'inspirations'? Inspirations—pah! Two hundred and forty-three thousand francs, exactly. That's all you have after two years of what a girl with brains would have turned into millions. Millions! A man who has an expensive foreign car! And a chauffeur! And pretty as you are! And twenty! Not yet of age! Why, if you'd been a secretary or a shop-girl, or I don't know what, you'd have made more! But no doubt they wouldn't have hired you! Or you'd have found a way to work for nothing, it's so much more refined, I suppose that's what you think?"

The beautiful dark eyes had filled with tears, but Madame Prêtre had no more pity for Sylvia than for herself. For Madame Prêtre blamed herself, blamed her own vanity which as a girl had made her set her cap at Jules Prêtre, that handsome and rather stupid boy all the girls were crazy about, instead of trying to captivate some middle-aged tradesman already established in life! She was paying for that mistake today—and Sylvia was paying for it, Sylvia was like her father, only better looking and even more stupid. "Well, that's what you wanted," Madame Pretre had told herself as Sylvia grew up, realizing that she herself had to limit her genius for intrigue to the bounds of a concierge's lodge. And she had ardently wanted, for Sylvia and for herself, some revenge on life. She had believed the hour of that revenge had come with Henry Stass.

"Now, now, don't cry," she said in a voice that still shook with controlled anger. "We'll try to set things right. Don't cry. What did you say when he told you that?"

"I . . . I said . . . that it was too bad!" sobbed Sylvia.

"And you cried when you said it?"

"N . . . no. . . ."

"And you wait to cry now! Oh well, let's forget it." Madame Prêtre had recovered her calm; once again she became the scheming old diplomat. Henry Stass was Sylvia's big chance. And that chance must not be allowed to slip through her fingers. "Now, that model. Naturally, it's a woman?"

"He didn't tell me."

"And you didn't ask! Oh, my poor child. . . . But we must find out who she is."

"Why, Mamma?"

"Why? To get rid of her! The woman's bound to have a man somewhere in her life, maybe she has a husband. . . . We must . . ."

Sylvia brooded, staring blankly ahead. She was no longer thinking about Henry Stass; nor was she thinking about the freckle-faced young photographer she had met centuries ago in Bourrély Square.

It would be hard to put her confused thoughts into words; at best, one might say she was feeling very discouraged, and that she was thinking that no matter how hard she tried, nobody was ever satisfied. Madame Prêtre sat there reflecting, calculating, elaborating in her suspicious mind some artless and complicated plans.

"Oh, I'll think of something," she said.

The mere prospect of having to put her shrewd mind to work once more had already restored a little of her serenity.

Madame Prêtre once again waited motionless, on sentry-go, settled in her wicker chair like a monstrous idol. She was hoping to satisfy a simple curiosity and at the same time to avenge Sylvia, who still lay in her pink taffeta temple, answering the magazine quiz.

To take any active steps herself or bustle about in any way would have been contrary to Madame Prêtre's nature. However, she had called upon Mademoiselle Marie to do certain things for her; Mademoiselle Marie, friend and helper in time of need, was used by Madame Prêtre much as the ancient Spartans used their Helots. Having done this, she took up her look-out duties in the wicker chair, sitting in the damp summer heat, day after day, noting almost mechanically the comings and goings of the occupants of the building.

On this particular day nothing much happened. First to leave was the fair-haired young man, Mademoiselle Lethuit's tenant, surely a foreigner from whom she must get a very high rent. Next came Gérard Ducas, going off somewhere with one of Jean Cadou's paintings under his arm; later on he returned, still carrying it. Then Madame Morani left the house. That was at three in the afternoon; she was wearing lipstick, and carrying a new handbag; she was certainly not on her way to the Turkish baths. Later, Monsieur Morani came home from work, only to go out again with the Fortin girl who never let him out of her sight, he'd have a hard time getting rid of that one. Dr. Fisher then went out, returning soon afterwards with a bottle under his arm, wrapped in tissue paper; that must have cost him something! So, he was no longer satisfied to do his drinking at Socrates' bar. There's a man who must have committed some crime or other in the past, Madame Prêtre told herself, almost with sympathy. Why condemn him? That's the way the world was made. She was almost grateful to anyone who confirmed her in the rough and ruthless image she had of the world. Adultery, sexual anomalies, crimes, frauds had for her a colour and perfume, an almost poetic attraction. She felt at home in that world, among her own kind, her equals. The feeling was all the more strange since she herself had committed few of those sins—but she had always felt capable of committing them. As a sickly child, standing motionless at the window, she had already learned to detect in others the germ which would burgeon into the bloody and sordid adventures that she would read about in the evening papers. So in this sea of humanity that ebbed and flowed at her feet, she represented a kind of benevolent bard. She spoke, and her words poured like water down the rue d'Odessa, indifferent and slimy as the gutter, spreading impartial information from door to door.

Madame Prêtre waited. Less calm, however, than usual. Now and then her voluminous bosom palpitated under the influence of an unfamiliar passion: indignation. From her point of view, there was only one crime in the world: an attack on Sylvia. Sylvia, who seemed calm enough and was intently reading an article on "The Life of Whales". "Little fool, little idiot!" Madame Prêtre mused. "She's been dropped and her chances are spoilt. I suppose she's not good enough for him, that disgusting old swine. And she does nothing, just sits there reading!" And the monstrous, benevolent idol, the sniffer of gutters, the wily protector of iniquitous lives, momentarily bowed her head before the continual humiliation inflicted upon her by the object of her irascible love.

Bruno stepped off the kerb, on to the crossing and went round behind the Edgar-Quinet metro station, on his way to the pork butcher's in the rue Delambre—his actions were compulsive—where he bought the frankfurter sausages for the sauerkraut they always ate on Mondays. Every Monday—and today was Monday.

He enjoyed this walk in the evening, about seven o'clock, and never varied the route. He liked sauerkraut. And Jacquotte, who was waiting for him in their furnished room, cooked it to perfection in white wine seasoned with dried juniper berries. Before Jacquotte, he had been obliged to get rid of a mistress because she was such a bad cook. What was the point of getting the landlord's permission to have a gas-ring in the room, if it wasn't put to good use?

Bruno walked down the right side of the rue Delambre. Sometimes he amused himself, as he had done as a child, by shutting his eyes and reciting the names of the shops as he touched them with his hand: Gobert, the dyer and cleaner; the Café des Artistes; the sweet-shop, Au Bonbon Praliné. Knowing them by heart delighted him. He also knew by heart the names of the shops in certain streets where he would have liked to live. As he took his place in the queue that had already formed at the pork-butcher's and saw that he would have time for such thoughts, he began his favourite game, which was to go over in his mind the shops in some of those streets: Hermès, Lanvin, Pharmacie Saint-Honoré . . . Résidence Auteuil, Blanchisserie Mozart, Au Petit Roy. If Bruno had had more imagination, he would have attempted to wander in spirit through the places he dreamed of most, Hollywood, the stars' swimming-pools, Clark Gable's mansion, Frank Sinatra's . . . but he lacked imagination. So he had to be satisfied with the streets he had already seen, the names of shops he had read in passing by. Something, however, interfered with even this humble reverie, as if he had tied a knot in his memory. In vain did he try to remain mentally in the Avenue Mozart or to haunt a residence with a view over the Bois de Boulogne. Jacquotte had said, "Don't forget . . ." But don't forget what? And the pork-butcher's voice dragged him definitely back into the rue Delambre.

"Two pairs of frankfurters, as usual?"

"No, today give me four pairs. And four slices of salt pork."

That was what he had been told to remember! He must not forget to buy extra portions for Stéphane Morani and Martine Fortin, who were to be their guests. He hurried home. He must help Jacquotte arrange the room. Not that Stéphane was so difficult;

but Martine . . . it had been Jacquotte's idea to invite her. Certainly
it was awkward to invite a man without his mistress, but when she
was as glum as Martine Fortin, you were tempted to forget her.
Stéphane, it seemed to him, could have done better for himself, even
Toni would have been an improvement. . . . Oh, well, everybody
to his own taste! When you'd been a man's friend for eight years,
you didn't criticize him for his taste in women! You waited for
him to find another girl-friend.

Bruno himself had never made any bones about changing his
girl-friends; although he was a man of ingrained habits, buying the
exact replica of a necktie when the original one wore out, he never
hesitated to break off an affair with a woman, for, as he said, "that's
the way artists are". True, like the neckties, Bruno's mistresses
always ran to type, plump little brunettes with a fondness for
garlic. Jacquotte, who now opened the door to him, was a sample,
although she added a touch of dignity to the prototype which
rather impressed Bruno, just as he was impressed by Stéphane's
cultured air. He attributed his poor success in the art of crooning
popular songs to his lack of education, thus showing a dauntless
confidence in the degree of culture possessed by successful singers.
And Stéphane's example did nothing to disabuse him.

"Look what I've done, what do you think of it?" asked Jacquotte.

Bruno glanced round and was delighted with the intimate look
she had given the room. On the chest of drawers, some daisies
queened it in a red and blue Bohemian glass vase, making quite a
display. On the walnut table, slightly scaling, a crocheted doily
beneath each plate and glass produced a sumptuous effect. The
smell of sauerkraut escaping in thick clouds from the kitchenette
was very appetizing, and around the standard lamp Jacquotte had
draped a kind of Spanish shawl embroidered with big red flowers,
which gave an artistic note to the *ensemble* and drew the eye away
from the screen that hid the wash basin.

"Come to think of it," said Bruno, marvelling, "this is a nice
enough place to invite friends to."

Jacquotte smiled. She had done everything to get him to say just
that. Although Bruno was quite unaware of it, she had decided to

marry him. By combining forces, according to her way of thinking, the two of them could live quite comfortably, and she was waiting for the right moment to play her trump card: she had a half-dead aunt living in the rue Daguerre who could be evicted from her flat without any trouble. Jacquotte had already made enquiries as to the conditions for buying a washing machine on the deferred payment plan; already she knew the names of the shopkeepers in the rue Daguerre and could list the amenities of the district. Her guns were loaded and in place; she was merely waiting for an occasion to open fire. Inviting Stéphane Morani to dinner seemed to provide her with this occasion. And so she had dressed accordingly. The blue faille silk skirt, tight over her ample hips, the yellowed lace blouse (handed down by her mother) and fastened with a coral brooch, her little hands loaded with artistic rings, she looked (so she thought) very much like a woman of the world. Bruno admired her without the ghost of a presentiment.

"I warn you," said Stéphane, as they arrived in front of the lodging house which for years had had a placard up announcing that all the rooms were occupied, "we mustn't expect much from that poor devil of a Bruno and his girl-friend! I imagine their place must be pretty dreadful, with a fake Henri III buffet and flowered wall-paper, no doubt. I'm sure I don't know what gave Bruno the idea of a dinner party. It's the first time it's happened in all the eight years I've known him. How could I refuse? It would look as though I thought them beneath me, and I wouldn't for anything want to give that impression."

"Of course," said Martine, "we couldn't refuse."

Their long conversations on café terraces had preserved them from being prostrated by the heat. They were becoming intoxicated with words, Stéphane quite innocently, Martine with a vestige of uneasiness; for she was not an ingenuous person.

They climbed the winding little stairway which was clean enough, despite its frayed carpeting. Stéphane rested his weight upon Martine's shoulder, making boyishly mischievous remarks. They were both enjoying the adventure.

"We're going to have fun," he whispered. "Do you know what she does? She's a sub-editor on one of those women's magazines, runs an agony column, called "Affairs of the Heart" or something. . . ."

Martine smiled.

"And I suppose she signs her name 'Aunt Louise' or 'Rose Thorn'? I'll bet she's tall and thin, with buck teeth, like an English-woman."

"No, you're wrong. That's not the type Bruno likes. I'd say she goes in for ear-rings and an inspired look."

Stifling their laughter, they reached the third floor in the midst of a constantly stronger reek of sauerkraut.

"Sauerkraut," said Martine, with a grimace, "do you suppose that's for us?"

"I'm afraid so," he whispered. "Come, have courage! Forward march to the sacrifice!" (He did not dislike sauerkraut.)

Valiantly he knocked at the door. They entered, immediately drowned in the dense smell and the warm radiance of the Spanish lamp.

"Come in, come in!" exclaimed the simpering little Jacquotte, darting to shut the door. "It's such a pleasure to meet you at last, I'm longing to know Bruno's friends!"

Martine detested her on sight. Stéphane ceremoniously kissed the plump little hand with its exotic rings, and shook hands with Bruno, as though perfectly delighted.

"Why, your room is charming!"

Martine looked at the draped lamp, at the tiny kitchenette, no more than a cupboard, standing half open, at the screen, at the walnut table. . . . Oh, to be back in her own clean bare room! To be talking on a café terrace or on a park bench; anything rather than this dinner with two fat little creatures who pretended to be amateurs of good cooking, to be anywhere other than in these stuffy rooms where the heat was intense and where one had to look at that Spanish shawl! (The shawl was the decorative detail that most irritated her.) Oh, to be talking with Stéphane. It was so much more beautiful, so much richer. . . . Stéphane's words were like food to her.

But the little creature was bustling round Martine.

"Do take off your coat. . . . Now, do sit on the bed. Yes, we're a little short of space here, but . . . It's going to be a real doll's house dinner-party. . . ."

Her black hair was set in tiny curls. She was powdered with very white powder, like one of those fly-blown Oriental pastries and a big brown mole on her left cheek looked like a raisin.

"What? What? What are you men saying?"

Bruno, very red in the face, had just been told by Stéphane that Martine did not like sauerkraut.

"But what does it matter, Bruno?" said Stéphane, patting him on the back. "We've come here to see you, not to eat sauerkraut."

But Bruno was inconsolable.

"I might have guessed as much!"

There was a moment of confusion. Martine sat stiffly entrenched in sullen silence, unwilling to talk either to this woman she disliked or to the profusely apologetic Bruno. Jacquotte fluttered about eagerly, wagging her hips, wagging her bosom, reminding Martine of a concierge's wriggling little dog, and trying all she could to make the party go.

"We'll manage somehow," said Jacquotte, "won't we, Martine? You don't mind if I call you by your first name, do you? We'll open a tin of peas and call it a day. Have a glass of Banyuls! It's excellent, a friend of mine brings it to me from the Midi every year. . . . What about a biscuit? We're very short of space here, for entertaining, but we must make do. I've told Bruno a hundred times we ought to . . . And I imagine you two would like . . ." She changed the subject abruptly, falling back in her chair as if suddenly pierced by an arrow. "Oh! Stéphane, what you do with your piano, it's just sheer magic. . . . Yes, of course, I've gone to hear you, but you shouldn't be playing in a café-restaurant, you should be playing in a concert hall, yes that's where people should be listening to you. . . ."

And she talked and talked in a piping little voice, with a great rolling of the r's, determined to make an impression on Stéphane, determined to charm him, so that he would have to congratulate

Bruno upon having had the luck to find a woman worthy of him. And she poured out the Banyuls, smiling distractedly, filling the silence, calling them by their first names, ferociously resolved not to let them be bored for an instant. And Bruno, still unsuspecting, drawn by degrees into the obvious trap, thought to himself, "She certainly knows how to entertain! What a wife she would make!"

They drew their chairs up to the table. The sauerkraut which had until then been only the ghost of a smell, appeared at last, smoking hot, crowned with sausages, very impressive. Stéphane pitched in with a will: the little woman's eulogy had awakened his appetite. Moreover, he was enjoying himself, already thinking up humorous remarks he would make to Martine when they left, while playing his rôle of a prince visiting a cottage and condescending to chat with the cottagers.

Bruno was radiant with refined satisfaction. He would never have imagined that Jacquotte could rise to Stéphane's cultural heights. But they seemed to be getting along marvellously well.

"You're one of those women who . . ." Stéphane was saying.

With his usual blindness, he had already classified the little lonely-hearts chronicler (as he now thought of her) among the inferior creatures, rather comical but harmless, whose admiration was something he considered his due, and whom he quite gratuitously imagined to be completely impervious to his irony. Impervious? Already Jacquotte had the feeling that she had done enough, as far as Stéphane was concerned; sooner or later he could be brought to say to Bruno, "After all, why don't you marry that girl?" So she decided to turn her guns upon Martine. The disagreeable remarks of a mistress can sometimes puncture all the praises in the world. Martine must be brought over to her side. And what more natural than a solidarity between two women who were in practically the same situation?

"And of course, Martine," she said, withdrawing herself and Martine resolutely from the conversation of the two men, "You, too, I imagine, are very fond of music?"

"Why . . . yes . . . ," Martine muttered, rather disconcerted.

"Oh, music!" Jacquotte continued in a tone of complicity. "The

great consoler! How well I understand you! I don't mean to be
personal, but well, I, too have suffered. . . ."

Martine winced, as if to defend herself against so much familiarity.
"I don't see what . . . ," she began, casting a glance at Stéphane.

But Stéphane and Bruno were deep in an argument over what
fee to ask for an evening performance at a reception to be given in
the Ile Saint-Louis to celebrate a young girl's eighteenth birthday.
An engagement obtained for them by the agency.

"Oh, now, between women . . . ," the insinuating voice was
whispering, "I'm aware that I shouldn't notice, that I shouldn't say
anything, but . . . Oh, above all, I don't want you to think me
prying. . . . But I like you so much . . . instinctively, I understood
from the first minute. . . ."

She smelled of jasmine and beer. Martine was not taken in by the
falseness of these dubious and lukewarm demonstrations. This was
the sort of thing she loathed, it matched the bad taste of the room,
the lace doilies, the middle-class cosiness, the omnipresent bed.
But at the same time she was gradually fascinated and disarmed.
That "between women", with its background of rather tainted
complicity provided a kind of warmth she was not used to. And
gradually she succumbed to the temptation, allowed herself to be
snared and as if hypnotized by the murmuring voice, finding the
room was less ugly than she had thought, feeling the warmth of the
evening less oppressive. Still awkward and unused to such conversation, she began a few sentences, uttered a timid confession, caught
herself, stopped, went on again, encouraged by Jacquotte's murmured words of understanding. . . . And her plain face became
suffused with waves of colour, which gave it a kind of beauty, if
fleeting and remote.

"Yes, of course," said Jacquotte, who was barely listening, so
happy was she over the victory which now lay within her grasp.
And she judged the moment ripe to offer her guests an admirable
and enormous moulded rice pudding surrounded with apricots.

"But, my dear girl, this is a veritable feast!" exclaimed Stéphane,
who quickly became familiar; moreover, he was fond of sweet
things.

"What wouldn't we do for you, Stéphane Morani," she simpered, "and for this charming young lady! I may as well confess to you that she and I have been doing some talking, your ears must have burned."

Stéphane burst out laughing.

"Don't think, my dear, that we ourselves haven't been exchanging a few secrets, eh, Bruno?"

Stéphane slapped the tubby Bruno's shoulder with a rather forced and condescending familiarity, which was so convincing that even he himself mistook it for genuine affection.

"Oh, my dear friends!" he exclaimed, with a sudden melancholy that transformed his expression in an instant. "How delightful it is to see you two so happy, so united, entertaining us with such charming simplicity"—the word made Jacquotte frown slightly, but Bruno was blissfully unaware of any slight—"I, who am practically alone in the world and homeless, alas, there is no need to hide the truth from such faithful friends, find it particularly comforting to be with you here in this pleasantly modest home!"

The remains of the sauerkraut languished on the table. The rice pudding, vigorously attacked, had disappeared, leaving behind it only some tiny white fragments floating in a glaucous juice. The evening air grew cool, and Bruno shut the window and drew the flowered curtains across it. The table lamp garlanded with red paper, cast an intimate and pleasant glow. The aroma of coffee filled the room, making it suddenly comfortable. Stéphane felt surrounded by friends, listened to, admired. Martine also appeared to be relaxed. He let himself go in a flood of confidences which were welling up in him.

"I, too, once enjoyed this sort of thing. Oh, those peaceful evenings, the certainty of being understood. . . . How naïve can one be! But I can't blame anyone—all my bad luck is the result of my own stupidity. I remember what I was like as a young man: as loaded with illusions as a Christmas tree with candles, I was perfectly ridiculous, with my head in the clouds and my feet not entirely on the ground. And that idealist that I was, that lunatic dreamer, took it into his head to marry the most matter-of-fact,

the most earthy creature in the world. . . ." He paused a second,
then went on in a great burst of lyricism and charitable feeling.
"But I still tell myself today that she wasn't to blame for anything
at all. She didn't want much, poor thing. I offered her flowers, I
offered her the stars, I offered her music, a life full of dreams and
illusion, what I offered was perhaps chimerical. . . ." He raised
his eyebrows and smiled with ironic resignation. "Yes, I offered her
all that. And all she wanted was what any middle-class person
wants: success, a motor car, a fur coat. Oh, my poor wife! She
wanted bread, and I gave her cake. I played the rôle of Marie-
Antoinette, and so I have my prison!"

His laughter exploded, he was frankly amused at his own dia-
tribe. Bruno listened meditatively, without feeling any of the barbs
in that speech. Yet he, too, wanted nothing but middle-class
success and a car. The barbs did not touch him, for he had the odd
quirk of regarding everything Stéphane said as the outcome of a
tremendous amount of culture, but a way of thinking that need not
affect his own most profound convictions. Who in the world would
refuse a motor car if it were offered to him?

The conversation was not taking the turn Jacquotte wanted.
This recital of Stéphane's marital misfortunes was not calculated to
encourage Bruno along the road she wanted him to follow.

"Yes," she said, "you've had bad luck. Oh, I know there are
women like that. . . . But fortunately you've found a consolation,
someone who understands you. . . ."

Martine flushed.

"A fine consolation!" sighed Stéphane. "A fine consolation to
spoil a life, to absorb the youth of a pure and ardent person to
whom, once again, I can offer nothing but dreams, poems,
music. . . ."

This time Jacquotte felt near her goal, and lost a little of her
caution.

"But love, Stéphane? Don't you count love for anything?"

"Love, yes, obviously. . . ."

He was rather uncomfortable.

"Love, yes," she said. "And believe me, there is no reason to blush. A life in which there has been love is never spoiled." This was one of the themes she wrote about in her weekly column. "Naturally, it would be better . . . I mean, when it's possible, it is so much better to conform. . . . But when one is broadminded, couples like us . . ."

Stéphane turned upon her a look more surprised than shocked.

"I don't see at all," he said urbanely, "what you mean by 'couples like us'?"

There was an unbearable moment of silence. Martine flinched, then blushed deeply. There; it had happened again. She had let herself go, and as always it ended up with her being snubbed, and feeling ashamed as she had felt after the scene on the stairs, a scene she would never completely forget. Bruno lowered his eyes, Jacquotte lowered hers, Stéphane alone seemed merely astonished.

Martine, searching in vain for something to say that would break the silence, repeated over and over to herself, "He's right, there's no reason why we should feel ashamed. Our relations are so much finer . . . there's no reason to be ashamed!" But those two stupid creatures, whom she despised and detested, were for all that a real couple, yet they sat there with averted eyes. "There's no reason to be ashamed! Oh, if they'd read Stéphane's diary, as I have done, oh, if only they'd read his diary!" But they hadn't read the diary, and she was filled with a devouring shame. And the moment of silence grew longer, as they sat there before the ruins of the rice pudding.

The summer heat became drier, and the rue d'Odessa more peaceful. Madame Prêtre sat in her wicker sentry-box and Sylvia lay on her bed facing the mirrored wardrobe, reading. And Socrates watched Constantine and Dimitrios devour the meals he offered them, gloomily resigned as they consumed his profits. And the young man who rented Germaine Lethuit's flat had turned out to be a Swede. And at the Brasserie Dorée there was a different type of customer: fewer commercial travellers, office workers, family gatherings, and more tourists, who mistakenly imagined that Gloria Grétry was a sought-after figure in the Parisian entertainment world. And Stéphane and Martine still lingered on the terrace of the Café Dupont, without noticing the changes taking place in the population of the quarter.

Indeed, for them, Paris did not exist. The houses they saw were the houses of Signac, the passers-by were the people Stéphane had encountered in the course of his life, and Martine, the plain and unwanted girl, had become his family: his old one-eyed grandfather, his father, his mother, his wife, and society, as well. She was the silent tribunal before which Stéphane had pleaded his cause for years, a tribunal which he believed he had at last succeeded in isolating and concentrating in one single person, upon whom he was lavishing flattering attentions and, in his turn, absolving. For he had become her schoolmaster, her unworthy pharmacist father, her contemptuous friends, and even all that faceless multitude who had connived to prevent her from enjoying life to the full; he was all those doors that had been shut before, or rather he was the proof that she was not rejected, not isolated: she had only to look about her to realize that there were no more shut doors, that the hostile band of people no longer existed, and that they both circulated freely in a world they had freely chosen.

Meanwhile, in her suburban home, Germaine Lethuit was shutting some ancient piece of luggage and giving advice to her sister Pauline, congratulating her upon having divorced a crook, thus making it possible for the three of them to spend their summer holidays together in a dignified and respectable manner at a seaside resort in Brittany.

And Madame Prêtre's friend, Mademoiselle Marie, was taking a bus going towards the Étoile, with the object of gaining the confidence of a certain concierge in the Avenue Carnot. . . .

And Bruno was worrying, for he had seen through Jacquotte's designs; at the moment he was trying to persuade the manager of the Brasserie Dorée to let him do more singing than before. But he was denied this happiness, and Jacquotte wanted to marry him! The summer heat, too, got him down. Men were certainly creatures to be pitied, especially himself and Stéphane, he thought, for it was clear that Martine wanted to marry Stéphane. But Stéphane, no doubt, would be able to defend himself better. It would also be easier for Stéphane, since a divorce couldn't be got all that easily. Bruno warbled his refrains more lamentably than ever and one day. Marcel cast him into the depths of despair by saying, "You have a real comic gift."

And Jean Cadou went on painting big silver triangles on a reddish or bluish background.

"At last," said Gérard Ducas in his genteel little voice, "we are ready to go. These holidays are a great treat for me. A time comes when one has an absolute physical need to see farther than the other side of the rue d'Odessa."

"The need felt by office-workers at this time of year," growled Jean.

He carried on painting as the antiquary came and went, packing their clothes with meticulous care in a very impressive wardrobe trunk.

"Perhaps," Ducas conceded.

He loathed quarrelling with Jean, and sometimes, in order to avoid a quarrel, he was obliged to be extremely diplomatic. Jean was so highly strung! These artists. . . . Ducas always found the best possible reasons for justifying his friend.

"Well, did he accept my painting?" asked Jean, disagreeably.

For the last half-hour, ever since Ducas's return, he had wanted to ask this question. That, of course, was why he had talked of quite different things. And Gérard had suspected nothing. Jean had a wild urge to break something.

"Why, yes!" the antiquary replied enthusiastically.

He had kept the news back, waiting for Jean's bad temper to pass.

"He even said he considered it excellent, very stark and uncluttered, in your new manner. He believes he has an American buyer lined up for it."

"It's always Americans!"

"Yes, they're very fond of abstract painting over there."

"Not half! You can palm anything off on to them! These dealers, they'd like to get rid of me, to make room for their own little pals with French buyers, anything to keep my name from being known here!"

Ducas said nothing. Decidedly, Jean was in one of his black moods.

"Cliques, always cliques, with their plotting and scheming! To hell with them, I'll not descend to their level. They're after my hide, but they'll not get me!" He rumpled his already dishevelled hair, and threw down his brush.

"Aren't you looking forward to seeing your family?" Ducas dared to remark. "Down there you'll be able to paint, get an exhibition together perhaps."

Nothing could have been more unwelcome than these words, and Jean immediately exploded. "An exhibition! Why? For the sensation I make when I exhibit my work? For the money I realize on sales? Tell me why!"

Since his arrival in Paris ten years previously, Jean had had three exhibitions, thanks to some complicated intrigues on the part of his friend Gérard Ducas. Ten years already, mused Ducas sadly. Yet Jean had not changed. The thirty-two-year-old Jean could almost be taken for the twenty-two-year-old Jean, sullen and shy, with his tousled hair and dirty fingernails. "A Rimbaud!" the dazzled Gérard Ducas had exclaimed. However, despite all the gossip, he had never thought of himself as a Verlaine. When Jean's family, respectable dealers in wall-paper, had lavishly given their offspring the flat in the rue d'Odessa, he had merely gone to offer his services to the young Rimbaud, whom he had found sitting on a pile of packing cases, looking like an untidy undergraduate, biting his fingernails and glowering. The young man looked extremely romantic, thought Ducas.

"Can I help you in any way, is there anything I can do, my dear boy?" he had asked.

"Help me, my eye!" the voice of the poet had muttered.

Rather taken aback, the antiquary had turned to go. "As you like. I merely thought I might be able to help you unpack. . . ."

"Oh, if it's to unpack, that suits me," Rimbaud had declared.

Gérard Ducas had unpacked for him. A few days later he had suggested taking the young man's soiled linen to his own laundry-man. In his graceless way, Jean had accepted the offer, apparently with no intention of repaying Ducas for the laundry bill, an oversight that overwhelmed the antiquary with delight. He had an abiding need to do things for people. He joked about it himself, saying he had inherited the trait from his exemplary mother, a humble gate-keeper at Saint-Jean-le-Vieil, who had brought him up in the religion of "the finer things of life", honesty and virtue, that mother who seemed to have "stepped right out of an old-fashioned calendar", as he still said, recalling how she fed the pigeons and cultivated roses.

How antiquated all that had seemed to him when he had first arrived in Paris to take an advanced degree in History. How old-fashioned and ridiculous and shameful was the tenderness. that welled up in him even that day as he packed the wardrobe-trunk, at the mere reference to a mother, a little village, roses. . . . How he had joked about those things—while feeling deliciously sacrilegi-ous—with the other young fellows in their sub-surrealist group! What a beautiful epoch of discovery and revolt that had been, an epoch of ill-paid tasks and evenings of exalted talk in a café! What fun they had made of him with his brand new diploma! He had renounced the idea of being a schoolmaster and instead had com-bined forces with that half-mad old Russian woman who had an antique shop in the rue de Rennes. It was the glorious period of Montparnasse, and he had felt so very much in the centre of things, so much a part of "the movement" (what movement?), had seen famous people (without ever having the courage to speak to them), and painters' models, girls who would have been scandalous in Saint-Jean-le-Vieil (and was attracted to them only aesthetically, he reflected, for one of the ideas instilled in his youth was that men "caught nasty diseases" from going with such girls. His mother had told him that, blushing, at the moment of parting), and he had settled down to a chaste and orderly life (in reality if not in thought, a life he could have had by remaining an old bachelor in Saint-Jean-le-Vieil. But that never occurred to him). He wrote to his mother without really thinking of her, imagining her always with her roses and her pruning shears, like a picture in an almanac, and her death did not affect his life except that he had no more letters to write.

The old Russian woman left him the antique shop and disappeared towards her drug-addict's destiny. Time passed, and the other young fellows got ahead. One of them became a Communist, another married, a third won the Prix Goncourt, a fourth, younger than he, went to the colonies to teach, and Weiss, the most intelligent of them all, the only one who had known André Breton, died in 1941 in a concentration camp. He continued to live with his youthful illusions, still dazzled, still scandalized, until he suddenly perceived that the mystic, mysterious, secret language employed by the group he had belonged to, with the feeling of belonging to a class apart and of possessing a miraculous golden key, was now the language of everyone, that even the posters were now surrealist, that men of the working class no longer respected their mothers, that the milliners' apprentices knew who Louis Aragon was. . . . And he had to pretend to be glad about it, to consider all this quite natural.

But what, then, had happened to delicious sacrilege! Where was the dangerous secret! Where was the language for the initiates! There remained only one more convention, a convention of anti-conventionality, there remained only twenty-year-old virgins who blushed at being so, young fellows who affected equivocal manners, and an old man who sometimes recalled, embellished by distance, the roses of Saint-Jean-le-Vieil. No doubt he had waited too long— he had been afraid of becoming involved, of being gulled, and after all he was not too discontented with his life. He enjoyed it slowly, sipping it like a good wine. And his devoted and affectionate feelings for Jean were likewise, no matter what the gossips said, the sentiments of a connoisseur, innocuous and pure. The antiquary believed in Jean's talent. It proved to him that his youth had not been wasted, as the affection he had for the boy somewhat redeemed all those years without tenderness. But though Gérard Ducas's admiration was indispensable to Jean, his affection often irritated him. And in Jean's worst moods, he enjoyed wreaking violence upon it.

"Oh yes, the summer holidays!" Jean was saying, "and the beloved parents! And what has our dear little Jean done this year, Monsieur Ducas? And is our little Jean making good progress? I

can just hear them, and it's revolting! And you play their game!
'Oh yes, Madame, Jean eats regularly. No, no, he doesn't drink....'
A wall-paper dealer and an antiquary, they go well together. Our
dear little Jean! All three of you sanctimonious characters out of a
prissy story-book for juveniles!"

"Jean!" said Gérard Ducas sorrowfully.

"Yes, yes, you adore that virtuous and provincial family atmosphere. That's all you really like. But what about the crowded
train, the suitcases, and the boredom. . . . You know, I think I'll
chuck the family this year, get myself an American car, and drive
off to Deauville, following the Morani woman's example."

"Is Madame Morani going to Deauville?" asked Ducas, less out
of curiosity than to change the subject.

"I don't know if she's going to Deauville, but I do know I saw
her getting out of a Cadillac yesterday afternoon."

"Poor Stéphane," sighed the antiquary.

Jean seemed to be calming down.

"Oh, you and your poor Stéphane, either he doesn't suspect a
thing or else he finds it damned convenient."

"Oh, Jean!"

It was the roses-and-pictures-on-almanac Ducas that was shocked,
the Ducas of the earliest years.

"Why not?" said Jean spitefully. "Fewer expenses, a little more
spending-money. . . . He certainly must be short of money to
make him sell the maid's room to that little Fortin monster. One
really wonders what he does with that creature. I know what I'd
do: I'd exhibit her in a circus, she's weird enough."

"Jean, you're unjust both to Monsieur Morani who is a very
honest man and to that girl who, though obviously not very
pretty is . . ."

"The image of a monkey," snickered Jean.

"But she is a great admirer of your paintings."

"They all admire my paintings, don't they? Even Socrates, who's
hung one up among his mandarins. Even Germaine Lethuit
admires that painting of mine, thinks it's exquisite! Exquisite!
Even . . ."

Again the situation was perilous. Jean was decidedly in a black mood. He was subject to these moments of "depression", as the antiquary qualified them, when he would say really the most hateful things about the respectable people of the building, and even about his own paintings, and about Gérard Ducas himself. It sometimes ended up in a bout of drinking, with Jean returning home at five o'clock in the morning, making a rumpus on the stairs.

"He's like a big wild horse," Ducas said to the other tenants of the building, "you must excuse him. An artist. . . ." And they excused him. And Jean resumed his morose silence, his glum self-sufficiency, accepting everyone's compliments, the devotion of Ducas, the purchase of his pictures by Ducas's friends, as his due, and despite their good will, the occupants of the building and the regular customers of the Café Céleste could not keep from remarking "How self-satisfied that young Jean Cadou is!"

However, it never occurred to them to be surprised that Jean Cadou, with a flat at his disposal, a substantial allowance from his parents, and the talent they ascribed to him, still seemed to have no friends outside their little group. The question they never asked (and why should they ask questions about Jean Cadou that they did not ask about themselves?) was whether, despite the smug admiration of his parents, the devotion of the antiquary, and their own optimism as to Cadou's talent, the surly manners of the artist did not conceal some doubts as to his superiority, if submitted to outside judgement. They did not enquire and Jean Cadou himself would never have dreamed of asking himself such an awkward question. Yet this very remote, obscure awareness of his nonentity which sometimes made this sullen, lazy young man so cruel, alone animated him like some monster roused from the ocean-bed, was the same emotion which occasionally and almost imperceptibly inspired Jean Cadou's flat, gloomy, lifeless paintings with a desperate flash of life, like that momentarily human expression one sometimes sees in the eyes of a caged animal.

Now Stéphane was preparing to leave. Cadou and Ducas had left, Mademoiselle Lethuit had left, and Dr. Fisher had left (at dawn, quiet as a cat, no one having even heard his tin trunk on the stairs), and Socrates became silent, liberated for a few weeks from Constantine and Dimitrios who were busy with other prey; and Madame Prêtre, in her wicker sentry-box, appeared to doze. Stéphane was going! Martine came down from her room and braved the Hydra in the Morani flat. For Louise was there, placidly packing Stéphane's bags.

"Why of course, say goodbye to Stéphane," she said without a hint of irony. "I'm finishing his packing and . . . Would you like an apéritif? I happen to have a bottle of . . ."

She folded a pullover, then took two glasses and set them on the kitchen table. Her every gesture was possessive, commanding, a guileless insult to all Martine's endeavours. Martine had come to see Stéphane for a last time, to hear his voice, to be reassured, to lay in a stock of words and phrases on which to feed and sustain herself until his return in September, and yet she did not look at him and scarcely listened to him. She only looked at and listened to Louise.

"I'm putting in your heavy walking boots, you'll need them in the mountains. And your grey pullover, I mended it yesterday. Be sure to get a porter to carry your bag, it's rather heavy, and it would be unwise for you to try to carry it yourself. . . ."

She came and went in the kitchen, where Stéphane and Martine sat with their glasses of wine before them, as self-conscious as they would have been in a railway station waiting-room. She came and went, paying them only an absent-minded attention. Things began to fall into place around her, the gestures she made seemed to form neat patterns around her, not graceful, but assured, charged with an insulting calmness, as if proclaiming that those objects and those gestures were hers for all eternity, were identified with her, that indeed she herself was there, calm and eternal.

Grief and wrath surged anew in Martine, whose whole soul proclaimed, in desperate rebuttal, "She's not beautiful! She's not beautiful!" And then, looking at Stéphane, she noticed that his eyes were averted. He, too, although perhaps more obscurely, felt the same embarrassment and humiliation at facing that triumphant woman. She laid her hand on his. "I understand you, Stéphane," she thought ardently, "I understand you. You and I have right on our side. Some day . . ." She was quite incapable of imagining what that day was that she yearned for, that they yearned for. No doubt she would have been incapable of recognizing it if it had come, all of a sudden. But she yearned for it intensely.

"You mustn't miss the train," said Louise. "Do you want me to call a taxi?"

"Perhaps that's a little too extravagant," he murmured. "I can walk as far as the station, you know. . . ."

Martine's own suffering and humiliation were forced upon her, she did not really possess them. But she could appropriate Stéphane's humiliation and suffering, could feed upon them. And with that nourishment she must be satisfied, until his return.

"Then I'll go with you," said Louise. "I don't want you to carry that suitcase. Are you going down, Martine?"

Martine went downstairs. She wanted to endure all this to the end, the constrained goodbyes on the doorstep, under the amused observation of Madame Prêtre, wanted to see them cross the boulevard together, side by side, Louise carrying the suitcase. . . .

"She can very well bear the burden of his suitcase," said the oily voice of Madame Prêtre, as if responding to Martine's thoughts, "since she makes him bear other things. . . ."

Socrates, who was setting out the three tables on the terrace, burst out laughing. Martine made no comment. Near the taxi rank, Stéphane deposited a kiss on Louise's forehead.

"You know," murmured Madame Prêtre, "I'll bet those two live together like brother and sister. . . ."

Martine tore herself away from the scene on the boulevard and, without a word, went down the rue d'Odessa. She was not going to the Prisunic, for she, too, was on holiday. She had no intention of leaving Paris. Where could she go? And with whom? She would wait, she would try to preserve the little she had to preserve, she would try not to live or breathe or budge, so as not to crack this thin veneer of peace, this frosty peace that covered her burning suffering. . . . Once again she would have to endure hostile faces, colours, smells. Oh, if only she could live this month with her eyes shut, quietly, in a plant-like slumber.

Since it was noon, she would have her lunch, she decided, at the vegetarian restaurant. There everything was pure, inoffensive, without taste or smell. After that, she would sleep in the stifling heat of her little bedroom. Or she would try to sleep.

It was pleasantly cool in the studio. Louise had a vague hankering for some lemonade. But she did not want to disturb Henry who seemed to be sleeping. They would have a drink together in a while, and they might even have dinner, though they had already lunched together, since Stéphane had gone away. She wondered whether she would return to the Céleste that night. Henry would probably ask her to stay here. But Madame Prêtre would be quick to know, and spread the word around; Louise never slept out, she had accustomed herself to her brief Monday pleasures. Though, if she worried at all, it was for Stéphane's sake; personally, she cared very little what might be said about her in the rue d'Odessa; being regarded with respect was one of the blessings she could most easily do without.

She had very beautiful hair, thought Henry, who was only half asleep. Beautiful hair, beautiful face, beautiful breasts. To be sure, she was no sweet-and-twenty, but . . . Thus, from time to time, he felt the need of justifying himself. After all, the important thing was that she suited him. He had been hesitating for the past few days whether or not to leave Paris and go to his house in Provence. To go away with her, of course, for he had no idea of leaving her.

He mused a while over the possibility of that move to his country place, imagined Lou's lovely bare feet stepping on the stone pavement of the patio, on the red tiled floor of the bedroom. . . . But hot weather did not bother him, and he had begun to love Paris again. He enjoyed going to Montparnasse to fetch her, liked, while waiting for her, to stroll about in the quarter. Whatever had made him settle in the Étoile section of town! There in Montparnasse he had found again an atmosphere he loved, the railway-station, the travellers hurrying towards the suburban trains, the news-reel cinema where they showed rainy old films; the typists in their crudely coloured tight sweaters, jade green, pale mauve; the omnipotent café proprietors; the Breton hotels and cafés. . . . He even liked the office workers with attaché cases so torn and shapeless that they looked like something cast up by the sea (Henry always wondered what those attaché cases contained: a fortune, perhaps, or the amputated foot of a woman?).

The luggage room, he even liked that! The greenish luggage room, the refreshment bar, the magazines people read on trains, their alluring covers always depicting a pair of pretty legs beside a revolver. . . . And the cyclists on Sunday, with their tricoloured sweaters; and those stout-hearted, heavy, stupid locomotives with round eyes and sputtering snouts playfully ejecting a little quite innocuous smoke. And the *Folies Montparnasse*! That music-hall was a treasure-trove of subjects for sketches, and he sketched without any intention of putting the material to use later on, but rather for sheer pleasure, like a child. . . .

When everything is going well, best not to budge but just let things be. The spells of depression had taught him that. And so, for the time being at least, there would be no bare feet on the porous stones of the patio or on the glazed red tiles of the bedroom, for the time being there would be no Mediterranean. There would only be the cool and quiet studio, the music-hall and the contorted bodies he liked to sketch, the narrow and humid streets, the distant sky. Since she was free now, she would come every morning to pose. She could prepare the lunch, that would be a change, for he never lunched at home, and it was pointless for the two of them, to go to a restaurant every day: pointless and costly. Through the open window hardly stirring the curtains, came the syrupy undisturbing warmth. The days would go by, but they themselves would stay quietly, and nothing would happen. Better still, that very evening he would tell her to spend the night here with him. He would not ask her to, he would tell her. And after a minute's hesitation she would say, "Why, of course, Henry." He would see her fall asleep, hiding her face in the crook of her arm—she always hid her face to sleep.

And he would say aloud, for himself alone: "It's crazy how peaceful the summer can be."

Quite serenely, Madame Prêtre had been prepared to hoist her great bulk to go and reveal the scandal that tarnished a respectable family—if the guilty party happened to belong to a respectable family. Quite serenely, Madame Prêtre had contemplated sending an anonymous letter to the lover or husband of the guilty party—if in fact she turned out to have a lover or husband; and even, if the anonymous letter brought no result, to produce a signed denouncement. With a completely clear conscience she would have made it her duty to reveal to Henry Stass, by the same means, that the guilty party had a "protector" to whom she handed over the famous painter's money. This last did not require the actual existence of such a "protector"; if need be, Madame Prêtre felt ready to invent one. But she could not accept serenely the revelation Mademoiselle Marie brought to her, sweetening it like a pudding with compassionate exclamations. And even, so great was her bewilderment (or perhaps it was an instinctive reaction and less inoffensive than it seemed), that she called upon Socrates to bear witness, for the revelation had been brought to her on the very spot where she reigned supreme, the terrace.

Socrates felt that the least he could do was to offer her a pick-me-up, and to his great surprise, Madame Prêtre accepted it. She rarely entered the bar except for the literary reunions on Mondays, at which she deemed her presence indispensable. But it was impossible, after that piece of news, to remain calmly in her wicker sentry-box, beneath the gaze of the passers-by, with the news idle in her hands like a ridiculous and worthless object, a mockery to all her loving efforts. For what else was it, she asked—and Mademoiselle Marie agreed, raising her arms to Heaven and wailing contentedly—what else was it but an insult, a slap in the face for Sylvia, the detested and the adored, the bedevilled and the bedecked Sylvia, who was waiting in the concierge's lodge (reading *Vogue* today), confidently waiting for her mother's decision? Sylvia flouted! Sylvia disdained!

Madame Prêtre, her throat tight, her bosom on fire (or at least the heart that throbbed far beneath that heavy flesh), downed a glass of rum, in the Dr. Fisher manner; then collapsed on the banquette, under the calendar and the mandarins. Looking like a dragon herself, she was better adapted to the décor than they were.

Meanwhile, Mademoiselle Marie continued her sympathetic lamentations. Tall, flat-chested, with pretentions to elegance—she was a dressmaker and the wife of a sergeant of the Garde Républicaine, from whom she was separated—thickly powdered, pale of lip, pale of eye, with her grey hair parted severely in the middle, but waved—Mademoiselle Marie, who could not tolerate being addressed as Madame, prided herself on being tender-hearted. Was it because of all those inarticulate little grunts she made, her mouth full of pins, in response to the complaints of her customers? Or was it a habit she had acquired when the sergeant had left her, going off with a girl from the Auvergne (a major grievance for Mademoiselle Marie, who prided herself on being "a thoroughbred Parisian")? Whatever the cause, she had a taste for tears. This propensity did not keep her from being on very good terms with Madame Prêtre, for whom she turned out, each year, one of those interchangeable black dresses that the concierge wore as a kind of uniform. As for her own frocks, Mademoiselle Marie allowed herself some flights of fancy, restricted, however, to tones of grey, beige, brown and to fabrics that might be striped or stippled but never, never, flower-printed. For, said Mademoiselle Marie, who expressed herself well, "My heart is in mourning." Madame Prêtre provided Mademoiselle Marie with subjects for lamentation, as an audience provides a flamenco singer with themes for his songs. So she now gratefully attacked the present theme: rarely had she found a finer occasion. And although Madame Prêtre might have wished for a little less inspiration on the part of her friend, Mademoiselle Marie chanced to feel particularly inspired that day. As everyone knows, inspiration is a capricious wind, blowing where it lists.

"Oh, the poor child!" moaned Mademoiselle Marie, as Socrates looked on admiringly. "Oh, the cad who led her astray, who promised to marry her, who filled her young heart with love, only to abandon her now! And for whom? For whom? For an old woman, a sly creature, a married woman, a woman whose husband is an invalid, and absent from home, a woman who isn't even pretty, who . . ."

"Oh, she's not so bad looking," Socrates cut in. He had a weakness for rather plump brunettes. "For my part . . ."

Mademoiselle Marie glanced at him wrathfully.

"A woman," she went on, "who has deceived her husband for years, a woman who was, as we all know, a street-walker, a collaborator. . . ."

"Yes, that's true," said Socrates, impartially. "She brought me a ham once. But I'd say she went in more for black-marketeering than for collaborating, as you put it. The price wasn't too high."

"Oh," said Madame Prêtre, who was beginning to feel more cheerful, thanks to the rum, "I'm sure she knew some Germans. . . ."

"The way she dresses is scandalous! The way she talks to the Arab fruit-seller on the corner of the boulevard is a disgrace! And now to steal from that poor innocent child, that lamb, that dove, a man who was going to marry her! Poor, unfortunate child! Supposing she had been pregnant! Oh, how unfortunate we are! The world is nothing but injustice. . . ."

Madame Prêtre did not much care for this way of presenting Sylvia in the rôle of victim. "Unfortunate child" was what she herself had always called Sylvia; but she alone had the right to pity her daughter.

"I wonder how the woman managed it," she said pensively.

She did indeed wonder, her wrath was mingled with admiration, and Socrates and Mademoiselle Marie bent closer, enraptured by this new theme.

"Those street-walkers," said Mademoiselle Marie, in a definitely less elegiac tone, "have certain ways of doing things, it seems. . . . Of course I have no personal knowledge, but from what they say . . . I'm sure the woman from the Auvergne used some such means to lure my husband away from me. At night, when I approached him, he always pushed me away. 'Marie,' he said, 'I cannot . . .' "

"Some women cast a spell," Socrates observed. "In my country . . ."

Madame Prêtre did not believe in witchcraft nor in any other means than those of flesh and blood, filth and money.

"She seems to know her way about," she conceded. "Of course, Sylvia's young . . ."

"An innocent flower!" Mademoiselle Marie threw in.

"Shut up Marie. All the same, you'd think that a man over sixty . . ."

"Maybe that's why?" said Socrates, naïvely. "Maybe he thinks she's more suitable?"

"More suitable? That old swine? He *has* to like a twenty-year-old girl better than a woman who's . . . who's fifty perhaps? They're all the same at that age. Either they don't think any more about such things or else they're ready to go for a girl of fourteen."

Madame Prêtre laid down this credo in a rage. Everyone knew that men of sixty went for young girls. She'd always noticed it, and she'd built on it and now they were talking to her about suitability!

"Idiot!" she said aloud.

No, in shame and anger she had to confess, positively admit that the question of age did not enter into this. What was involved was plain gumption. Madame Prêtre had never under-estimated Madame Morani, and today she saw that her instinct had not betrayed her. That woman was quite capable of anything.

"She must have wormed his address out of Sylvia, and then gone there. . . . A man she knew twenty years ago! Some people would do . . ."

"Anything and everything!" finished Mademoiselle Marie, on her high horse again. "And you'll see, she'll hang on to him by appealing to his sensuality, that's the only way a woman of that age can hope to hold him. And you'll see, she'll ruin him! She'll wreck him, she might even kill him, who knows! There are women who do that, I assure you. With pills . . ."

For a moment Madame Prêtre lulled her grief with these alluring visions. But only for a moment.

"What are we to do now?" she groaned bitterly. "What *can* we do? I'd hoped . . ."

"What will become of the poor girl?" Mademoiselle Marie went on, as if echoing Madame Prêtre's thoughts. "Will she ever get over it?"

"Marie, be quiet! There's no question of getting over it. The question is . . ."

But Madame Prêtre herself did not know what the question was. For she did not see what pressure she could bring to bear upon Louise Morani. There was no respectable family involved, no fear of what people would say. Madame Prêtre knew Louise only too well. There was certainly no "protector". A woman of that age was only too glad . . . and Henry Stass must know her past. As for her husband. . . .

"Poor Monsieur Morani!" said Mademoiselle Marie, as if anticipating Madame Prêtre's thoughts. "Cuckolded by a man older than he is!"

"With the little money she has, she'd have a hard time finding a young man," said Madame Prêtre, but she was too hard hit to take any pleasure in her own spitefulness.

"And he doesn't even know it?" said Mademoiselle Marie, by way of a suggestion.

"That wouldn't get us anywhere," said Madame Prêtre, coming straight to the point. "What would you expect him to say to her? She's the one who holds the purse strings, the flat is hers. He earns almost nothing, he's a sick man, what could he say to her?"

"Poor man, poor man!" said Mademoiselle Marie, more out of a sense of duty than from any real interest in Stéphane. What interested her was Madame Prêtre and the disasters she would cause, giving Marie the chance to exclaim, "Don't, oh don't do that!" But with the best will in the world, Madame Prêtre did not seem able to think of any disaster to bring about. Mademoiselle Marie was very disappointed.

"But if he knew?" she persisted.

"Maybe he'd be pleased?" said Socrates with his usual dismaying naïveté. "That famous man makes a lot of money, doesn't he?"

This question revived the pain of the wound, and Madame Prêtre uttered a groan.

"Sylvia wouldn't know anything about that," said Mademoiselle Marie shrewdly. "The poor child was quite incapable of taking such a thing into account."

Madame Prêtre exploded.

"The poor child, the poor child, I'm fed up with hearing you say that. She's not an invalid, yet! She'll find ten men for that one, let me tell you!"

"Oh, yes, yes," said Marie, smiling sweetly, "of course she will. Poor outraged mother!"

But the poor outraged mother had painfully raised herself from the banquette and was going back to her lodge, to avoid giving her friend too obvious a subject for lamentation: Madame Prêtre's shrewd little eyes were brimming with tears of rage. The door of the lodge banged. Mademoiselle Marie and Socrates stared at each other.

"What self-control! What courage! She refuses to admit her grief!"

"Poor woman," said Socrates, speaking sincerely. For he had a kind enough heart when he thought about it. And, from habit, he added, "Would you like a glass of something?"

"Something sweet, then," said Mademoiselle Marie, who felt very well indeed. "A little benedictine . . ."

In the lodge, Madame Prêtre surveyed her daughter. "What beauty! What beauty!" she repeated despairingly. And Sylvia was there, beautiful indeed, in striped corsair pants and a salmon pink low-necked blouse, her dark hair well cut and expertly tinted to give it a very faint tawny sheen. Yes, she was beautiful with her golden brown eyes, her adorable little nose with its slight upward tilt, and her peach-bloom complexion, like a Hollywood star, and her figure, slender yet rounded, with such pretty arms. . . .

"What are you doing?" asked Madame Prêtre in a choked voice.

"I'm looking at the new collections," said Sylvia sweetly. "The
autumn fashions will be very becoming to me."

"And what'll you buy them with, your new autumn fashions?"
her mother thought wrathfully, but she said nothing. If she had
spoken, she would have said too much. She needed to pull herself
together a little before saying anything, before making any sug-
gestions. This was not the time. She was overwhelmed just now by
this world in which men of sixty-five preferred a Madame Morani
to her Sylvia, where a married man could "say nothing" because
it was his wife who had the money, a world where a Mademoiselle
Marie could whimper "Innocent as a flower!" while thinking,
"Just plain idiotic!"

She was all the more overwhelmed because basically, she felt that
world to be right. She had tried to conceal the fact, but she had
always known that her beautiful and adored Sylvia was not made
to triumph in this world where Madame Prêtre herself was so
much at home. If Sylvia had been anyone else's child, she would
have thought it quite right for her to be superseded, even by a
woman of Lousie Morani's age. She had always known it, even when
Sylvia was only ten. Despite her love, she had in a way condemned
her. By her words, her own taste for this hard and ruthless world,
by her curiosity, and her spiteful, sagacious and limited outlook,
she had condemned Sylvia. And though she might not consciously
know it, at least she sensed it from the conflicting emotions she
always felt in her daughter's presence, a feeling which was the only
high-minded reaction ever experienced by this base creature. For it
made her suffer to bestow her love on someone who, according to
her own moral code, did not deserve it.

Later on she would talk to Sylvia once more, forcing herself
to be gentle. She would try to convince her that she should return
to Henry Stass; but better to wait a while. If he had tired of Sylvia,
he would also tire of Louise Morani. She would then coach Sylvia
as to her every remark, her every gesture; and they would see
whether she triumphed or not! But that would be later on. Today,
Madame Prêtre could not have summoned up the strength. Her
affection for Sylvia weighed her down like a crushingly heavy

burden, and if she had let herself go, she might either have slapped her or taken her, sobbing, into her arms.

She went into the dark alcove, into voluntary confinement, and lay down. She did not weep, but deep within her there was a kind of long, monotonous lament. The cat jumped up on the couch at her feet, but she made no sign. She gave herself over to that lament, hugged it close, as she had hugged Sylvia, without understanding. She was sure that no one would disturb her; almost all the occupants of the building had gone away, and when Sylvia was looking at clothes, she could be counted on to keep at it for the entire afternoon.

Why can't one believe? Martine asked herself. Why is it impossible to believe absolutely and unquestioningly as the Faithful believe in God? Why can't one exist blindly, vigorously, finding life enough in itself, as animals do?

If one could have seen a cross-section of the house or formed an accurate picture of the lay-out of the place then one would have seen at once that Martine, lying on her narrow bed in the stuffy attic, high up beneath the burning roof, was immediately above that other small cool room, with its slight smell of cat, where Madame Prêtre lay nursing her sorrows. Such parallel sorrows could never meet. And, on a larger scale if a cross-section of the street or an accurate picture of the lay-out of the town was available, one would have seen that their two sorrows and their two bodies were exactly parallel or perpendicular to many other sorrows and many other bodies. And supposing a graph had been drawn of all this, a stylised, symbolic affair, with lines for the bodies and circles for their sorrows, then any one of these bodies with its attendant sorrow would have seemed relatively unimportant. Or perhaps, on the other hand, might it not have acquired additional significance? Might not the entire graph change, as a coherent and finished painting may change, by the simple placing of one single line in its composition? Quite possibly! But if the eye turned from the graph of the town to concentrate on a street, on one single house, if the line became a body again, the circle a sorrow, and if that body and that sorrow became your own, then it would be no comfort to know the place they occupied on the graph, to know which line and which circle had held you prisoner. Martine would be there, before your very eyes, you would be Martine. And there was nothing you could do about it.

She lay there on her bed, utterly undone, a castaway. She was Martine. Why could not one believe? Or exist? Her hand slid under the pillow, grasped the blue exercise book, her lifebuoy, her hope. There were other similar notebooks on the unpainted wooden table. But this one was the last, the one in which her name figured prominently on every page. Proof that it was possible for someone to love her, and for her to love in return. Who, not knowing her, upon reading these pages, would not have imagined her beautiful? She herself, for a day, a week, a month, had seen herself there and had believed herself to be beautiful. From where, then, came her present distress, this returning doubt, swelling ever bigger and bigger, like a heavy sea driving the foam along before it, and, as apparently ebbing, is all the while gathering strength for its highest wave?

A short while ago she had washed out a petticoat which now hung on a stretched cord in front of the small window. For a long moment she stared at that spot of white, and it did her good. Perhaps, if she had been less hot . . . she thought of going downstairs. But where could she go? In the bar? There she would be exposed to Socrates' chatter, to his loud commiseration. . . . A stroll up the street? She had a horror of crowds, of the narrow passageways steaming with heat; by the time you reached the boulevard you were soaked with sweat, and exhausted by the combination of dust and sunlight.

For a moment, in some part of her mind, too vague to be called a thought, there was a room with a tiled floor, cool and dark, with a very special smell. . . . The word "Pharmacy" suddenly loomed up and she could see that cool dim room where she had played as a child, squatting on the floor, her toys old boxes marked "poison"; the image no longer pleased her. Her mother must still be there, no longer as the wife of the pharmacist, but as an employee, managing for someone else what she had once owned. Her mother, always complaining, always, as she put it, "upset", and yet a woman who had once been pretty. Did the bedroom still exist, with its flowered wall-paper, where her father (poor swindler of limited intellect), had taken the law into his own hands and done away with himself? Martine remembered that room because it had been hers, and because it was there, in a hidden corner, that she had discovered a yellowed old photograph of that young and pretty mother, that mother she blamed for not having bequeathed her at least some beauty. The cool room vanished from her mind. A faint breath of air stirred the white petticoat. But it made no difference to the stifling atmosphere.

She took the notebook out from beneath the pillow and leafed through it, reading her name. Her name: Martine. The day she had first seen it there, it had seemed to prove something to her. It would still seem like a proof, had Stéphane been near. But he was not, and it was only a week since he had left; less than a week. Not a fourth part of the time she would have to endure alone, that she must get through alone, time which seemed in her mind's eye to be as hot and unbearable as it was that very minute.

No, she must not go out. She already knew that downstairs the world that awaited her was again closed and hostile. She already knew that again, the protection offered by Stéphane having disappeared, everything would seem to her as aggressive and insulting as Louise had seemed a few days before. She must remain here, on this bed, beneath this burning roof, burdened with this spent and puny body, and holding this notebook in her hand. Upon this immobility and this glimmer of hope, upon this small amount of breathable air in an unbearable atmosphere, depended her very life. And she wanted to live.

She pressed her cheek against the page where her name was written.

"I want . . ." she sighed, "I want . . ."

Her fervent murmur was almost a prayer.

They called it, because of the potted palm trees that were crowded into it, "the winter garden". It was quite a small hexagonal room, opening out upon a veranda. Here reigned the eternal wicker

armchairs, along with last year's magazines; and on the window-
panes was pasted the inevitable filigraned paper, yellowed with time,
letting in a doubtful glimmer of light (the same imitation stained-
glass paper flourished in the antiquated w.c.s and bathrooms), but
shutting out no view, since the window did not overlook the sea,
as did the veranda, but opened out upon a rather sordid courtyard.
The potted palms, because of the film of grey dust covering them
and because of their impassive rigidity, caused, no doubt, by the
cold, were the least Oriental trees one could imagine—nothing,
absolutely nothing in their grey and stunted rigidity could possibly
recall the scent of sandalwood, the houris of a harem, or the sun,
alas, try as you would to evoke such visions. These were palm trees
native to Brittany. The veranda, too, despite its exotic name, was
indubitably Breton; fishing nets accumulated there, the property
of the paying guests; these nets were innocent of any catch (save
perhaps that day, recorded by a camera, when a dull grey shrimp
was found there), even though they gave off a strong fishy smell.
The stairs (not to mention the clutter in the cloakroom of sou'-
westers, umbrellas, boots and various odds and ends) were indisputably Breton, if only because of the smell that hovered there,
which, it must be confessed, was the odour of rancid butter (it was
very hard to obtain fresh provisions in this remote seaside place).

   Then, there was the rain, the fine, light rain of Brittany, as
diaphanous as the fairies one hopes to see dancing in the cromlechs
(and they will be seen just as soon as the Tourist Bureau organizes
the "See Brittany by Night" committee, still in gestation), the rain
was labelled, patented, one would almost say kept in reserve for the
summer visitors. As soon as the visitors began to arrive that summer,
one of those famous Breton fishermen you see on calendars advertising Brittany, was there to comment, "People come a long way to
see this!" And, incredible as that would seem, it was true. They
came from quite far away. Only the night before, an autobus had
brought twenty or so trippers from Angers, who had come to
appreciate, like true connoisseurs, a rain slightly different from their
own (there must surely be some special words to qualify these subtle
differences of rain, as for wine the "bouquet", the "body", and

other niceties; and if there are no such words in French or English then there must surely be in the Breton language). For, as the proprietress had ritually said, "It's raining everywhere, this year." And the rain-connoisseurs, with Basque bérets on their heads—the one false note—had gaily gone out to enjoy the treat of this exotic rain.

The Gentleman was doubtless not a connoisseur of rain. He had remained at the hotel, as Pauline Lethuit had done. He could enjoy, without stirring, the odours of fish and rancid butter, enough to make him realize that he was spending the holidays in Brittany. The Gentleman had taken one of the wicker chairs, cast a glance at the sea (across the veranda) and settled down very seriously to read in a year-old magazine about the birth of Lollobrigida's baby. Pauline was knitting. She was knitting a bolero jacket with a tightly twisted wool yarn. Naturally, her father and Germaine had dashed out after the Angevins towards the sea, the fugitive shrimps, and the conversation of the Typical Fisherman (whom one eventually suspected, since he was never on the sea, of being paid by some special organization, perhaps the Tourist Bureau). Every day since their arrival they had made a dash for the sea, but particularly today, for they were not going to be outdone by some Angevins! And Germaine was so athletic! Pauline sighed. Although she owned a sou'wester, she was not the athletic type. The sight of the sea made her feel romantic, made her long to play some Fauré or Debussy. Unfortunately there was no piano at the hotel. She thought of her husband, the swindler, and wondered if he was having his holidays. Even swindlers had occasional holidays, she imagined.

"It seems they're having wonderful weather in Paris," said the Gentleman, his voice hoarse from timidity. And he added, as if to excuse himself, "This is the first time I've ever come to Brittany."

Pauline blushed. Despite her forty-odd years, she always blushed when a stranger addressed a word to her.

"We come here every year," she said, however, terrified at the prospect of another afternoon of solitude.

She knew Germaine and their father; you literally could not drag them away from the delights of the rain. They walked miles to eat pancakes that were less good than the ones made in the hotel kitchen, or to see cromlechs identical to those they had seen the day before (one could almost believe those huge stones were moved during the night to provide goals for the tourists' excursions), and they never wearied of it; one might have thought they were Breton-born.

"For my part, I always go South," said the Gentleman with a mournful air. "To the Midi. But they say that Brittany is healthier."

"Oh yes, very healthy," said Pauline with no less melancholy.

The Gentleman must be some fifty years old, but he was well preserved. A short, wiry little man, a vine-grower, she imagined, in Anjou, of course. . . . Meanwhile, he was intent on rectifying a possible misunderstanding.

"I go to the Midi, but not to the Riviera. Smack in the middle of the land."

"How nice! There must be plenty of sunshine. . . ." ("Smack in the middle of the land," an odd expression. Yes, surely, he must be a vine-grower. However, he seemed to be rather refined and delicate for such heavy work.)

"Too much, Mademoiselle . . . or Madame?"

"Madame," she said regretfully.

He was going to think that she was there with or waiting for her husband, and would go back to his reading of the magazines. But not at all, he went on chatting. Perhaps he was an adventurer?

"Too much sunshine. My health—I'm very delicate, very. . . . My health suffered there. My work is hard, I take two months of real rest every year, and in that sunshine . . ."

Yes, that was it. A farmer. But Pauline had never imagined that rough workers of the soil looked like this. He must be the proprietor of a vineyard, must employ others. You could see by his worried look that he had responsibilities.

"Are you going to stay two months here?"

"Oh, no," he said, with a shiver. "Too damp, much too damp. My health . . ." He gave a glance towards the veranda, and the fine, light, fairy-like rain that was falling beyond it. "I think I'll go to the Midi."

There was a silence. Pauline lowered her eyes to her knitting.

Last year, she had knitted a whole dress with the same kind of yarn; that summer had been particularly rainy. She had worn the dress all winter. The thought made her pensive. It would be so nice to go south one year. But her father and Germaine were so happy in Brittany! And then, the prices were reasonable.

"Is the cost of living high in the Midi? I don't mean on the Riviera, but there where you go. . . ." She paused, blushing at her audacity. "I mean, where you go, smack in the middle of the land."

The Gentleman looked at her with some surprise. No doubt he fancied that in order to come every year to Brittany one needed a particular kind of temperament which could not endure any other climate. He observed her more closely and saw that she was still good-looking, pleasantly plump, and that she had some qualities he considered important, a very gentle expression, in no way aggressive, no make-up, or almost none, and he liked the old-fashioned way in which her fair hair was arranged.

"It's a little dearer than here," he said, adding at once, "but arrangements can be made, you can find lodgings in a private home. . . . And then, there's the fine weather."

"I thought the sunshine was bad for you," said Pauline shyly.

It had been ages since she had had such a long conversation with a gentleman at least, such an aimless conversation and one which might have seemed to people who did not know her, somewhat frivolous.

"Yes, but the rain!" said the Gentleman. "I have a very delicate constitution."

"Your work must tire you," said Pauline adroitly.

He smiled shrewdly, exactly as she had expected.

"Oh, no! So you've guessed what my work is? Still, what a numbskull I am, you must have seen my case in the entrance? Yes, I'm an agent for a firm: a commercial traveller. Brushes, floor-polish, all kinds of cleaning products, but no vacuum cleaners! I brought my case along because even on holiday I sometimes manage to sell one or two things. . . . Your husband may perhaps know my firm by name, Mirbien Products?"

"I'm not married," Pauline confessed. "That is to say, I'm divorced."

The Gentleman heaved a sympathetic sigh, pursed his lips in a melancholy way to show his pity, then, averting his eyes, made his own confession.

"As for me, I'm a widower. With a young son, at a boarding school in Angers. . . ."

The essentials had been exchanged, and the rain, the fairy-like rain of Brittany, stopped.

What was the sequel of this idyll in the Brittany of the *korrigans*, those evil sprites, where the weather was fine for ten days running? What of the excursions they made together, holding hands in the char-à-banc, the stroll they took on the breakwater (where the suspect fisherman drew their attention to a cormorant "the first of the season, that brings good luck to sweethearts") and the avowals that followed?

"I've never dared tell Germaine," murmured Pauline, "but I've never been able to understand the difference between a cromlech and a dolmen. Have you?"

Yes, at the end of only a week in Brittany, the Gentleman—who was not called Octave or Ernest, as one might have expected, but Jean, quite simply—had understood.

"You know, what I like about Brittany," he confessed, in his turn," is that everything is clean. The bad smell comes from the butter, that's all. In the Midi, everything is wonderful, yes indeed; but when you look a little closer . . . Now, take the toilet facilities. . . I do like a clean house. When you've been travelling a whole week, you like to come back to a clean house, it's only natural."

"Yes, indeed it's only natural," she sighed.

This profession of commercial traveller was, after all, romantic. The wife of a traveller. . . . The clean house. . . .

"Not counting the fact that I have all my own cleaning products, of course. . . ."

The practical side must not be neglected. She had still not dared to ask the name of his little son, but she had already found out that the boy was ten, when Germaine noticed what was going on.

"Pauline," she said with restraint, "you are compromising yourself with that man."

Pauline stood up for herself furiously. She had wanted to see the cromlechs of Carnac again, the Gentleman (was Germaine by any chance referring to Monsieur Jean Le Blanc?) happened to be in the char-à-banc, was that her fault? And as for the walk on the break-water, she hadn't been able to avoid talking to him, surely Germaine wouldn't have wanted her to be rude, would she?

"Pauline," said Germaine Lethuit, "you're a child." (This was a fact that had always been recognized in the Lethuit family: Pauline was a child. Only once in her life had they let her have her way, and she had married, and what had been the result? Her husband had robbed the Post Office.) "Don't you see? That man wants to get you into a situation where you cannot refuse him . . ."

Pauline, blushing guiltily, still demurred. There was no question of such a thing, Monsieur Jean had behaved in a perfectly correct way. . . .

"Why, of course. At your age, he'd not try the same methods he'd use to seduce a young girl. But didn't he let you understand that he was in very good circumstances?"

"Why, I mean to say. . . . I believe he makes a good living, yes. . . ."

"Ah!" exclaimed Germaine, in the tone of someone who has made a point. "And will you kindly tell me just what are his cir-stances?" (This question was purely rhetorical. But then, Germaine's questions almost always involved an answer furnished by herself.) "He is a commercial traveller! Always away from home—he was unable to hide that from you—and with commission earnings, that is to say, irregular, and his wife left alone at the house to make both ends meet. Anyway, travelling, he'd have expenses, he'd account for them however he liked, wouldn't he?"

Obviously, presented in this light. . . .

"I don't believe he's that kind of man," she murmured. "You seem to be saying . . . I don't believe he's a man to . . . I mean, he's not a Don Juan. . . ."

"Now let's look at things frankly, as they are," said Germaine. "And above all, Pauline, don't think I'm trying to influence you. You wanted to marry the first time, I predicted that you'd be unhappy, but I gave way. So now I'm giving you my opinion, and you can do as you like." (Germaine was always saying to mothers who refused to let their children be vaccinated, "I warn you, you're taking a risk, but it's entirely up to you," and she would make a sign to the nurse.) "You say that this man is not a woman-chaser. You may be right. He's not the same type as your husband, fortunately. But please note that we sometimes feel reassured by people's looks, and then. . . . Well, we'll say he's not a woman-chaser. Good. But why?"

Pauline was quite incapable of replying to this type of question.

"Why? Well, I suppose because he . . . because he doesn't think much about women."

"Exactly. He's a man who lacks vitality. All you have to do is listen to him. The rain makes him feel bad, the wind makes him feel bad, the sun makes him feel bad. And at fifty! Just look at Papa and all the things he does at his age! A walk in the wind holds no terrors for him! 'Wind whips the blood,' he said to me only yesterday, when we went out for crabs. But that Jean Le Blanc of yours . . . I'm not one of these women who think a man ridiculous because he wears woollen underwear, those things don't count, but after all, in summer!"

"It's not his fault if he has rheumatism. And it wasn't as warm as all that, yesterday."

"Oh, my dear! You're so touching! You're so frail, yet you have this urge to devote yourself to someone. I remember that day when you attended to our poor Minou's ears, you were admirable! But you're used to being spoiled, my dear Pauline, and I'm not reproaching you for it, we do spoil you, Papa and I, as if you were our child. Our little artist, our little bird, our darling. Think of your health, my dear. A bad marriage is harder to bear than relative solitude. . . . Just look at our poor dear friend Stéphane Morani. Do you think he's happier as he is than he'd be as a bachelor, surrounded by the affection of his little circle of friends?"

Germaine was sincere, she did not suffer from her celibacy. As the head of the family, ruling a father still vigorous physically but less gifted than she in financial matters, and a sister who gave singing lessons (but in Meudon young girls who took singing lessons were rare, and rarer still were those who paid decently), Germaine Lethuit had all the preoccupations needed for a tranquil life.

"All the same, Stéphane Morani's not alone," Pauline insisted, still feebly defending herself.

"Alas! Do you imagine that the companionship of a woman as vulgar as she is, and who behaves as she does . . . I'd prefer not to talk about it, but do you imagine such a wife is any real comfort?"

"Then why does he stay with her?" said Pauline, who had these moments of revolt against her sister's friends. "It's idiotic."

"That's none of our business," Germaine observed. "Anyway, from what I know of Stéphane Morani, it could only be for good and high-minded reasons. We're getting away from the subject. That little son you don't know anything about, for instance. But don't think I'm urging you to . . . anyway, don't believe that. . . . Look, all I'm asking you to do is, reflect!"

Pauline reflected. She was fond of comfort, she was timorous. Monsieur Jean Le Blanc reflected. He didn't like families and he certainly didn't like bossy sisters. The rain began to fall again, all the more inexplicable since, according to the hotel radio, which they listened to every night, sitting between the two potted palms, it was frightfully hot in Paris. His rheumatism returned. And so Monsieur Jean Le Blanc disappeared one day with his valise on which was displayed the trade-name *Mirbien*—a name that haunted Pauline's thoughts for several weeks afterwards. She returned to her knitting, which had been somewhat neglected. She would never know the name of the little boy who was at a boarding school in Angers and who had the habit of biting his nails. Pauline's father was a splendid sight with his beautiful moustaches as he left at daybreak to go shrimping. And there were bright intervals. Two days before returning to Paris, the motionless fisherman on the breakwater dispelled their suspicions and revealed the truth: he was not, after all, employed by the Tourist Bureau. He was a war veteran,

enjoying his pension. It was his own affair if he liked rain and conversation, wasn't it? At any rate, it was for this he had left his native
town of Agen in the Bordeaux region to come to Brittany to live.

Martine resolved to go down and brave the judges of the nether-
world.

The weather was torrid in Paris, as the radio had said. And the
radio also said that even those planning to leave Paris in September
might still expect good weather, for the heat was going to last.
Martine finally plucked up courage to descend the stairs, a blue
exercise-book in her hand.

Madame Prêtre was not in the bar, but in her lodge, with
Mademoiselle Marie. Sylvia, in the company of a long-haired
youth, was at a preview of some documentary films on which the
young man had done some kind of work. Not much could be hoped
for from this contact, but one never knew, and meanwhile. . . .

So there the two women were, the one short and stout and shrewd
with a sensual mouth and eyes almost hidden under heavy lids, her
throat clasped by the usual black ribbon with its cameo; the other
woman as lean and pale as a dab, with little white bows on her dark
grey dress. . . . No, Martine could not have chosen a more dreadful
tribunal, could not have flung herself with more courage at anything she feared more. But courageous though she was, that day,
she stood hesitating in the doorway for a moment, as one hesitates
before plunging into icy water. Then she went in.

They were perfect. The bottle of Dubonnet was brought out
as if automatically, and they each had a glass, a big one, to encourage
Martine. Questions were asked, and all Martine had to do was
reply. It was all quite natural, they said; they had known it; nothing
astonished Madame Prêtre, and Mademoiselle Marie was ready to
sympathize with any kind of distress. So, Martine was not Stéphane
Morani's mistress? They understood. She was troubled? They
understood. Here and now they were ready to swear to it—oh,
they had been absolutely sure, for it would have come to their
ears—that he did not have a mistress. That was something, at any
rate. You couldn't say that of every man. But surely he had a kind

of feeling for Martine. . . . Oh, as to that, they would swear to it. A feeling! Mademoiselle Marie's eyes rolled heavenward to express the intensity of that feeling. Madame Prêtre's plump little hand fell upon Martine's thin shoulder.

"All the same, there's bound to be a gesture of some kind some time, something or other that makes you feel there would be more to it if he were only free, eh?"

Martine was in the water up to her neck, in the icy and slimy water. She had wanted it, she could no longer escape it. She sought judgement from those she feared and hated most, from these women whose butchers' hands weighed her doubts, the burning agony of these past days. . . . They would condemn her, perhaps. . . .

"Oh, come, I'm sure there must have been a little kiss. . . . After all we're women of experience, a mother understands. . . . There's nothing to blush about. . . ."

"Not one kiss?" insisted Mademoiselle Marie.

"No."

She had confessed. She had said "No." She was quite tense with the effort, her courage at breaking-point.

"Madame Prêtre," Socrates came to say, "there's a customer who wants to use the telephone and mine's out of order. Can he use yours in the lodge? He says it's only for two seconds. . . ."

"It'll be thirty francs," said Madame Prêtre, and she followed the man into the alcove where the telephone was.

"Poor Madame Prêtre!" murmured the dressmaker, like a well regulated machine. "You're not the only one to suffer, my poor young lady. . . . Oh, we all have our troubles!" (But time was pressing, so she would refrain from talking about her own troubles, she would not talk about the woman from the Auvergne.) "Between you and me, that poor little Sylvia isn't entirely normal. But to be abandoned for a Louise Morani!"

"Who abandoned her for Louise Morani?" asked Martine mechanically.

But she was so absorbed in her torment that she did not even raise her head at the mention of Louise, thereby greatly disappointing Mademoiselle Marie.

"Why, the famous painter they were so proud of, Sylvia and her mother. It seems that Madame Morani was his model years ago. But don't say anything about it. The poor mother is suffering the seven sorrows, and without a word . . ."

Madame Prêtre put the thirty francs in her purse.

"Now, let's get back to you, my dear Martine." It was the first time she had ever called Martine by her Christian name. "I don't like to see you upset like this. . . . Do have a little to drink, this wine is excellent, isn't it, Marie? And we'll have a good long talk. Of course you're unhappy, because he's away, but he'll soon be back. Why, it's the second week of August already. And he's missing you, I'm sure. What about all those letters? I recognized his writing, you see!"

Yes, he had written. But if the journal couldn't console her, how could the letters, lined up on her chest of drawers, still unopened?

"And in another ten days he'll be here, think of that, and you'll have your little rendezvous, and your evenings out together again . . you often meet at the Café Dupont, don't you? *I* know. You see how fond he is of you."

But this was not the test she had set herself, it was like holding a red-hot iron at arm's length, instead of summoning up courage to press it quickly against her wound.

"Madame Prêtre, you know about life. . . ." It was hard to get the words out. "Would you have a look at this?"

She was holding out the blue exercise book, upon which she had so often laid her head to sleep.

"It's his journal . . . and I'd like you to tell me . . ."

"That's pretty clever," said Mademoiselle Marie. "But how did you manage to get into the flat?"

Martine flushed bright red.

"Oh! Why, it was Monsieur Morani himself who . . . I'd never dream . . ."

"Why, for heavens sake, of course, Marie!" said the concierge, good-naturedly. "Is Martine Fortin the type of girl to break into a flat and take something? Give that to me, my child. We'll read it, and we'll tell you frankly what you can expect. Is that what you want?"

Martine bowed her head. Yes, when it came to it, that was what she wanted. If those two women, sly and malevolent and smugly pitying as they were, could be convinced, why then . . . How many days would it take them to read the journal? How long to talk it over between themselves? Two, three, four days? A week, perhaps, during which time there would be something else to wait for besides Stéphane's return. She longed to be convinced, to believe he was utterly sincere. But doubt had exhausted and bewildered her. She heard herself mutter, "Take your time. . . ."

But she still had the strength to flee.

"Well! If someone had told me that, I'd never have believed it!" The dressmaker poured herself another glass of wine. "That Fortin girl in your lodge! A girl as proud as that!"

"Coming into my lodge is nothing to be ashamed of," retorted the concierge. She did not, however, allow herself to flare up, but instead settled down at the table for a good talk. "And besides, what won't people do when they're in love!"

"Oh, that poor girl! And so plain! She can't have any idea how plain she is. . . ."

"Oh, she's not the first one. . . . Possibly he's not slept with all of them, but God knows he's had plenty of girls crazy about him."

"Perhaps it's our duty to tell her," Mademoiselle Marie suggested.

"And why, please? What do you expect would happen?"

"Oh, I don't know. Well, at least she's had a little happiness out of life. What are you going to say to her about that thing?"

Madame Prêtre's disdainful hand lifted the exercise book, as if weighing it.

"Why, of course, that he adores her, and so forth and so on. What she wants us to say, poor creature. Live and let live, that's my motto."

"You're not even going to read it?"

"Indeed I am. . . . There must be some funny things in it, it will give me some ideas. . . ."

Even in the concierge's lodge it was hot. The alcove where Madame Prêtre slept smelt of cat rather more than usual. A little before seven o'clock she would use a deodorant spray in there, for Sylvia detested the cat smell.

There they were, the two of them, peaceably sitting with the journal on the table between them, commenting on Martine's unexpected visit, like two gourmets before a tasty dish from which they intend to extract the maximum flavour. But the overpowering heat was a bit depressing.

"He doesn't care a rap for her, he's trifling with her," Mademoiselle Marie began, languidly.

"How right you are!"

These were the first chords, the instruments were tuning up for the great symphony of scandal-mongering and slander, of gratuitous lies which they would both enjoy and to which each would add her touch, her note, Madame Prêtre's being heavier, more highly coloured, more brazen than Mademoiselle Marie's, which would be sweeter and more treacherously sentimental.

"She obviously filched that diary from a desk drawer, while his back was turned."

"Obviously."

It was a good theme, and despite the heat, they courageously set about to elaborate it.

The days went by, not flowing past, but ranging themselves one after the other like blocks of stone. They were like dolmens, inscrutable stone gods, grey in the summer heat, terrible to some people, favourable to others.

For Henry and Louise, the long stone vista of summer days had been propitious, they wandered along it at a leisurely pace, looking back now and then to see how far they had come, almost persuading themselves that, if they liked, they could stop or even retrace their steps. And added to this perspective, was another, more distant still; of those days at Signac when they had felt so "right", as Lou put it, with quiet dignity. It even seemed as if they could return to that pleasant time, and that between the two vistas there had been but a momentary halt, a rest in the cool shade, necessary but unexciting.

Now, with refound freedom, Louise's hands touched the pots and pans in the little kitchen which Henry had never used. In the studio, the long grey curtains were drawn apart, the windows were opened. The welcome breath of air that occasionally found its way in seemed the only cool breeze in all Paris. She brought the carafe of ice-water, the bottle of *vin rosé*; she laid the table which was used for the still-lifes; they sat facing each other to eat their meals, at times a little perplexed by this utter, undeserved peace. The silence was too full, too rich, it had to be broken.

Henry finally confessed that he had never liked the pompous English furnishings in the bedroom at the far end of the studio, that bedroom where they never slept. The furniture had been forced upon him, as suitable to a bachelor. They slept and ate in the studio, and already in one corner there was an accumulation of empty bottles that Lou always forgot to take downstairs. Henry had dismissed his charwoman, killing two birds with one stone: when one had a woman in the house, it was wasteful to pay out good money to a daily help. He had wrapped a woollen scarf around the telephone, and when it shuddered imperceptibly they looked at each other and laughed. He did not reply to letters. The invitations he had accepted for so many years because he thought it necessary if he wanted to get on, and then had gone on accepting out of sheer force of habit—protesting all the while that he "couldn't stand those people" and yet secretly flattered to be so sought-after— and afterwards had still accepted because he didn't know how to fill in the time when he wasn't painting and because he was bored and couldn't use up his surplus energy staying up late and drinking too much—with what pleasure he now saw those invitations pile up in the cut-glass bowl he disliked so much. That bowl had been a present from his sister who had profited from his success to come to Paris, where she had met and married a distinguished music critic, Professor Fuchs, and who now actually had a *salon*! He reproached Lou for not throwing out the invitations and letters, as he reproached her for the accumulation of bottles. She really was too neglectful! Three or four times they had quarrelled over this sort of thing, and now, between them, there was that bond of affectionate hostility that unites real married couples.

It pleased him to note that Lou also had not the least idea of how to kill time, once she had finished her household duties. She still went punctually to the Montparnasse music-hall, and he went just as punctually to fetch her, sometimes watching the show, sometimes spending the evening at a cinema. She already knew all the trades-people in Henry's street, the Avenue Carnot, and talked to them; he learned with surprise that they had their opinions on his painting and on the life he led. He was annoyed when Lou, who had gone out to buy bread, did not return until three-quarters of an hour later, buzzing with the details of the misfortunes of "that poor little dry-cleaning man"! His life was becoming filled with people. He had never known the art of making friends and had none. He was solitary by nature, as his father had been, before him; his father had been a mill-hand in one of the spinning mills of the north, a sober labourer who never set foot inside the taverns but came home and ate his supper without saying a word, leaning his elbow on the oilcloth-covered table, finding his only pleasure in the little back garden where he grew vegetables.

Like his father, Henry was a little troubled by a superabundance of energy, for he never went with prostitutes. Henry was a dedicated man, a man with a task to accomplish and a need, a real physical need, to accomplish it. And now, his work done, he was like the peasant who sees his wheat sprouting at last, his apple-trees laden with fruit, and like the peasant he dared not take that rest, that glance towards the horizon which prompts the uneasy murmur, "Next year, the harvest will be bad." He, too, needed that anxiety which the earth sagely dispenses, to enable him not to see the calm of the horizon. But his harvest had been garnered once and for all, and where, now, could he find that daily anxiety which conceals the fear of the future?

And the black mood, the "spell", was upon him again, that first day of September. The weather was still hot, and one evening at the theatre, he had gone out for a breath of air at the intermission, and was surprised, upon leaving the damp heat inside to find the same humidity outside. One would have had to rise very high above the narrow streets, along which the windows were gaping wide like dead fish, to find a bit of air that was breathable.

The now familiar bell pealed, signalling that the curtain was about to go up, and the crowd, athirst for nudity, rushed back again into the oven. He, too, went in, although he was beginning to experience the hollow feeling that heralded a black mood. But superstition drew him as far as his seat in the stalls, he still had faith in habit.

However, everything went off well. For once the girls were keeping time, and he was able to lose himself in the contemplation of abstract pattern. Admirable, that geometry of the legs rising simultaneously, some too heavy, some too sinewy, all of them tanned by grease-paint. Admirable the way the curves responded to the thin diagonals, admirable, too, those lines of flexed feet terminating, like a sudden chord of music, the long arch of legs and insteps; the backward curves of bodies finishing in those elongated ovals that were faces. He had amused himself hundreds of times with those lines, or had been upset by a broken line or flaw in the composition that was taking shape. Then it suddenly became worse: there was no composition, no harmonious whole, and the geometry was ruined by those elongated ovals which had suddenly become human faces, by those diagonals which had suddenly become legs. . . . As if by magic, the chorus girls seemed to be revealed, all at once, stripped of their true form (what he called their true form) and invested, to his profound indignation, with a mediocre and superfluous individuality which became insistent and dominated everything, thus "upsetting the whole works", as he said in his perhaps wilfully inadequate language.

Insistent, yes, like those bores who sometimes cornered him to tell all about the death of their mother, their army experiences, and how glad they were to meet him while he weighed up the pros and cons of outlawing himself from civilized society by strangling the insufferable person on the spot, there behind the couch in Professor Fuch's *salon*. One after another the girls, beginning with the ugliest ones, obtruded themselves upon his consciousness as personalities.

He had but to see a mole on a leg or a forgotten string of beads around a neck: suddenly the lines and curves had taken on humanity. How stupid of him to sit in the front row! But how could he have guessed that even this habit would betray him? Yes, that necklace, that mole were enough. They insinuated themselves into his imagination, those girls with their thin or flabby limbs, their lodging-house life, their ready-cooked food bought at the pork-butcher's—"No garlic in the salami today, I'm meeting my boy-friend"—their permanent waves, their badly bleached and dried-out hair, their fake jewellery, their clothes, their muddy high heels, their carefully made-up faces, doubtful underwear, and cheap scent, that "*fleurs du muguet*". Two or three of them were rather pretty—the Sultaness, the Bird of Paradise, Eve in the first Tableau Vivant. But then he thought of them with their little motor cars, their shop-keeper "protectors" who were only too glad to take out an actress on the cheap—the days of wild extravagance were no more. Two or three of the girls were married, had children, virtuous women who saw nothing wrong in nakedness. The husbands, perhaps a cashier in a bank or an assistant stage manager or an employee in a big store, came to fetch them—and Henry thought of them stopping at the chemist's on their way home to buy the child's cough medi-cine, and of how those husbands, when they made love to their wives could not help thinking, all the same, about all the men who had gazed with desire at those untouchable bodies, and of how they would resolutely announce, "I can't wait to get you out of that cheap music-hall!" One of the girls, Lou had told him, was a Swede, very Left Wing, and a medical student who believed in women's rights. She lived in a small top-floor bedroom, impeccably clean, with a reproduction of an abstract painting on the wall, and it was there, that she liked to be made love to.

Yes, there they were, all those girls, asserting themselves as people. Nothing could be done about it. And what a sickening idea that all those naked bodies were thinking organisms, had brains, individual-ities, pretensions. "I want to be loved." "It's five thousand francs."

"Oh, until something better turns up, I'm willing to take a bit-part, it's better than nothing." And a mole on the right calf. Babies, abortions, unhappy childhoods. An old mother. The number of old mothers there were in the world! The lowest pickpocket in the metro or at the races had one. Or a "cultural circle", like Sylvia. Tacking up on the wall above her cheap bed a clipping from a woman's magazine: "How to Cultivate Your Personality". And if a man beat them, did they love the man or the blows or both at the same time? To the most self-seeking girl there came a day when she refused to accept money. The ugliest girl is apt to fall in love. And the stupidest girl, too, who knows she is stupid. Infallibly, inevitably, there came that day of pity, of inane emotion, when you raised your eyes towards the sky. . . . Oh, the purity of curves and angles! The certainty of matter, of weight and flesh, of heavy feet set on the ground, of superbly ponderous hips, of human beings as impervious as earthen vessels. . . .

He would have to begin all over again, would have to go on struggling. He took out his sketch-book. It was all right. For once in a way they were keeping time, toes pointed, slightly bent, curves, ovals, not faces any more. . . . And then the music stopped, they bowed and went off, backs bent, thin arms hanging limply. Twelve faces, twelve different bodies. His sketch was a failure!

There remained one final test: Louise. He would go back-stage for her, as he did almost every night, though she might find him a little more taciturn tonight, and he would take her home in the beautiful limousine with its green leather upholstery which must have cost a great deal, as she had admiringly said. He would take her home, as he did every night, under the now resigned eye of the chauffeur—though he hadn't a charwoman, he had a chauffeur, for he had never learned to drive. Tonight, he thought, the chauffeur would also, no doubt, have a face. He would take her home with him, and there . . .

All this was accomplished without incident. He had managed to avoid several hazards: the face of the chauffeur ("Good evening, Jean," without looking at him, thinking vaguely of dismissing him; "The boss must be in a touchy mood tonight"), had avoided

a too protracted silence that might have alarmed Louise and made
her say "What's wrong with you?", had put the key in the lock,
managing to find it at once, and as he lit the lamp in the studio he
had managed to throw out a very convincing "Naturally, you've
still not taken down those bottles!" It was as good a way as any to
keep her from asking questions.

"Oh, they can wait until tomorrow. . . ."

She undressed. Her dressing-gown now hung in the cupboard,
already she was at home here, placidly settled in. Was it true? Or
would she, too, let him down? He would try everything to test her,
put her to every kind of torture to free himself of all doubt. And if
torture were not enough . . . the gramophone record was there,
covered with dust, hidden under a magazine: that record, that magic
thing, that talisman. "What a fetishist I am, after all." And she,
stretching her arms, was standing there, her heavy breasts and wide
hips not those of Venus but of Ceres, the Mother-Goddess, the
Earth-Goddess, who reigned over the somnolent wheat-fields. . . .
"Strange," he thought for no reason, "strange that she's never had
children." He had turned on the gramophone; gently lifted the arm
with its tiny sapphire needle, and set it in the first grooves of the
thing made of vulcanite, no, they didn't make them of vulcanite
nowadays, it must be some kind of plastic, set the needle in the first
groove of the magic thing. And he waited, like a savage waiting
for the Oracle to speak.

"I like that music," she said. "It's pretty. It's a little sad."

Goddess! There was the music, as solid and sedate as a piece of
furniture. And his melancholy was there, just as motionless. He
could walk round them, touch them, handle them. So, music and
sadness were just that—mere things?

Without a doubt, had he been that savage, he would have knelt
down at her feet.

"Fine, fine," he said aloud.

"What's fine?" she asked, startled.

"All this," he hazarded, "you, the studio. . . ."

"Nothing very new about us," she smiled. "Aren't you sleepy?"

"I need a drink. I feel a hell of a lot better than I did. Where's that bottle? You didn't . . .?"

"It's with the other bottles."

She had gone to bed, and after some fumbling had managed to reach down and pick up a newspaper lying on the floor beneath it.

"You might at least separate the empty bottles from the full ones. I have to hold them up to the light!"

"Lack of instinct. . . ."

He filled a glass, happily watching the flow of the dark red wine. He had made his decision. He would continue to wait for Louise in the badly lit passageway back-stage, along with those young fellows in their Sunday best, almost choking in their tight collars, and bright cheap ties, who always laughed too loudly. Those young fellows were life. They were the same fellows you saw on bicycles at dawn, in their loud-coloured sweaters, gaily flashing through the grey mornings like the cries of birds. The same fellows, a little older, took their wives out for a good dinner in a tavern, bragging that they knew "how to live". You saw those same young fellows at the music-hall in the company of a slightly tipsy Grandpa and a sickly little son they'd brought along, because he'd enjoy the scenic effects and he'd "see nothing bad in it, bless him!" And in the interval the child would ask for caramels and wait patiently though a little mournfully, for the time when he too would be ready for the grosser pleasures of the grown-ups; the simple enjoyment of the show, of the crowd, of the feeling that one was part of it all. Henry had lost that joy for a time, but now he was going to recover it.

He was in no hurry to tell Louise, but was anticipating with pleasure her surprise, the clamour an astonished woman made. She might perhaps want to stop working. That was natural. In that case they would go to his farm in the Midi, where she would at once get to know all the neighbours, who now kept away from him, perhaps frightened at what the villagers said about the luxury of his bathroom. Or they might even stay on here in Paris, and he would go on grousing about the bottles and her long scraps of gossip.

"What are you reading?"

"About the Pacy-sur-Eure crime. They've arrested the postman."

"Was he the one?"

He kept putting off the pleasure of asking her, perhaps a little out of fear that once again the remedy would turn out to be inadequate, fit only to stave off his hunger for a few minutes.

"No, I don't think so," she said with conviction. "If postmen took it into their heads to kill people, there'd be no peace for anyone."

She did not raise her head; she was frowning with concentration, and over her forehead fell the long black lock of hair.

"Lou?"

"What?" she asked sleepily. "Aren't you coming to bed?"

Sleepiness gave her eyes a softer expression. He looked into her face, contemplating the lines of sadness, the peaceful, serene mouth.

"Do you like it here, too?"

"Like what?"

"All this. Us." Then, hastily correcting himself, for he felt that what he had said was too sentimental, "I mean, the way we live...."

"Why of course, Henry, it's very nice," she said serenely, "except for the bottles...."

They laughed. But Henry still felt embarrassed.

"Even the bottles, I think I can get used to them. Well, then, you'll stay?"

She frowned again, not understanding:

"What do you mean by that, 'you'll stay'?"

Her expression had hardened again, as if she had been expecting this moment when she would have to take up arms once more, as if she had always known that their summer was only a respite, a temporary shelter. She assumed once more the expression she had held in those first days, a beautiful mask, full of courage and maturity.

"You don't understand," he hastened to say. "What I'd like is——" He paused. He had never felt so foolish in all his life. "I'd like you to stay on here with me ... always."

"Here?" she asked, as if the place had some importance.

"Here or somewhere else. You could go on working at the music-hall if you liked, but we could also go down to my property in the Midi."

He never used the word "property", but today he had the feeling
that it sounded rich, and would impress her with its seriousness. He
himself had been impressed when the building contractors had told
him, "Those outlying farm-buildings are indispensable to your
property." Result: the "property" was much too big for him, far
too luxurious, and had cost him an insane amount of money.

She leaned on her elbow, half sitting up in bed, and thought.

"In short, what you're saying is . . ."

"An offer of marriage," he said, with a forced laugh. What an
idiotic situation! And all this on account of that gramophone
record. She would of course imagine God only knew what sentimental inanity. Even so, he admired her for her calm; she must be
weighing everything up. Perhaps she would actually want him to
marry her, would want to get a divorce, all the complications.
"A left-handed offer," he added. "You would be 'the painter's
companion,' as they say in the obituaries. What do you say to
that?"

"But you see, I'm married. . . ."

Yes, she was admirable, meeting so calmly such an unhoped-for
offer. She must want him to marry her! Even if only for what she
would inherit. Surely she was afraid he would change his mind?
But you couldn't ask a reasonable woman to exchange even an
unsatisfactory husband for a man who refused to marry her.

"Very well," he said resignedly. "Let's say, then, that I'm making
you an outright offer of marriage."

Had she thought he was joking, up till then? She gave him an
astonished look.

"You want to marry me?"

"I've been telling you so for an hour! I'm ready to marry you,
there now! At the town hall, in a church, in a mosque, anywhere
you like. Is that clear?"

He had been undressing as he spoke, and now he slid between the
sheets, pushing her towards the wall.

"You might at least show a little affection," he said, jokingly.
"Isn't that the proper thing to do?"

"You see," she said, "I must think it over."

He admired her. Decidedly, he admired her. She was surely going to hold out for . . . well, perhaps a month. But why? Even the Mozart record took second place, disappeared from his mind. Was it a touch of jealousy? He fell asleep, agreeably preoccupied with the thought.

Stéphane at last had returned and was with them again! How happy he was to see them! How he had missed them, this little circle of his who sustained him and buoyed him up. Detesting solitude and silence he now felt wonderfully reassured, fearing unknown faces and unknown questions he now felt mercifully protected. At last he was home, in this phoney Chinese restaurant ("Greek Cuisine"), in this big adopted family ("We Celestials"), who greeted him with an affection that seemed sincere enough.

"So here you are last, Morani!" Ducas said in his mannered voice.

"Can I offer you a drink, Monsieur Morani?" said Socrates.

And Jean Cadou deigned to pronounce distinctly a "Hullo, there!"

Sylvia was ecstatic, beneath the disapproving eye of Madame Prêtre. "Oh, how beautifully tanned you are, Monsieur Stéphane!"

"I'll have a spot of rum, Socrates. Yes, we had a very pleasant holiday," said Dr. Fisher. "We even had a few visitors, eh, Morani?"

Beneath the slanting eyes of the mandarins, Stéphane was surrounded, congratulated, as though he had just given a performance. Even Germaine Lethuit had made a point of taking a later train to Meudon for his sake.

"Dear friends! How good of you to welcome me like this. Really . . ."

He had to sit down. He felt less rested than usual from his holiday. More than once, recently, he had felt this heaviness in the legs, as if they were leaden, this sudden, imperious, embarrassing need for sleep. He tried to pull himself together. Somehow he must respond to this touching eagerness of his friends.

"Socrates, I believe I'll have a cup of coffee. . . . Now, what about you, my dear Ducas, did you have a pleasant vacation? I imagine our young friend has brought back some splendid canvases. How sorry I am, Germaine, that you had so much rain! Is your sister as pretty as ever? And your father. . . . Well, well, Madame Prêtre. You've been hiding! I haven't yet seen you to say how do you do!"

With a stupendous effort, he got to his feet, for he did not want the concierge to think that he attached less importance to her than to the others.

"Come into the light, Madame Prêtre! Tell us about Arcachon?"

"We didn't go away this year," said Madame Prêtre, a little against her will. Her eyes avoided Stéphane's, but he did not notice it.

"Didn't go away! Why, what a shame!"

"Sylvia's future might have been at stake," Madame Prêtre murmured. "She attracted the attention of a film producer. . . ."

Stéphane turned enthusiastically towards Sylvia. "What's this? Our little Sylvia is going to be a film star? That's what I call wonderful news!"

"Oh, I only had a test," said Sylvia. She was rather embarrassed at her mother's cold manner, although Stéphane had not noticed it. But Martine's entrance now distracted his attention.

"Martine! My dear!"

His feeling of fatigue was increasing; she would think he took no pleasure in seeing her again. He felt almost guilty about this tiredness that paralysed his mind, overcoming him with torpor, and causing a subdued roaring in his ears.

Martine smiled, apparently relaxed. "You look wonderful, Stéphane! And you, too, Dr. Fisher. I'll bet you went on some nice little excursions together, didn't you?"

Stéphane was infinitely relieved. He had been afraid he would find her changed, overwhelmed once more by that black mood which he had seemed to feel reviving in her letters. But there she was, smiling, even rather gaily, with a kind of femininity (as if she had been wearing a new frock) that he had not seen in her before. Besides, he was too fatigued to analyse Martine's state of mind.

And it seemed to him that all these friends of his were talking very loudly.

"I'm very sorry," said Germaine Lethuit, "that the young man did not want to join us." She was referring to her tenant. "Fundamentally, those Nordics . . ."

Socrates brought the coffee.

"I wanted to go to Deauville," he said in his heavily smug way, "but I said to myself . . ."

Dr. Fisher nodded gravely. "Curious," he reflected, "how one becomes immune to alcohol. In the long run, one has no reaction of any kind. I must find something else."

"With a painter as abstract as Jean, it's odd to note the influence an environment has on his work," Gérard Ducas was saying smoothly. "In the country, I noticed the effect of nature on his paintings. They're much more airy, much more . . ."

It was incredible to feel as sleepy as this. Stéphane could barely hear what was being said around him, despite the coffee which he had drunk mechanically. The mandarins seemed to file past him, and the young girl with the nenuphars on the calendar seemed to smile. Above the bar, the god whose name nobody knew, glimmered in the shadow, serene and futile. Around Stéphane, words continued to interweave, forming a disagreeable kind of music. "An orchestra of coffee-grinders," he thought absurdly. Absurd also this sensation of seeing mouths opening and shutting without hearing what was actually being said. He would have liked to ask their permission to go upstairs, but the very thought of opening his lips and of composing the words, which he imagined infinitely long and containing an endless number of syllables, was too much of an effort. Better just to stay there, at the risk of falling asleep on the banquette, beneath the gaze of the young girl with the nenuphars.

They were all glad to see him again. Germaine Lethuit had composed another poem; surely, a special meeting must be called to have it read. This poem was about alcoholism in France, a burning question.

Ducas was sure Stéphane would like the latest canvases painted by Jean, that he would also understand his own confidential remarks on his two months' vacation spent with Jean's family, among the apple orchards; how nostalgic it had made him, and how handsome Jean had been in shirtsleeves. . . .

Sylvia thought the cinema director was rather flighty and inconsiderate. It was hard to pose in a bathing suit, for shots that might never be used, and act in short film tests with a great many pretty girls, who, said Sylvia, had almost nothing to say that was worth listening to. Yes, it was hard to take the Seventh Art very seriously. She was sure that Stéphane would give her a reason to feel less clumsy, less useless, than the servants of that art had made her feel in the midst of all that discouraging pushing and shoving.

Martine sat beside Stéphane, but did not look at him. She was re-experiencing that moment when Madame Prêtre had handed back the blue exercise book, with a surprised and almost hostile look. With one of her sudden flashes of insight, Martine had penetrated to the depths of that gross soul: *What, this plain girl inspired such pages, while Sylvia* . . . Delicious moment of triumph! Delicious hostility, and delectable the words spoken by Madame Prêtre: "Oh, but if you believed everything a man writes . . ." Martine had realized then that enthusiastic affirmation would not have given her as much satisfaction as had Madame Prêtre's reticence. She did not need to look at Stéphane.

Clearly, rum was no longer enough. Yet Dr. Fisher was tired and in that state of mind when very little is enough to make a man drunk. It had been a very good summer: he had passed it in a state of intoxication which had made him, usually so silent, talk as they were all talking here today. Yes, he had talked a lot, and always to Stéphane who, as he had discovered for the first time this year, since they were almost always alone together, was a good companion, listening, agreeing, letting him drink—as good a companion as if he had approved without listening or hearing at all. Those holidays must have used up the power of rum, however; he must soon find something else.

In Stéphane's ears words kept on rumbling, but he still could not grasp what was being said. It was almost funny to see their lips move without hearing anything but this rumbling, this confused sound that filled the bar. It was calming, now that the noise had become just one loud roar and he was no longer able to distinguish a solitary word. His eyelids drooped, would have closed, had he not suddenly been disturbed—yes, it was certainly a sensation of disturbance he felt at the sight of her—by the entrance of Louise, disturbed by that curt voice which cut through the soothing and muffled uproar, and penetrated the dense and compact tumult, and which he could not but understand despite all the fatigue in the world.

"For God's sake, can't you see that my husband is going to faint?"

Why couldn't one believe absolutely, as the Faithful believe in God? That moment had come for Martine. As a thin column of incense rises, while a pinch of dust is consumed, she had believed, for a moment she had been consumed with pure joy.

She was now sitting on the red leather banquette of the Brasserie Dorée, listening to the sentimental songs, as indifferent to the purple nudes and the lunatic harlequins on the walls as they were to her. Toni was circulating through the crowd very adroitly with her tray. A sallow-faced man ordered a Pernod.

She had come yesterday, as she had come today. Toni would bring her a pint, Bruno would bow to her with respectful familiarity. . . Even Marcel recognized her now. And Stéphane would have the boyish smile he had on his good days, and would propose that they do something "absolutely mad", go to the cinema perhaps, or have a cocktail at another café.

As the thin column of incense rose, as the pinch of dust was consumed . . . there she was, sitting on this banquette in her own right. As it was her right, she would put her hand on Stéphane's sleeve and press his arm, would remind him to take his medicine, would ask some intimate question to which he would quite naturally reply. Did she not feel that they should stop at this point, go no farther?

"Here's your pint," said Toni. "Shall I mark it up?"

Put it on Stéphane's bill. That seemed natural to them. Did she not feel that she should stop here? She had her niche at the Brasserie, her niche in Stéphane's journal. She was in Stéphane's confidence,

she was in Madame Prêtre's bad books. Why did she always want
something more?

Bruno sawed away pathetically on his violin. Marcel, looking
disgusted, drummed on the case of his 'cello. Stéphane was playing
the piano lazily, but without displeasure. He had easily slipped back
into the friendly atmosphere of the Brasserie; Bruno's innocent
prankishness, Marcel's smiling indifference filled him with a careless
and unrestrained gaiety and a kind of relief that he did not find at
the Café Céleste.

"Suppose we play The Gondolier?" Bruno implored.

That piece gave him three opportunities to sing. Marcel gladly
put down his 'cello. He considered himself a first-class guitarist and
was always running down "fellows in café orchestras who try to
play more than one instrument."

"Right you are, we'll take The Gondolier," Stéphane sighed.
"And from that, what about going on to The Last Mambo?"

Bruno made a wry face. He only liked sentimental songs.

"Ready? Let's go. . . ."

Martine listened to both songs while thinking about what she was
going to do. She had already thought out what she was going to ask
him, what she still wanted to get out of him. Yes, she was in his
confidence, she had her place in his life, but there was something
else, she wanted the final crowning triumph. What she wanted
was . . .

Bruno had sung the three refrains of The Gondolier which were
his by right. He now approached the piano and shook the maracas
while Marcel went up to the microphone and played a surprisingly
expert number on the guitar; he really had enough talent to be a
star attraction, and moreover, he played in a Left Bank night club.
But these afternoons at the Brasserie gave him a fixed salary and he
preferred not to drop the job until after the birth of his child, whom
he was confident would be a son. He had decided to call him
Django, in honour of Django Reinhardt, if the authorities would
let him.

"Have you seen her?" muttered Bruno to Stéphane, shaking the
maracas. "She's here."

"Who? Madame La Crémière?"

"Why, no! I mean your girl-friend. With a new frock, I'd say. Yellow. And I mean, yellow!"

"Poor girl!" said Stéphane, smiling.

He was in a good mood. The orchestra was going to make some extra money that very night playing at a dance—not a fortune, they were simply to be standbys for a jazz orchestra and fill in when the jazz instrumentalists took a rest—but it would bring him in a small sum. There was no need to mention it to Louise, who must have put aside some money herself, since she was having the kitchen repainted.

"Yellow, a real yellow. She might have done better than that."

Stéphane had a pang of remorse and raised himself up from the chair (he used a chair instead of a stool, by special favour of the management).

"Not too bad," he said without conviction.

"When you're in love," retorted Bruno.

Ever since Marcel, who was not yet thirty, had begun to make recordings, Bruno had become sarcastic and bitter, and his bitterness was not at all assuaged by Marcel's advice. "I tell you," Marcel was always saying, "your talent's for comedy!" To which Bruno always replied, "Maybe that's my talent, but it's not my ideal."

Stéphane shot another glance in Martine's direction, and she smiled at him.

"Clothes don't make the woman," he said, with a feeling of compunction.

"No, but it's the woman who selects the clothes," said Bruno. "But since you like her as she is . . ."

Evidently Stéphane would have to explain yet once more that Martine and he were only good friends, that . . . But he hadn't the strength. Anyway, what did it matter? "As if anyone couldn't see," he told himself, as he sat down beside her half an hour later. And it was true, yellow was not becoming to her.

"Well, my dear little Martine! How good it is to see you here. Thank God, we're falling back into our old habits. And my work is all the more bearable for it."

"I'm glad, too, Stéphane. Are you quite all right after that faint-ing attack you had the other day?"

"Yes, quite," he said hurriedly. "It was nothing. Just the fatigue of the journey. Let's talk about something else. Let's talk about you, for instance. Have you put these few weeks of respite to some account? Did you visit any of the museums? Have you read a good book? Sometimes I envied you your solitude, a rich solitude, I'm sure. Dr. Fisher is as good a soul as one could find in the world, but he's tiring. He goes on and on telling about his experiences in the war. I'll confess I only listened to a quarter of them, but he was absolutely determined to tell me everything. Wasn't it odd, though? He's usually so disinclined to talk."

"No doubt he drank a lot."

"Well, we must admit that our excellent Doctor has a slight weakness in that direction. I was telling Louise . . ." He stumbled on the name, paused a second, watching for her reaction, but she did not blink. "I was telling Louise yesterday that if he'd been a surgeon, his hand trembles so much now that . . ."

"And did you find your wife well?" she asked maliciously.

"Oh yes, Louise is always well. You know, Martine, that may explain her—well, her hardness of heart. She can't understand other people's sufferings. I've often had the rather consoling thought that ill health, perhaps, develops in us a keener sensibility, a kind of second sight."

"Well your wife certainly doesn't sin by an excess of sensibility," said Martine. She was not even tempted to tell him what she knew about Louise. For the moment she was satisfied with Madame Prêtre's hostile look, and with what she intended to get out of Stéphane.

"Unfortunately we're all incomplete in one way or another," he said. "I'm only too well aware of my own shortcomings on the practical side, and that is what counts with Louise."

He had come home to Louise without too much displeasure, contrary to what he had feared. She seemed calmer than usual, almost absent-minded, and she had given him his drops and taken care of him after his fainting spell, and had done this with more grace and kindness than he had known before. True, there were all those plans of hers to repaint the kitchen, to make new curtains for her bedroom, but after all. . . . It rather amused him to realize that she had been hiding a part of her earnings from him, as he hid a part of his from her.

"But let's talk about you, Martine. Were you able to go back to work without disliking it too much? I know how hard it is to mix with the crowd again."

Dislike it? No, she couldn't say she had felt reluctant to return to her job. She had been thinking of nothing but this plan of hers for the past fortnight, ever since Madame Prêtre had given her that hostile look. She had kept the plan to herself all this time, caressing it, shaping it like a ball of clay, playing with it, modelling it in its diverse forms, enjoying the knowledge that from this modelling clay, malleable and yielding to her all-powerful imagination, would be born that achievement, that crowning triumph, which had begun with Madame Prêtre's surprise. And she waited one more minute to reveal it, to persuade Stéphane, waited for the sole joy of feeling within her that seed from which would spring the dreamed-of apotheosis.

"Stéphane," she said at last, "I must confess something to you."

"How serious you are, dear Martine!" he said, smiling indulgently. "A confession! What folly have you committed besides buying this new dress which is so becoming?"

"I wouldn't like to have you misinterpret my motives, Stéphane."

"Martine! Why, I know you so well; how could I imagine anything but purity and goodness coming from you? You're blushing! Why, what can this folly be? Is it of a . . . sentimental nature?"

"Oh, Stéphane!" At any other time she would have been offended. But her present desire blinded her, and anyway this was not the moment to be annoyed at trifles. "You remember that you entrusted something to me, before you went away—something you held very precious. . . ."

"My journal!" he exclaimed. "And you've lost it!"

"No, no, don't worry. Lost isn't the word."

"No?" He was seriously disturbed, she could see it by the way he was nervously twisting a button on the white jacket he was still wearing. "Why, what do you mean? You can't have forgotten it somewhere? And which notebook?"

"I didn't leave it anywhere, don't worry. I'm not in the habit of losing things. It's only—you're going to hate me for this—it's only that someone begged me to, and I was perhaps indiscreet. I lent the notebook."

"To someone who's lost it!"

"No, no, no, Stéphane. Your notebook—this concerns the last one—is in my room with the others, and I can return them all to you whenever you like. I was simply afraid . . ."

He was visibly relieved.

"Yes, quite. Quite frankly, Martine, I would have preferred my journal to remain between us two. But since you thought it best to . . . well, would you tell me to whom you lent it?"

"This will give you a shock. I lent it to Madame Prêtre."

"To the concierge! Oh, really, Martine!"

"Stéphane, you can't imagine the good it did her to read it. She was desperate. Sylvia had just broken off her affair with that painter. . . ."

"The poor child!" he said, his thoughts already distracted from the notebook. "Naturally, he was the one who dropped her?"

"Naturally," she said, smiling in spite of herself. "And of course one can hardly blame him. Apart from her aesthetic charms, poor Sylvia . . ."

"I admit she's really stupid. What a blow it must have been for poor Madame Prêtre. But I don't see in what way my journal——"

The moment had come to convince him.

"Stéphane, you can't imagine the effect an example such as yours can have on a poor woman who, we must admit, has never in all her life known anything but material cares."

"Yes, but really, Martine. . . ."

"It was a real revelation for her, and also, I dare say, a kind of consolation. Yes, Stéphane, you can't realize the splendour, the radiance of a personality such as yours, of thoughts . . ."

With what diabolical cleverness she had seized his own weapons!

With a cleverness of which she was unconscious, she had identified herself with him, had employed his words, his phrases, even to the intonation which was characteristic of him; and he did not take fright in front of that mirror, but smiled complacently at the reflected image which he found pleasing without realizing it was his own, as one appreciates on someone else the coat one has chosen for oneself, provided one has a generous nature, and Stéphane did have a generous nature.

"What you say is very touching, my dear. I can scarcely believe . . . You see how we are, how I am. Presumptuous. For a moment I felt disturbed at the idea—I feel ashamed to say it—that my concierge had read my journal. My concierge. As if we shouldn't think first of all about just such people."

The mirrors, the chromium, sparkled; the soft music poured out in floods. The members of the Hawaiian orchestra shook the dust from their *pareos*. Not far from them, a man in a skimpy jacket was listening enraptured. His tired face, his hands with broken fingernails, no longer existed for him, nothing counted but the enchantment of alcohol and bad music.

"I've thought what a good example your life could be Stéphane, if it were known to our friends. I mean, if each of them could have this communication with you."

"You want me to lend the journal to all our friends? Why, that's insane, it's . . ."

She did not become impatient or annoyed. The memory of Madame Prêtre's astonishment sustained her, filled her mind, as did that more than half convinced "How is it possible?" which she had read in the concierge's eyes. That moment had been wonderful; in an instant she had been showered with blessings. Had she been pretty, she would never have known such triumphant pleasure. And she was grateful to Stéphane for having obtained this for her. His phrases—in which she no longer believed, or at least which were no longer alive for her but were dead, dull and cold, had suddenly, under that look in Madame Prêtre's eyes, recovered their power and magic. It was no longer Stéphane alone who could for so many obscure reasons, delude her, but now Madame Prêtre also saw her in a flattering and different light. She went back again and again to that moment when, with an expression that one could only call vexed or even envious, Madame Prêtre had looked from the journal to Martine and back again, as if comparing them, gauging them, and finally—with what displeasure!—being obliged to identify the actual Martine with the girl described in the journal. They were one and the same! She was that "little Antigone" Stéphane wrote about, that "wonderful friend", whose features one could only imagine as serene and beautiful. . . .

It was then the new desire had been born, so complacently fondled since, so repeatedly dwelt upon in moments of weariness: her desire to be seen in that same light by all "the Celestials".

The dream was innocent enough, it was the dream of a little girl, a dream right out of a fairy-story, the Ugly Duckling at last recognized as a swan, Cinderella no longer filthy with ashes. It was the dream of an unhappy child, of the Little Match Girl, starving, and seeing roast goose stuffed with apples, it was the tale of diamonds falling from the lips of the pauper-woman, thanks to a good fairy. . . . One might say that it was an inoffensive dream. But Martine's ardour, the immoderate hunger inhabiting that puny body of hers, a hunger which she promised herself to satisfy one day, that pride of hers which spread itself the moment the least space was provided and which always demanded more and more space, these were perhaps, not so inoffensive. And that stubborn will, driving straight ahead, allowing no loop-holes of escape, no by-passes; which took every method, from the gentlest to the cruellest, to accomplish its end, was that inoffensive?

"Do please realize that I'm not suggesting this if it would be unpleasant to you, although from the literary point of view your journal deserves to be read."

"I never intended anyone to read it," said the poor man, taking every turn of the road she was leading him along, falling into every trap she set, with an innocence that should have aroused her pity. "I swear to you, Martine, when I wrote the journal I was far from having any literary aspirations whatsoever."

"I'm sure of it, Stéphane. And that's why I don't advise you to present it as a work of art. What I do advise is that you present it as a case history, a human document. As such, I'm sure it would have enormous value to our friends."

An inoffensive dream, the dream of a plain and humiliated and neglected little girl, of the lucid child who sat in judgement on her father and mother, condemning the one as a cheap swindler, the other as lazy, useless, complaining, a mother who had not even handed down her beauty to her daughter. But this vestment of high-minded words which she put on so easily, with a kind of malicious pleasure, was surely not inoffensive. Nor was the keen attention with which she surveyed Stéphane's confusion and his childlike pleasure.

"Yes, I see, as a human document. . . . If you put it like that. By choosing certain passages. . . . But where my wife's concerned I wouldn't want it to look . . ."

"Naturally. The last one or two notebooks would serve the purpose, perhaps. There is nothing in them that might embarrass your wife. Oh, Stéphane, that passage on solitude is so beautiful!"

Her soft and admiring voice, the very voice needed to persuade Stéphane, was it inoffensive?

"Do you really think it would interest our friends?"

"Tremendously, Stéphane! I don't believe you realize how much influence you have."

Stéphane weakened. For his part he would have been quite happy to go on humming to himself the little cradle song with which he had tried in vain to lull his suffering. But since she wanted it to be heard by others . . .

"Perhaps you're right; perhaps I am in a way duty bound. . . ."

The idea began to please him, and in a few phrases, timidly at first, he began to develop the theme. She had won. She would have her triumph, she would see astonishment in all their eyes, and perhaps envy. She would see others do as Madame Prêtre had done, waver between her and the notebook, and back again, and then that identification of the two Martines, that surprise, that apotheosis.

The mirrors and the chromium sparkled. A swarthy young woman with an Italian accent had come forward on the platform and was singing "I'm a girl of Hawaii", undulating her hips, wrapped in a kind of *pareo*. The man in the skimpy jacket looked at her in ecstasy and with great dignity signalled to the waiter: "Same again, please." Martine gave herself up to a feeling of well-being. Tonight, while waiting for her fulfillment, she, too, could enjoy the delights of the Brasserie Dorée. She, too, could give an order with a commanding wave of the hand, could delight in the multicoloured *pareo*, the bland voice, the mirrors and the lights; she could even momentarily forget the pleasure of having Stéphane at her side, Stéphane relaxed, confident, talkative, and she need not even listen to what he said. Tomorrow she would be happy. Tomorrow, tomorrow.

Something in Madame Prêtre's enormous and malodorous person had changed. She moved about more slowly, as though her mass of dark clothing weighed more heavily upon her; the arrogance of her big diplomatic nose was less apparent, the shrewdness of her colourless eyes was veiled, and she did not raise her head when a stranger climbed the stairs—a grave symptom. Even the hand that wielded the broom (sweeping, this way and that and into corners, a ten-year accumulation of dust) seemed to be altered: usually haughty and careless if not disdainful and wrathful, that hand now seemed flabby and resigned. Pensively, she swept pieces of straw and bits of paper into one single little pile which she then surveyed with a sigh.

"What now, Madame Prêtre? Not feeling well?"

It was Ducas, for ever courteous, who had just started up the stairs. Slowly, as if she were carrying an immense load, Madame Prêtre raised her head, mournful with curl-papers, those badges of rank about which she no longer cared.

"None too well, Monsieur Ducas, I thank you."

"I hope nothing's happened to our little Sylvia?"

"No more than usual, Monsieur Ducas. You've heard the latest?"

Ducas looked embarrassed. Socrates had not spared him the least detail, not even the name of the woman who had replaced Sylvia in the famous painter's affections.

"Unfortunately, yes," he murmured. "But if Sylvia could break into films," he suggested.

Alas! The film tests had led to nothing. Had they been merely a pretext for that young fellow (surely a young man without any income) to take Sylvia out?

"I don't like Sylvia going about with that crowd, not at all. But the last word's not been said. That woman won't keep him for long, you can be sure!"

"Of course not, Madame," said the antiquary, going up a few steps.

But Madame Prêtre followed him to the bottom of the stairs, broom in hand. "Do you know if *he* knows what's going on, Monsieur Ducas?"

The antiquary came down a step to whisper: "Our poor friend Morani? No, I don't think so. He seemed very serene, very calm, when I saw him. They say she never slept at home one single night while the poor man was away for the summer?"

"Not one single night! And now she's having her kitchen re-painted. And she's wearing a new coat, very smart. It's enough to make you wonder if he has eyes in his head!"

The last words were said in a such a snarling tone, so viciously, that Gérard Ducas was surprised. "The poor man's really not responsible," he ventured, gently.

"We'll see about that!" was Madame Prêtre's surprising reply, and she went back inside the lodge.

Gérard Ducas climbed the stairs to his flat, greatly surprised. Although Madame Prêtre was naturally talkative, extremely curious, no doubt a scandal-monger or even sometimes a back-biter, she was not by nature ill-tempered. She couldn't bear the idea of people being secretive with her, but she seemed to be satisfied with merely knowing their secrets. What, then, had caused this sudden change in her attitude to Stéphane Morani? Peace-loving by nature, Gérard Ducas did not like to feel surrounded by aggressive people. "Her stomach must be upset," he reflected, as he entered Jean's room, "yes, poor woman, it must be her stomach." He himself suffered from indigestion at times.

But it was not indigestion. After having continued in the same stricken way to sweep the pile of dust and straw into the gutter, Madame Prêtre had finally gone into her lodge and there, letting herself fall upon the pink bed, but avoiding looking in the mirror, she heaved another sigh, a long sigh. Where was Sylvia?

Most likely with that assistant-to-God-knew-what. That contact would give Sylvia nothing but a vocabulary. But what more than that had she got out of Henry Stass? About two hundred and forty-three thousand francs which were devaluing in the bank. Quite different from what she had hoped. Oh, how good it would be to forget all this and not to keep on saying, "If only she'd been a little cleverer!" Sylvia was *not* clever, and that was a fact. A fact. But if Madame Prêtre had constantly kept that fact in mind, would she have had anything to hope for? Would she have gambled on her daughter's virginity? But suppose Sylvia could make someone fall in love with her. . . . Madame Prêtre sighed and sighed again. After all, more unlikely things happened. Take Martine Fortin, for instance. Who would have imagined that with a face and body like hers a handsome man like Stéphane Morani (for you had to admit, if he had been a little less thin—and even as he was, he was still a good-looking man), who would have imagined that a handsome man like that could fall in love with a girl as plain as Martine Fortin?

But the illustration proved nothing. For clearly Stéphane Morani was not in love with Martine Fortin. He said all that in his journal . . . but why? She could not understand it, and this set her against him. Why did he have to go and fill notebooks pretending he was in love with someone if he was not? True, he did not say she was his mistress. She was not, and this surprised Madame Prêtre who had always been convinced that Martine was Morani's mistress, that he slept with her because it was convenient since she was in the house, but Madame Prêtre had never supposed he was in love with the girl. And now, all her suppositions were upset. In any case, if such a thing was possible, if Martine Fortin was loved by a man, all the more reason to think that Sylvia, pretty as she was, could also be loved by someone. And so, Madame Prêtre had been right to gamble on her daughter's virginity.

Right—and logical. Sylvia could still win out. A man was in love with Martine Fortin. It was reasonable, then, to . . . But Madame Prêtre must not let herself go on thinking about it. All the same, it was preposterous! Not that Sylvia . . . No, but preposterous about Martine Fortin. Madame Prêtre would have sworn that Stéphane Morani still had a kind of sentimental feeling for his wife. Of course, it was in his own interest. . . . But in that journal there had been no question of interest. Which proved that everything in the journal was just a tissue of lies. Why would Monsieur Morani go on living with a wife who bored him—she gathered from the journal that she bored him and did not understand him—if not out of self-interest? It was clear as day. The journal was nothing but a great farce, and she had been wrong to take it seriously.

Wrong not to admit the facts. Sylvia was not . . . Beneath the layers of shawls, oh, the pain that fact caused, always the same, and always as oppressive! Sylvia was not like anyone else: she could only be loved by an idiot like that photographer, who earned sixty thousand francs a month by working himself to the bone, and would have given her a brood of children as stupid as he was. (Madame Prêtre thought: "stupid as he", then, "as she", and the pain revived, tenfold.) She had been wrong. Girls like Martine Fortin could not make men fall in love with them, men like Stéphane Morani could not be unselfish, and her child was born to be the wife of a local photographer!

Oh grief! As she had this terrible thought, she saw Sylvia's little face before her, adorable with its dark, astonished eyes, the rosy mouth, ravishing complexion, that slightly raised upper lip which made her look like a child of ten. "Is it true, Mamma? But I think he's so nice." Yes, she thought the sixty-thousand-francs-a-month-photographer was nice. She would have gladly lived in the back rooms of the photographer's studio, with its stink of chemicals, would have gladly heard the photographer assuring the mammas of the quarter, "Why no, Madame, the child didn't move, he's adorable, that baby." She, the fool, thought he was nice! Even as she herself had once thought an innocent little cabinet-maker nice! Madame Prêtre had suffered enough over the niceness of that young fellow, Jules Prêtre, who had had the grace to catch a cold and die of it a few months later. Should Sylvia have been allowed to have her photographer? Madame Prêtre had been unable to tolerate the idea. It would have meant admitting total defeat, admitting . . .

She would have liked to read that notebook again, and now reproached herself for having given it back to Martine too soon. Perhaps, after all . . . He said that he had not made Martine his mistress because of "scruples" or some such la-di-da. Could that be true? There were people like that; Madame Prêtre had never believed in them much, but perhaps she had been wrong. There must be people like that. And if Stéphane Morani was that kind of person, then you could say that Martine, although she wasn't his mistress, had at any rate made him fall in love with her. This idea was quite a new one for Madame Prêtre. And, in order to believe in Sylvia, she had to believe in a world in which a Martine could be loved by an unselfish Stéphane Morani. This seemed to present an insurmountable obstacle, one which her whole past experience forbade her to overcome. . . . Yet had she not surmounted it without hesitation when she had told herself, at the beginning of Sylvia's affair with Henry Stass, that after all Sylvia was "no stupider than the next one"?

Her head ached. She was not in the habit of dealing with such problems. That detestable journal—and to begin with, who ever heard of keeping a journal?—was at the bottom of it all. She was steeped in contradictions almost without noticing it. For a moment she detested Martine, Stéphane, the notebook, and "put them all in their place", that is to say, relegated them to their usual place. Then came the moment to think about Sylvia, in *her* place. No. Better admit, no matter how it hurt, everything that her reason refused to admit: every human creature—even Martine Fortin—could be loved.

She sighed heavily after this effort. Yes, even Martine. And Stéphane and Sylvia too. Each of them could be loved. If she could hang on to that idea, all her problems would disappear. Even Martine and Stéphane and Sylvia. Madame Prêtre was unaccustomed to such tolerance, but for her daughter's sake she was ready to deny her basic conception of life. And so, having thought things out, she rose from the bed, feeling less overwhelmed, went into the alcove where, between her bed and the telephone, was a very simple gas-ring, and reached out for a saucepan. One final thought lingered. "Even Martine and Stéphane and Sylvia." Since it had to be. "Even Martine and Stéphane and Sylvia." "Oh, and the photographer," added a small voice, maliciously, coming from Heaven knew where. . . .

Seized with sudden rage, Madame Prêtre hurled the saucepan to the floor. The cat fled, miauling.

"You've not forgotten my special bread?" Stéphane called out from his bedroom.

"No."

"Did you pick up the new prescription?"

"Yes."

She had remembered everything and she was now standing in the newly painted kitchen surveying the table, set for their evening meal. The yellow melons cut in two, the dark Parma ham. The brown flecked eggs were for their breakfast, but she had not been able to resist the temptation to pile them, pyramid fashion in the fruit bowl. There was the beefsteak for Stéphane. And the mushroom salad: she was especially fond of mushrooms, not merely their taste, which was always a little earthy, but she also liked to wash them, to hold in her hand those little round heads that had pierced the ground with a strange blind force. . . . And the wine, a bottle of very good wine, which she hoped might still be a little cool. In this flat, where each of them had a separate bedroom, but were obliged to eat in the kitchen, the kitchen was the only room where she felt comfortable. Stéphane's reproaches and insinuations had ruined the pleasure of having a home. But she still liked these moments of calm in the kitchen, while she was preparing and serving up their simple meals. She had forgotten nothing, that evening, as she surveyed the table. But she was thinking of something else.

She was somewhat surprised.

Were the dice loaded? Had she misunderstood the rules of this

Game of Goose, in which the piece is moved from square to square, advancing or retreating according to the throw of the dice? For her part, she believed she had always played fair, observing the rules to the best of her knowledge, going from square to square on the giant board of life, retreating when she had to, without complaint. From the factory to the Hôtel de la Paix, from the Hôtel de la Paix to marriage, from marriage to the war—the war had only been another square of the game, for her, a little more highly coloured perhaps, but no more important than the square called "prison"— and finally from the war to her job at the music-hall, to this invalid husband, to this life which was barely easier than the life she had lived in her youth.

She was a stout-hearted player, ready to be sent back to the starting point or near it, according to how the dice fell. What she disliked in Stéphane was exactly this: he was a poor loser. She was quite ready, now, at the next throw to pass into the square "old age", and she was not even greatly impressed by the square at the extreme end of the board, the "cemetery", with its picture of a hilarious death's head and a weeping-willow. It even amused her to think that in ten throws of the dice or in a hundred, and no matter what the course run, one always ended up there. But tonight, she was a little surprised.

The order of things, the events of her life, had left her not so much submissive as intact. At least, so she believed; she unconsciously endured the imperceptible wound inflicted by Stéphane throughout the years. She had cleared a path for herself through a hard and definite world, where she believed she knew the rules. And now everything was topsy-turvy, the bad cards won, and the game that had been lost could begin again. She looked in vain for the explanation.

Already, and more than once, she had scrupulously reviewed the time she had spent with Henry, in the present and in the past. She had accounted for them, evaluated them. She had not found the explanation. Henry was asking her to marry him: this was not in the rules. There was something abnormal about it, something miraculous, and even when miracles were in her favour, Lou did not like them. She remained motionless, standing there by the table, again searching her mind.

She had accepted without surprise the money offered her, and the pleasure. She had enjoyed their infrequent conversations on those warm summer days; she had been astonished at so much passion, at the gentle look in his eyes after their love-making, eyes that were tolerant of her thickened body, the body of a woman past forty, and at his generosity. However, without pride or humility, she judged herself physically superior to a great many young girls, and had therefore not been too surprised—just when she was gathering her forces together for a long solitary journey— at encountering an unexpected respite, a halt on the road which risked leaving her weak and deprived of courage. It was that risk which had been vaguely unpleasant: the idea that she would need all the more courage to set out again. But after all, a halt was something that could be expected; not so, an arrival. It was too much. She almost wished—she swore to herself that she did wish it—that the whole thing was nothing but a sudden whim of Henry's. He would soon change his mind, and the only benefit she would have derived from the adventure was this repainted kitchen (as a matter fact, since the workmen had left some materials she might have her bedroom done as well), and that new coat (like Sylvia!), and a slightly augmented bank account. Nothing exaggerated. The normal balance-sheet of such an affair. And the pleasure, too, that tenderness between them which had come so easily. But all this did not justify such an offer. Heavens, if you had to marry all the men you liked to be with! Thus thought Lou, standing in front of the table.

"Wool-gathering, Louise?" Hunger had drawn Stéphane into the kitchen. "Not bad, the kitchen painted in blue," he added, "rejuvenates it."

"If we could only do the same for ourselves," laughed Louise, collecting her thoughts.

"Why, what's this, what's this? Such splendours!" He was pretending he had just noticed the food set out on the table. As a matter of fact he had seen it the minute he entered the kitchen, but had been uncertain how to react.

"A little treat," said Lou without emphasis. And she thought, "Of course he makes a show of trusting me. That justifies him. After all, why complicate life? But to the others I'm a lost woman and he is an unfortunate man who submits to everything without complaint."

"Naturally," he thought, "she's making another display of generosity. She must always stress the fact that she earns more than I do, that I'm good for nothing."

But their mutual resentments were more ritual than actual; neither of them was by nature aggressive. They sat down to table in the neat kitchen with a shared feeling of pleasure.

"It's nice of you to remember to buy my bread," he said, with a courtesy that still had something vindictive about it, because it implied that she might remember the enriched bread, the thermometer, the sickening medicine, but that other needs, more essential, more spiritual, were overlooked.

Even so, his sour intonation was less marked that evening, and he was almost worried at the way Louise let it pass.

"It's excellent, this Parma ham with the melon," he said, giving her a slyly inquisitive look. "They eat ham this way in Italy, don't they?"

"And with figs, I believe."

Decidedly the atmosphere was serene, that evening. Why shouldn't it be? Through the tiny kitchen window came a cool breeze, rising from the trees in the avenue. A beautiful autumn. The other night, returning from a dance at which the Trio had played, he had felt very exhausted, and again had had that strange feeling of faintness and desire to sink into sleep. Bruno had had to bring him home in a taxi. But during the past few days he had felt well enough; these September days were mild, Martine was in a radiant humour—he was really abashed at her devotion, and at that touching idea of hers of sharing his journal with the others. . . . Louise herself was doing her best, no doubt, for since his return from the mountains he had had a quite new impression of comfort and tranquility. He looked at her as she ate, sitting there in silence, that lock of hair as usual fallen over her forehead, her brows knitted as if she were thinking. Poor Louise, thinking! How he had tried, years ago, to help her to think! Looking at her, he was amazed to see how much she resembled that younger Louise, who had used to pout, leaning her elbow on the table, refusing to talk to him. But then, months passed nowadays without his having the impression of really seeing her.

"Lou?"

She looked up, surprised. He was not in the habit of calling her by that "vulgar diminutive", as he said. It was a part of his principles to call her "Louise", in a slightly affected way which seemed to embarrass even himself.

"Turn on the radio, will you?"

Without moving from the table, she stretched out her hand towards the enormous and decrepit old radio, which was a sputtering mass of atmospherics beneath its scaling rosewood. Then she reached for the bottle.

"The wine will be too warm," she sighed, "but never mind. . . ."

"I say," he exclaimed, handling the bottle, "you've adopted some luxurious habits during my absence. It's vintage wine, now, is it?" Automatically he glanced towards the corner where she placed the empty bottles. "And you've tidied up the bottles!"

For no apparent reason she burst out laughing. "That surprises you, does it?"

She uncorked the bottle, filled the glasses, slowly. It was Monday, her night off. She was in no hurry, and Henry was dining in town that night. She would go early next morning to the studio and they would have breakfast together. But suppose Henry talked again about that idea of his?

"It's a really remarkable wine, this," said Stéphane. "Besides, there's nothing to equal French wines. Those Italian wines, those Chiantis, they're all ordinary." He was decidedly feeling well, the radio was playing softly, the air was pleasant and cool with an odour of leaves that filled the bright clean room—that shade of blue was pretty, and Louise, no doubt affected by the renovated kitchen, had finally got round to scouring the saucepans. "One could recreate a whole civilization beginning with its wine, my dear. Fundamentally our sense of taste has as much importance as our sense of hearing. Which proves, among other things, that so-much-discussed superiority of the French. Take cooking anywhere except in France. Take those ragouts and stews of the Italians and the English, they are as lacking in finesse as their mumbled languages, Italian a trickle and a dripping, English something cautiously chewed, compare that with our French as spoken in Touraine, for instance, so limpid and clear, or as spoken in Provence, so rich, so nourishing. . . .''

He was hypnotized by his own words, enchanted at not being interrupted.

"That's the absolute truth," said Lou contentedly. She was drinking one glass of wine after another. As long as it gave him pleasure to talk. . . . She must learn to listen to Henry in the same way: surely his plans were only daydreams. She poured out another glass of wine for herself, then for Stéphane.

"You want it well done?" she asked, rising lazily to cook the steak.

"Not too much. And under the grill, please."

Yes, he really felt well, really relaxed tonight. He did not even feel like going down to the bar where the others would soon be waiting for him. "*Quand j'ai ma petite canne à pê-ê-chê . . .*" the radio measured out rhythmically.

"That's what Bruno ought to sing, eh?" he said, smiling. "I think I'll buy the music for him tomorrow. He'll be furious!"

She yawned and stretched. The odour of grilled meat filled the kitchen. He recalled their first days together in Paris when, in their tiny hotel room, she would yawn and stretch like that, and recalled how it had stirred his desire. It was now more than a year since he had touched her, all that had ended with one of their quarrels, apparently insignificant, but which had suddenly become violent. He had wrapped himself in dignity and afterwards had found himself locked in it, feeling a little crestfallen at noting how apparently little she minded. His conviction of having been right in that argument—as always, he had the unpleasant feeling of being right, but of being unable to convince her—forbade him to make the least placating gesture. But perhaps she had thought it over during his holiday? And perhaps she was trying, by all these little attentions, if not to admit herself in the wrong—from what he knew of her, she would rather let herself be killed than admit that—then to bring him back to her?

"Here you are. Is it the way you like it?"

She held out a plate on which she had served up the steak, garnished with salad.

"Do you want coffee? I'll put the water on. They'll be waiting for you downstairs, your little pals."

He wasn't annoyed. Perhaps she was just a little bit jealous? She was wearing a sleeveless frock, of a rather pretty shade, olive green. "She's stopped wearing that vulgar red dress," he reflected. Was it perhaps to please him? And she appeared to be gentler, too, even her gestures seemed to be rounded and slowed down. . . . He himself had been more patient since his return, he would pay himself that compliment. Perhaps he had sometimes—but with what good reason!—lacked tolerance and understanding? "So little is needed," he thought, "to make her happy, the poor, misled creature. A little love, a little patience. . . ."

"A little wine," she thought, "a little of this warmth that comes from Henry's money. . . . And we can live without quarrelling at least."

The kettle sang. She did not get up. The radio dispensed in a muffled voice some useful hints on what to buy, mingled with sweet music and splutterings. The bottle was empty. They felt comfortable. Across the table their hands met, and clasped. It was not a gesture of tenderness, not even a gesture of friendship. Rather, it was an instinct of animals used to the same lair and, having fed, used to drawing close to each other without knowing whether for love-making or sleep. Even so, they made that gesture, and held it for a long while, in that indifferent feeling of peace.

However, at the Café Céleste, they were waiting for Stéphane.

"Now that Monsieur Morani's come back, they'll not feel so free, don't you see?" said Madame Prêtre. "And so, you'll go there. . . ."

"But what about Albert?" asked Sylvia, with a little pout.

"What Albert?"

"My boy-friend."

"How many times do I have to tell you that this Albert—I'll bet you don't even know his family name—is not your 'boy-friend'! Your boy-friend is Henry Stass, whether you like it or not!" As she spoke, she reflected that Henry Stass especially would have to like it! But it would never occur to Sylvia to raise such an objection.

"Albert told me . . ."

She was stubborn! God knew what nonsense that Albert had stuffed her head with. Here was another affair just like the one with the photographer, all over again! In another minute Sylvia would again be whispering, "But he's so nice!"

"Sylvia, you've let a man get you all worked up again! That Albert will get you nowhere. Can't you see he's just fooling round with you? All those cinema people . . ."

"Not Albert," murmured Sylvia obstinately. "He's not like that, at all, he told me so. He's so nice. . . ."

Bah! She would have sworn it! So nice! Madame Prêtre lost all patience. "I tell you he's trifling with you!"

"No, he wants to marry me."

"How you do fasten on to men!" shouted Madame Prêtre. "First there was that down-at-heel photographer, then Henry Stass—but there, that was a man worth having—and now this Albert! If you were allowed to, you'd marry ten times, eh?"

Sylvia's eyes were brimming with tears. She was quite aware that her mother was not entirely wrong. A man had only to be a little nice to her. . . . "As for Henry Stass, it's not my fault," she sobbed, "since he didn't want to."

Madame Prêtre softened. "He didn't want to because you went about it all wrong, my poor child. Do you think he could be seriously in love with Madame Morani, when he had a pretty girl like you? Oh come, now! I'm sure he thinks about you every day, that he misses you. . . ."

"You really think that?"

Sentimental arguments always shook her.

"I'm sure. And he's the one who must have thought that you didn't like him much. You weren't affectionate enough. That must have hurt him and he wanted to have his revenge and so he took up with the first woman that came along."

"Do you really think so?"

Sylvia had stopped crying. Such a complexity of emotions made her marvel. Madame Prêtre went on improvising with brio, concealing her impatience.

"The proof? Why did he take Louise Morani? A woman of that age, you can be sure it isn't for her good looks!"

Sylvia's eyes widened in total stupefaction.

"It's because she lived in this house, that's why!" Madame Prêtre declared. "So you'd know of it! He wanted to find out if you're really in love with him!"

This finished Sylvia. She lay on the bed, holding her head in both hands, Madame Prêtre also sat down, exhausted by her imaginative efforts.

"And you," she went on with less warmth, "you don't even cry. You say goodbye as if seeing him off for a stroll, and you don't give another sign of life. What do you expect him to think?"

There was a silence while Sylvia let this sink in, and while Madame Prêtre recovered her strength.

"And Madame Morani?" Sylvia asked all of a sudden. "You think she doesn't love him either?"

Madame Prêtre was so accustomed to Sylvia's absurd questions that she was ready for this one.

"Madame Morani's a devoted wife," she explained brilliantly. (In the last number of the magazine, *Confidences*, this subject had been treated at great length.) "She's devoted to her consumptive husband, whose earnings aren't enough. You know as well as I do that they had to sell the maid's room last year. She's devoted to him, she adores her husband, when all's said and done, and she suffers. You must explain all that to Henry Stass."

"I must explain that to him?"

"Yes. He's breaking up a happy home. If he would give them a sum of money and not have anything more to do with Madame Morani, he'd be doing a good deed! A good deed! The Moranis adore each other. Louise Morani cries her eyes out every night. You'll remember to tell him that?"

"Yes," said Sylvia, much impressed. "I'll remember. Is it true that she cries?"

"Since I tell you so, it's true."

Convinced, Sylvia said nothing. Madame Prêtre could see that she was apparently much affected. Yes, she'd remember. She would telephone Henry, ask to see him, and would tell him what she had to say. Then, they'd see what would happen. Madame Prêtre felt she had earned a reward and went towards the alcove where she had put the bottle of Dubonnet.

"Aren't you coming with me to Socrates', Mamma?"

"That's true. It's Monday. But I feel pretty tired."

"Oh, it's going to be wonderful tonight! Stéphane Morani is going to read some pages from his journal. Martine Fortin told me she'd read it and that it just bowls you over!"

Madame Prêtre sprang from the alcove, wiping her mouth on a corner of one of her shawls.

"Oh no, thank you! I know all about his journal, I know all I want to!"

"And can't I go to the meeting?"

"Oh, go if you like, you'll not understand a word. But as for me, no thank you. You can say my stomach's upset. Oh, no thank you, I can do without knowing anything more about that journal!"

She had turned herself inside out to think up an idea that would convince the girl. Enough of all these complications! Disgruntled, she went back to the alcove and took another long pull at the bottle.

Beneath the gaze of the mandarins, the young girl with the nenuphars (or perhaps after all they were lotus flowers), beneath the gaze of the nameless god, Stéphane was reading, and his vibrant, well-modulated voice filled the dim little bar. He was reading slowly, skipping a passage now and then, taking pleasure in the reading. After all, this was an excellent idea of Martine's, surprisingly so. He had experienced a slight nervousness when he began, but gradually, with the unfolding of the sentences, he had recovered his self-assurance. Now he was surprised at the charm and facility of his writing; there was nothing perfunctory in this, the sentences flowed harmoniously. And did not some writers publish their intimate journals?

Dr. Fisher, to Socrates' great surprise, had not ordered a drink; yet he was floating in an agreeable dream which Stéphane's voice became part of rather than disturbed. That resonant voice recalled other voices, so fervent and convinced, and the back room of a dim café almost identical to this one (excluding of course the mandarins; but the other café had also had a gilded god of sorts in a corner, an unknown icon). His own voice had been raised among those voices, articulating words in capital letters, and a great warmth had filled him, as it must now, this evening, be filling Stéphane. He had loved mankind, had desired its happiness. Not that he had loved precisely such and such a man (although he had been extremely fond of his neighbour the cobbler, and of his own wife, with whom, though he loved her, he had often quarrelled). No, he had loved all mankind, humanity united in one vast and indistinguishable flock, its very indistinguishableness making it all the more touching. In that other dim café he had been that tall, fair-haired young man talking eloquently and glancing at himself furtively in the mirror on the wall of that back room, where he had harangued his comrades as he would have liked to harangue all humanity. He had returned home still in an excited state, still in a sweat, and Anna had said, as every woman in the world says at some time, "Oh, politics!" as she wiped his forehead with a handkerchief.

It was rarely that he thought, now, of the man he had been. But today the recollection amused him. To hear again those words in which he had once believed, and to know what he now knew about himself and mankind. . . . The chaste friendship, the chaste love of men, how fine that was, seen from the outside! And how pleasant the feeling! All one had to do was look at the face of that Morani chap, flushed with pleasure, and listen to his vibrant voice, the distinct articulation of the words . . . even to the occasional shortness of breath, which was becoming less bothersome. A session of this kind from time to time would do him more good than a whiff of mountain air. Yes, men were extraordinarily entertaining. It had been pleasant, in the old days, to be among them, a jelly-fish among the lot of jelly-fish, and to get excited talking, and to feel of primordial importance in the mechanism of the universe. But it was also pleasant to have become a spectator; to compare that great exaltation with its small causes, its paltry effects. To know, he alone among them, how hollow and vain and stupid all this was. There was even a kind of intoxication in it. For a moment he felt divinely well, floating in space, contemplating them from on high with pity, free of bonds, free of responsibilities, free. . . .

During the reading, Gérard Ducas had unconsciously laid his hand on Jean's, as he sometimes happened to do at a concert, when he was moved. And he was moved, quite in spite of himself, by this reading. Oh, the poor dear Stéphane Morani, with his big phrases, his out-dated formulas, his swollen metaphors. It was exquisite in its ingenuousness. No one better than he appreciated this type of "museum piece". "Absolutely the journal of Queen Victoria", he would say to Jean later on. And yet he was moved, with the same kind of emotion he experienced when he thought of his mother and the roses of Saint-Jean-le-Vieil. After all, it produced an inimitable melody, this sort of thing, this combination of high-minded provincialism, this whiff of lavender between the sheets, this oafish uprightness, ponderous with very ample and well-balanced comparisons.

"It's both ugly and touching, like the village monuments to the war-dead", he would tell Jean. He could have hoped that Jean would understand, would share his emotion. But Jean did not always understand such things. "If I'd had a son," Ducas reflected, "he wouldn't have understood, either." Besides, wasn't Jean like a son to him? Those worthy wall-paper dealers could really not play the part of parents except in a music-hall skit. He alone had really understood Jean, understood what torment lay hidden in that apparently thankless nature. The parents knew this, moreover, and thanked him. "You're like a father to Jean, Monsieur Ducas. We

don't know what he'd do without you." What greater joy could he
have derived from fatherhood? Not to mention that he would be
burdened with a wife, a loud and disorderly woman like that wife
of poor Morani. He detested that woman, although he appreciated
the motives that had led Stéphane to marry her. All that was
delicious, too, so Queen-Victoria (in reverse, naturally, in the
Dostoievskian manner, but it came to the same thing). Delicious
and tragic, for the poor charming fellow must have always detested
that frightfully common creature. It must have been—indeed,
the diary let this be supposed—a kind of unconsummated marriage,
or almost. A *mariage blanc*, without blemish. And it was better so.
White as the shirt Jean wore that summer day when he was painting
in the apple orchard.

Gérard Ducas liked to watch him paint for hours, contemplating
with pleasure that stubborn profile, that diligent hand, that open
shirt revealing the bare chest. Thus his own mother must have
watched him, when he had been a student in that little house in
Saint-Jean-le-Vieil. Even a mother likes her son to be handsome.
There was nothing equivocal in that. He felt, now, that Stéphane
would have understood. Yes, despite the poor fellow's lack of taste,
he would have understood the feeling Gérard Ducas had for his
Jean. "Chaste and passionate," he sighed to himself. "Chaste and
passionate." How he wished that Jean himself could understand it!
How he wished that the atmosphere that reigned between them
could have been more serene, more tender, less stormy. . . . The
atmosphere of the Morani diary. . . .

"Crazy how the man believes in his own stuff," Jean thought.
"It can't be denied, there are still some naïve people in the world.
A decent bird, though, essentially. Screamingly funny, of course,
this journal stuff, but authentic. A first-rate thing, in its way,
Gérard must be wild over it, just the kind of dinkus he adores.
Good old Gérard, as wide-eyed as a cow in a field. "You're evolv-
ing, Jean, you'll soon be ready for another exhibition." And he
believes in the rubbish, too. Certainly must, to go to all that trouble
to find buyers for my stuff. Considering what he gets out of it!
You have to be in love with painting. It's like this decent, down-at-

heel Morani, who sticks to his worthy wife . . . although the girl's no more appetizing. But if he doesn't sleep with her, then he must sleep with his wife.

"She might not be too bad in bed. Some men like fat women. Gérard's not one of them! Whenever they meet on the stairs, the looks he gives that woman! If looks could kill! True, women, as far as Gérard's concerned . . . What he needs is a handsome fellow like me. 'Oh, I insist, give me your shirt, I'll wash it for you.' A real Angel in the House. After all, he doesn't give a damn for my painting, like this chap doesn't care a damn what we think of his intimate journal. Intimate, my foot. The truth is, he must like his Lou quite a lot, in bed at least. And as for Gérard. . . . He's certainly waited a long time if . . . Ever since we've known each other. I've got to be fair. He's always behaved like a gentleman, he's been a good sport. And he drools with admiration over everything I do. Besides, the stuff I turned out in Normandy's not too bad, really. We might try that little gallery in the . . . Oh, the poor Gé-gé! His eyes are full of tears over that chap's blah-blah. And here I was, thinking . . . There's not an ounce of viciousness in him. Or in the other chump, either. The two of them off their rocker, that's all. Yes, the little gallery . . ."

Germaine Lethuit was thinking they might very well have read her poem today. After all, she had mentioned it before this business of the journal had come to light. She had priority. But, naturally, the minute Stéphane Morani said anything. . . . True, these reunions had been his idea. But did that give him the right to monopolize things? Not counting that Gérard Ducas was still waiting to read his paper which he had been polishing for months, "The History of a Louis XV *bidet*". And Jean Cadou's canvases that they ought to go upstairs to see. When would they let her read her poem? Well, she wouldn't allow herself to mention it. She would wait. She was used to self-sacrifice.

And all the more since, in all fairness, this intimate diary was an interesting psychological case-history. Germaine Lethuit had made a close study of the rehabilitation of unmarried mothers, and had been able to appreciate the difficulties. Obviously Louise Morani wasn't an unmarried mother, but her case was similar. And the effort to rehabilitate her had met with total failure. But then, Stéphane hadn't gone about it scientifically. His so-called mystical impulses, his pious decisions—more often than not the result of adolescent insecurities, as Freud had pointed out—could not be expected to have a satisfactory effect. And there you had a life ruined simply because of a defective early education in a church school.

Not to mention the rather suspect part played by that little Martine Fortin in all this. Antigone, Antigone. . . . Why, everyone says she's his mistress. If he simply abandoned that wife of his, a quite uninteresting woman, a hopeless case, and lived openly with the young Fortin girl it would be more reasonable and dignified. But expect reason from these mystics! They enjoy suffering; they are all introverts. Take Madame Guyon, for instance. Or those monks who flagellated themselves. No, no, Germain Lethuit would not allow all that. There were enough things to do in the world, schools to construct, hospitals crowded with invalids needing care, political problems to solve. . . . And men like Stéphane Morani chose to sacrifice themselves, to live with a wife they hated, to exhaust their strength, and why? Out of pride, simple pride, for the most part. The Pharisees! They liked to show themselves superior to the simple materialists who made an effort to find a little happiness on earth. However, one must remember that all sacrifice was not of this type. There were admirable examples of self-sacrifice. Saint Vincent de Paul, for instance. And among the laity even finer examples, because such people did not expect a reward.

Did she herself expect anyone to be grateful to her for sacrificing her life to her old father and to Pauline? No. And she derived no vanity from it. She had never tried to marry or to leave France. Of course she could have found a husband for Pauline, but she wanted an honest man, she wanted to prevent Pauline from making another mistake. One had one's responsibilities. From that point of view she could evidently understand Stéphane Morani. Once he had married his wife, he could not throw her out on the street again. Without him, she would no doubt have reverted to her evil ways. True, she was little better than a street-walker, as it was. That new coat of hers, those new shoes! It was a kind of prostitution. But after all, the presence of her husband obliged her to put up a respectable front, to lead a regular kind of life. But perhaps the Fortin girl was not his mistress? Merely a kind of moral aid? Recalling the weighty feeling of responsibility she herself had for Pauline, Germaine Lethuit was inclined to be indulgent. To be sure, if Stéphane believed it his duty . . . She thought of lending him a very interesting book, *Ten Years of Prison Life*, written by a female supervisor in a women's prison, all about how she had tried to give the prisoners some political ideas—which had brought about her dismissal. After all, the intimate diary of Stéphane Morani described an effort as worthy as any other. She was ready to take an interest in it.

"It's lovely," murmured Sylvia, her eyes brimming with tears. "It's so lovely!"

And Socrates, more jaundiced than ever, more melancholy, echoed her words: "Lovely!"

It was all madly romantic. It was something of which Sylvia had always dreamed. Oh, to have a man say things like that to her, and what would it have mattered if she did not understand the words too well, so long as they were tender? To have a man who would love her like that, sacrifice himself for her, as Stéphane did for Louise Morani, or else a man who would not demand anything of her, like Stéphane with Martine Fortin. Yes, it was lovely, those words, those phrases moved her to tears. She had always hoped that Henry would talk to her like that! It was really unfair that Stéphane was not famous like Henry. He should have written novels or maybe operas. They could then have gone out together without any objections from Madame Prêtre. Stéphane never seemed to expect her to say anything more than what she said. He did not stare at her in that strange way Henry sometimes did. He did not make her feel that deep anxiety, that resentment which her mother's outbursts caused her. He talked to her as he talked to everyone. How she wished he had been famous!

It was lovely, too lovely. If life had been like that, Socrates reflected, it would be easy to live. But he was not deluded. A Greek knows what beautiful words are. When you want to sell something, you must wrap it up with care. He knew all that. But just the same he was charmed by such lovely words. He knew that if he'd been able to talk like that, he would have managed to cope with Constantine and Dimitrios, he'd have been able to convince them that he was a respectable man who had had misfortunes and was not merely a pauper who couldn't afford to offer them a free drink. But the trouble was that Socrates himself could barely distinguish one from the other. Oh, if he had Monsieur Morani's ability! Just listen to those words pouring out! How convincing! If he could only talk like that to Constantine and Dimitrios! If he could talk like that to himself, convince himself that he was the same man now in this forsaken little bistro that he had been in the sparkling and prosperous restaurant with its white tablecloths, its enormous kitchens, and in that Athens flat with its plush armchairs, its Parthenon made of sugar! Oh, to have again that feeling of security that had surrounded him, and the unshakable conviction that he was Somebody! How could anyone manage to be Somebody without giving dinner parties, offering drinks, dominating a circle of sympathetic admirers, discoursing before a respectful assembly? Who would listen to Stéphane Morani himself if he did not own his flat? How to be somebody of importance without money, without an audience, all alone? Socrates was well aware—for in trade you become sharp—that it was impossible. And yet, he listened to Stéphane as if listening to music. It did one good, at times, to forget the impossibilities.

Stéphane continued to read in the silence. He had rather forgotten the time, he suddenly realized. Might he not be boring them? He raised his head to look at his audience. Gérard Ducas had hidden his eyes with one hand, as if he were moved. Cadou, who was often so disagreeable, smiled good-naturedly at him. Sylvia was devouring him with her eyes. Socrates was listening with an almost painful attention delineated on his fake pirate's face. Germaine Lethuit was nodding her head in approbation. At seeing them all so attentive to his words, he became curiously uneasy. The sentences which had been rolling out a moment before without any difficulty, charmed as he was by their rhythm, their felicitous turns, now suddenly became audible to him, as they were to his listeners. He stumbled on first one word then another, and as he read, his mind began to follow the words, and dub in other thoughts, spoiling his pleasure, disturbing his peace. "What are they going to think of this? They're going to think this a little too . . . After all, they don't know Martine and Louise as I do, and this may risk . . ." This was something new for him, to set up a parallel between his real life and what appeared of it in this indulgent mirror, his journal. It was perhaps this confrontation of the two selves that bothered him, dimmed his eyes and blurred his speech, as if he felt, while talking, someone standing behind him and about to tap him on the shoulder.

"Well, I think that will be all for today. . . . Please remember that the passages I have read are mere jottings. . . ."

He felt obliged to stop. But even before he had time to wonder why, there he was, being surrounded and congratulated. Sylvia, enraptured, threw herself on his neck—even kissed him.

"You should have been a writer, Monsieur Stéphane! You would surely have won the Prix Goncourt!"

"Deeply touched, very deeply," muttered Ducas, clasping his hand. And Jean Cadou, jovially: "Good stuff, that!"

"What a wonderful document!" breathed Germaine Lethuit. "It seems to condemn certain methods . . . a great deal could be said as to that. But what human warmth and sincerity."

"It's very well turned, Monsieur Morani," Socrates declared. "Really well turned! And it makes you think. . . ."

With difficulty, Dr. Fisher emerged from his fog and came to shake Stéphane by the hand. "Morani, my dear fellow, that's very fine, very fine." (Dr. Fisher's thought was: Let him rest in peace, poor fellow, let him never suspect. . . .)

Stéphane was profoundly moved by these marks of affection. His secret uneasiness sank out of sight, disappeared into those regions he would never again approach. His face was radiant with happiness, and he could only stammer his thanks.

"This is too much, too much. You're too kind, all of you."

He had not been as happy as this for a long time. He felt as relieved as if he had just passed an exam. And perhaps it was the examination he had always dreamed of: to be at last interrogated on all these doubtful things, on all these obscure points, and to provide an answer, his answer, and to be finally condemned or absolved. Those attentive faces around him, of which he had for a moment been afraid, had he not always needed just that? To be listened to, to be allowed to explain his case, to be judged at last, given a good or bad mark which would be there permanently, would classify him for ever as inferior or superior to the average, a mark that would speak for him, act for him, accomplish everything—as the final report card of the year, whether good or bad, defines, catalogues and classifies to the accompaniment of speeches and prizes, the entire school year—so that he would never again have to think about anything but the year when he had had the third certificate of merit in Latin. An examination. A judgement. God! How happy he was tonight!

"My friends, just a moment . . ."

He called Martine over to his side. Was she not the one who had had this idea, who had procured this relief for him? But Martine was not as relieved as he was. She wanted more talk, more discussion. She wanted to put questions: "What do you think of this, or that?" As if it were not enough, this great collective demonstration of approval, this great general absolution, with Dr. Fisher smiling, Gérard Ducas nostalgic, Jean Cadou at last cordial, Sylvia overwhelmed, Socrates thoughtful, Germaine Lethuit giving, after mature reflection, her *approbatur*. As if that did not suffice, that intense assuagement which he suddenly perceived he had longed for all these years, not only morally, in this demonstration of friendship and confidence, but almost physically, as well, in that vision he had had upon raising his eyes from the notebook, that row of faces, of bodies held motionless in close attention, motionless except for Dr. Fisher's fingers tapping on the table, that physical form of examination where the tribunal he had seen a hundred times in reverie—and actually, in that infernal tribunal of his childhood, Old One-Eye and, on either side of him, his parents, tearful and silent, which had condemned him. . . . "This boy's no eagle. . . . He's only seventh in class!" Was it in a dream that he had heard those words, or in reality? Had he heard them only once or a hundred times? It mattered little today. That impenetrable silence of Louise which had appeared to him like a judgement, had he only dreamed it, sensed it, had he been mistaken as to its meaning? It mattered little now. He was finally absolved. And just as, after an examination, one wants to forget all those dates, all those facts which might have been wrong, he now did not want to look back.

"Thank you, thank you, my friends. . . ."

As if that weren't enough! In his total abandonment to a feeling of physical well-being, he noted with annoyance that Martine still wanted something. How unpleasant she was, with her eternal dissatisfaction, her for ever unslaked thirst. She was like a sullen beggar, always asking for more and more.

"But don't you think . . .?" she was saying to someone.

He cut her short, almost rudely: "Frankly, Martine . . . I can't take any more tonight. This has cost me a great effort. I believe for once I shall leave you to your discussion and go upstairs to bed." He did not even meet her eyes. That evening he could not endure the existence beside him of someone who was not utterly gratified. And, curiously enough, the others also seemed eager to separate, to carry away a portion of this satisfaction and cordiality that had filled the dim little room with a vague and heavy excitement.

"I'm pretty tired myself," said Ducas.

"I think I'll take a turn on the boulevard," said Jean.

"I think I'll close up the place, since everyone's going," said Socrates.

"The last train . . ." said Germaine Lethuit, gathering up her hat, a little plumed felt like a Musketeer's.

"Mamma, her stomach . . ." Sylvia murmured.

All the same, thought Martine, she wasn't going to stay alone in the deserted bistro. She hadn't much choice though in the general atmosphere of satisfaction. She couldn't even sulk at Stéphane, who . . .

But Stéphane had disappeared, he was already going upstairs, humming a tune, despite his shortness of breath, and he reached his floor before she did and, invisible, was calling down to her as he turned the key in the lock, "Good night, Martine!"

As a precaution, Stéphane shut the door behind him. In the dim
light of the little foyer, where the smell of hot oil still lingered, he
hummed his tune. Cautiously, he opened the door of his bedroom,
after hesitating a moment. But Louise must be asleep. Otherwise,
he would have felt inclined for a little talk with her. Still pervaded
by that feeling of calm and assuagement, he began to undress. He
would go to bed and fall asleep at once. Tonight he need not fear
the return of those childhood dreams of terrible sessions in the
shabby drawing-room and the one-eyed old grandfather looking at
him with insulting indulgence. Tonight Stéphane had had his
revenge. Wasn't that it? Or was this feeling of indifference, of self-
certainty the state of mind that Father Mourron had called a good
conscience? "From the minute you do your best, my boy, and your
conscience is clear . . ." Was that it?

Everything had been ready since the previous day: the white
arm-band, the scarf, the missal. His new suit was, as Stéphane's
mother had remarked to the seamstress, a little too tight.

"And I told you, Gertrude," she said to the maid, "that I knew
it would be."

There were white flowers in the dining-room, where the luncheon
was to be given, and a ray of sunshine fell on the well-polished
red-tiled floor.

"We're having Madame Cassou, and Papa," said Madame
Morani in her prettily drawling voice. Her hair had not yet been
arranged, but hung down her back, and she was wearing a loose
dressing-gown. "And just imagine, the Duffys, whose little boy is a
classmate of Stéphane, have asked permission to join us, supposedly
because they haven't enough room at their house for a party.
What they really want of course, is for their little boy Paul to be
in our Stéphane's circle of friends."

"The paint-dealer's son!" Gertrude exclaimed.

"As I told Stéphane, he ought to get to know the Stievrain boy,
or the pharmacist's little son, or the Varlot boy, I forget his name.
But not Paul Duffy! And now, that boy's going to have his First
Communion party with us! But how can we say no to them?

They have no sense of the proprieties! Now, take me, do I try to mix with the Nersons?"

"No, Madame, certainly no one could say . . ."

Madame Morani fluttered about, and a fresh scent of orris-root came from her unfastened dressing-gown.

"I know my place," she said, "even though my family was one of the best in town, as I can say without boasting, I came down in the world when I married my husband. I don't hide the fact, I came down in the world."

"That's so, Madame, that's so," the maid impartially agreed.

"But I have a sense of the proprieties. I mix with my equals, and I'm happy to do so, Gertrude. You wouldn't see me going to the Nersons, pretending I didn't have room, and asking them to be so kind as to include Stéphane. If I had not married my husband, I could have done so. . . ."

"To be sure, Madame."

"But now I cannot, and shall never reproach him for it, Gertrude, because I love him."

"My dearest!" said Monsieur Morani tenderly. He had entered the room unnoticed. "My dearest!" And he took her into his arms gently, with veneration. Never could he love her enough, considering all she had done for him. She had had to defy her own father. And so exquisite, so pretty!

"What did Papa do?"

This was the little Stéphane speaking. Until then he had remained sitting quietly on a chair, stiff as a mummy, in his new suit. They had forgotten he was there, and now they all burst out laughing.

"Why, nothing at all, my angel," said Madame Morani. "But it's his fault if we have to lunch with those dreadful Duffys! And now, I must get dressed for them."

She fled, with a roguish laugh. Monsieur Morani watched her go, as if dazzled. So pretty, so fresh. Her perfume, that scent of orris-root, still lingered in the room. Her reproachful remarks—which were not so much reproaches as innocent chaffing—occasionally hurt him a little. However, it was quite natural that she should regret the fine society in which her parents had moved. In Signac, social rank was so strictly defined. The wife of a schoolmaster had fewer invitations than the daughter of a shipowner, even a bankrupt one. And Estelle was made for society—what grace she had, and how well she was able to dress on nothing (fortunately she had learned how to sew, as she often said, one would have thought her marriage was foreordained)! Yes, what more natural than those little sighs, those little impatient remarks that sometimes escaped her? They made him prize her all the more for having married him in spite of everything. To the very end of his life, the unassuming man told himself fervently, he would serve her, pamper her. From the next room her pretty voice, just a little sulky now, called out to him.

"Joujou!"

His name was Georges, but she called him by the baby-talk word, Joujou. What could be more endearing, what could be more like her?

"Joujou!" She was becoming impatient.

"Coming, my love," he called, and hurried off to join her.

"And now, young Master Stéphane," said Gertrude, as she arranged the flowers, "are you quite ready?"

"Yes, Gertrude." He was fidgeting on his chair.

"We're all very proud of you. Only yesterday I heard Father Mourron say to your mother, 'That boy is the most pious child in my class. The Nerson boy is nothing by comparison.' What do you say to that? Does that make you happy?"

"Yes, Gertrude. When are we going?"

"You have all the time in the world, my lamb. Another little half-hour. A bit nervous?"

"Yes, Gertrude."

"That's only normal, my lamb. But a boy like you, I'll say this, you're not vain, you have nothing to fear from your First Communion. It'll go off without a hitch. You're not like that Peyron boy, Marcel Peyron, you know his story, about how he . . ."

"Yes, Gertrude."

He was not afraid, but he was waiting. "You should be filled with a marvellous happiness, Stéphane, you so pious, you the honour of my class," the Abbé Mourron had said, and he had replied, "Yes, Father." But he was still waiting for that dazzling white light they all talked about. Would it come to him now, in the small room with the red tiled floor, which was already infiltrated by the smell of cooking; or outside, in the full sunlight and the dust of the boulevard lined with chestnut trees; or while the organ played and as he walked towards the altar on the red carpet used on festival days that he had noticed rolled up, ready, in the sacristy? Or would it come to him at the luncheon party afterwards? Or later on, that night in his bed, while reciting his prayer, would that light suddenly . . .?

"We knew it," Gertrude was saying: "Madame Bisserand and I knew he hadn't gone to confession; and we said, 'He'll never dare receive Holy Communion.' Why, he had killed the cat only the night before, and he knew that we knew it. But morning comes and there's our Marcel Peyron, all dressed up in new clothes, exactly like you, and trotting off to church with the others. We couldn't believe our eyes. No, it wasn't possible, the good Lord would not permit . . ."

Tirelessly she went on reeling off the inevitable story of wickedness reserved for these occasions. The little boy sitting there was not afraid and barely heard her, for he was waiting. He had been waiting for a good week, now. Yesterday, in the narrow confessional, he had almost believed. . . . He had lingered, enumerating more and more faults. . . . The Abbé Mourron had become impatient: "Stéphane, my child, you are being too scrupulous, really, you must calm down. The good Lord loves you, my dear child set your mind at rest." Then, changing his tone, he called out suddenly: "Next!" For a queue had formed. This morning, as he looked at himself in the mirror . . .

"He was blue in the face!" exclaimed Gertrude. "Half choked to death by the Host! 'I knew it,' says Madame Bisserand, 'I knew this would happen!' They stretched him out there, they made him throw it up, and would you believe it? The Host came out whole, it wasn't melted or digested at all! What do you say to that?"

. . . In front of the mirrored wardrobe, in his new suit, the sacred new suit, he had looked at his face, had joined his hands together, had shut his eyes. It hadn't come. Not the right moment, perhaps. Not the hour. He had to take Communion first.

"But you don't risk having such a thing happen to you. The good Lord loves you, as Father Mourron said. Wouldn't you like to be a priest, dearie, when you grow up?"

"No, Gertrude."

"You're right. There have to be priests, but . . ."

But Etienne Nerson had said that it had come to him a week ago. Maybe it wasn't true? After all, when he came out of the confessional yesterday, he was quite pale. Whereas Stéphane felt really just as usual, except for his anxiety. It wasn't fair.

"You're not listening to me, Master Stéphane? It's because you're all worked up, aren't you? Me, I remember . . ."

Etienne Nerson had one of the lowest possible grades in Geography, a 3, and his conduct marks were almost as low, often below 5. And he did not know his Catechism. Surely he was telling a fib, to please his parents. Or else, there were other rules for the Nersons, because they lived in the biggest house in town? And so "it" came to the Nerson boy automatically, despite his bad marks and his Catechism exercise-book where anyone could see, there in broad daylight, the notation: "inattentive pupil". Madame Morani was in the habit of saying, "Don't imitate Etienne in any way, my dear. The Nersons obviously don't have to exert the least effort to be respected! In the old days, I could have associated with them, and you could have allowed yourself to . . . But I would not lower myself for anything in the world to try to insinuate myself with them now. Isn't that so, Gertrude?" Stéphane felt confusedly that the gay and inattentive Etienne could, in fact, get away with anything. The masters were indulgent, the Abbé Mourron resignedly so. . . . He could even have made his First Communion without having felt "that indefinable joy" the Abbé Mourron talked about with fervent tears brimming in his brown eyes, which were wide open and gentle. So then, why should he have lied? Like everything else, the "indefinable joy" was bestowed upon Etienne Nerson unfairly. And supposing—all of a sudden, little Stéphane was imagining the worst—supposing he should never experience that joy?

"You're not listening to me, Master Stéphane? Oh, my God, just look at him, Madame!"

As for him, he couldn't get away with anything, as Mamma said. So, if "it" didn't come to him . . . Father Mourron would hold it against him, no doubt. Would suspect him of a wicked action, hidden, who knows? But God must know that he had nothing to reproach himself with, nothing. Mamma examined his exercise-books so carefully in the evening. "All our hopes rest on you, Stéphane," she was always saying. "Your grandfather counts on you, my angel. Oh, the house we used to live in!" He said his prayers with her, snuggled against her perfumed dressing-gown. "And, O God, make everything as it was before," she always made him add. The photograph of Grandfather in the days of his splendour was hung above Stéphane's bed. As a quite small child, he had for a long time believed that all that was expected of him was for him to grow up to be a man like that, with the same frock coat and perhaps a single eye—this detail rather frightened him. Now he was aware that something else was required, and he now sometimes looked with repugnance at Grandfather's portrait. They wouldn't have expected so much of him if "the crisis", that mysterious thing Mamma was always talking about, had not broken the proud bristling of that moustache. And what about Papa? In what way had he been responsible for that "crisis"?

"Oh, Joujou! Come, look at the child!"

He was well aware that they were fluttering round him, but first of all he wanted to solve the mystery, wanted to understand. And so, voluntarily, he prolonged the torpor he had fallen into—due to the restless night, as well as to fasting, for he had been so anxious and tense the night before that he had been unable to swallow a mouthful. Yes, if Grandfather had known how to escape the "crisis", if Papa had not committed that mysterious crime to which they always alluded without naming it, Stéphane would that day not have been required to give, as Father Mourron had said, "a good example of piety" to the whole Catechism class. With desperate intensity, he was still seeking within himself that joy, that celestial peace they had dinned into his ears, and the drowsiness which had invaded him the night before, snuggled against the dressing-gown impregnated with the scent of orris-root. . . .

"Stéphane! My love, my angel-child, why, you make me afraid! Talk, say something to me!"

"What? What is it?" he stammered, instinctively exaggerating his alarm, so that no one would guess. . .

His mother had tears in her eyes. "My baby, my dearest Stéphane! Are you better, now? Did you see him, Joujou? An angel, a verit-able little angel!'

"He looked like a little Saint John," said Gertrude, in an ecstasy.

Papa looked slightly uncomfortable. "Is everything all right, my dear boy?" he asked with timid anxiety.

But Mamma did not let him have time to reply.

"Oh, my God!" she exclaimed. "There's Father Mourron come to fetch him!"

She dashed to the door. In the narrow hallway she could be heard whispering. Stéphane could distinguish a few words: ". . . extra-ordinary . . . so sensitive . . . he was transfigured, if you had only seen him . . ." Without a doubt, Mamma believed that "it" had happened. What a bore! He examined his memories, stumbled upon those few seconds of agreeable drowsiness. After all, how could he be expected to know? The marvellous peace. . . . It might just be a way grown-ups had of talking, they always tended to exaggerate, to begin with. (All that fuss they made over a school-report!) In short, that peace was like going to sleep. This theory stated, Stéphane's conscience was at rest. He *had* felt what he was expected to feel. His apprehension diminished. He replied to the Abbé Mourron, who was calling out to him. The other boys who were waiting outside must have heard something, for they were whispering. Father Mourron surveyed him with emotion, his big brown eyes still wet with tears. Stéphane lowered his eyelids, filled with a feeling of triumph. He no longer argued with himself. That was "it", that was certainly it.

He kept on repeating this, and when he arrived at the church, convinced, he was able to receive without any disturbance at all, and as a certain reward of merit, the savourless Host.

Part III: AUTUMN

"MONSIEUR PÉNARD has already written up my studio for his magazine," Henry said to Louise.

"But I think that with the material I have today we will be able to do something quite amusing," said the young man. (He was very natty, and Henry decided that he was not too unlikeable.) "We have at our disposal, a very handsome reproduction of your first portrait, Madame. What a pity the Maestro has not completed this one! But we can still make a rather amusing plate from this sketch. Perhaps you may have a photograph of yourself and Madame at the period of the New York painting? I understand that painting was made in Narbonne?"

"At Signac," said Henry, very ill at ease. He was always uncomfortable with reporters, horribly embarrassed at having to answer their questions, yet afraid to throw them out, having a kind of superstition about it, close to what he felt about extravagance with money. He couldn't quite accept that he no longer needed publicity any more than he needed to practice economy.

"And haven't you kept some little photograph of that period, Maestro? Or perhaps you, Madame Morani, have something of the kind? You must have treasured the memory of having had your portrait painted by the great man!"

He talked to them as if they were six-year-old children, patiently, bringing himself down to the level of their understanding.

"Heavens, I may still have some photos," said Louise. "Remember, Henry, the ones taken at the Fair, in the shooting-gallery?"

The young man gurgled and exclaimed as if she had just presented him with a mud-pie. "Oh, that would be wonderful! Do you think you might find that snapshot for me? Do try. He must have been superb at that period."

"I'll look for it," she promised. Henry noted with pleasure that she was as disconcerted as he was by the young man. And the young man, very kindly, tried to put them both as ease.

"Now, let's see. Have we remembered everything? We're going to do a very nice story for you, with superb photos, the two paintings, the photo we took of Madame today, the photos of Narbonne . . ."

"Signac," said Henry, as upset as if he had made the error himself.

"Signac, of course," said the young man who was not in the least embarrassed. "Some very fine photographs of the locale where the portrait was painted, beside a railway station, I believe?"

"A bridge," said Henry mildly.

"A bridge, of course. You see, I'm not the one in charge of the illustrations. But everything will be well taken care of, don't you worry."

"Oh, I'm not worried," said Henry, resignedly. He was getting used to the young man, was actually becoming rather attached to him, simply because he had seen him more than once. "Would you care for a glass of something?" He had laid in some whisky for the occasion. The young man accepted.

"What a wonderful story yours is," said the young man enthusiastically. "Twenty years later, Henry Stass paints a new portrait of Lou. That's almost a ready-made heading. You aren't by any chance thinking of getting married?"

"Oh, no," said Louise hurriedly.

"Too bad. That would make it even better. You'd immediately get four pages in our magazine, with both of you in the cradle, First Communion, and everything, and a title such as, for instance, 'At Last Fate Reunites Them!' "

"That's not a reason to marry," said Henry good-humouredly. "But if we ever do decide to, you'll be the first to be told, I promise."

They all laughed heartily. But meanwhile the young man continued to look about him, still hunting for something that would make another story. Not finding anything and seeing his glass empty, he took his leave, giving Louise a last reminder: "Do please remember to look for that photo, Madame Morani! It would be very naughty of you not to do that for me!"

The door closed, they looked at each other and burst out laughing. "What a lot!" said Henry. "But he's a decent enough young fellow. And think of it, two big pages, what publicity!"

"You don't really need it, do you?"

"You never can tell," he said, mistrustfully, and she nodded assent, helping herself to another glass of whisky.

Henry didn't like the stuff, but she appreciated it. As for him, he wandered about the room, tidying up, for everything had been moved to take the photographs, easel, brushes, even the divan which had been turned in another direction. He pushed it back where it belonged. He had a horror of seeing things out of their proper places.

"You oughtn't to drink that stuff," he said. "Who knows what's in it! And it's expensive."

"Exactly," she said, with logic, "and for that reason it can't be bad. Anyway, you drink cognac."

"It's not the same," he said, obstinately.

In what way it was not the same he would have had a hard time explaining. But he had these absurd ideas which twenty years of going out among society—twenty years during which he had seen people drinking whisky and none the worse for it—had in no way altered.

"It's because you don't like it that you make such a fuss," said Lou, not without a vague desire for an argument. "If you liked it as you do cognac, it wouldn't matter to you what's in it."

Henry looked at the rain falling on the rooftops. It had been raining for almost a week, now.

He liked the rain, liked autumn, for they recalled the scenes of his childhood, the northern towns where the rain seems to be always falling upon the red brick houses. He remembered the big loose clogs they had worn, remembered the little kitchen where they had crowded round the oilcloth-covered table in a steamy atmosphere of damp coats drying. . . . His had been a happy childhood, on the whole; a childhood that had been lulled by this cradle-song of the rain. He was beginning to recapture that peace, that mindless silence, with Louise. And the faint murmur of jealousy within him was somehow as reassuring as the rain.

He went over to the window. Tepid putrefaction of autumn, mellow forsakenness of wet streets; the dubious odour of dead leaves; the reassuring stench of stables in the metro; in all these things, in the musty and deceptive country smells everywhere, in those little trollops of clouds drifting across the sky, you saw signs and portents of a revenge that was preparing, the revenge of cities which, for a moment in the spring and autumn, are divested of their ferocious power. Straight lines and angles would soon take their revenge, and the pitiless geometry of intersecting streets, the shut house-fronts, the checker-board pavements thirstily drinking up dreary snow, and a stiff wind cutting through the still soft air, all these things would soon have their revenge. The city would triumph, in all its chromium-plated caverns where people crowd together for lack of anything better to do; it would triumph in all the wide cinema screens and in the muffled roar of the shops and market-places, in all its amalgam of rubber and plastic and aluminium, of cash-registers and table d'hôte meals, of pasteboard and cardboard, of grinning gigantic mouths on the sides of buildings, of hot grogs and waiting-rooms and hotel bedrooms. . . . Then it was that a man found himself alone in the midst of the dwelling-places he had built for himself, as in the midst of a sumptuous and ridiculous palace of mirrors where he collides at every turn with his own image. And if the shelter built by his own hands did not shield him, if his image in that mirror seemed to him solitary, if his refuge could not protect him against one single season, what then could protect him through the longer winter?

But the rain was gentle and apparently everlasting.

"Would you like me to pose?" she asked.

"Yes, perhaps. Yes. But won't you be cold?"

The central heating had not yet been turned on, and it was not warm in the studio, despite the humming of the electric radiator.

"If I get cold, I'll drink some whisky," she said with a laugh.

She undressed and slipped into her yellow and red dressing-gown.

He looked discontentedly at his sketch. She was there, sitting on the divan, half naked, the dressing-gown falling around her, elbows on knees, fists closed, that heavy body with ponderous and peaceful lines, posed there without grace but with a static dignity. . . . What he had done wasn't what he had wanted to do, not at all. After a while, she came up behind him. He dropped his arms in discouragement.

"But you've changed almost nothing!"

"I've been working on the background."

"A grey background! As if you need me to pose for a grey background! Cold as it is!"

She had acquired, from her life with Stéphane, his sensitiveness to cold, and prolonged poses irritated her. He burst out laughing. Louise's bad tempers always amused him.

"But it's not so easy! There's always a reflection, your eyes, your hair, your dressing-gown, to make my grey go bluish or yellowish. It's quite hard to make a flat grey that stays put."

"Then why do you try? It would be just as pretty if you painted the divan, and the dressing-gown, and . . ."

"And the window, and the Eiffel tower, and the little bird sitting on top? Why not, indeed?"

Vexed, she said nothing more. He continued idly to survey his canvas. That background existed, in spite of what he'd tried to do. He had tried to separate that body, that face, completely isolate them, show them intact, as they were, detached from everything surrounding them. What he wanted to signify was the female object, the Louise-object, cut off from everything that could explain it or destroy it. For a moment he had seen what the picture could be, that naked, heavy body, miraculously harmonious, absurdly miraculous, and surrounded by a dull, cold grey . . . the grey of death as one would like death to be.

His thoughts wandered, returned into the past, to the pedestrian painting of Lou leaning against the bridge at Signac, with a background of green foliage in the worst possible taste. And to think, that painting hung in a big New York gallery, and was going to be reproduced in a magazine article! He couldn't think of it without a smile. And yet, on second thought, he was quite sure that when he painted it he was trying to express . . . no, rather, he was expressing spontaneously then what he was now trying to express, what he had been trying to express ever since . . . since Mozart. A crazy way of evolving, he ruminated, as he laid his hand on Lou's shoulder. You'd think that in the course of one's life one would more likely try for a long time, under various forms, to express something, and that, with the advent of old age, one would not have to do anything more than repeat the discovery that would at last be clear as day. . . .

"Will you take the pose?" he said, with assumed impatience.

He was going to work on that background again, despite Louise's objections. Slowly he set to work and his thoughts, as slow and intent as his brush, returned into the past. In the old days he had not needed a grey background, to isolate people and things. Lou's hands, her head turned aside in the crudely purple shadow, the cold greens, the warm greens, each ingredient lived its distinct life, apart, without contagion, without collusion. His thought slowed down still more, moving as if in a tangible and compact element—and his brush came to a halt. How remote from him now was that ease, that independence, that untroubled irresponsibility! How much harder this grey background was to toss off than had been the trees of Signac! Yet he had known that peace, that freedom, he had lived life up to the hilt, and to find all that again, today, he must withdraw from everything that was life. . . . Was it possible that what had been truth and innocence at a certain age was no longer so at another age?

"Don't scratch your leg like that when I'm painting, that's an unpleasant habit of yours," he said with unjustified irritation.

"I suppose that keeps you from working on your background?" The cold made her sarcastic.

There must have been some precise moment when the break had occurred, when the limit had been reached and crossed, when he had found himself involuntarily on the other side of something. . . . A day, an hour when he had ceased to paint with total innocence, but had begun to paint with intention? An instant when the brush suddenly had not guided the hand but the hand had guided the brush? Mozart must have come to him a little after that moment. Mozart was like an admonition, an infinitely faint lament, a fugitive glimmer in the warm and quiet obscurity. . . . It would have required so much time, so much attention, to hear that lament, really, to discern that glimmer, really. . . . Does one thus, at sixty, with one's life-work accomplished, start off again, in the wake of a child who is singing?

No, no, he would be rational. Mozart, his difficulties, the lament and the glimmer, they must be due to his age, the result of a precocious fatigue, exhaustion perhaps, of the creative power. . . . That, too, was in the nature of things, it had merely come to him very early. Suddenly he felt worn out.

"Rest a little, the work's not going well. You can cover yourself up. We'll have another try after a while."

He went over to sit beside her, as if approaching a fire to warm himself. And at once he felt more relaxed.

"What about your husband?" he asked suddenly.

"What about him?"

"Have you told him?"

She shook her head.

"Oh, look here, Lou! Sooner or later you must. . . ."

"I don't see why," she said, stubbornly.

He flared up with a superficial anger, a welcome distraction.

"After all, you can't just pack your bags one day and leave a note on the table, Lou. That's not done nowadays."

"But I don't want to pack my bags," she said, rather uncertainly.

"What a silly you are!" He smiled. He was sure she'd finally come to him, he was sure of it. Indeed, it was one of the rare things of which he still felt sure. But why drag it out? "Do you still love him?"

"I don't believe I was ever in love with him." One day, however, on the bridge—the same bridge which figured in Henry's portrait of her but she did not think of that—they had run towards each other. They had been eager to be in each other's arms, and she had murmured, her lips against his, "How handsome you are!" And one day she had wept, on the bed of a little hotel bedroom, because she had not understood what he wanted. . . .

"You feel sorry for him, then?"

"Sorry? Why?" she asked with sincere surprise. No, illness did not arouse pity in her, nor did poverty. She had never been sorry for herself, why should she be sorry for him? Evidently, if she left him, he would be alone; but he would still have the flat. The Fortin girl could take care of him, or else Madame Prêtre. Or he could go to a sanatorium, as Dr. Fisher had been advising him to do for a long time. This was not what tormented her, nor the prospect of all the discussions ahead; for there would be discussions. He would cling to her, of that she was certain. Although he posed as a martyr and complained to his friends—she was sure he did, simply from the way everyone in the house stared at her—he would not let her go without making an issue of it. He was a man who loved to make a fuss. Besides, looking at the thing fairly, how would he manage without her? His earnings were ridiculously small. "No," she said aloud, "he'd manage without me, I believe. But . . ."

Henry, becoming impatient, let himself be drawn. "Well, then, I can only suppose that you sleep with him!"

"No. Not for . . . some time."

"A likely-sounding state of things! He's young, handsome . . ." She burst into a laugh. "Who told you that?"

"That child Sylvia."

"Oh, yes. She must be in love with him. You can't imagine how many young girls are in love with him. A little monster who lives in the house, for instance, has taken it into her head to . . ."

"I haven't the least desire to hear about the romantic triumphs of your husband, my dear woman," he said with a vehemence that did him good. "If you refuse to come here to live with me, it's for a good reason, is it not?"

A reason? She could find no other than a vague and quite confused aversion to doing as he asked, because she did not understand exactly what he wanted of her that she couldn't give him every day, and the absurd suspicion that such a marvellous offer must have a hidden motive.

"Later on," she said, "perhaps later on. . . ."

He left the couch and began to pace the floor.

"That's it, later on. When you're ninety years old. Then the journalist will be able to make a pretty heading: 'They Waited Sixty Years!' Provided I'm not already buried by that time, in which case you will pay me a visit every Thursday, with a bouquet! I say, aren't you a little crazy? Do you think you're Greta Garbo?"

She bowed her head, sincerely ashamed, for everything would have inclined her, on the contrary, to feel unworthy of such a generous offer, and to accept it gratefully, had it not been for that secret feeling of mistrust.

"Forgive me," she said, truly abashed. "I don't know what's wrong with me."

"Very well. We can postpone the psychological discussion of your case. When you've come to a decision, send me word, and I'll tell you if the bedroom is still free. While waiting, I'd be grateful if you'd allow me to work a little more. . . ."

He had taken up his brushes. He felt better. Now he could see what was needed: it was that dressing-gown that ruined everything. Without protest she had resumed the pose.

"I say, throw off that dressing-gown, will you. That red and yellow, it's frightful. And please do me the kindness of buying another one in blue . . . or green. For the time being, pose like that."

Submissively, she cast off the dressing-gown. Her face was calm. Her body appeared, as steadfast and reassuring as a rock.

In imagination, Martine drew them around her once more, a family circle, a bulwark of people. Now she no longer had to invent motives and witnesses. There they were, real living people with identities and professions, a part of that crowd whose opinion she had dreaded. First of all there was Madame Prêtre, then Sylvia. They certainly had no reason to lie to her. She had not imagined the stupefied expression on Madame Prêtre's face, nor the oily amiability that had followed. She had not imagined the tears in Sylvia's eyes as she said, "Oh, how lovely it is, Martine, how happy you should be!" True, Madame Prêtre did not like Louise, and true Sylvia shed tears every day over things she read in the evening papers. . . .

But then, there was Germaine Lethuit, a superior person, who devoted herself entirely to others, to her father and the sister who had been unhappily married, and to the disinherited of the earth. Her devotion was incontestable, unassuming and indicated a forthright mind. Well, it was not towards Stéphane that Germaine had gone but towards Martine herself. "My dear girl," she had said, "how congenial I find that atmosphere. . . . The part you have played, your devotion, and his, to an idea. . . . Evidently, your moral scruples are not entirely mine, for I would not have blamed you if you had decided to live together without benefit of clergy; for my own part, I have always preferred not to marry, but instead to remain faithful to those who need me. But at one point all doctrines meet, don't they?" Germaine's kiss had been sincere, the warm handclasp she had given Stéphane, and her words, too, had all been sincere. "All doctrines meet," she had said, and with that had returned to Meudon. No, Germaine Lethuit had not lied.

What about Gérard Ducas? A highly educated man, who was not an old maid, who had no taste for exercising authority, had made no sacrifice that needed to be justified. Martine recalled his fine-featured but rather characterless face, with its expression of sincere emotion. "Stéphane, my good friend, I am profoundly moved. . . . It is infinitely touching. It's . . . isn't it, Jean?" She could hear him again: that emotion had been sincere, and so had Jean Cadou's cordiality. "Amazing, that stuff," he had said. And they had gone upstairs together, followed by goodnight wishes. No, they were blameless.

And Dr. Fisher? A mature, courageous man, a man who had suffered. He would certainly not consent to do mere lip-service, he who had lost all for an idea.

Or Socrates? A simple man, incapable of . . .

No need to go on. This was not the sort of reassurance she wanted. Had there been a hundred people, she would have felt the same anxiety, the same deception. What had caused her present feeling was the haste, yes, the haste with which they had all exclaimed, congratulated, and then gone away. . . . They had fled from her, literally fled from her and her questions and misgivings. "You know how splendid we think it is!" they had seemed to say; "You know we're all agreed on it!" And Stéphane himself had hurried away, satisfied and relieved, as she had seen by his smile.

Would everyone, then, except Martine herself, feel eternally satisfied and relieved? Was there a conspiracy against her? They had eluded her, but not Stéphane. Yet they had heard what Stéphane read, had congratulated him on that journal in which she constantly figured. They might have . . . they might have . . . She wept with rage, her head buried in her pillow. To think that she had imagined she was going to enjoy a triumph! "Why, naturally, we always knew," that was their attitude. And Stéphane, how she hated him today for approving, accepting. . . . She had expected a lightning flash of revelation, and nothing had happened, nothing was changed. She had been wrong to insist upon that reading. She might have guessed that it would change nothing either for them or for her. "This is what I'm really like," she had wanted to tell them, "you've never really seen me, now look at me!" And they, with disgusting complacency, had replied, "Why, of course, we've always known," and had even refused to look at her.

No, she was wrong. She would start over again: there had been Madame Prêtre, Sylvia. . . .

The rain was falling outside, with an exasperating gentleness.

The bar smelt of wet dog.

"Drink it up, drink it up, my lad," said Socrates benevolently, but his benevolence was wearing a little thin. A beggar, down on his luck, was drinking hot coffee in very little sips; he had played that game for the past few weeks. When he had finished, he would tilt the glass and lap up the last drop; then he would sit there quietly waiting. Intolerable! Finally, when he was quite sure this was not to be the day when Socrates would keep his promise, he would slowly stand up and, dragging his feet, as slowly go out, and Socrates would see him turn back to cast a last look at him through the window. Then Socrates would feel ashamed, as the beggar intended him to. By next week, Socrates resolved, he would have bought the coat he had promised to give the poor devil. But this was the fourth week since that Monday when he had rapturously promised to give him a coat, and each week he had postponed the project. Having exhausted the pleasure of giving before actually doing so, he did not now want to go through with it. But the beggar had no idea of this, and firmly believed in Socrates' wealth.

Now he coughed raucously. It was a tearing, whistling, gasping cough, a veritable model of a cough. "Just see how much I need a warm coat," that cough said. Socrates was enraged.

"The weather's mild," he said aloud. That was his reply to the cough.

"Oh, but winter's almost here!" said the beggar.

"We have a lot of mild days ahead of us," said Socrates stubbornly.

The beggar said nothing, for he had a feeling that the Greek would seize the least argument as an excuse to throw him out, and he was determined not to be thrown out until he had that coat. He stretched out his legs towards a fleeting ray of sunshine. His shoes were far too big, his feet were innocent of socks. From time to time he trembled slightly, like an old animal about to die. Socrates averted his eyes, so as not to see this discreet complaint. But despite himself he kept looking at those ankles, doubtfully clean, goose-pimply with the cold, and his anger grew. The beggar was staying on there solely to flout him, to irritate him. But what could Socrates do, how *could* he give the beggar a coat? There was only five thousand francs in the till. Humiliation washed over him. Five thousand francs. He who had been born with a silver spoon in his mouth! He who had been a part of the Gilded Youth of Athens! He who had counted at his table dozens of parasites whose names he didn't even know! Thinking on his ruin, sometimes he saw himself as the victim, sometimes as the cause, but no matter which, he never escaped its consequences. He could not even command the respect of a miserable beggar nowadays. And since he had never, for his own part, respected anything but wealth, he quite approved of the beggar's attitude. But that man must stop staring at him, he must stop coughing and shivering.

"I'm going out," said Socrates, without much conviction. "I've a call to make."

"I can take care of the café for you," said the beggar sweetly.

So, he wouldn't go away! Socrates decided to make a supreme sacrifice.

"What about a sandwich?" he suggested, almost obsequiously.

There was only one sandwich left, and if a customer appeared . . . But that beggar had to go away and to go away satisfied.

"No, thank you," said the beggar, "I don't feel any too well."

Socrates almost broke down and wept from sheer exasperation. The refusal of the sandwich was a serious matter. It indicated that the beggar counted on staying there, if need be, until evening. God! How he cursed the moment when he had promised . . . when he had said, "My poor fellow, you must be cold, come next Monday and I'll give you a good coat, I have more coats than I know what to do with, I've already given away more than half the coats I owned. Oh, you should have seen me when I lived in Greece. I had forty suits, and so many pairs of boots that when I'd worn them three times I gave them away. I was always saying, 'Here, chum, take these boots, take this suit, take, take!' Sometimes, when I went for a stroll on Constitution Square, as many as ten men would be hanging round me. And it was 'Socrates, how about offering me a glass of coffee!' or 'Socrates, buy my sponges, it'll bring you good luck.' And I paid and I bought, and all those fellows wore boots I'd given them."

Socrates had ended up by believing all this himself. He had been King of Athens. And today he did not have one single coat to give away. And this lousy beggar, scratching himself in the sun, was going to judge him, Socrates! The peace he bought so dearly from Constantine and Dimitrios, the consideration and respect he begged from others and did not have for himself, all this was falling apart with every second that passed, with every second ticked off loudly by the big wall-clock, all this was wearing thin, powdering into dust under the increasingly anxious gaze of the beggar, the accusing look in those rheumy and inquisitorial eyes. . . . No, it was impossible! Socrates felt he could not go on enduring this torture until evening. He could not confess the truth, could not destroy the intricate structure of lies that was his life.

He poured out a glass of wine and drained it at a gulp. The seconds were hurtling past, the beggar continued to stare at him. No, no confession, not that! Socrates staggered to his feet, struck by a sudden idea. Monsieur Ducas. That gentleman never bolted the door of his room. Socrates' key would suffice. Monsieur Ducas had two topcoats. He would think that a burglar had broken in. . . . The beggar would not come again, he would forbid him to return. The seconds being ticked off were now a deafening roar in his ears. Socrates stretched out his hand, hesitated another instant. The beggar's eyes followed him, filled now with hope. Yes, certainly, he believed that Socrates was going to his own room to select one of his forty suits. . . . If the beggar had seen the little closet where three shirts hung alongside the one and only gabardine suit Socrates owned and which he had no idea of giving away, why, the man would have believed that robbers had cleaned out the Greek. The street was crowded with people, the stairs were deserted. By slightly forcing the lock . . .

Already, with the intensity of a drugged person waiting for the dope to take effect, Socrates was imagining the beggar's thanks, his confusion (imagine having thought that Socrates could be close-fisted about a coat!), his stammered apologies, which would restore that lost sovereignty. . . . Already the key was in his hand. He took a step towards the rear of the little room, then another step. He felt the beggar's gaze upon his back like a weight—then all at once, oblivious of everything, Socrates darted into the stairway and climbed to the third floor where he was soon standing in the narrow corridor, trying with shaking hand to find the keyhole. Suddenly he had pulled, pushed, had entered, run to the wardrobe, opened it. It was empty. Empty! In a flash he recalled having seen Ducas that very morning carrying something over his arm as he went out. Certainly it was his coat that he was taking to the cleaner's.

Still with a wild look in his eyes, Socrates opened and shut the drawers of the chest. But the antiquary was an orderly man. If the the coat was not in the closet, it was at the cleaner's. Socrates remained there motionless for a long moment.

He was in possession of all his faculties as he went downstairs again, slowly and heavily, and re-entered the bar. The beggar, with the subtlety of the abject at once saw that something was wrong. He gave a despairing yet disdainful look at Socrates' empty hands. Then he stood up and went out, without even bothering to cough. Socrates collapsed on a bar-stool. It was all over. Never again would he be, in the eyes of that beggar, a wealthy man. A tear slid down his cheek.

The rain was falling again with exasperating gentleness.

"May I have a hot grog, Socrates?" Martine demanded.

He served her in silence. She, too, said nothing for a long while. And yet there seemed to be some kind of understanding between them, which became so obvious that after a moment he felt obliged to raise his eyes.

"Well?" he said brusquely. "What's wrong?"

Her anxiety must have been obvious if even Socrates, usually so self-absorbed, saw it and reacted to it. Her hope was restored.

"Nothing," she said, however, to reassure him. "I was only wondering . . ."

She sought in her mind for a way to touch him, to surprise him before he could arm himself with his usual insulting courtesy, before he could assume his usual smiling task. She thought him stupid and credulous, and chose her method accordingly.

"I say, Socrates, tell me about your young days in Athens. I love to travel, and perhaps sometime I may go to Greece."

But for the moment Socrates was broken and crushed by the final arrogant look the beggar had given him.

"Oh, you know, Greece . . . when you're there . . . You hear so much about Greece, but it's just words, words. . . ." (Oh, he'd not have said that in the time of the plush chairs, the well-lit restaurant through which he walked as master, the kitchens where the pale carcasses of dressed fowls were heaped on the marble. . . .) "People talk, talk. And when we meet with misfortune, Mademoiselle, we see that all this talk amounts to nothing. It's worthless!"

Worthless, that pride in his country, in his origin; worthless, that pleasure of being a man, of walking across the sunny square, well-dressed, freshly shaven; worthless, that easy sympathy for all those who depended upon him; worthless, Socrates himself, who no longer inspired respect in even a humble beggar. . . .

"Worthless, Socrates? Oh yes, of course, all that literature. . . ." Furtively she brought the subject round to what she wanted. He couldn't escape her. She'd soon find out. . . . "But don't you think all the things people say . . . and write . . . For instance, that reading from the journal. Tell me what you thought of Monsieur Morani's reading the other night?"

She was surprised at the vivacity with which he turned towards her. Perhaps she should have waited, have been more circumspect? But she was too impatient.

"What do you mean by that, Mademoiselle? I don't quite understand. Why, I—I thought it was very nice, as everybody else did!"

"Yes," she insisted, losing all sense of modesty, "but 'very nice' doesn't mean anything. I want your honest personal opinion."

"It was very nice," he said slowly, his face turned away from her again, and speaking as if with great intentness, "it was very nice, very well said, well turned. There: that's all I think about it. I don't see what more you want me to say. You're like Madame Prêtre!"

"Has Madame Prêtre talked to you about it?"

"People always talk too much," he said gloomily.

"But what, exactly, did she say?"

In her exasperation she had seized him by the sleeve, trying to force him to look at her, while he continued to avoid her eyes.

"Well, she said the same, Mademoiselle Martine, that it was well said, all that. . . . Will you please let go of me? Let go!"

But she clung to his sleeve, staring into that bland face to which she had never paid much attention before, and beneath her gaze it seemed to her that the poor fellow's mask was falling apart, that she could see through all those artless boastings they had laughed

at so many times, as they had laughed at the calendar girl with her
nenuphars and the gilded god; today she was at last seeing something
else, more troubling, almost terrifying. Was it a sign? Was she
going to break down that barrier which as she had imagined it the
other day, separated her from the truth?

"Didn't you wonder why he read all that to you, and why he
wrote it?"

Was it fear that she read on his face? If this thing—vaguely and
obscurely sensed, like an object one touched in the dark without
being able to imagine its exact form—if this sign on his face, which
she thought she read, with sudden clairvoyance, were not there;
if it were not a kind of fear she was tracking down in him, but
instead only the annoyance and uneasiness caused by the expression
of a sentiment you do not share and cannot imagine having; if all
this were nothing but a wobbly edifice fabricated by her imagination, then did her question have any meaning?

Socrates remained mute. Why does she ask why? he wondered,
foggily. What does she want exactly? Before, he would have
demanded an explanation, asked her straight out. But now he was a
broken man. Obsessed by the memory of the beggar, he felt limp
and helpless. She had said "Why?" The question, to his mind,
applied to everything. *Why* had he known this distress? Was it
really he, Socrates, who had climbed the stairs in haste, had
shaken the antiquary's door, looked for a coat in order to steal
it? Why? Why?

"For heaven's sake, answer me!" she shouted, beside herself.
"Answer! What Morani read the other night didn't mean a thing,
did it? There was nothing in it but words, words, words, meant to
hide . . . to hide . . . "

The beggar had vanished and would not return. Gérard Ducas's
door was shut again, he would not notice anything. It was not
Socrates who, overwhelmed by an insane terror, had climbed the
stairs. That had been someone totally different, a being created by
the desperate need he had so unwisely fostered, by the pitiful vanity
which, gradually devouring him, had become a kind of second self,
an outsider impelling him to act, to such an extent that what

remained of his real self could only despairingly observe the incomprehensible metamorphosis. . . . No, the beggar had not existed. Only Socrates existed, standing there now in the bar, with but one desire, which was not to be pestered with questions. . . . By a supreme effort of will, he managed to thrust aside his terror and to resume his personality, to reintegrate, to some extent, the body that had acted at the behest of something other than his own will.

"I think you need a rest, Mademoiselle Martine," he said with sudden calm. "You ought to go to your room and lie down. This autumn weather is treacherous. You must be sickening for something."

"You really think so, Socrates?"

She went on asking questions, went on sitting there on a bar stool, looking fixedly at him with imploring eyes, as the beggar had done. For a second, with a flash of intuition that was too fleeting to be called a thought, he felt she too was being driven at that moment by some "thing" outside her will-power, as he had been on the stairs. But it was only a lightning sensation, like a stab of pain against which one presses the hand after it has vanished, a kind of sudden fellow-feeling immediately denied . . . already denied. He smiled at her, with less difficulty than before, and his face was that of the everyday Socrates, with the exaggeratedly dark brows and eyes, the too strongly marked features.

"I assure you, there's some kind of sickness going round. I've served at least twenty hot grogs today. Let's hope it's not that Asian 'flu they're talking so much about. I believe . . ."

She had gone out, her shoulders bowed.

"I must be mad, or sickening for something. Yesterday at the store I was in a draught. I'm cold, I'm shivering. It must be the 'flu or something. I ought to take a sedative. . . ." But instead of obeying her thoughts, she stopped outside the antiquary's door and knocked. There was no reply. She took another step and knocked at Jean's door, without reason or thought except the need to see a door open.

"Do you happen to have some antihistamine?" she asked when the door finally opened. "I'm feeling so bad that I can't face going out again——"

Jean was wearing a kind of overall splattered with paint and he seemed to be in a satisfied mood.

"I have some 'maxiton', but . . . Come in, come in. Look, I've just been working on my last thing . . . it belongs to my 'green period', as our friend Gérard says. He's not come back yet, a pity, for he would certainly have some antihistamine, some anti-what-ever-you-like. He believes in taking care of himself! But Morani must have some, too. Oh, they're absolutely alike, those two old boys. Gérard's out, arranging things for my exhibition."

"May I sit down a minute?" she asked.

"To be sure. Sit down. Why, poor Martine! You're as pale as a ghost, you're as green as my painting! I'll give you a slug of rum, that'll put you to rights."

"But, I'm not used to drinking," she vainly demurred, for he had already brought a bottle and a dubiously clean glass.

"Nonsense, drink it up, that'll kill the microbes."

He poured out a stiff tot which she tossed off at once. If that didn't cure her, and the hot grog inside her as well, it was decidedly not the 'flu. He surveyed her, amused.

"Is this the first time you've ever drunk rum? What a face you're making. Believe me, that's better medicine than your antihistamine."

"You think so?" she asked. Already her head was swimming. But she did feel much, much better, and she said with somewhat exaggerated fervour, "Jean, you're really a wonderful person!"

"Oh, take it easy," he said with a laugh. "Don't be unfaithful to old Stéphane, eh? I hope you didn't burst in here to seduce me!"

She laughed uproariously, without being shocked at his coarse-ness. "Oh, that's an idea that would never occur to me! It would be too—too hopeless." The idea struck her as very funny, and she was surprised when Jean Cadou did not laugh.

"What do you mean, hopeless?" he snorted. "If you're alluding to your type of femininity, you're devilishly right. But if you're daring to imply . . ."

She could never have imagined finding herself in Jean Cadou's room squabbling with him! But now she had the 'flu, she repeated to herself, as if that made the thing reasonable. "Oh come, Jean,"—

she had never before called him by his first name—"supposing we talk frankly, for once."

"What do you mean by frankly?" he stammered, put out of countenance.

She wanted to see him, too, as she had had the impression of *seeing* Socrates. And all at once—it may have been the effect of the alcohol—she felt it would be easy.

"Why, yes. Suppose we tell each other some home truths? No more politeness, like the other night. When he read that journal, you didn't believe in it, did you? It was the same thing as with that nice old Gérard, your boy friend. . . ." She roared with laughter. Everything was so funny tonight. And if she hadn't spoken the truth, why did Jean, red with fury, try to convince her she was wrong?

"I don't know what stops me," he growled. "You're drunk, otherwise it's incredible. Listen, Martine: Gérard and I are good friends, nothing more. Friends. Do you understand?"

Yes, why did he tie himself in knots to convince that ugly girl sitting there on that chair, laughing, her whole face lighted up with a kind of ridiculous gloating expression?

"Friends," she said, still with the same laughter on her ghastly pale face, "oh yes, just friends."

"He admires my painting, and that's why . . ."

"Oh of course, of course," she said, with a burst of laughter that bordered on hysteria. "They're all good excuses. Words, words. Always the same thing. It's just like the journal. Everyone's the same."

"Get the hell out of here," said Jean, his eyes flashing, as he grabbed her by the shoulders, "and quick!"

They all said the same thing, even Stéphane. She was a nuisance, she disturbed them. But Jean was frank, at any rate.

"You're frank, at least," she said, still laughing, as he shoved her towards the door. "You're outspoken, aren't you?"

And she had also seen *him*, him too, seen his naked face convulsed with anger and fear. So much for their complaisant smiles. They were all afraid, all of them. That was why they drove her out: she upset them. This idea which had distressed her a few hours before now enchanted her and, outside the shut door, she went on laughing, sitting on one of the steps, incapable of getting up. She laughed and laughed, hearing her own laughter spiral up the stairway, knocking at every door, defying everyone. Let them answer her, at least! Stéphane must have come home, surely he could hear her. And Louise, the calm Louise! And Madame Prêtre downstairs, and Sylvia, on her pink bed, surely they could hear her. And was the antiquary never coming home? And Socrates, sheltered behind his chromium bar, did he not hear her? And Dr. Fisher, so dignified with his white hair, would he not come out and say, "What's going on? Does someone need me?" She laughed and laughed, unable to stop. Why didn't one of the doors open? Would no one wonder what was wrong, and come to ask her?

But the doors remained shut, the dusty stairway remained empty, and it was only much later, when silence was restored, when already, sitting there on the frayed carpeting, her head in her hands, she had stopped laughing for centuries, that the fair-haired young man, Germaine Lethuit's tenant, came downstairs and tactfully pretended not to see her.

The continuing rain filled the Brasserie Dorée with an unusual crowd of people who were all sniffling and blowing and calling for hot grogs. "One hot grog!" rang out time and again. And Bruno had stage-fright because, overcoming his prejudices, he had decided (with the manager's permission) to sing the comic Panama-postman song, *Le Facteur de Panama*, in its entirety. Toni, the waitress was in the best of spirits. "Would you like a hot grog, too, Monsieur Stéphane? I've served thirty-three in the last two hours! Nice and hot, with sugar?"

"They certainly take good care of you," muttered Marcel. "What about me? Don't I get anything?" He was worried, his wife was having a baby, it might be born any minute now.

"I'll see to you later," laughed Toni.

But it was only a pretext; everyone knew she had a weakness for Stéphane.

It was pleasant in the restaurant, among this unaccustomed rush of orders, with the trio doing its best to accelerate the usual lackadaisical rhythm, taking some liberties that the stout, pale-faced manager approved with a nod of his majestic head as he stood at the end of the room. Toni and the two afternoon waiters were also feeling the heartening effects of numerous tips, and called out their orders in louder voices: "Two bock beers, one hot grog, make it two hot grogs!" On the wall where the photograph of Gloria Grétry had hung, was now the picture of a beaming Breton tenor, another young hopeful, who sang "the repertoire of Frank Sinatra", announcing his songs in a jolly way that quite won over his audience.

"Well," whispered Stéphane, "are you going to sing it?"

And Marcel, still on the look out for a summons to the telephone, said, "Come on, let's have *Le Facteur de Panama!*"

With a swagger, Bruno approached the microphone, cast a bewildered glance over the room, rolled his big eyes. There was a ripple of laughter. He who so yearned to charm and to move, aroused laughter. He began:

> *C'est le facteur, c'est le facteur de Panama*
> *Qui sait danser, qui sait danser le cha-cha-cha . . .*

His singing was banal, without spirit or dash, despite the laughter that burst out here and there, despite the murmured words of encouragement from Marcel and Stéphane. Toni stopped to stare at him above her tray, bubbling with laughter. "Couldn't you just die laughing at him?" she muttered to Stéphane as she passed by the piano.

"And to think the poor fellow fancies himself as a second André Claveau. . . . Let's jazz it up, boys, let's play a joke on him. . . ." Stéphane was in fine fettle, ready to laugh at anything, and the piteous expression on poor Bruno's face, as he waggled his hips in a cha-cha-cha, to the delight of the crowd, tickled him greatly. "Marcel! Psst! Marcel!" He signalled to Marcel to pick up the beat, and Marcel agreed with a nod. They quickened the tempo.

Qui sait danser le cha-cha-cha . . .

Bruno showed signs of distress. Marcel, for a moment distracted from his worries, stifled a laugh behind his guitar. Stéphane, who was having a wonderful time, hurried the rhythm still more, transforming the cha-cha-cha into a frenzied dance, with Bruno unable to keep up with the tempo, to the great delight of the audience who thought the effect was intentional.

Qui sait danser, qui sait danser . . .

"He's priceless!" whispered Toni, determined not to leave her observation post.

Thunderous laughter greeted the end of the song, and Bruno stepped back, out of breath and furious.

"You two bastards. . . ."

But the manager was making his way to them through the crowd. "That's not at all bad," he said. "You ought to work up a repertoire of that sort of thing. Then maybe, some evening or other . . ."

"Evening?" Bruno flushed with pleasure.

"Why yes, who knows? Of course, you must try it out in the afternoons, to begin with. But if it works . . . Oh, I forgot, Marcel! I didn't want to interrupt. Marcel, you have a baby daughter. They telephoned."

"You might have told me straight away!" the guitarist said, indignantly. Then, "A baby girl . . . I wanted a boy. . . . Is my wife all right?"

"I imagine so," said the manager with a vague shrug. "Get on with the music. . . . Oh, Morani, before you begin again, I want to ask you something. Is it your wife who's in this number of *Paris-Monde*? If it is, here, take this number, I'd be much obliged if you'd get her to sign it for me. My granddaughter collects autographs. And if Madame Morani could get the painter to sign it too, that would be fine. Go on, gentlemen, go on with the music."

He withdrew, still ghastly pale and fat and sad, but conscientiously giving Toni a pinch as he passed her.

"The usual selection from *The White Horse Inn*," said Stéphane. "Better not risk giving anything new to our beloved public. And congratulations, Marcel!"

"Congratulations . . . for a girl baby."

"Oh yes," said Bruno, who had recovered his optimism, "a baby girl's much nicer. What are you going to call her?"

Stéphane put aside the illustrated *Paris-Monde*, and leafed through the music.

"Marcelle," said the guitarist, blushing. "What's in *Paris-Monde* about your wife, Stéphane?"

Stéphane held it out to him.

Marcel whistled. "I say, she's not bad! But, no offence intended, the painting is pretty rotten. And it says here that it's in a museum, what about that!"

Bruno approached. "Let me have a look. Say, she's an eyeful there. She must have been a beaut at that age, eh?"

"A real beauty," said Stéphane sincerely. "And with a look in her eyes. . . . You'd have thought . . . "

"The bosom especially," said Marcel more prosaically. "But she's not bad now, considering her age. The proof is that the painter fellow is doing another portrait of her. And in the altogether. Oh, I'm sorry!"

Stéphane gave a melancholy shrug. "If I'm obliged to let my wife pose, you can be sure I expect such comments, my dear Marcel. I know you don't mean to be spiteful, so it doesn't matter. And I would certainly not have authorized my wife to pose in that . . . rather daring way, except for a painter as eminent as he is, world-known. . . . "

"Oh yes?" said Marcel, with a doubtful grimace.

Once more they attacked the selection from *The White Horse Inn*.

Martine was not waiting for him, when Stéphane left the restaurant, but he was not unduly disturbed by this departure from routine. He was still laughing to himself over poor Bruno, over some of Marcel's remarks as they had tossed off a couple of drinks in celebration of the newborn baby, at Marcel's expense the first round, and Stéphane's the second—such an expense was unimportant now that Louise was posing and bringing home extra money. They had laughed and joked in the midst of floods of *czardas* poured out by the new "regional orchestra", they had drunk to the health of the baby Marcelle, to the health of *Le Facteur de Panama*, and to "the portrait of Lou"—he had felt it out of place to object to this, on seeing their eagerness to drink the toast. In the doorway of the restaurant he hesitated a moment at sight of the rain still coming down. But the weather was mild enough, so he turned up his coat collar and plunged into the crowd. It was raining too hard to loiter. He would not go round by the vegetarian restaurant to see if Martine was there. Nor would he climb the stairs to her room; despite his good humour, his legs felt heavy, and there was a slight roaring in his ears. He had no desire to have an argument with Martine over some God-awful foggy notions of hers. The very thought that she might be waiting for him somewhere disturbed his peace of mind, and reduced his good humour. Really, some people did not know how to live, he reflected with serene pity, and she was one of them. He had done everything for her, and she still managed to be dissatisfied. "Poor Martine!" He was still thinking of her as he mounted the stairs and it spoiled the pleasure of his return to the flat, which seemed brand new with its freshly painted walls.

He opened the door, hoping that Martine was not listening for this small sound to bring her down from her room. Louise's presence almost gave him pleasure. She was walking about with a saucepan in her hand, half-dressed, as was her custom. For years he had reproached her for her lack of modesty and orderliness. Oh well! Tonight he was inclined to be indulgent.

"Well, my dear! Is it you or what's in the pan, or both of you, that smells so good?"

"The Chanel scent, that's the saucepan; the onion smell, that's me," she laughed. "I'm hurrying, for I'm having my dinner in town tonight."

"Hurry up then. But you'd go faster if you didn't try. . . ."

"To do everything at the same time, I know. You're a fine one to complain, I'm cooking your dinner. Mushrooms *à la grecque*, ravioli, potatoes with onions. . . . And I've bought you a good bottle of wine."

"That's nice of you."

He carefully shook his shabby old topcoat before hanging it up in the tiny entrance-way, where they bumped into each other.

"What weather! Oh, I must tell you some news, my cellist-guitarist, if I may call him that, has a baby daughter."

He liked to refer to Bruno and Marcel like that, with the possessive pronoun, and Louise sometimes referred to the instrumentalists as "his", but derisively. Tonight, however, she did not laugh, but stood there in her petticoat, the saucepan in her hand, undecided.

"What will the baby be called?"

"Marcelle."

He went into the bedroom, leaving the door open. If Martine passed by in the hall, she would hear the sound of conversation and would not come in. No, he had no desire for argument this evening. At least, Louise's talk did not tire him. It was about mushrooms, about wine; nothing more intellectual than that. She did her best. . . . He lay down on the bed, too tired to take off his shoes. Later, later. . . . An appetising odour came from the kitchen, but it was too much to think of getting up and going in there to eat, it was too fatiguing to think of taking one more step or making one more effort.

Louise came to look at him from the doorway.

"Not feeling too well?"

"None too well."

"It's this humidity. Tomorrow morning I'm going to buy you a new topcoat. That one's had its day. And you need a new sweater and a new pair of socks. . . ."

"Easy, easy. But I forget, you're a celebrity now. I say, while I think of it, you'll find three numbers of *Paris-Monde* in my coat pocket, you're asked to sign them! And if you can make the great painter sign them, too . . . But these won't be the last ones, I warn you."

"How silly!" she exclaimed, as if a little embarrassed. "Now, Stéphane, I'm going to take off your boots."

She drew near the bed. She must have bought herself some new underwear, too, for he now noticed that her petticoat was not the kind she usually wore, and he did not need to be an expert to see that it must have cost quite a lot. She bent down. He reproached himself for feeling a little excited by her. Already, the other night before going downstairs, he had had the same sensation. Sedately, she untied the laces, pulled off one boot, then the other. Was she also a little stirred, he wondered? If there had been one thing he was sure of, in the old days, it was the physical ascendancy he had over her.

"Are you in a great hurry?" he asked.

"Oh, I still have time," she said, straightening herself. She did not look at him. She was subtle enough to feel the presence of his nascent desire, and simple enough to be moved by it.

"Sit down beside me for a little. It's been such a long time since we've had a good talk, Louise."

She had liked his voice in the old days, liked it instinctively, sensually. She had listened to him talk as if enchanted, without hearing what he said. He knew that power of his. She sat down on the bed.

"I think that not talking to each other is the cause of a great deal of unhappiness in marriage," he said, "much more than the inevitable rows and real differences of opinion. Married couples stop talking to each other. And in our case fate obliges us to do work with no glamour attached to it. Why don't you lie down beside me for a little while?"

She hesitated.

"Why don't you lie down beside me for a little while?"

Many years ago he had said those same words in that same warm voice whose power he knew so well. And she had burst into tears, had said, "No, no, no! I hate you!"

Poor Lou, she was crying. He was terribly upset. This was the first time he had ever seen her cry.

"My dearest, you misunderstood . . . do believe me."

It was his fault. He should not have taken Louise to meet his little circle of friends. Upon coming to Paris, he had found that it was easy to make friends, that was what was wonderful about Paris. But they were all so likeable, those young people he had met in the corridors of the broadcasting studio, where he had landed a small job. There were two young actresses who were absolute dears, there was Pierre, a music student at the Conservatory, who set himself up as a Communist and sang revolutionary songs of his own composition, and there was a young sound-engineer. What more natural than to want them to meet his young wife, Louise?

Their group had got into the habit of meeting in a little café, where they talked about their vague broadcasting projects—indeed, they had carried out one of them, "Voices from the Clouds". He had urged her to go with him: "It's very important for my future, Louise. Just fancy! I may make a career in radio broadcasting! Besides, they're absolutely remarkable people, yet very simple and charming. . . ." To them, he had told certain things in confidence, had forewarned them of the situation, to avoid conversation that would be over her head and also, perhaps, because of that desperate need he had for approbation and friendship.

"If you love her she's one of us, Stéphane," Jeanne, one of the actresses had said, in a rather supercilious way. (Jeanne, a flat-chested but rather pretty little blonde, was from the North, and she pronounced his name in a kind of whinny, flattening the "a". She aspired to have a stage career without compromising herself.)

"Why do we need an excuse to include her in our circle?" Pierre had exclaimed fervently. "Jeanne, you're behaving like a typical reactionary. You're prepared to accept a proletarian, a victim of society, yes, but solely because she happens to have married one of your friends. For my part, even if she was once a tart . . ."

"Pierre!" the young actress had exclaimed, blushing. "Stéphane, forgive him, he doesn't realize what he's saying."

"But I'm not offended by what he's said, Jeanne! Yes, my poor Louise has known every temptation, every humiliation. I don't hide the fact from my self. And I may say, it was for that very reason, Jeanne, that I fell in love with her. I'm expecting trouble in the future, I'll be put to the test many times, and I may not even succeed in the end. But my life will not have been lived in vain if . . ."

"That's all very well," interrupted Pierre, to Stéphane's obvious annoyance, for he hated to be interrupted—"but of what importance is one woman when what's needed is to reform the very structure of society?"

"Stéphane didn't marry the entire social order," said Jeanne drily.

"I'll bet she's jolly pretty," muttered the other young actress, a tall brunette who was still rather self-conscious about her opulent bosom.

The sound-engineer said nothing; he rarely spoke.

"Oh come, Catherine, don't be silly," said Jeanne, as she always did. And she added, regally, "It's quite all right, bring her along whenever you like. We'll try to tame your savage Louise."

"I don't like to hear you talk like that," said Stéphane.

He was not quite sure whether to be annoyed or secretly flattered by her lack of feeling, for he knew she was in love with him. But she did not attract him, with her thin and frail little body, her fair hair, her fine straight nose; she had a certain distinction that Stéphane approved on principle, but the appearance of Lou in his life, radiant and impetuous, had immediately moved him, whereas Jeanne only inspired a kind of bored respect. Lou! Whenever he suddenly thought of her, no matter where he was, in a café, or during auditions as he accompanied a singer, or during rehearsals, his heart was torn with desire and tenderness. What a need he then felt to be with her again quickly, to assure himself that she was still there, still belonged to him, that she had not deceived him, that she was not unhappy because of the poor way they lived, so different from the hopes she had entertained when they left Signac for Paris. But no, there she was, innocent, neither sad nor guilty, smiling with as much assurance as ever, and with so much pride that he was both humiliated and dazzled. And while he was still worrying over looking like a provincial, or getting lost in the metro, still suffering over the protective way people had of saying to him, "Oh yes, you've just arrived from Signac", she already knew everything, knew the local tradesmen, the number of the autobus they should take to go to the rue Francois-Premier, knew the names of his employers. He maintained his superiority over her only in the realm of culture, and was always advising her to read this or that book, visit this or that museum, spying upon her reactions. "You ought to . . ." And she, full of good intentions, obeyed him, sure that she had only to enter a museum to see, and had only to read a book to understand. And she would say to him: "Oh, I saw that, I like it," or "Oh, no, Manet, I don't like him."

She was different from him, for he was always afraid of making a mistake. And so he tried to reassure her, console her, and, incidentally, to reassure himself. "You're wrong, Louise. When your eyes have become educated, you'll understand Manet. And you didn't do anything else?"

No, she had done nothing else, and she did not like Manet. She liked red. She liked Rubens. And she remained faithful to Stéphane. She was intact. She was as impervious, as solid as a rock. It almost irritated him to see how simply she existed, for he himself was always wondering what he ought to think, and what other people thought. Manet, for instance: he did not like Manet either. Looking at a Manet, that moment of dazzling illumination never came. He was in despair over this. Yet Manet's paintings were beautiful. He did not argue with the world's judgement. Fundamentally, he was an unassuming man. And a little upset over the injustice done to him, doubting himself, and annoyed at doubting. She never doubted, but then she had no ideals. This, Stéphane reflected, was the terrible consequence of the life she had led. Her eyes were shut to the perils of life, and so she had false assurance, false happiness. He must dedicate his life to this task: *he would open her eyes, gently*.

"What I'd like," he said to Jeanne, "is to see her develop a taste for higher things, I would like to see her read, go to the galleries and museums. Often a cultural advance can bring about a moral one. And in any case it would prevent a possible relapse into her former ways."

"Oh, she wouldn't do that!" said Catherine, who was good-hearted and never understood anything, "why, she loves you."

"Alas, love is not always enough. In each one of us there is the primeval slime, my dear Catherine. Slime returns to slime, if the soul does not sustain it and raise it up."

"You've set yourself a very admirable task, no doubt, but I'm afraid it's beyond the strength of any man," said Jeanne, who had adopted Stéphane's vocabulary. "Don't think for a minute that I blame you: we ought to make an effort, all of us, to serve, even beyond our strength. I admire you, Stéphane. You are more courageous than we are. You are superior to us and our poor earthly wisdom."

She had dropped her hand on his arm, and was gazing at him with admiration in her cold blue eyes. Even Pierre, the Marxist, was affected; he read a great deal of Dostoievski, and books with titles such as *The Prostitute* or *The Anarchist-Assassin* entered into his personal pantheon. The sound-engineer asked flatly: "Is she a good-looker?" But no one ever listened to him.

What a wonderful thing friendship is! Stéphane had thought, forgetting that he had known these people only six months. And he had taken Lou to meet them.

He had to do justice to Jeanne: she had behaved very well, had offered them tea in her room—she lodged with an aunt. "We're delighted to know the wife of our beloved Stéphane, at last!" said she. And Catherine had thrown herself on Lou's neck. And Pierre had kissed her hand, perhaps rather ostentatiously: he was showing respect to this "victim of society" and was at the same time experiencing *Crime and Punishment* intensely. The sound-engineer, Archambault—they always called him by his family name—gave a misplaced whistle of admiration. But he was quelled by a glance from Jeanne and went no farther. And finally they had tied themselves in knots to create an understanding atmosphere around her. They had not smiled at her opinions on the Parisian museums, nor had they smiled at her accent which, unlike Stéphane, she had not managed to overcome.

Jeanne served tea a little early; conversation languished because of the tactful precautions they imposed upon themselves. Only Catherine seemed to be at ease; she actually gave Louise the address of a little dressmaker. Lou greatly admired the tea service, which Jeanne had inherited and Jeanne smiled affably.

"At the Hôtel de la Paix in Signac," said Lou, "they have a tea service like this, do you remember, Stéphane?"

Stéphane assented briefly. There was a chill in the air, but Louise was completely oblivious to it.

"Oh," she went on, "in weather like this, how I miss Signac! The trees must be all in flower there, now. You know, Stéphane, we really should go back for Easter."

"Perhaps, my dearest, perhaps," said Stéphane, with some embarrassment. "But that can wait!"

The hot-headed Pierre spoiled everything. "For my part," he exclaimed warmly, "I think your wife is right. You should go back to your miserable little town and brave public opinion. Let them see how happy you are! And people with really free and liberal minds will see . . ."

"Pierre, you're ridiculous," said Jeanne curtly. "You always think you're acting on a stage, at the beginning of a brilliant theatrical career. I think, on the contrary, that Stéphane and . . . Louise . . . acted very wisely in leaving Signac. It's no use exposing yourselves deliberately to the misunderstanding of narrow-minded people who, after all, are the backbone of society. In Paris . . . "

Innocently, Lou interrupted her. "What misunderstanding?" she asked in surprise. "Have you some reason for avoiding Signac, Stéphane?"

Stéphane reddened to the very ears. Jeanne gave a short laugh, quickly suppressed. Catherine didn't understand a word of this exchange, nor did the sound-engineer, who timidly echoed Lou's words: "Oh," he said, "have you some reason for avoiding Signac, Stéphane?"

Pierre jumped to his feet and frenziedly shook hands with Lou, who was tremendously surprised. "Bravo!" he said fervently. "Bravo! That's the way to see things! You are a character right out of Marx, conscious, aware, resolute, and without that frightful Christian guilt-complex."

"Guilt-complex?" said Lou, surprised beyond measure. "Why, what have I done to have a guilt-complex?"

These words fell into a total silence. It took her nearly a minute to understand, for she was not as stupid as Stéphane seemed to think.

"And so," she went on slowly, "all that fuss is beginning again? What have you been telling them?"

"Louise!" he implored.

Her temper flared up, all the more fiercely since she did not understand, could never manage to understand, the importance he attached to what he called her "past". As if that meant anything! And several times already, she had guessed, from the embarrassment of certain passing friends, that he must have talked to them in this strange way. . . .

"Stories you've made up, naturally!" she exclaimed. "As if my life is any business of theirs! As if it's of any interest to them! Of course it isn't, but Stéphane Morani is determined to tell them all about it. . . . He is so proud of it, just imagine! His wife wasn't a virgin! What a rare thing! And do you imagine these young ladies here are virgins?"

"Lou!"

The sound-engineer was laughing innocently. Louise, under the spell of her own fury, let it loose, as one frees an animal held captive for too long.

"And you exhibit me, like a curiosity! Why not put me in a circus? At least that would bring in more than the admiration of your little friends! Well now, look, they've had the show, and you can take up the collection!"

She had gone out and banged the door. He had mumbled something into the deathlike silence and then dashed out into the stairway after her. He had not had the courage to stay and meet Jeanne's eyes.

Louise had walked very fast down the street bordering the Luxembourg Gardens, without looking at him. Breathlessly he had followed her—he was often breathless.

"Louise, my dearest, I assure you . . ."

She had not listened to him, and she kept on muttering indignantly to herself. "This is really too much! This is really the limit!"

They arrived at their little hotel.

"Dearest, don't shout in the stairway, I implore you. . . ."

In their bedroom they had not spoken for a long while. She was too unfair—another fault of hers. After all, he had only wanted to avoid some uncomfortable moments. Then, he liked to talk about her. What was wrong with that? And, after all, he could not pretend. . . . He had wanted his friends to understand their wonderful romance, for to him it was a truly marvellous memory, that day when he had asked her to marry him and when she had seemed surprised. . . . But perhaps he had been wrong to tell his friends about such things. . . .

"Louise!" he pleaded, making an effort.

"What?" she said, in a voice so strange that he looked at her.

She was crying. For the first time she was crying in front of him. And also it was, no doubt, the first time she had cried since her infancy: she was not one to shed tears. Stéphane's heart was broken. He who, in the depths of himself, accused her of being insensitive! If only he could feel that she was as sensitive as he, how he could love her, and how much more freely!

"Dear heart, don't cry, I beg of you, you're hurting me, my love. . . ."

But she had already dried her tears, and was now merely sniffing prettily. "Well, what? Try to explain. You must admit that . . ."

No, he was mistaken. She was not, as he had feared and hoped, deeply wounded, she was not hurt, in any way he could understand. He could not console her, could not take her into his arms, could not confide to her, "I am like you." Why, then, had he married her? After all, though, she had cried. . . .

"Well, really, Steph, it was stupid, after all."

Stupid, he thought with rage. Stupid, like the questions he asked, stupid, like the precautions he saw fit to take with her, as if she were a sick child. . . . This was all nonsense, according to her. This was making a fuss over nothing. They loved each other, they were happy together, it would have been better for him to get on with his work. . . . But no, he did not want to live in peace, like the rest of the world. Then why had he married her?

"Why?" she asked. "Tell me why?"

He had no idea. He did not understand it himself. But did he at least love her, did she love him?

"Why don't you lie down here beside me for a while?" he had asked her in that warm voice whose power he knew so well.

"No, no, no!" she had said. "I hate you!"

He knew that she could not resist him for long, that for a moment they would both be able to forget. . . .

"Come. Come."

She approached the bed, still sulking. "All the same, admit, Stéphane, you have a strange disposition." She, too, had given up trying to explain her feelings. He had "a strange disposition" and that took care of everything for the moment.

"That's so, my dearest. Please forgive me."

He was already holding her in his arms. She asked for nothing more. They would know a moment of peace, but afterwards, lying there motionless, half asleep, they would be unaware of the bitterness slowly forming between them like a barrier, against which, three days later, they would once more crash.

"Why don't you lie down here beside me for a while?" he was again asking.

She hesitated. For she now knew that these things had no lasting power, that they were only moments of sombre peace in the midst of harassing days. But a moment of peace is, after all, good to have. . . . Henry was waiting for her, and again he would make those insane offers. Like the young woman of earlier years, she was in a quandary.

"Later," she murmured. "Later. I—I forgot, I left my iron heating. . . ."

And she bounded into the kitchen. "I'll bring your dinner to you on a tray, don't move!" she called.

She had a sudden furious need for activity. All these men! Still fuming, she ironed the olive-green dress that Henry had chosen for her.

Outside, it was still raining. But inside the Prisunic, beneath the glaring white lights, autumn flaunted itself with insulting virulence in the displays of purple underwear, the stacks of orange-coloured ashcans, the mounds of multicoloured sweets, multicoloured socks, multicoloured dustcloths. . . .

Martine had come to an end of her self-questioning and was ready for action. They'd asked for it. Since they'd obliged her to do so—and "they" applied to the sarcastic shop-assistants as well as to the smiling "Celestials", including the placid Louise and Stéphane himself—she was going to act. She was going to force them all to abandon that slippery smile and confess the truth. She would make Stéphane face up to himself. And even though the truth thus unveiled might prove to be unendurable, she would somehow endure it. She would endure anything rather than this conspiracy, in which, but for her pride which forbade such a thing, she might have played a part.

She had asked for the afternoon off. Now she no longer trembled or doubted. They should have what they wanted. She preferred public derision to this conniving approbation. Did they think she was so stupid, so voluntarily blinded? Oh, it now seemed to her that she had never had any hope. With disgust she cast off her naïve desire for a splendid climax, a crowning triumph. She had never wanted this—this affability, this too easy assent. What she had wanted (she no longer dared confess it to herself) was to be this other kind of being, for whom there would have been no need of affability or assent, who would have derived her joy from knowing what she was. Such a person she could never be. She would be Martine to the end, plain, perhaps ugly, frigid, introverted. She would be Martine to the end, and would never again try to be anything else.

She was, to outward appearances, calm as she left the Prisunic. And she was calm, too, as she stood waiting on the street corner for Louise to leave the house. She was ready to wait, without suffering, for an hour or two hours. But in less than a quarter of an hour, Louise left the house, as if in obedience to Martine's wishes.

It was raining, so Louise took a taxi. "To the Avenue Carnot," she said to the driver.

The taxi moved off. It was not the first in the line of taxi-cabs, but the third. Louise chose it because it had a glass top that would let some light filter in. Martine took the first cab in the rank, an ordinary taxi, and shamelessly said to the driver, who made a joke of it, "Follow that car," exactly as they did in detective stories.

Unhurriedly the two cars moved round the station and entered the Avenue du Maine. Martine could see Lou's head resting on the cushions. No doubt she was already dreaming about that ugly man whose features Martine had intently studied in a magazine. No doubt she was dreaming. . . . Like Louise, Martine leaned back against the torn upholstery and sank into a dream of anticipation, living in advance what she was about to do; it belonged to her as that man belonged to Louise, that man whose name Louise was perhaps murmuring as she thought of his hands on her impatient body.

In front of the École Militaire, the two taxis were caught almost side by side in a traffic jam. But no wave of hostility passed between them, no envy agitated Martine's thin little body, tense with the need to get to grips at last with the carnal world which had rejected it, and no misgiving disturbed the other woman voluptuously leaning back in the taxi she had taken without thought of the expense, dressed in a new tailormade achieved without sacrifice or the least feeling of guilt, so she was able to relax, as if already given over to the sure and steadfast pleasure that awaited her. . . .

The two taxis crossed the Seine. For a moment Martine's surged ahead, as if impatient. "Wait, hold back!" she called. "They're going at a snail's pace," muttered the driver. "I'm in no hurry, either," said Martine. If Louise was still enjoying her reverie, having no doubt repeated the same words to her driver, "I'm in no hurry", then why shouldn't she, Martine, go on dreaming a little before the arrival of that moment which was certainly more important for her than the moment of love for the other woman, that moment which Martine intended to make decisive?

But the two taxi-cabs had now skirted the Étoile and were entering the Avenue Carnot, where first one cab and then the other, stopped in front of a certain house.

"You're getting out here?" asked Martine's driver, with malignant interest.

Martine got out and paid.

The driver was hoping to witness one of those all-for-love crimes, but to his disappointment he saw his fare go to a nearby café and take a seat on the terrace, while the other lady entered the house through the handsome grey door. The driver started up his car and went off, slowly.

Martine sat there waiting, without anger or impatience. She was not acting against Louise or against the unknown man who was now holding Louise in his arms. She had always known that there was a world of this kind which she could never hope to enter, a world in which human beings embraced quite simply, slept and ate quite simply. The people of that world had never promised her anything. If she hated them, it was with an impersonal, cold, almost detached, hatred. They had never deceived her. They had not held out to her the fallacious hope of a place among them. She did not have to be revenged on them.

She waited, calm enough even to read, to order another drink, and to take an interest in the people coming and going in the street. She had become herself again; had found herself again, almost with a feeling of relief, if not of well-being. Except that, from time to time, as she remembered the past summer and all her efforts to become apart of a world which she had not yet realized was non-existent, and at the thought of that moment at the Brasserie Dorée when, with such intensity, she had believed her metamorphosis possible, her body trembled in a long shudder of shame.

She was prepared to wait till evening, and if need be to return next day. She wanted to make sure of not meeting Louise. That man whom she did not know, who was famous and no doubt wealthy, did not impress her. But Louise . . . that Louise could for a moment suspect that she, Martine, had been the dupe of that husband whom Louise must have condemned long ago. . . . This would be the supreme humiliation.

She did not have long to wait. She would not have to come back next day. At the end of scarcely two hours, Louise emerged from the house, looking just the same, her face calm, her beige coat floating around her as with the same careless mien, she walked unhurriedly through the rain, glancing in the shop windows as she went.

"Will she be so unchanged tonight, though?" thought Martine harshly, before crossing the street.

To reassure Stéphane, she had wanted to have this setting that he liked, the pink-shaded lamps, the fake Breton ware, the check tablecloths, the copper casseroles that were never used, all the hideous cosiness and semi-luxury of the little restaurant that was too expensive for them. Leaning on the table, she had nonchalantly ordered an expensive dish. Confident that her face was flattered by the dim rosy light, she relaxed and smiled. She was not any prettier than she had been; but she was more alive.

"Well, Stéphane?" she said with a smile, and despising him a little for not seeing through it. He smiled too, delighted to see that she was not still sulking. Life would be simple if only people would make a little effort.

"My dear," he said, "shall we really splash out and have some oysters?" He was full of good intentions. Not without a secret feeling of guilt, he was intensely enjoying this dinner in a good restaurant, this "mad escapade" which would later on call for some clever juggling in his accounts. Not that Louise would worry much about accounts this month.

The oysters were brought. Stéphane made a point of eating them with great deliberation.

"Did you have a good day? It was rainy again," he said mechanically, without looking at her. "You ought to have a breath of fresh air occasionally, it's so hot in your aquarium."

Martine lowered her eyes. She did not want to play her cards at once. "I didn't go to work this afternoon. I had asked for some time off to go to the dentist. A fictitious dentist, naturally."

She attacked an oyster with the tip of her fork; the oyster resisted. Martine was clumsy. Stéphane looked at her in surprise.

"Then that's what's made you so gay, you frivolous girl? No, not like that . . . slip the fork under the oyster, like this. Watch. And it comes away easily."

"Thank you. Yes, I went for a breath of fresh air, took a stroll. It was very instructive." She gulped down some wine. But nothing would intoxicate her today. Should she speak out at once? There was no opportunity, for Stéphane, having dexterously emptied and stacked the oyster shells, was beginning on one of his favourite themes.

"Ah yes," he said, "that's one of the pleasures, for us poor devils, to stroll about Paris, head up, watching the pageant of the streets, the houses; if those old stones could speak, they could tell us more than any books. Nowadays I tire quickly, get out of breath. But in the old days I often took Louise out, and tried to make her understand. . . ."

Today he had not hesitated to mention his wife's name. Martine seemed to be in such a good humour, and as for himself, he had been feeling relieved and relaxed for some time. All he wanted now was to be surrounded by peace and harmony. He had believed he sensed the same desire in Louise. And now Martine too, after one of her frequent and incomprehensible periods of sulking, (surely due to her health, he told himself), seemed eager to relax, He was very glad of it, as he sat there unreservedly enjoying the dim light, the gleaming copper, the attentive head waiter, the appetizing smells that came from the kitchen. For the moment all his problems seemed to be resolved. In a surge of sympathy, he took the bony little hand lying on the tablecloth and pressed it in his.

"You're right, Martine. We should let ourselves go occasionally, have a little treat, as my wife says, get out of the rut. After all, we're not ants, but grasshoppers! So let us take some advantage of our deplorable reputation for frivolity! I sometimes allow myself to be oppressed by cares and preoccupations. You always set me to rights.

And hurrah for oysters! And what care we for our daily bread!
Would you like some champagne? Waiter!"

"Oh no, no, be sensible!" she protested.

He was smiling, exerting his charm, and in a way perfectly
happy. Happy! But if she were to draw near him ever so little, he
would give that involuntary start, that look of horror. . . . How had
she been able to forget that? At present, she told herself fiercely, she
did not loathe his stupidity and mediocrity as much as she loathed
herself for having been taken in and for having struggled all summer long to be duped by him! But today. . . .

He had not listened to her protests, but had called the waiter.
He wanted champagne, he wanted to laugh, to talk. . . . Everything
had gone so well since that reading! Everyone—his friends, Louise—
had been so good to him; only Martine had been a little sulky.
But he was ready to forget all that; he forgot disagreeable things
very quickly.

"Champagne, waiter! And a good one. Let me see the wine card.
That's it, yes. A half bottle? Oh no, let's have a whole one. Eh,
Martine?"

She could not check a nervous laugh. He was so contented, so
natural. But that naturalness no longer had any power to attract
her, for she knew it was merely one more way of keeping her at a
distance. And would he be able to refrain, a few minutes later, from
mentioning his wife? Oh, no! Martine had not failed to notice that
recently he complained less of his wife, or complained simply as a
matter of course. A shudder of repulsion and shame took hold of her
again. To have believed in him, to have begged for a smile from
this man!

Stéphane watched the glasses being filled. With boyish pleasure
he raised his slightly.

"My very dear friend," he said, "let us pay tribute to custom and
drink a toast. To your twentieth birthday, to this little celebration,
to our friendship, to anything you like. While we're about it, to my
poor lungs! To your daily martyrdom, to your poor eyes that risk
being blinded by coloured plastics, to your martyred eyes and my
martyred ears! I say, that's what I call a good toast, eh?"

"Excellent," she said, smiling. She was going to destroy that face. Socrates had defended himself, hit back; so had Jean Cadou, although she had read the truth in their eyes. But Stéphane would not have the strength to hit back, she knew it, she felt it. And this time she would have no pity, either for him or for herself.

"And above all, above all," he said enthusiastically, "to your excellent idea for today, that we poor devils should throw money out the window for once. Let's have some lobster, some duck, some . . . Are we not rulers of all we survey in the Brasserie, in the Prisunic? Have some more champagne. And in it we will dissolve some false pearls. . . ."

Even his face was taking a holiday: the hard lines had disappeared, permitting the rebirth of the handsome, if nerveless young fellow that he must have been, the handsome, immature, spineless person he would always be if . . . If? Who could ever reply to this question, to all the questions? No one. She knew it now. They all had too many reasons to set themselves against her, humouring her with the same politeness they would show to an invalid or a lunatic. Leaving between her and them that glass partition, that bulwark which, they imagined, she would never succeed in crashing through. They thought they were safe from her! They thought she was made of the same stuff as they were! She was carried away in a wave of wrath.

"Stéphane, I have something to say to you. . . ."

The words came out despite herself, and she wanted to unsay them as soon as they were spoken. But it was too late. She had committed the basic mistake, the only one that he noticed and that really offended him: she had interrupted him. Stéphane frowned.

"What else have we been doing for the last half hour but talk?" he asked, with mingled annoyance and a kind of apprehension.

She would have liked to take advantage of this sentence and of the attitude which he implicitly prescribed; she would have liked to wait a little longer. But she could not hold herself back, now. "I want to talk to you about something in particular, which won't perhaps please you."

The words were those of an anonymous letter, they were stupid and melodramatic. But they had been said, and they gave her a certain relief. Stéphane, however, was annoyed.

"Oh, I see," he said, edgily, "the little celebration was not without a purpose? You brought me here with dark designs, you wanted to take advantage of a little intoxication? Then, my dear girl, you should have waited until the dessert! I am innocence itself, I suspected nothing." The sarcastic lines on either side of his mouth became more pronounced, impressively indicating restrained bitterness and exquisite irony. "The condemned man was to have his cigarette and glass of rum, was that the idea? And what, I beg you, are you going to tell me? It must be of some importance to justify such stage-setting."

She waited, seemingly impassive.

"To think," he continued, "to think that I was talking about light-hearted grasshoppers! Well, it's clear now that the grasshopper turns out to be nothing but a frightful little ant. Come, say what you have to say, now that you've put me in a good mood for it. But do take it easy; we're only at the hors d'œuvres, don't forget."

She knew him well. First, let him have his outburst. Already the impressive mask was falling apart, allowing his anxiety to appear. His own anger was running away with him.

"You must admit now, Martine, that you've shown an extraordinary lack of candour. To ruin my one moment of relaxation by . . . Why didn't you tell me whatever it is at once?"

Already his voice was weakening, and the entreaty in his eyes was barely veiled. "Frightful little ant," he had said. But she was already avenged. She was watching him weaken. His weakness compensated her for her ugliness. In another moment . . .

"Confess, my dear, that your attitude is surprising, to say the least. Dissimulation is perhaps too strong a word, but I do not understand, I cannot understand. . . . Martine?"

Ugly? Perhaps. But so very much stronger than he. She would make him confess. Make him. . . . Her thin little hands were clenched under the table.

"Martine, I'm sorry, I let myself go. I've said things I shouldn't have said, things I didn't really mean. If I have offended you . . . I quite understand that you may have wanted a moment of intimacy to . . . Well, my dear, what's up, now?"

Now. The word had escaped him. Would he never be rid of her? Would she always be harassing him with her demands, her fancies which he found incomprehensible, without reflecting that her submission to him was still more incomprehensible? All at once he looked very tired.

"Come to think of it," she said, "what I want to talk to you about is a bit of good news in a way. . . . It concerns your wife."

"Louise?" he asked, this time with real anguish. "You've spoken to her?"

"No." She replied slowly, patiently. She had the feeling of setting up her words like bricks, with which she was free to build as she wished. And she still hesitated how to place them. Which first? This or that? But in her mind, the edifice arose, was already completed. "No, I didn't speak to your wife. But I've thought carefully about your situation."

"Still the same, alas," he sighed.

His sigh was one of relief, she felt. Since she only wanted to talk, there was nothing to worry about. . . . But she would show him that words too, could be weapons.

"You've often talked to me about your wife, and we've deplored the rift between you—for which she is completely responsible— and we've tried, in vain, to find a way out. . . ."

"There is no way out, unfortunately, my dear," said Stéphane, who was recovering his self-assurance.

"That's what you've always said, Stéphane, and I agreed with you. But today I'm no longer of that opinion."

"I don't understand," he stammered.

"I think that now there is a way," she said, very gently. "And I'm sure that our friends will agree with me. Things have reached such a point . . ."

Stéphane appeared to be excessively embarrassed. Forlornly, he carved the fowl that had been set on the table before him. "Martine," he said, "I keep nothing from you, as you know. But

I will confess, this subject is extremely painful. There are certain wounds . . . "

"I suppose," she said in a voice that was smoother, if possible, than before, "I suppose by 'this subject' you are referring to the *Paris-Monde* thing."

"Yes, of course, all that publicity is very unpleasant." He was still staring gloomily at the bird he was carving.

"Of course. But don't you see that it gives you the opportunity you've been looking for?"

Contrary to what she had expected, Stéphane's reaction was aggressive.

"I suppose you mean by 'opportunity' the chance to get rid of my wife?" he asked, speaking vehemently and raising his head with a kind of jerk. "To get rid of her, to abandon her, to accuse her before everyone? I don't doubt your good intentions, Martine, but I have a greater sense of responsibility than that. To take advantage of a foolish act on the part of my wife—whom I could reproach for quite a lot of other things—to take advantage of her rashness to drag her shamefully through the courts, to free myself at her expense—I'd never do that! No, never! I will shield her from her own foolishness. And besides, she may not be as guilty as she seems. She may have acted out of a simple impulse of vanity, the wish to be seen in the company of a famous man. . . ."

Martine was on the point of making an angry retort, but she checked herself. Would he always find a way out, then? Oh, no! She was all too sure of her ultimate victory. She would corner him, force him to admit the truth: it had to be. With restraint, therefore, she went on with what she had to say.

"You're admirable, Stéphane. But I'm sure that, deep down, you'll be relieved to know this: your wife does not need your protection. There is no question of abandoning her, of bringing accusations against her, of spying upon her, and all the rest. Henry Stass wants to marry her."

"What?"

"You heard me. That painter, that Henry Stass, in whose affections (if you will excuse the term), your wife supplanted that girl

Sylvia, wants to marry her. So you see, your wife runs no risk of being abandoned."

There, at last, she had him, uncertain and stupefied! This time he could not pretend not to have heard or to have misunderstood, could not befuddle her with fine phrases, "Do read my journal", could not thrust her behind a barrier of smiles and pretexts.

"You're out of your mind, Martine! It's impossible, such an assumption."

"It's not an assumption."

"By what right, then. . . ? Who has been telling you such things?"

"Who? Why, Henry Stass himself, my dear Stéphane."

For a second his throat was too tight to speak, and he paled visibly. "You . . . saw him?"

"Yes. There's nothing so extraordinary in that. Besides, he's much less awe-inspiring than one would expect. A very nice man, very simple." The words were coming easily now, were pouring out. She felt suddenly liberated, capable of surmounting any obstacle, without effort, gaily. "He told me quite categorically that there's only one thing he wants, and that is, to take care of your wife's future."

"He wants to take care of . . . Why, this is preposterous! How could you have discovered his address, and how could you have spoken to him? You're pulling my leg, aren't you?" He passed a trembling hand over his forehead, then seized her hand feverishly, only to drop it at once. He swallowed some wine, avidly. "Tell me the truth, Martine. This is a frightful . . . no,—you must be joking. But tell me why? It's impossible. And what are you trying to get out of me?"

"I found out where he lived," she said calmly, "by following your wife. I did not have an appointment. I simply went in when she left his place, two hours later. He himself opened the door. I told him about you. I told him of your concern, your uneasiness. He declared that for weeks he had been expecting you to take action of some kind or other."

"Action?" He could say nothing more.

"Yes, actually, he expected you to do something about it. I described your feelings, as we know them through your journal. He quite understood. And he replied as I've told you, that he'd come to a decision, and asked nothing better than to take care of your wife."

"You followed her! You waited till she came out!" Stéphane muttered.

"Do I have to repeat it a hundred times?"

"How could you do such a thing?"

At last, at last he had no reply to make to her. At last she had got at him. What would he do now? She was well aware, it was clear as day, that he did not want to leave his wife. Martine also knew that he loathed her, that minute, for having intervened, for having broken into his agreeably fictitious existence. But she wanted him to admit it. Oh, let him at last tell her that all she aroused in him or had ever aroused, was aversion, repugnance! Let him at last recognize himself for what he was, as she had been forced to recognize what she was. If only now, after having tried so hard to share his delusions, she could draw him to her and consume him in her lucidity! Then she would have won the battle.

But he said nothing. Must she goad him still more?

"Aren't you glad, Stéphane? Aren't you relieved of a great burden? I hope so, for I wanted to help you. I wanted to free you from your scruples. . . ."

Her irony was obvious. And yet, was it not the truth? If she had absolutely believed in him, would she not have done the same? And if his feeling for Louise had really been what he made it out to be, if he had been the man he pretended to be, would he not have wanted her to do just this? A dead silence fell between them. They were almost alone in the warm room, with its sparkling copper, the clock in its antique case, the check tablecloths, and the champagne bucket between them. . . .

"You seem upset?" she said. "Is it by any chance . . . "

A murmur came from the wireless. Some people at a distant table were lingering on, still talking. Stéphane pushed back his chair and got laboriously to his feet.

"Waiter! The bill," he said in a muffled voice.

His face was ravaged, frightening. He paid in silence. Was he going to make some kind of reply?

"I misjudged you," he said all at once, speaking very fast, in a panic of fury. "You're nothing but a little schemer. You've concocted all this for some sordid reason, Heaven only knows what. You're disgusting. To think that I believed I could depend on you, trust you. . . . To think that I . . . Your soul matches your face! Your face sums you up! You . . . "

No, he could say no more. His whole body was shaking, convulsed with fear and revolt. And also with incomprehension. To think that she who had been so trusting only a week ago. . . . To think that he had been so happy at the prospect of this evening at this restaurant, to think . . . Tears came into his eyes. He lurched out. The waiter muttered something to the cashier, and they laughed. Martine could easily guess what they were saying.

But what did it matter? She had triumphed at last. She had got at him. She had got at them. And she had still not said her last word. She had not mentioned that blue notebook she'd left behind her in the painter's studio, remarking, "This will no doubt interest Madame Morani." It scarcely mattered. She had seen his face distorted with rage and fear, stripped of all that pretended sweetness, that assumed patience. . . . And that face was surely as ugly as her own. She would unmask them all. From now on the world would be peopled solely with real faces, faces without beauty. The world would be nothing but ugliness, from now on.

Down there, behind the Montparnasse railway-station, in the tranquil rue Bourdelle, and in a no less tranquil little photographer's studio, a young man was imploring a grumpy little boy to "look at the little bird". One after another, three locomotives rumbled disdainfully away, as if regretfully, well aware they were only going as far as the suburbs. The platforms were deserted at this hour of the day.

Sylvia stood hesitating at the corner of the Boulevard Edgar-Quinet, uncertain whether or not to take a taxi. It was not raining, and she was in no hurry. Just as well, then, to go on foot part of the

way, that would give her time for thought. Slowly she walked
down the rue d'Odessa, jostled by the crowd, brought to a halt by
every window display, automatically looking at her reflection in
every expanse of glass, deciding that the pale yellow tailored costume
under her dark coat was a little too light for the season. One after
another, the "novelty" shops held her attention. She examined
minutely, with her beautiful vacant eyes the dozens of skirts hanging out in the open air, and the noisy merchandise of the dealer in
radios held her fascinated for a long while. Whistles of admiration
sounded as she passed by a café terrace, and she smiled. In front of
the Prisunic she instinctively quickened her steps, but soon afterwards slowed down again to examine the pictured tiles on the
façade of the Turkish baths, then moved on a little farther to
stop first of all before the display of a street-hawker who was
selling piles of synthetic sponges in exquisite tints of orange,
mauve and green, and then to look at what the flower-sellers had
to offer: scentless dahlias that had been sprinkled with water. Then
on a few steps more. . . .

Sooner or later, she would have to take a taxi, would have to
direct the cabby "To the Étoile", would have to get out at . . .
Her appointment at the hairdresser's, the light tailormade in which
she was shivering, the instructions given by her mother all led up
to that. . . . Sylvia's soul was too gentle to hold a feeling of revolt
or repulsion; but she none the less felt a kind of distress which slowed
her steps, and her natural indolence made her welcome with
pleasure all the diversions offered by the rue d'Odessa. And when,
despite so many shop windows on both sides—she had crossed and
recrossed the street three times—despite the colours and shapes she
felt constrained to linger over, she arrived in sight of the station,
she stopped for a last time, convinced that it was cold and that she
should have some hot coffee. What would her mother have said
to this? For Madame Prêtre had expressly enjoined her daughter not
to dawdle on the way. Even so, Sylvia went into the gloomy little
café and sat down at a bare wooden table which smelled of potas-
sium-chloride and took the glass of pale and bitter coffee they
brought her. Mechanically she picked up the evening paper,

France-Soir, and ran her eyes over the alluring headings: "Man Watches Wife Drown Without Trying to Save Her"—"The Pacy-sur-Eure Postman's Alibi: Is it Sound?"

"I love," thought Sylvia, "the long limousine with its smell of leather. I love the studio with its smell of turpentine. I love the bedroom with its English furniture. I love my fur coat. I love to have Mamma happy, Henry happy, everyone happy. I love to do what people expect of me, what ought to be done, I love to do the right thing. I love to see smiles around me, the smiles of the waiter hurrying to help me out of my coat, of the journalist who knows Henry and already recognizes me. I love . . . I loved the prize-givings at school and the masters who patted my cheeks, I loved my first prize in Conduct, in Gymnastics, in Sewing. . . . And yet . . . "

Her mother was always saying, "The world would never get a clean bill of health from me." Why, wondered Sylvia, why was her mother never satisfied? Sylvia had always done her best. . . . Her eyes became glued to the fashion page.

"I love," she thought, "the little tailored costumes with their unfitted jackets; yellow and pink suit me, but not blue. I love to be well dressed, clean, and nice-smelling. That ought to be enough for them. I love to be looked at, I love to have a man tell me he loves me. I love to know that I'm with a man of position, and for people to see I don't go out with just anyone . . . and to be treated with respect, and talked to. I love, yes, I love to be talked to."

At the bottom of the page was a questionnaire: "Are you able to hold your own with your husband?" Although quite devoid of a husband, Sylvia set to work on the list of questions, not without some underlying remorse. Time drifted by.

"What are the duties of a President of the Council? Oh, I know, Albert explained that to me. All you have to do is listen carefully, and remember. Now I can talk about painting, about the cinema . . . I can . . . But Henry's to blame, for he never wants to talk. And Mamma won't talk, either. Life, my poor child. . . . That's all either of them finds to say. But life's something else: jollier, more . . . exciting."

Life was exciting, she was sure of that. Her favourite magazine, *Marie-Christine*, affirmed it once a week. Life was exciting, the air was exciting, passion was exciting. Every reader of *Marie-Christine* knew that. It was as obvious as the need for brunettes to have a touch of yellow in their clothes, the need to use Tone-Citron for rough hands. This was the sort of thing that kept a troubled Sylvia in her chair in the dim and protective little café.

"But," she thought, "Henry isn't exciting. Henry isn't *at all* exciting. Yet he's a famous painter. He's been photographed for *Paris-Monde* twice. The studio has been photographed for *Paris-Monde*. Louise Morani has been photographed . . . "

And how furious Madame Prêtre had been! "Why couldn't you have managed to get yourself photographed?" she had said. "I suppose she's prettier than you are? Oh, my poor Sylvia."

She had to go there. If her mother was to be believed, Henry would ask nothing better than to have her again in his arms, in his studio, in his car. But despite *Paris-Monde*, the prospect of such a thing was not at all exciting.

"Try," Madame Prêtre had said.

"People are always saying that," thought Sylvia, "and I try all the time, and what good does it do? They go on calling me 'my poor child'. And I get no thanks. None? There's the fur coat, but . . . "

But she was well aware that when something really *really* exciting happened, all the rest, the fur coat, the car, the studio, and even—she shivered at her own sacrilege—even *Paris-Monde* amounted to nothing. For instance, when the young photographer had declared that he would kill himself for her. Or when Stéphane Morani had read his diary. Or even just when she read in *Marie-Christine* some love-story that made her cry, or when she answered all the questions in one of those educational quizzes, or when she read in *France-Soir* about some touching episode, yes, then she really felt there was a world quite apart from the one her mother or Henry inhabited, a world the right size for her, where she belonged and was loved.

"Come to think of it," mused Sylvia, "they're rather alike:

never satisfied. But a man like Stéphane Morani, on the other hand . . . How exciting it was that evening, with everyone pleased and agreeing with each other. No one asked for anything, demanded anything. Whereas Mamma . . . and Henry . . . with them, I always feel I've done something wrong. But what? What?"

She absently scanned the newspaper. The manageress of the café stared at her suspiciously. But Sylvia did not budge. By nature she was incapable of deciding, contrary to the obedience she owed her mother, that she would not go to the Avenue Carnot. But the repulsion she had felt for a long time in her subconscious slowly emerged from those dark waters, becoming perceptible, fascinating her, and holding her there.

None the less, the limousine, the fur coat, *Paris-Monde*, all pleaded for Henry. And those young women in *Marie-Christine* looked so smart! And in the serial stories they were always getting out of a blue Buick or a Chrysler. But the painters—and there were some painters in the stories—were so much more attractive than Henry! Shocking and cynical, no doubt (although in love with the heroine and revealing it to her at the very end, after having experienced the torments of jealousy), but declaring on all crucial occasions, "My art comes first", in such a noble way. You could easily imagine Stéphane Morani declaring that, tossing back his thick dark hair, gesticulating with his aristocratic hands (for he did have aristocratic hands, *Marie-Christine* would have agreed on that point. Whereas Henry . . .).

The secret repulsion had come to the surface. Sylvia even discovered with stupefaction that this repulsion included not only Henry but her mother as well. Was it possible? What then had been taking place unnoticed inside her mind while she blithely continued to obey her mother, going to the hairdresser's, putting on the yellow silk tailormade. . . . And when, submissively, she had almost taken that taxi, to Henry's to deliver the speech that had been drummed into her dozens of times. . . .

No, she was not in love with Stéphane Morani. If her thoughts dwelt on any image, it was rather on that of the freckled-faced photographer, who had talked one day of killing himself for her (and had not done it). But all the same, Stéphane Morani had something to do with this feeling of revulsion, this obstacle against which she had stumbled. It was the exciting scene of that reading which, today, had made her drift from the path of duty, had made her conscious of the profound uneasiness she had always felt with her mother and Henry.

"That was a magnificent hour I experienced," she told herself. Yes, that hour, the intonations of that warm voice, those too sonorous words, those too polished sentences; those bald affirmations; that general and perhaps suspect sympathy; that pleading of a cause, those sham smiles, that sham absolution; all these things that had been the damnation of Martine had spelt salvation for Sylvia.

At last she had felt sure of herself. At last she had glimpsed, so she thought, happiness and truth. No, she was not in love with Stéphane Morani. But he was a saint, of that she was sure. Her mother's suffering, Henry's pity—she had always felt them, without understanding, like almost imperceptible yet unpleasant shades of feeling, and she could now reject them, with the bright, clear images furnished by Stéphane. And her feeling of revulsion grew until it gradually attained the strength of a decision.

She would not go to Henry's. She would not return home to her mother. Both of them had tricked her. They had taken refuge behind motor-cars, furs and *Paris-Monde* to set her mind at rest.

"When you come to it, they're not *authentic*," she decided.

The big word was said. In Sylvia's mythology and under the influence of Stéphane Morani, Goodness, Poverty, Sacrifice came to take the place of Art and Success and Beauty. She was already quite prepared to dedicate herself to these new gods with the same humble and mediocre application that had been the despair of Henry Stass. As a child, she had bent over some embroidery, or a page of writing with the same application. "As long as they don't ask her to understand," her mother always said. Perhaps Sylvia was incapable of understanding; but she was capable of choosing, and she had now chosen her new gods.

She left the table, paid her bill. Poverty and Sacrifice were

already before her dazzled eyes, in the form of a freckled-faced
photographer. She would be poor and happy; contemptuously she
left the rôle of Muse to others. She would write to *Marie-Christine*:
"My mother wanted me to marry an aged painter, immensely
wealthy. I preferred a young photographer, poor and honest."
And she was sure that *Marie-Christine* would applaud her action.
The new gods also figured in *Marie-Christine*, which was all to the
good, since *Marie-Christine* was a microcosm.

She went out. And already, in her more modest mien, in her way
of lowering her eyelids, one could read a subtle change.

Down there, behind the railway-station, in the tranquil rue
Bourdelle, a photographer was imploring a grumpy little boy,
sitting on his mother's knee, to "look at the little bird", never
guessing what happiness was coming towards him, armed with the
adjective "authentic" and dressed in a very light costume of
yellow silk.

"Oh, you know," said Louise, "we all have our faults."

She yawned. She was sleepy. She really wanted to go home, but
Henry didn't like her to be the first to talk of going. And if she
didn't get home soon, there'd be a fuss; Stéphane would play the
martyr. Not that he wasn't aware of what was going on, of course,
though he was behaving with quite a lot of tact, she'd give him that
much credit.

The studio divan was piled with sketches for a ballet, and because
of this, they had slept in the too elegant bedroom, with its shining
mahogany furniture, the milk-glass lamps, the brass fittings of the
little portable bar that had once been a part of a yacht's furnishings,
and the *toile de Jouy* curtains. Louise was rather fond of this bedroom.
She could imagine with pleasure waking up here, going to sleep
here. Yes, she could imagine it. But she had not yet made up her
mind. Every day, however, she inclined more and more towards a
favourable decision, and Henry could not help being aware of it,
from the questions she asked. "Where did you say your property is?"
"Do you still have your old studio in the rue Lhomond? Why not
sell it?" She knew all about his business affairs, which were not very

complicated anyway, and took an interest in them. She would go
to the theatre for the rehearsals of the ballet when they began.
She would give him her opinion on everything and they would not
agree on anything; in short, all would be well. But now Henry
was annoyed with her for not admitting . . .

"Faults, faults, how can you say that! And you consider it quite
excusable I suppose, for that two-legged little monster to burst into
my studio and order me to marry you and then, incidentally, to
leave that wretched notebook behind?"

"I suppose she wants to marry him," said Louise vaguely,
yawning again. "And she thought I'd be annoyed. . . . It's jealousy,
such an old story! Old as the hills."

Henry propped himself up on an elbow. His broad chest emerged
from the sheets, that chest which always made people think he
must be a giant when they saw him seated, and he looked at her
sternly. "And of course, you're not annoyed?"

Lou shrugged, exasperated. "How do you expect me to feel
about it? Besides, I haven't time to talk, I must go."

"You've all the time in the world. Well, now! You've read that
stuff and you think it's all quite natural? You're called by every
kind of name there, and you find it quite natural."

"I really don't see how it can matter to you," said Louise, dis-
engaging herself from him irritably.

"Well, it does," he shouted in sudden wrath, "I don't like
imbeciles! And I don't like to see my wife—shut up—my wife
treated like a reformed prostitute, like . . . I don't know what!
It does matter to me: if you're not as revolted as I am, then it means
you're completely gone on that fool, and I'll not have it! Not in
my own house! So there!"

In his fury he had got out of bed and was now pacing the floor,
seizing the milk-glass lamp, putting it down again, hesitating
whether or not to break it.

"It's for you to decide," said Louise, who was growing sleepier
all the time but who, in her turn, was getting angry. "You must
decide whether you look on me as belonging here or would like
to see the last of me?"

He sat down on the bed and took her hand in his. "Really, Louise, don't tell me you're not furious."

"Oh, you know . . . I'm used to it."

"Used to it, used to it! How in the world have you managed to live for years with that fool and his eternal twaddle! You only have to read three lines of that stuff to see . . ."

"You always exaggerate," she said calmly. "Stéphane isn't a fool, you know."

"Oh no? Then perhaps *I* am?"

"Why no, Henry, neither of you is a fool. People can't help the way they're made, that's all. I really don't see why you're making such a fuss."

"So I'm making a fuss! There's nothing to make a fuss about! You'll drive me crazy! Once and for all, admit that he's an idiot, that husband of yours, an irresponsible lunatic, if not a dangerous crack-pot, and then let's say no more about it."

He was standing up again, looking a little ridiculous, wearing only the lower half of his pyjamas, his legs short, his shoulders broad, his face that of a shrewd peasant. . . .

"Have it your own way," she said wearily. "Let's say he's a madman and leave it at that. Now, let me dress."

He stood still a moment, not watching her while she gathered up her scattered clothing. Then he put a curt question: "Well, if he's a fool or a madman, why did you marry him?"

She stopped, bent over as she was, with her skirt pulled halfway over her hips. Then she slowly straightened up. "Henry, are you making fun of me?"

"I'm asking you why you married him?"

"I married him because I wanted to, so there! And it occurs to me that I didn't have to ask your advice, did I? I hope you're satisfied?"

"No," he said, gritting his teeth. "No." And he walked up to her and seized her by the wrist. "I'm not satisfied. And you're going to answer me. He impressed you, didn't he? You liked his fine words. I suppose, it flattered you to play the part of a Magdalen. The rôle fits you like a glove! Magdalen before the repentance, naturally!"

"And so what, so what? I've already told you it's none of your business. Surely you're not going to make a scene over something that happened fifteen years ago, are you? Right, I married the fellow, I've slept with him, and if I wanted to do it all over again, I'd do it, and it would still be none of your business! Who do you think you are? My father? You . . . "

Her voice had risen, it was the shrill voice of a matron who has nothing to fear, who will not let herself be intimidated by anyone, and her words became punctuated with far-fetched exclamations, in an overflow of indignation that revelled in its own force. In this vehement outpouring, Henry again found her, a little stupid, a little vulgar, but still totally free of all the things he really disliked. Gradually he himself calmed down, his anger merging with a feeling of amused tenderness. She had not even understood what had so enraged him in that wretched notebook, still lying there at the foot of the bed, had not understood the insinuations in that affected writing which had aroused in him this fierce indignation. She had not understood. That was all he needed. He could have soothed her with a word, but he listened to her storm of indignation with a kind of pleasure. She was again "behaving like a woman", that creature who shouts to no purpose, to whom one does not listen, but indulges like a household pet that is something of a nuisance. Her protestations were weakening, moreover. To the "No, really!" screams of a fishwife, the auction-room shouts of "This is a bit thick!" she descended to "You must admit", accompanied by shrugs; she shook her dishevelled hair to make it clear that she'd never let herself be led by the nose; with a look she defied him, with a gesture provoked him; and finally came the moment when she sat down with dignity to pull on her stockings, and invited him at last to say a word or two.

"All the same, Henry, if you could explain what got into you . . ."

Could he? Could he explain to himself the sudden turmoil of wrath and doubt that had overwhelmed him upon reading that harmless, that childish notebook? What power could there be in those swollen phrases, that guileless dissimulation. . . . After all, as Lou said, what business was it of his?

"Look here, what upsets me," he explained hesitantly, "is that you could be taken in by all that twaddle."

"It just isn't important," she said, buttoning her shirtwaist. "Jealousy! How absurd it is. . . ."

Jealousy? Yes, it was certainly a kind of jealousy that had seized him as he breathed what seemed to him, the thoroughly unhealthy air of Stéphane Morani's journal. He feared that she had been infected by it, was no longer herself . . . but she had not even understood. The man was quite simply a crack-pot, if he wasn't a hypocrite. For surely he must guess something from the late hours Louise was keeping.

"Does he know . . . ?" he began, but immediately checked himself. It was futile to begin another argument now. She seemed determined not to answer him. Later on he would have plenty of time to ask her this question, and others, more adroitly.

"Does who know what?" she said, going to pick up her blue jacket that had been thrown down on the chest of drawers.

"Nothing, nothing. I was thinking aloud."

"Oh, you men, with your complications," she sighed, adjusting the jacket, contemplating herself in the mirror with some satisfaction.

" 'You men', what men?" said Henry, who was putting on his dressing-gown, to accompany her to the door.

"Why, you, Stéphane, and the others. . . ." Then, fearing she had annoyed him by this association, she added, "You're not vexed?"

"No, of course not!"

They were leaving the room, and he turned out the light at that very moment, so she could not see his face.

Within its peaceful dark red walls, beneath the slanting gaze of the mandarins, the Café Céleste stood unchanged, just as it had always been since the day when Socrates' Turkish uncle had been beguiled by the gilded god and the girl with the nenuphars. As usual on a Monday night, the chairs were stacked in one corner of the room, forming an inextricable jumble, roughly pyramidal in shape. The fish in the aquarium conscientiously followed their unchanging routine. It would soon be time to tear a page off the calendar; then the young girl with the nenuphars, and wearing a bon-bon pink tunic, would smile above October days.

Outside, the rue d'Odessa was a blaze of light, some motor-cars passed slowly by, hampered by the crowd of pedestrians; from open windows the ringing of bells pierced the tumult; radios were blasting away; and despite the fact that night had fallen, some coster-mongers were still selling a sunset-glow of neckties heaped in a big inverted umbrella. The ill-fed and over-painted prostitutes who came and went in the dense shadows of the wide boulevard had renounced their summer attire and were now bravely sporting some pitiful fox furs to protect them from the gentle rain. All the neon signs were on parade, reflected in the tiled frontage of the Turkish baths. A great many shop-windows were still lit up, and the passers-by stopped to gaze, in spite of the rain, for the evening was almost warm.

In the alley-way, mothers were calling their children, gathered round the window display of a radio shop, where a television was in operation for the first time. "Rob . . . ert! Jeann . . . ot!" On the screen, flickering cowboys pursued each other. The hot frankfurter sausages and potato chips which could be had at an open booth had attracted a group of the ill-fed girls with the dilapidated fox furs. The doors of the small cafés were wide open, and the loud voices of card-players could be heard: "I tell you, four aces!" Two young fellows in shirtsleeves could be seen playing a game of billiards, and despite floods of sweet music provided by the management, the click of the colliding balls could still be heard, and the greenish light of the backroom had a peaceful look.

Someone knocked on the ground glass door of the Café Céleste. With a careless gesture of the thumb, the same gesture he had made throughout the years, Socrates indicated the placard "Closed Monday". The man shrugged and went away. Socrates offered a round of white wine to the group of people who were waiting for Stéphane.

A big Technicolor film was being shown at the Miramar

Cinema: "Deep-Sea Romance". On the posters, two men in skin-divers' outfits were plunging, hand in hand, into a bright green sea where an enormous shark was awaiting them. The mother continued to call: "Rob . . . ert! Jeann . . . ot!" Robert did not budge from his position in front of the television set where the phantom cowboys were massacring phantom Indians. Jeannot, chewing a caramel, was absorbed in contemplation of the shark. The green cross of the pharmacy winked at the red disc of the "Melody" music shop opposite. The Oriental restaurant, Sultan Dinn, competed vainly with its distinguished pale blue sign dripping sadly down the front of the building. In a bright white light, the three show-windows of "Christina's Dress Shop" still displayed tempting beflowered creations. An indignant mother came out of the alley, dragging a smaller child who was struggling to free himself from her grasp. "I knew it!" the mother's voice screamed. "Wait till you hear what your papa will say! After dark! It's . . . " Her voice merged with the loud roar of the street. "I want some chips!" clamoured the youngster. A few well-dressed couples entered the Sultan Dinn restaurant, laughing loudly. At the end of the street the poor little pale neon sign of the Café Céleste could not even be seen.

"What about another bottle of white wine?" Socrates suggested. They were still waiting for Stéphane.

Madame Prêtre was in a gloomy mood. Tactfully the antiquary was trying to comfort her. "Now, dear Madame, what do you expect? All children do foolish things. Sylvia will come back to you. And there's no reason to think that the young man won't marry her. Obviously it's not the match you hoped to make for her, but . . . "

Germaine Lethuit intervened, not so tactfully. "And even if he doesn't marry her," she said warmly, "what's wrong with that? She wanted to emancipate herself, that child, to emancipate herself and lead a free life. Well, I approve!"

"Emancipate herself!" Madame Prêtre forgot, in her indignation, the tacit understanding that Sylvia was a subject to be talked about with care. "Emancipate herself! That child! You, who know her, presume to tell me that to my face, me, her mother? Why, that girl's never been able to come to any decision by herself, as you perfectly well know. She has the brains of a kitten! Emancipate herself! Really!"

Ducas, somewhat embarrassed, gave a little cough. "You exaggerate, Madame Prêtre, you exaggerate."

"Yes indeed," said Socrates, supporting Ducas, and filled with good intentions. "I've even heard her say very sensible things sometimes. As Monsieur Morani said to me . . . "

"Oh, no, don't tell me about that! I've had it dinned into my ears. I don't want to say anything against Monsieur Morani, but he didn't realize . . . "

"I don't see the connection," said Gérard Ducas.

"There isn't any. Poor old chap, he wasn't the one to lead your daughter astray," said Jean Cadou, smiling, for the idea struck him as funny.

"It's not anyone's fault," murmured Dr. Fisher airily. "No, thank you, no wine."

"I didn't say it was his fault. Of course, Monsieur Morani didn't want to . . . But she lost her head, she got all worked up. . . ."

Despite everything, a note of rancour sounded in her voice. Madame Prêtre would have been hard put to it to say just how Stéphane Morani was responsible for Sylvia's flight, but instinctively she blamed him for it.

"And after all," said Jean Cadou thoughtlessly, "what interest could poor Stéphane have had in . . . "

He checked himself, rather appalled at their silence. "I could do with another glass of wine," he said, to cover his confusion.

And there was silence again. Dr. Fisher smiled vaguely and Socrates moved his bottles about for no reason at all. Gérard Ducas had prepared a charming and witty essay (the famous "History of a Louis XV *bidet*"), which he had wanted to submit to his friends for criticism, perhaps before having it printed and published on fine paper at his own expense; it would make an attractive slender volume. Jean would design the cover. Germaine Lethuit was thinking about her poem, which she had in her handbag: four pages that had been typed at her office. It would make such a lovely subject for discussion. Perhaps they would have time to read it, if Stéphane didn't keep them too long. . . .

They went on waiting for him.

Martine's bedroom overlooked the alley-way. By leaning out she could see quaint little courtyards with rickety sheds, studios which hummed and buzzed with voices during the day. But the voices were stilled now. The mothers had collected their children and were now, to the accompaniment of screams and shouts, stuffing them with supper. From her window Martine saw lights moving, and occasionally glimpsed one corner of a lit room. A child's cry rose up to her, a man's voice came up from one of the miniature courtyards complaining: "Where have you put the thing this time?" A great red glow hovered over everything, coming from a high electric street sign which Martine could not see. In her bedroom, the light was not lit, but the window was open and Martine was looking out. The door was locked. A quarter of an hour earlier, someone had timidly knocked at that door, but she had given no sign of life.

"So you've had a spat?" said Louise, with a knowing smile.

Stéphane hadn't the courage to take offence. "She complicates life so," he murmured uncertainly. "You're going out again?"

"Any objections?" asked Lou, ready for a quarrel.

"No, no. I was only hoping . . . You could have kept me company for a while."

"But you have your friends downstairs, haven't you? It's Monday."

"I'm so tired. . . ."

She examined him with an alert, intelligent look. He must have been getting himself into trouble again. Of course it was that Fortin girl. Louise had never liked her. "If you would just tell me what's wrong," she said.

"Why nothing, my dear, nothing. Merely what one meets with so often in life, scheming and self-interest, where one hoped for friendship and devotion. Once more I've been too naïve, that's all. So I must put up with the consequences."

Once more. That must be an allusion to their marriage, she supposed. That was certainly what he seemed to be saying in that famous journal of his. She felt embarrassed over having read that notebook; especially because she did not understand. That he should talk to her like that—well, she had always accepted it as his way of affirming his superiority, a tactic to assure him victory in their disputes. But that he should have taken the trouble to write it down in those notebooks. . . . That meant he believed in it a little. So then, he really had been unhappy? She had never suspected it, seeing in his attitude only a pose, a strategem. And to discover that he had been half in earnest (no matter how little), filled her with mingled disgust and pity, as if for an invalid disfigured by a disease, frightful to look at.

"You mustn't take it to heart," she said awkwardly. "She's not worth much, that Fortin girl."

They were both a little embarrassed by all the words they left unsaid. Stéphane had no inclination to discuss Henry with her. Besides, Martine was quite capable of having embroidered the facts. What was there to prove that anything was involved except a long standing affection?

"The nuisance of it is that she'll not leave here," Stéphane reflected aloud.

"How can that affect you? You needn't speak to her any more."

She had always been superbly indifferent to the opinion others might have of her, to gossip, to the attitude of the neighbours, and this indifference irritated Stéphane.

"But you don't understand! God only knows what rumours she'll spread about you and me. She's capable of setting the whole house against me."

"That wouldn't be such a loss, you know."

"But really, Louise, you don't understand, such things are foreign to you. . . ." He was on the point of flying into a temper, his eyes were filling with tears of exasperation.

"Now, now," she admonished him soothingly. "Don't get angry.

She can say what she likes about me, I don't mind at all, since I never speak to those people anyway. And what gossip could she possibly circulate about you?"

They were waiting for Stéphane, and *Paris-Monde*, the magazine, was lying on the table.

"He must have 'flu," said Socrates, tired of moving about pointlessly behind the bar.

"Then Martine Fortin must also have 'flu," snapped Madame Prêtre.

"I'll bet they're up there together, holding forth in noble language," said Jean with a laugh. "I can just hear them: 'My little Antigone!' 'My great big Oedipus!'"

"You always get everything mixed up," said Gérard Ducas, smiling indulgently.

But Madame Prêtre exclaimed with unaccustomed virulence, "Oh, no, they're not together. I don't know where Martine Fortin is, but I know that Monsieur Morani is still with his wife."

"They may be having a discussion," said the antiquary as if with compunction. "In which case, suppose we begin the reading without him?"

"A discussion?" said Madame Prêtre, still on the war-path and speaking with feigned astonishment. "What would they be discussing?"

"They never stop, apparently," said Germaine Lethuit. "It's only to be expected; a marriage of that kind can't last."

"Our friend, with his admirable if slightly Utopian fervour, certainly flung himself into a complicated adventure that time."

"Lots of married couples yammer at each other from morning till night, and yet manage to get along pretty well," said Jean, with a shrug. "Utopian fervour or not, you can get fed up with having the same face in front of you all the time."

"Are you thinking of Madame Morani or Martine Fortin?" asked the concierge.

"What do you mean by that?"

"Well, if there's one face Monsieur Morani's fed up with, I can tell you it's more likely to be Martine Fortin's."

"Oh? Have they quarrelled?" asked the antiquary with interest.

Louise, wearing her olive green frock and beige coat, was ready to leave. She looked slimmer and somehow more alive, thought Stéphane. That painter must have been giving her advice on how to dress. Of course, she would listen to him because he was a famous man; but when he himself had tried to advise her, he had had a cool reception. Not that this proved anything.

"You know, this evening," he blurted out, "I knocked at her door, to remind her of the Monday meeting, and would you believe it? She didn't answer. Yet I'm sure she was there."

"Go without her."

She must have changed her hairdresser too. It seemed to him—but he knew so little about such things—that, although she still wore her hair knotted at the back of the head, there was a kind of wave at the temples. She noticed his gaze.

"Do you like it?"

"Yes, it's nice. It's . . . softer. But it may be those colours that give the effect."

"Pretty, isn't it?" she said, turning in front of him.

"It must have cost a lot?" he asked, averting his eyes.

Martine, too, had surely noticed this additional elegance, and had felt jealous.

"Rather expensive. Well, as long as it lasts. . . ."

She did not seem in the least embarrassed. He let the subject drop.

"But if I go without her, they'll all wonder . . ."

The thing that most embarrassed him, and which he could not explain to Louise, was the reading of the journal a fortnight before. Having publicly treated Martine as his "little Antigone" and "one of the Elect", it would be hard to back down without explanations.

"For heaven's sake," she exclaimed with her usual indignation, "it's none of their business! After all, you've not slept with that girl!"

"Louise!"

To be sure, she reflected, if he had slept with her, it would appear in that journal! What foolishness to write everything down in a notebook! And to get so excited over a little horror whose impossible character, she, Louise, had guessed from the first minute. Oh well, he must have believed in that, too. Poor Stéphane! He was now assuming a gentle and wheedling tone she had not heard from him for some time.

"Listen, Lou, really, I don't want to go to the meeting. I don't feel well, you see, and if . . . If you would be so kind . . ."

The fluorescent light above the bar sizzled, the goldfish dutifully pursued their rounds, the silly young girl with the nenuphars smiled imperturbably. The god did not manifest himself. Was it perhaps the God of Waiting? His patience led one to suppose so. The idea pleased Dr. Fisher, who was floating in space like the fish in their water. *Paris-Monde* was open on the table.

"There's no disgrace in that," said Socrates, benign as usual. "Take me, now, when I lived in Athens . . ."

They all interrupted him at once, wishing to avoid hearing about the charms of a princess with fabulous diamonds—Socrates seemed to have been more smitten with the diamonds than with their royal owner.

"All this is absurd," piped up the antiquary. "I quite understand your grief, Madame Prêtre, and I never had a liking for that . . . that woman," he said, waving his hand towards the open magazine. "But this gives us no reason to suppose . . . er, no. Our friend is so remote from such material questions that I'm sure he never even noticed . . ."

Madame Prêtre guffawed.

"It would be very natural," said Socrates.

"What would be natural?" asked Germaine Lethuit.

"Uh, well, that they'd make it up if . . ."

"At the very moment when that woman is publicly flaunting her affair with the painter? Oh, come! Thank goodness, Stéphane Morani's standards of morality are too high to permit . . ."

"But it's clear," said Gérard Ducas. "Stéphane, the poor dear fellow, doesn't suspect a thing. I'm persuaded that he believes models are extremely well paid for posing, or that *Paris-Monde* has paid her a large sum. You can be sure that she makes him believe whatever she likes."

"He's certainly ready to believe."

"And why not?" exclaimed Jean Cadou. "What do you expect the poor devil to do? Do you expect him to get up on his high horse and declaim, 'Leave me, unfortunate woman!' and the whole shebang of classical drama? The flat belongs to her, you might almost say he doesn't work, he's a sick man, where would he go? But I'm sure he's the wretchedest man on earth."

"Why?" asked Socrates naïvely. For him, money sanctified everything. Oh, if only he were still in Athens! The restaurant, the dazzling white tablecloths. . . . He sank into his dream.

Dr. Fisher, still soaring, was supremely indifferent to what was being said. He liked to hear people making sounds around him, that was all. So many words for nothing! Sound effects.

But Mademoiselle Lethuit was worked up with indignation. "Jean, I don't understand your reasoning. Now, take my sister: in giving her a home when she needed it, I knew perfectly well that it meant my renouncing marriage, renouncing a normal life. Well, I didn't hesitate a second. I said to her, 'Pauline . . . '"

"Why of course," the antiquary put in eagerly, "of course, that's what Morani would do. I mean to say, he wouldn't take into account any material considerations, and if he had any idea . . ."

"And he hadn't any suspicions when the flat was repainted?" said Madame Prêtre bitterly. "And he doesn't suspect a thing when he sees his wife dressing like a princess? Or when she gives him rumpsteak every day for dinner?"

"He eats rumpsteak every day?" asked Socrates, interested.

"And he drinks vintage claret, Mademoiselle Marie told me that, she's seen the woman-in-question doing her shopping."

That rumpsteak, that claret, those luxuries, had all been stolen from Sylvia, according to Madame Prêtre's way of thinking. It all went to prove that Sylvia was a ninny, that Sylvia would never make anything of her life, that Sylvia would become the wife of the detested photographer. . . . And when that little ninny had tried to justify herself, she'd not been able to talk about anything but Stéphane Morani, while those Moranis (Madame Prêtre did not dissociate the two) sat eating rumpsteak at her, Sylvia's, expense.

"That doesn't prove a thing," said Ducas. "For my part, I never notice what I eat."

"It doesn't prove a thing," said Jean, "and anyone can see he's horribly upset. All this publicity. . . ."

"It doesn't prove a thing," said Germaine Lethuit. "Stéphane never had a practical mind, he's one of those rare souls . . ."

Even Dr. Fisher came down for a moment from his clouds. "It doesn't prove a thing," he said, smiling at the girl with the nenuphars. What *did* prove anything on this earth?

"Oh, of course," said Socrates, conciliating as usual, "it doesn't prove a thing." But to himself he thought that a handsome woman who brought money home was a godsend. Although it seemed doubtful whether Monsieur Morani liked money. To Socrates it seemed impossible that anyone could not like it, and yet . . . He remained thoughtful.

Madame Prêtre clenched her fists. Were they all against her? All against Sylvia? All of them ready to agree that Sylvia belonged where she was, in the arms of the photographer, in his miserable little flat, surrounded by family photographs, and with the cinema on Saturdays, and furniture on the instalment plan? Sylvia herself admitted defeat, was content with that niggardly life, implicitly recognized that she was made for nothing better, that Madame Prêtre had brought her into the world, cared for her, brought her up, suffered for nothing more than that destiny which was the very pattern of the commonplace. Shame and anger burned within Madame Prêtre. They seemed quite convinced, however. . . . But weren't they also convinced of the high-mindedness of Stéphane Morani, who let his flat be painted at the expense of his wife's lover? Oh, the world, as she often said, needn't ask her for a clean bill of health! Sylvia had succumbed. Monsieur Morani, too, would succumb sooner or later, and people would see what he was worth.

The door opened.

"If I'd be so kind as to what?"

Louise gave a last look at herself in the mirror, then put on some lipstick.

"To tell them . . ."

She smiled at him, a kind smile, when all was said and done.

"I'm to tell them you have 'flu. Right?"

"But when they see me go to work tomorrow?"

"Just wrap up well. That won't hurt you."

He stretched a hand out to her uncertainly.

"You're kind, Lou. Will you be home late?"

"Why—about the usual time," she said, a little embarrassed.

Averting his eyes, he pretended to riffle through the pages of a book on the table. "You might, perhaps, avoid . . . coming home in that limousine," he muttered. "They know that car, you see. It looks bad."

She turned her back, pretending to look at herself again in the mirror. "Right you are. I'll get out behind the station."

A vague, uncomfortable complicity hovered between them.

The door opened.

"My husband is very sorry," she said in her warm voice which seemed to fill the room, "but he can't come down tonight. He's afraid he has 'flu."

No one said anything.

Outside, tirelessly, the traffic lights signalled yellow, red, green, arrogantly dominating the paltry blue and white neon signs. From the shadows of the Boulevard Edgar-Quinet, the pale young women in high heels, looking paler as the hours passed, emerged as if from a dark lake. At the other end of the street, the Montparnasse station slumbered, with intermittent little snores, and the yellow arrow of the Café Dupont marked a mysterious boundary. This autumn was like the spring: rainy and warm. And through the gentle rain, in the warm night air, the crowds surged up and down the pavements of the rue d'Odessa, feasting themselves on lights and lustful desires, going in and out of the cinema and the cafés, dodging and holding up the advancing traffic. There had been a great deal of hot weather that year, but the forecast was for a change. Something in the air already seemed to indicate it. Avidly, avidly, everyone was enjoying this reprieve before the onslaught of winter.

The Brasserie Dorée is eternal. The torpor meted out by its syrupy refrains, the tranquillity born of a senseless act in which one freely participates, the warmth that springs from the assurance of being nestled in the very bosom of society, in what it has that is most inane and innocuous, is an eternal need. The office-worker with the bitten fingernails, slumped on the red imitation leather seat before a glass of Pernod, far from those "It's bad for your liver" remarks of domestic life, the young girls in slacks, humming the tunes, the gentleman who takes a newspaper from the stack provided by the management, and buries himself up to the ears in it, the travellers who dump at their feet the suitcase tied up with string that will burst open only when it reaches the station platform, the suburbanite without luggage and with a quarter of an hour to kill, the prostitute with the familiar fox fur, who glances round her nervously, for she is taking a bit of a rest in territory that is not hers, the worthy matron, some kind of local shop-keeper, who examines the wine card carefully then asks for something else, all this is steeped in a humanity that is dense without depth, a substance one might call peace if peace, for a moment, could be confused with somnolence.

And Stéphane, sitting at his piano, playing the most popular songs, *Les Lavandières du Portugal*, *Le Facteur de Panama*, and even, at times, giving a piano solo (with lavish help from the pedal) of medleys of his favourite composers (what a wonderful piece, that, *Night on a Bare Mountain*!), Stéphane, too, likes it here. The manager has a wink for Bruno, a smile for Marcel, but he greets Stéphane with gracious condescension, while Toni the waitress tries to pass as close as possible to him, and the music that pours out, flows on without stopping; it is eternal, and will prevent any word from ever being spoken.

Everything is in its place, everything is final. Now and then a pale
ray of sunlight filters through the rain from outside and quickens
the tarnished gildings and the spotted mirrors. A fine dust powders
the green plants that have been periodically replaced in the course
of twenty years and will be replaced again. On the walls, opulent
purple nudes cloak the harmless daydreams of repressed customers
with a respectable artistic pretext, (Oh, that purple! And look,
some of them, still more artistic, are frankly green! How marvellous!), just as the mirrors and plants satisfy less carnal desires.
And the music flows on, the nudes display themselves, filling empty
heads that would be horrified to know their own emptiness.

Everything is in its place. Stéphane plays a solo, variations on a
Chopin theme recalled from years long past. Tonight he does not
even trouble to revive his slumbering bitterness. Did he ever have
ambitions? Would he be happier, executing to perfection his
arpeggios and trills before a respectful audience in some stern concert hall? Did arpeggios and trills ever give him anything except the
mirage of admiring audiences in concert halls? Perhaps not. And
so, with the vanishing of that mirage, he placidly plays (inevitably
helped out by that precious pedal) a most melancholy concentrate
of Chopin. And when a woman begins to nod her head nostalgic-
ally, her hat oscillating perilously, he will not even smile. The fat
woman is eternal.

For the benefit of those people who might weary of the nudes
and demand something better, there are murals of moon-faced
Pierrots in a wild harlequinade, and on the tables artificial flowers,
plushily entangled, and Bruno, who now recites his chaplet of
songs (limp beads told in pseudo *Mexicano* accents):

> *Si tu m'aimais, le monde*
> *tra-la, la, la,*
> *Reprendrait ses couleurs*
> *tra-la, la, la . . .*

Oh, let not that voice impel the purple nudes to leave their
frames and revolutionize mythology! (Why, I thought it was
Pygmalion, and Orpheus? No, my goodness, Orpheus, that's

animals!) How scandalized the customers would be! Let us have dreams only, dreams only, if you please! Waiter, what does that mean? Stéphane would suddenly play off-key. What danger, what mystery in the body of a woman, in that brutal nakedness that allows no subterfuge! And how disturbing is the appeal of real music. . . . Let things stay as they are.

Let no word be ever again pronounced. Let the woman whose hat is trembling remain there, before her cooling cup of chocolate, an innocent, empty-headed puppet! Let the gentleman at the back of the room emerge at regular intervals from the depths of his newspaper and utter a chaotic discourse, of which nothing can be heard but words such as "Fatherland" and "Duty", worn so pebble-smooth that they are no longer even words. Let Chopin be martyrized without complaint by the foolish pedal, without daring to recall that he venerated Bach. Let the sexless Pierrot be all poesy, and let him pluck a branch of that odourless mimosa. Oh! Notary from the provinces obliged to wait for the train that leaves at twelve-two midnight, having come to Paris for the Montparnasse Follies' autumn show, remain forever provincial notary! Manager, remain manager, let only the well-worn words, "my position requires", fall from your lips forever, and do not tell us about your little girl or ask us anything, especially don't ask us anything. Sing, Bruno, with your best Mexican accent, those warbling words you so adore. Keep on singing, don't talk, and don't remain silent. Let the insipid sounds safeguard us all. It would need but a word or a moment of silence to . . .

The Brasserie Dorée is eternal. The Montparnasse music-hall is eternal. Faces without names, names without faces, words without flesh and flesh without words are eternal. Stéphane plays the piano. Stéphane writes. Stéphane talks. Stéphane's memories are set down in black and white and neatly stored in a desk drawer. Let music be eternal. . . . What other prayer could rise from all these drowsing people here assembled?

Autumn is even more melancholy in the suburbs, with their damp roads, their small houses bared of blooms, and Meudon, that particular day, had the look of a rarely visited cemetery. The road leading to the villa in the Jeanne-d'Arc Square was spongy, and Germaine Lethuit's heels sank into it with a soft depressing sound. After visiting so many hovels, after giving so much advice and engaging in so many discussions, she was eager to get back to the little sitting-room where at least the blue hydrangeas of the wall-paper were flowering in neat patterns.

She went into the little hall where, for economy's sake, the lamp was never lit, took off her overshoes, and for a moment stood there smiling, listening to Pauline's singing, which was punctuated from time to time by an approving grunt from the old man. Everything was peaceful in the cosy little house. To give herself a further illusion of secluded comfort, Germaine fastened the chain on the door and put on her house-slippers. Then, her briefcase under her arm, she entered the sitting-room, where a Mirus stove was roaring pleasantly.

"Here you are at last, Germaine!" exclaimed the old man, for whom a walk down the Jeanne-d'Arc lane at night represented a dangerous journey which he was all too glad to see his daughter survive, safe and sound.

"So soon, Germaine?" asked the soft voice of Pauline, who knew that it was Monday, when Germaine usually came home by the late train. But it would be useless to call the old man's attention to this, for his memory was failing. The two sisters exchanged a knowing look.

"Yes, here I am, my dears!" said Germaine, pleasurably aware, as every evening, that she was the most important person in the household, the one who returns from the outside world burdened with news and having escaped a thousand dangers. She flung the brief case on the piano, and sank into an armchair, with the theatrical exhaustion of one of the world's workers.

"A good day?" asked the old man, who had laid aside his news-paper.

"Not bad. I've finally persuaded that poor girl to keep her child with her. Having only one room is no excuse, for after all, many families have no more space and manage to take care of their children."

"It's the fault of a negligent government," said the old man, shaking his grey head. "If Jaurès had lived to see this . . ."

"We have no able politicians," said Pauline gravely. She was looking very pretty with her hair done up high and a fringe half covering her brow, in the old-fashioned way.

"There's little to hope for, either in the Opposition or in the Government. God knows, I did not approve Clemenceau's politics, but . . ." This was his favourite subject. "Yes," he went on indignantly, "Clemenceau was everything you like, but he was a man—a man! Today, all we have are limp dish-rags! Listen to this!" He brandished his newspaper, and in a blustering voice read an article aloud.

Germaine felt wonderfully relaxed. Even these fits of indignation, even these arguments and the raised pitch of her voice and Pauline's, calculated to reach the failing ear of their father, were all, in the long run, a part of the home, as surely as the paper on the walls, the roaring of the Mirus stove, the creaking of the old Breton cupboard. In a moment Pauline would introduce the name of Mendès-France into the conversation, since she considered him extremely attractive, perhaps because he looked something like her guilty husband. Dinner would be enlivened by a discussion of the cost of living, in the course of which the old man would repeat for the hundredth time (while the sisters exchanged compassionate glances), the things you could buy in 1891 for fifty centimes. Then Pauline would sing a song by Duparc, forcing her voice as much as possible, and her father, sitting close to the piano and cupping his ear in his hand, would mutter, "What a genius that Fauré!" while beating the wrong time. Peace and Virtue reigned over the Jeanne-d'Arc villa.

The old man had again plunged into his newspaper. "Today, Monday," he read in quite a loud voice, under the impression that he was muttering. "Is it Monday today?"

"Is it Monday?" Pauline repeated with well feigned artlessness. "Why, I don't know. Is it Monday, Germaine?"

"You're both crazy," said Germaine, smiling. "What did we do yesterday?"

"Oh, of course, our walk! What was I thinking of?"

"Of course!" said her father, reassured. "You must have mixed me up, Linette. But why did you come back so early, Germaine, if it's Monday? Didn't that little Monday meeting take place?"

Germaine shook her head. "No. I just went to see our tenant and settle a few questions with him. . . ."

"Is he nice?" Pauline sighed, trying to sound disinterested. But Germaine's reply proved that she had understood, as always, and it went directly to the point.

"He's twenty-five years old, and he's engaged to be married."

Monsieur Lethuit was not interested in the tenant; he was interested in those Monday reunions. "But what a shame," he said, "not to go on with them! I thought those friendly little meetings were so interesting, with everyone contributing his share of ideas, and collaborating in mutual good understanding. It was especially good for you, Germaine, you go out so little. It seems to me this is the second Monday without a meeting?"

"Is it because Stéphane Morani is ill again?" asked Pauline. She and her father never left Meudon, but they were acquainted with everything that went on in the Montparnasse quarter, most particularly in the rue d'Odessa. Pauline often thought about Stéphane Morani and Dr. Fisher and Martine Fortin while she nibbled at chocolates. But it must be admitted that the co-operative tenants of the rue d'Odessa seemed as remote to her as Monsieur Mendès-France. Obviously, she could go there and meet them. But Germaine wouldn't like that. And then, it was all so complicated; she preferred to hear about it in detail. "Well, Germaine?" she prodded.

"Ill? I suppose so. I saw his wife go into the chemist's."

"Oh yes, that woman . . ." said the old man.

"Does that still go on? Is she still with that painter?"

"Yes. It seems he knew her when she was younger."

"That doesn't excuse a thing," said the old man, severely. Partisan though he was of social progress, he came of a very strict Breton family, and there were some things he would never allow.

"But still, what a coincidence!" sighed the less strict Pauline, pushing back her stray curls with her fingertips. Though Pauline was forty and ate too many chocolates, she still had her dreams.

And all the same, she wore well for her age, was straight-backed and always remembered to hold her tummy in. Her pale blue eyes and rather full rosy lips may, however, have held an expression of regret. . . .

"What a disreputable woman!" continued Monsieur Lethuit, more Breton this evening than Socialist. "And her husband puts up with it?"

"Oh come, Father, he doesn't know about it."

"He'll certainly find out one of these days."

"If he knew . . . I suppose he'd leave her. . . ."

"But you say he's in poor health," murmured Pauline, sympathetically.

"He could go to a hospital," said Germaine crossly.

"Go *where*?" asked the old man, who had picked up his paper again.

"To the hos–pit–al!"

"Oh yes, that's so, the hospitals are magnificent nowadays. Thank goodness, slow as it has been, we've made some social progress after all."

Moving his finger down the page—his eyesight was also failing—he was trying to find the passage in his article where he had left off. Pauline, who was passionately fond of love-stories, moved closer to her sister and soon they were whispering together like two little girls.

"The hospital, how frightful!"

"But in any case, since he doesn't know anything, Pauline. . . . Be practical!"

"If he finds out about it, perhaps he'll not leave her, in spite of everything."

"I don't see what else he could do."

"But if he loves her?"

"If he loves her, if he loves her! What do you mean? Your reasoning is childish. *Can* he love her after all she's done? Take yourself, for instance, when you discovered your husband's wrongdoing. . . ."

Pauline glanced stealthily towards the wall where, ridicule

notwithstanding, she had hung the portrait of Monsieur Mendès-France, pretending it was because of political convictions. "No, to be sure," she murmured rather uncertainly. "But . . ."

"Oh come, Pauline! There's no 'but' possible. If he hears about it, he will have to leave her. All the more reason to, since the other man is free and rich and can take care of her. If he stayed with her, people could say he was benefiting by it! As people might have said —had you not left André—that you were willing to benefit from his thefts."

"But if he loves her," Pauline insisted, like a stubborn child.

Germaine was frankly irritated. She had a horror of people who argued and pretended they had a right to more family allowance than they received. And Pauline seemed to be hinting. . . . Germaine Lethuit made the mistake of raising her voice. "I don't understand what you're insinuating, Pauline! It's not for you to say such foolish things, you who, thank heaven, have built your life on solid foundations and . . ." She became rather mixed up in her fine phrase, and Pauline took advantage of it.

"Built, built, that's easy to say. But I don't see what good it's done me," she muttered. She would have been ready to drop the argument, however, had not Germaine continued to harangue her indignantly in a lowered voice, so as not to disturb the old gentleman who was reading.

"At least you haven't had to spend your life with a man who was robbing the State, my girl. And when you made your decision . . ."

"Oh! *My* decision!" muttered Pauline, sulkily.

"Surely you're not going to say that I forced you to get a divorce!"

They were both flushed with anger, now, as they faced one another; Pauline rather more sulky, Germaine frankly enraged, but they did not raise their voices, and they restrained their gestures, their tension showing only in the way their fingernails clawed at the tapestried arms of their chairs.

"All the same, you pushed me into it."

"I pushed you, I?"

"Yes!"

"And tell me why, please? Why would I have pushed you into it? I suppose it was to my advantage?" Germaine scoffed.

This reminder of her dependence upon Germaine made the sensitive Pauline redden. "You pushed me into it so you wouldn't have to remain alone with Papa!" she replied with a vehemence surprising in her. "You pushed me into it so that I'd become an old maid like you!" With this, since she could no longer control the pitch of her voice, she ran out to the kitchen, from which came a slight smell of burning.

The old gentleman raised his eyes. "Is something wrong, Germaine?"

She felt a little ashamed. "Nothing, Papa. Something's burning in the kitchen, I think."

"Oh, our little Pauline, always the same! What can you expect, my dear girl? She's like a bird, a little bird that sings and pays no heed to anything else. Oh, if we didn't have you, you and your sense of responsibility. . . ."

His gentle blue eyes rested on his daughter with tenderness. He adored his daughters, the one for her sweetness and beauty, her profound femininity, the other for her energy, her courage, and what he called her "sense of responsibility". There was no preference in his heart, as Germaine knew, and the admiration he felt for her— that father who, in his whole life had never been able to obtain a raise in salary, and was now satisfied with a meagre pension— because he considered her a hardy buccaneer of modern life, revived and warmed her every evening.

But this evening, Pauline's outburst had dumbfounded her. That sweet sister! Germaine did not hold a grudge against her for the tirade, even now she was ready to forgive. She could imagine how painful stories of love must be to that wounded heart. But Pauline's reproaches! With scrupulous fairness, Germaine examined her conscience. At the painful moment when the dishonesty of the Post Office employee had become apparent, had she felt some pleasure? True, she had always foreseen a catastrophe of the kind; the young man was not very reliable. But no one could say she had been pleased. Had she, as Pauline accused her, urged the separation?

Her advice had been asked and she had given it, nothing more. She had never thought to see the day when Pauline would reproach her for it, nor that her sister would regret the man who had robbed the State. Heaven knows what depths he would have sunk to some day! Besides the larceny, there had been that affair with the attractive little dressmaker; there had been no child but Germaine had been quick to see in it additional proof of her brother-in-law's corruption. He was dishonest, a woman-chaser; how, then, could such a man have made Pauline happy? It was only reasonable to alienate her from him. Germaine had only thought of her sister's happiness, and after all these peaceful years, she was not now going to question herself on these matters.

"And if he loves her?" She could still hear her sister's irritating voice, putting the question. It was this stupid romanticism that had driven Pauline into that deplorable marriage. Thank God, such crazy ideas had no connection with reality. Why, it was almost laughable, she decided, recalling the moving pages that Stéphane Morani had read to them the other day. To accuse her, Germaine, was as ridiculous as to accuse Stéphane Morani. Ridiculous!

Germaine Lethuit did not believe in absolute evil. The evil she discovered each day on her visits, she attributed to ignorance or poverty. Once and for all she had divided the world into categories: the unfortunates (who lived in cramped quarters, squandered their family allowances on drink, had too many children; to these people it was suitable to bring vaccines and kind words); then, there were the educated folk, nice people such as herself, Stéphane Morani, school-teachers, nurses; and finally there were the malefactors, people who robbed the State (Heaven knows why that seemed to her a degree worse than the mere robbers of individuals), and on the same plane, the members of the Government who did not do their duty. This classification had always seemed adequate to her.

"So I would remain an old maid like you!" Those words were incredible. Surely, Pauline herself did not believe in them. Anger. . . . Germaine Lethuit honestly examined her conscience. She visualized the Post Office employee, his attractive dark eyes—she had never denied that André was attractive. "Let me see her, let me explain," he had said. "No, André, better not see her." Had she been wrong to say that? Had she thought of anything except her sister's happiness? Had there been a tinge of jealousy? No. She had devoted herself to Pauline, had worked for her and fed her for ten years without one single regret or reproach. Even, with pleasure.

She had liked the decisions she had had to take, such things as selling one flat, finding another—so they need not sell everything that had come down to them from their mother. She had liked the responsibilities, had liked the feeling that everything depended on her. But from that to . . . No. Such devotion did exist. For instance, take Stéphane Morani. She always came back to that comforting sensation she had had when she had heard him reading from his journal. What a touching passage that was, in which he spoke of his solitude, of the spiritual aid Martine had given him. . . . But now it seemed they were at odds with each other? For a second Germaine forgot her own troubles to deplore the idea. She was fond of Martine. A serious and practical soul, with, evidently, a rather difficult disposition, but . . . They would make up their quarrel. All that wasn't important. Germaine Lethuit did not believe in evil. Or at least, if evil existed, it existed outside; checked, kept away from the little suburban house by the chain on the door and the closed shutters. Evil concerned outsiders, the people one didn't know. It could not exist within her. The kind smiles of her friends, her work that was so useful, so full of self-sacrifice. No. Evil was outside.

The old man raised his head and smiled. "Is everything quite all right, Germaine?"

The affection she read in his faded blue eyes moved her deeply. If he knew the crazy thoughts she had just been having! He, who had passed his life in honesty and virtue, sacrificing himself for his daughters. . . . She, too, no doubt, had done everything possible for him. No doubt one could say he, too, had not been displeased to have Pauline restored to him, thanks to her divorce, and to be able to live very tranquilly with his two daughters. She was at once ashamed of the thought. Decidedly she was not herself today. It must be this unusually mild autumn weather. . . .

"Have you read the article on Cuba, Germaine? I'd very much

like to have your opinion on it. Listen to this: 'The economic resources of the country . . .' "

Dear old soul! How fond he was of these harmless discussions during which he set all Europe and America to rights! She blushed over having had that doubt about him. Poor Pauline, she was nervous as she always was at the changes of the seasons. What more normal than for her to have thought in a moment of weakness, about her husband? The chaste Germaine Lethuit had read Freud and the medical books. She knew there were mental upsets that could be explained by physiology. Poor Pauline! Moved by a wave of generosity, she left her chair and ran into the kitchen where her sister was crying into the lamb stew.

"Pauline, please forgive me, I must be tired. . . ."

Pauline's sweet, puckered-up face cleared. "Oh no, it's my fault, my nerves . . ."

They hugged and kissed, they smiled at each other. In the sitting-room, their father, who had noticed nothing and still thought he was being listened to, went on reading about the resources of Cuba in his steady voice, articulating all the words clearly. Outside, the autumn rain continued to fall, on the arbour, the iris, and the terra-cotta dwarfs.

Let music be eternal. . . .

Eternal are the pleasures of the suburbs, the romances, the arbours, the little gardens, the hedge-clippers and the hedges clipped like poodle dogs, the blue bedrooms, the pink bedrooms, the doors locked at night against hypothetical prowlers. The not unpleasant humidity of cupboards that smell of mushrooms, the isolation and the silence (the train only ten minutes away), the shutters, the piano, the calendar with its pages kept up to date. And then, there are the planned vacations, the respected precedences, the birthdays of relatives one will never see; the good morning, the good evening, the manias, the habits, the chain, the lock, the keyhole. Who will enter, who will go out of a house so well guarded?

The eight-thirty-four train takes only twelve minutes to reach Meudon. Twelve minutes which stretch out like infinity between the exterior world and the little house with the iris. Twelve minutes —sufficient barrier behind which to thrust everything that one has seen or heard "outside". Let the wisteria bloom and fade, to bloom again. Nothing should ever harm them. Germaine would bring back to them from the outside world no blemish, no offending smell. Nothing that could be smuggled through the garden gate and disturb the spell-bound dance of the dwarfs. Names and figures, facts and even anecdotes; but nothing, nothing that could alter the wisteria, upset the tender image of Pauline singing, of their father reading near the stove, king in his small realm. No contagion should ever reach them: anything impure had been long banished from the peaceful garden.

Twelve minutes away is fear and pity and suffering; twelve minutes away there are, it is true, those hundreds of steps to go up and down, the body broken with fatigue, those words of comfort articulated a hundred times, nerves tense with fatigue. There are those little pleasures rejected, those little temptations waved aside, that constant generosity which again and again gives its time, its strength, its life. . . . Twelve minutes away. But fatigue is also an armour. Chastity and goodness, too, rise up like ramparts. Twelve minutes away. Nothing shall ever be put in question in the little house with the wisteria. Eternal shall be the peace agreed upon, everlasting the roaring stove, the respected father, the two sisters embracing in the kitchen. No germ has been able to infect them: their rigid armour is their protection.

Let music be eternal. . . .

How calm Dr. Fisher's study was! The heavy green curtains, the mahogany desk, the fine carpeting, all looked as though they had been placed there to be photographed. And the Doctor himself, always so neat and elegant (and to what, exactly, he owed that look of elegance was hard to say), seemed to be the perfect image of a text-book physician rather than an actual doctor. His air of detachment, his precise movements, were pleasant to see. One almost felt that he analysed his gestures so as to carry them out more deliberately, counting an imaginary tempo to himself, as if for gymnastic exercises. And he himself felt something of this. Even his words were now articulated without any trouble, almost without accent, and floated away, independent of him, with a dexterity of their own. . . .

"Sit down, my dear fellow. Now, what's the trouble. The usual discomforts. The heart is tired, isn't it? As it happens, a new preparation has been sent to me."

He stood up, walked towards the cabinet almost joyfully, found the medicine, explained the formula on the label to his patient. How easily he breathed and walked and talked! The atmosphere appeared to be so light, the air so transparent, that his body seemed almost weightless.

As soon as he could get rid of this patient, he thought, he would take a turn on the boulevard, for the sheer pleasure of feeling more weightless than all the others who lumbered along so heavily. For two pins he'd dismiss the man sitting opposite him, with a wave of the hand as if banishing a phantom. Would the man vanish into thin air? But the man seemed to be waiting for something more. Benevolently, Dr. Fisher indulged the patient's whim.

"Do you want me to examine you? The last X-ray, you know, wasn't too bad, considering everything. But if you like. Your blood-pressure, perhaps. . . . We haven't seen much of you these recent Mondays. Roll up your sleeve, please. And how is Mademoiselle Fortin? Is she well?"

He did not listen to the reply, but negligently manœuvred the little rubber bulb. "I have an insane inclination to go for a stroll on the boulevard," he could not keep from saying. "Yes, your blood-pressure is a little low. Do you take the tonic I prescribed, regularly?"

"Yes. But, Doctor, it's raining!"

"I don't mind rain at all. I'm fond of rain. Well now, there's nothing new in your state of health. I'll . . . have you the prescription?"

"My wife must have it somewhere. But I can go to fetch it."

The Doctor felt a dangerous impatience mounting in him, always an indication that his period of euphoria was coming to an end. It started with impatience, then anger, then the sluggish feeling returned, slowly regaining his disillusioned body, and finally there were the tears of exasperation over these sudden relapses. . . . If he could go out of doors quickly, the euphoria would last a while, would be maintained by the act of walking, and the silence. He drew a sheet of paper towards him and began scrawling on it with a trembling hand.

"I'll write a new one. Don't bother. Did you say Mademoiselle Fortin is quite well?" He spoke with feverish rapidity, to hurry things. Already he imagined himself on the threshold, bidding his visitor goodbye, giving him a friendly slap on the back; in anticipation he could see himself on the boulevard, a free man, inhaling deeply, a little intoxicated, walking in the midst of other people who would be nothing but shadows. The voice of the patient, heavy as lead, distressing to his rasped nerves, reached his ears.

"Frankly speaking, Doctor, I . . . I don't know. This may seem strange to you, but . . . I believe the poor girl is suffering a little from overwork, and is a little . . . well, in short, she's not quite herself. An inexplicable misunderstanding. . . ."

"Oh, very good, very good," said the Doctor hurriedly. "I mean, it's very regrettable, without a doubt. . . ."

"More than regrettable! I must say, Doctor, that I myself am amazed at the way she . . . well now, can you imagine, she walked right by me as if she didn't know me. . . ."

The Doctor got up, took a few steps towards the door. But Morani remained seated, Morani was hanging on, waiting for a reply. The Doctor stepped back and laid a hand on the poor fellow's shoulder. "It is certainly regrettable," he said, immediately conscious that he was saying the word for the second time. His irritation mounted.

"And I had such confidence in her! You see, meeting her was such an event for me. I believed in her, took everything to her, my illusions, my . . ."

"You should have been on your guard," said Dr. Fisher, in an oddly curt voice.

"On my guard, Doctor, that's what they've always told me.

But I've never learned to be mistrustful of people. From my unfortunate marriage to this last blow, I've always wanted to believe in the goodness of human beings, I've always wanted to preserve myself from being callous. . . ."

"Yes, it's pleasant, isn't it, to delude yourself with little bedtime stories. But you see where it gets you. . . ."

Stéphane appeared to be painfully surprised at the Doctor's asperity. "Yes," he said, thoughtfully, "events seem to have proved me wrong. But I won't lay down my arms, if I dare put it that way. If Martine is weakening now, I'd rather not know about it. I only want to remember the wonderful days when she was herself. . . ."

"You'd rather not know about it!" said the Doctor brusquely. "Then what are you complaining about? You're paying the price of your stupidity!" He seemed to realize the unseemliness of this outburst, checked himself, and continued in a gentler tone: "When she was herself! What do you mean by 'herself'? How can you know for sure what she is?"

What had happened to the supreme detachment he had felt during the reading of the journal? He had expected that one day or another events would open this fool's eyes to reality. But this stubbornness . . .

"As it happens," said Stéphane with dignity, "I'm one of those people who believe they can choose the part that is best in things and people. The odds, you know. . . ."

He wore the superior smile of those who know they cannot expect to be understood. This was too much for Dr. Fisher. The odds! As though he himself, in his way, had not bet on the odds! And how totally, how lamentably he had lost! The Doctor began pacing up and down the room, unable to contain the words that came to him; he had reached the degree of nervousness and exasperation when going out would no longer be of any avail. And it was this man who had brought him to such a point! The pleasant detachment, the feeling of winged weightlessness, had vanished, leaving only this acute nervous irritation. He clenched his fists.

"So you believe such things aren't dangerous? You actually think you can intoxicate yourself with words, launch ideas into the air, and live, like everyone else, at peace with yourself and others?" As he heard himself speak, he was horrified at his own words. And the fellow remained there, with that strange look of foolish amazement stamped on his face. That fellow who was the cause of all this, who had come here to badger him, persecute him with his big words and empty phrases, phrases that he had repeated many times, no doubt, but which Dr. Fisher was really hearing today for the first time.

"Why, Doctor, I don't understand. I've suffered enough for . . ."

"Words!" said the Doctor wrathfully. "Words, always words. I was like you, and may you never have the experience I had, may you never find out as I did what words can cost. You would do better to shut up for good and live quietly with your wife, of whom you haven't so much to complain, and whom you'd be very sorry to lose, yes, you'd be wise to live the tranquil little life that would suit you, and *shut up*!"

His voice had risen to a very high pitch; he could no longer control himself. The hand which he ran nervously through his white hair was trembling, and he mechanically loosened his tie. Stéphane's eyes still reflected nothing but that same rather shocked surprise.

"You surprise me, Doctor. Are there no other values for you than . . ."

"Other values! Imbecile! Terrible and dangerous imbecile! One day you'll see, when you're at the point of death (he stumbled on the word, and caught himself up), you'll see, one day. . . . Words will be of no use, then! No use at all!"

His fist came down on the desk with violence. All at once he heard his own voice yelling inarticulate words. The suffering this caused him did him good. He managed to get hold of himself. And yet, what good it would do him to howl in the face of everyone what he thought of them, to shout aloud his disdain and disgust! But the man in front of him was now very pale, although still staring with that stupid, idiotic astonishment. . . . The man would never be able to understand. They would never, any of them, understand his revolt, his wrath at being duped, at having sacrificed everything for a pasteboard idol. The poor fellow, with those wide open eyes of an innocent child, undoubtedly it wasn't his fault. Infantile mentality, poor health, necessary justification. . . . That intimate journal. . . . It was all more laughable than anything else. But today he felt it as a personal insult.

"Excuse me," he said in a voice that was still hoarse. "I'm feeling none too well today. But you should have the decency not to go about provoking people. . . . Excuse me." Little by little he returned to his usual tone, clear and precise. "I'm terribly overworked. The patients, my organization. . . . Do you know, we now have our own sanatorium in the Haute-Savoie? We didn't manage that without trouble! The authorizations. Here is your prescription."

Stéphane took it, still in a daze.

"And I beg of you, my dear chap, don't take to heart anything that escaped me. I suffer from a slight neurosis, you see . . . The things I went through. I hope that . . ."

"Why, of course, Doctor. I understand perfectly," Stéphane assured him. He had taken the prescription, had slipped it into his wallet, and was now looking for a banknote, while continuing against his will, to stare into the doctor's face.

"No, no, put your wallet away. We'll cancel this visit, what do you say?" said the physician, as he opened the door. "You know the way, I'll not show you out."

Stéphane made another movement towards his wallet, for pure form.

"No, no, I insist," the Doctor repeated with rather unnecessary emphasis. "Let's forget it."

For a moment more he remained on the threshold of the study. The outside door banged. Stéphane had gone. The Doctor shut the study door, crossed to the waiting-room.

"Next, please," he said in his precise voice.

But when he looked up, he saw that the little room was empty. He was alone in the flat, alone with the identity-card photograph, tiny and yellowed with age, which was lying in the lower drawer of the chest, the photograph he had not looked at for ten years. Why had he brought it away with him? He had had it on him when he fled, that was all. Why had he not thrown it away? Oh, God knew why ... and God knew why he had found peace for a moment four or five weeks before, in listening to the blah-blah of that imbecile, of those imbeciles. He should have shown the fellow the little photograph of a slightly plump woman, her hair dressed in an old-fashioned way, who had been for him all the love in the world. "All the love in the world" had not stood the strain. Nor had "love of humanity" or "a revolution true to itself" held out much better.... He should have shown the photograph to Morani, to prove to him ...

The Doctor shut the door to the waiting-room with almost excessive care, throwing the bolt in its catch, conscientiously, verifying that the door was locked, then verifying the other door. It was merely a mania he had, a tic, all these precautions, for he knew very well that he ran no risk. He went to sit down on the little green leather couch. His limbs were still trembling.

He should have shown Morani the photograph. What would you have done, if it had been you, pompous ass? What would you have said? Kill me, let me die with her, when it was so absolutely futile? Would all your big words have been any use for dying? And if you had gone off, as I did, crawling in the mud, hiding, suffering hunger and fear, suffering contempt and pity, and, after that, suffering the consulates, the standing in queues, the applications for this and that, the slaps on the back, of what use would your big words have been for living?

He knew he was right. To get all worked up was useless. But what put his back up was their obstinacy, the obstinacy of everyone, the determination of everyone to deny the glaring facts. Especially today. Yes, especially today. Confronted with the pig-headedness of that man, he'd flown off the handle. He'd like to see that fellow put to the test, see what he'd do in front of a human body gasping out its last breath in pain, a body that had nothing but a name in common with the woman in the yellowed little photograph. Imbecile, he had said, imbecile. . . . What good would it have done to expose myself? She would not even have recognized me. Yes, the imbecile would have found some big words for that, as well. To die for an ideal, he would have said, or not to abandon her in death. But it was not a dead woman that he had loved. With sudden malevolence, he wished that the imbecile would one day know this emptiness of mind and body. . . . Come, it was time to banish him from thought. All that had no meaning, no sense. It would lose its weight, its significance, and become diluted in space. It had to.

He stretched out on the little couch. The green leather was cold and smooth. He needed some rest. He extended his hand. The syringe was there, ready.

Eternal was the peace of the neat and dark little study. Eternal, the curtains that shut out the dazzling light, the locked desk-drawers which would never be opened, the shining and carefully cleaned instruments reposing in the glass cabinet. Eternal the mediocre sufferings which came in waves to break upon these shores, the invalids and those other sufferers stranded in a foreign land, the sufferers who had or did not have the right to some social aid (and after a moment of silence, surveying them with his pale blue eyes, Dr. Fisher examined them, and whether they were invalids or not, whether or not they had the right, he gave them that certificate, gave them that recommendation to the Ministry of Labour). Everlasting, the necessary social contacts, the official luncheons ("My dear sir, you as a distinguished foreigner should have the Legion of Honour, I really must do something about it for you. Your sanatorium? It's in the bag. However, we still need a few details, so come to my office. . ."). Eternal, the sovereign indifference and the contempt and still more indifference. He had stopped drinking now. This way was simpler. No one could buttonhole him any more, he would no more be the dupe of either people or of ideas. Jelly-fish. All of them jelly-fish. And the photograph would continue to lie quietly in the locked drawer. And the citation for brave conduct would lie dormant along with the Legion of Honour, filed away in his mind.

Eternal was the glacial sweetness of the liquid that was seeping into his thigh.

Everything was in place at the Turkish baths. The raised couches ranged along the walls, crude wooden benches, really, covered with thin mattresses, were ready for the naked bodies that would lie there and be kneaded by the aged masseuse.

Upon leaving the steam room, Louise had come, as usual, to lie on one of these couches, placing her wooden clogs on her left, her cigarettes on her right. While waiting for the masseuse, she had rolled over on her stomach and had placed in front of her, wide open, the detective story, *They'll Kill Me Tomorrow*. She intended to plunge into it, really plunge, for she wanted to avoid any conversation. "Things are all right as they are," she thought determinedly. The masseuse came up.

"Do you want your massage now, Madame?"

"No, not just yet. After a while, perhaps. But if you'll kindly hand me my dressing-gown. . . . Thank you."

She wrapped herself in it. It was not warm in the rest-room, and the humidity waiting for her outside in the rainy street made itself felt in the rather raw atmosphere of the room. Fortunately, the central heating would be turned on in another week. One could catch a cold the way it was at present. The rainy rue d'Odessa was waiting for her, and she had no wish to leave this place. Perhaps the massage would put her right. But she wanted to relax a little more, with her mind a blank. One could not keep from thinking during a massage, and these days she did not want to think.

It was not so much for the steam baths as for the silence that she had come here. In the hot-room beyond this one, the women were noisy, laughing in the clouds of steam, chatting, retailing the latest gossip, quarrelling now and then, and a naked woman, wringing out her hair, had angrily stamped her feet. But in the rest-room, where the mats seemed to be very cold, the silence was interrupted only occasionally by the groan of a woman being massaged with a little too much force. Silence. The woman lying naked on a couch against the opposite wall had a rather beautiful body, slightly plump, and very white, partly by contrast with the dark red wall, partly because of the talcum with which the masseuse was powdering it. There was no other woman in the room, now. It was still early, and many of the women lingered in the steam-room for hours. The windows were set high, like loop-holes in a fortress. Here one felt isolated from the rest of the world; that feeling of isolation was exactly what Louise had come to find. "For once, no men!" They were all—all of them—such bores. Take Henry, now, who was beginning to make scenes and stir up rows. She would never have believed that of him. Oh, well! She began to read:

Elaine listened, heard the creaking of footsteps in the hall. Suddenly she could not remember whether or not she had shut the door. Horrified, she stared at the oak panel. Slowly, the knob seemed to turn. Was the door going to open?

The next two pages were stuck together. Involuntarily her hand went to her hair in search of a hairpin, but she had let her hair down and the pins were in her coat pocket. She looked despairingly at her beige coat which was hanging too high up to be reached without standing. To get up was almost unthinkable. She considered the problem.

That beige was a smart colour, the coat was really pretty, and made her look more slender. What she would actually have preferred, though, was a leather coat from Hermès which cost two hundred thousand francs. She had been on the point of mentioning it to Henry, but after that scene he'd made the other day she had told herself that this was not the moment to talk about such things. However, when a man proposes marriage . . . She skipped the stuck pages, and continued to read the following page, with displeasure:

Elaine could not understand what had happened to her. The unknown man who had entered her room . . .

This was the inconvenience—and the attraction—of this kind of book: you could not skip one page. She adored these books which you could not put down once you had opened them, compelled to read to the very end. Stéphane had certainly tormented her enough on this subject, holding forth endlessly on the theme of "good reading"! Good reading, good social relations, good conduct. . . .

As if the world were a contaminated place where you risked catching the itch! And now Henry was beginning to harangue her, as well! Oh, men. . . .

Lazily she rolled over on her side and lit a cigarette. That must have made him wild when she compared him to Stéphane. She had sensed it the minute she had made the mistake, but she had expected that by the following day he would have banished the whole thing from his mind. Instead, he had demanded, "What did you mean the other day with your 'Stéphane and you, you're all alike, you men'?" She had been unable to keep from laughing. "Why, nothing at all," she had said, "I merely meant that you like to make scenes." "Scenes! So you think it's all the same as you put it! You mix me up with that fellow! You . . ." He had held forth for a good half hour at least.

If she'd understood aright, what he wanted to say was that it happened to be just the contrary. Stéphane was this, while he, Henry, was that. . . . She was convinced she was right, however: men were all alike, with them it was just one scene after another. Above all, she must not waste her strength trying to understand. She had suffered enough in the old days, without showing it, over the scenes Stéphane made. His questionings, his absurd demands, and that underlying, ever-present reproach, present from the first days of tender, burning love, in the miserable little hotel room where the entire furnishings were the bed and their two bodies. Even then, when he still loved her, when she thought him so handsome, there had been those scenes. "Oh, if only I had been the first man in your life!" He would say that, and then fly into a temper because she laughed. "We must make some worthwhile social contacts," he would say, and fly into a temper because she asked "Why?" She had cried over it several times. But she had been young then. Nowadays, she was quite determined not to listen or to worry about anything.

"Yes, you can begin now," she said to the masseuse.

Might as well have a massage, since it was impossible to keep from thinking anyway. She gave herself over to the strong hands of the masseuse. No use being stingy. She had ten thousand francs in her bag, and the very idea made her rejoice. Henry was rich, despite his moans and groans; he was well known, he didn't even have to work any more. He had everything he needed for happiness, as the saying was. He had still less reason than Stéphane to make scenes. Then why couldn't he be quiet? True, it was that journal that had especially upset him. He must have gathered from it that she still loved Stéphane. Poor Stéphane! God knew. . . .

The naked woman couched in the niche on the opposite side of the room also stretched her plump body, as if reflecting Louise's movements in a looking-glass. The oval of her face glimmered; she had perhaps applied some cold cream. It was too dark to see whether she were ugly or pretty. The woman's long, fair hair took on, at that distance, more importance than the face. It was unusual, Lou commented to herself, to see fair-haired women at the baths. The women who came here were more apt to be Jewish. Possibly the fair-haired woman was a local shop-keeper who had come here to enjoy some exoticism on the cheap. Or perhaps she had liver trouble and steam-bath treatments had been prescribed? Perhaps she was merely trying to take off weight. Lying on her side, like Lou, the woman was massaging her hips, an involuntary gesture of all plump women. . . . How good it was not to know her, not to know anyone, to be at peace there in the rather dim, raw, airless coolness of this place, as if at the bottom of a well. This was true repose, as refreshing as a drink. She preferred it even to the warm, dark void of sleep or love.

Silence was what she needed today. With a clatter of wooden clogs on the marble floor, another woman came to lie down not far off, draping herself in a kimono, hunting for her cigarettes. . . . Thank Heaven, the woman did not want to talk but was content to lie there sniffing a bottle of scent. . . . Gestures were so adequate, why did people feel the need of adding words? Lou felt very, very comfortable. The silent women, the distant sound of water which came from the shower-room, the wooden pillars framing the crude couch on which she lay, the mingy little fountain in the middle of the room, with discarded clogs stacked on the floor beside it . . .

and the tiny windows, placed so high that one might believe oneself in prison. The silence. . . .

Poor Steph! He could never have known silence like this. Why did some people feel such an urge to spoil things? For he had spoiled everything, even their amazed discoveries of those first days. . . . She had always believed, with a childlike resentment, that he "did it on purpose", that for some obscure reason he had a grudge against his very existence, that he was avenging himself on Heaven only knew what. . . . But today she thought he had also avenged himself on himself, if that journal spoke the truth. For what was that journal if not the proof that he had believed in his own nonsense, that he had wilfully refused to take life as he found it, refused to live simply? That he spoke ill of her in the journal did not trouble her, since she no longer loved him and did not have the kind of self-esteem that is easily hurt. She was now even inclined to forgive him; evidently he had not "done it on purpose", after all. Of course, Henry was right when he said it was nothing but a lot of foolishness. But Henry had also said that Stéphane was not such a dolt as he appeared to be, seeing that he had made no protest since their affair had begun. That was right enough . . . but perhaps it wasn't as simple as that. Poor Steph! Oh, well! All that was quite remote.

She was wondering whether or not to indulge in an alcohol rub. But why hesitate, when she had that ten thousand franc note? Henry always left his wallet in the bedroom. "Take whatever you like." She used a certain amount of discretion, but she helped herself, for she did not like the idea of being underestimated. That, too, posed some problems.

"An alcohol rub, Madame?"

No, she decided no, for it would wake her up and she had no desire to be wakened. A cup of mint tea, very sweet, would be better, and some cigarettes. She would not go to Henry's today. She would loiter on here, in the silence, in this cloistered and safe world where no one would talk to her, where no one would ask questions, where she simply existed without a thought and without any outside pressure. Gently she breathed, enjoying the slow expansion of the lungs, the movement of muscles, enjoying the knowledge of possessing limbs that were still supple and strong. She shook out her abundant black hair. She was thirsty. She was drowsy. In a moment they would bring her the mint tea with its refreshing scent. The wall clock made its regular ticking sound, letting the seconds fall upon her like dry little objects, like knuckle-bones falling into a plate. Minutes and hours were ticked off, during which she was alive, conscious of the passage of time and not caring. She, too, was nothing but a minute, an irresponsible minute launched into the void, and would disappear peaceably there, without leaving a trace. . . . Her head resting upon her arm, she fell asleep before she could be amazed at her own thought.

Eternal is the peace of sentient forms. Eternal the solemn joys of the earth, the dark viscera which do not prevaricate. Bodies exist; hours exist; and can confident footsteps on the dark earth ever be wrong?

The gilded god shimmered in the background. In the foreground Constantine and Dimitrios were eating. A real Greek dinner was set out before them. "They're eating *fêta*, they're eating *pasturna*, and they'll eat my very heart if this keeps up," thought Socrates with his usual grandiloquence. That same morning he had risen at dawn to earn some extra money at the *Halles* carrying crates of vegetables and fruit. Suppose someone had seen him doing porter's work! "Socrates, you're always the same! Yes, whenever I meet a Greek, I never fail to mention you and I always say, 'Socrates may not have many friends, for he's always been hard to please, but he treats what friends he has magnificently!'" "Yes, that's the truth, isn't it?" he always said, wanting them to repeat the words. Although their reply could no longer gladden him, he still needed it. Why, my God, why? Constantine and Dimitrios, for their part, were not ashamed to eat at his expense and live in sordid rooms with greasy wives, jingling with cheap jewellery and smelling like cold fritters. Why, then, did he feel as he did?

The real Socrates could not answer the question; only the foolish idol erected by his own hands could reply. That idol could not fall from high estate. That idol was a member of an important family of Athens—and as time went on it became ever more important —nor could that idol confess to poverty. Poverty! The word alone made him flinch, made him blush. Yet there were people who did not blush at that word, who pronounced it proudly He relived the scene of a few days before. He had been so shattered by that scene with the beggar that he had not been able to refrain from talking about it with Stéphane Morani. In the whole house, Morani was the only one to whom he could confide such a thing.

Stéphane Morani had tried to comfort him. "Why, my dear Socrates, since your intention was good. . . . I understand your sadness at not being able to help others; but there is no shame in that. Another man, more fortunate . . . Even Saint Martin was only able to give the half of his cloak. . . ."

The words "more fortunate" had affected Socrates like a slap in the face. It was easily said. Even the reference to Saint Martin had given him but moderate consolation. He refused energetically, with all his obtuse mind, to allow himself to be lured into the petal-strewn paths where Stéphane was attempting to lead him.

"But if you had seen me in the old days, Monsieur Morani! When I had forty suits! And so many pairs of boots that I didn't know what to do with them. Oh, if my father hadn't speculated! And now, to think that I haven't the means to offer a beggar a coat! What would my father have said! He, who committed suicide to avoid dishonour!"

"There's no dishonour in poverty, my good Socrates. Who knows, perhaps the gesture you intended but were unable to make may have touched that beggar all the same? Your charitable intention could touch him to the quick, it may have sown seeds . . ."

"He thought I couldn't afford it, I'm sure of it," said Socrates bitterly.

"And suppose he did think that, what does it matter?"

"It'll get talked about in the neighbourhood."

"And are you afraid of gossip? That story could only do you honour."

Stéphane himself saw in the incident the material for a nice little
edifying story. The way Socrates stupidly persisted in letting himself be caught in the web of his own weaving irritated him, to
begin with. Stéphane, had he been in Socrates' position, would
have submitted with grace, and easily adapted himself to changed
conditions! While Socrates continued to lament.

"When you think what I was, Monsieur Morani! Suits—I had
too many to count. And of good English worsted! There was a
blue, a grey, a Prince of Wales. And take my sister—I've quarrelled
with her—she had thirty-two pairs of boots and shoes. One day she
had luncheon with Princess Marina, and it was my sister who stole
the limelight."

His forehead was beaded with sweat, it trickled down on his
black moustache; his hands, clutching the jacket of the embarrassed
Stéphane, were trembling.

"I know I can tell you all this, Monsieur Morani, because you're
a fine man, educated, distinguished," he went on excitedly. "But
do you know how much is in my till this afternoon? Do you know?
Only two thousand francs! Two thousand francs! I, who was born
with a silver spoon in my mouth, you might say. And people will
hear of this! It will be known, sooner or later. I had to warn some
friends who come here to play cards not to come! I told them I
had a bad cold. What am I to do? What can I do?"

"My poor fellow, I myself . . ."

"Oh you, Monsieur Morani, you're comfortably off. You own
your flat, you earn a little money, your wife has a good job. . . .
Do you know that this café is mortgaged? Did you know that?
One day everyone will know. . . ."

"And what does it matter? Take me. Yes, yes, I assure you,
whatever you may think, I'm a poor man, really poor. And,
Socrates, I do not blush at the fact, I do not blush."

He had gone out, then. And Socrates had remained alone, in no
way consoled, merely disturbed because he had betrayed his secret.
But surely Monsieur Morani would keep his mouth shut. Why
should he spread the information? Oh, it was easy for him to talk!
"Really poor!" With a wife like his, he'd not die without a roof

over his head. Yet, just supposing that he, Socrates, found the strength to stand up and declare point blank: "I'm a poor man, really poor. Get the hell out of here."

No, it was impossible. He could already imagine the exclamations of pity, the sympathy extended, the "How did it happen?" questions, the long faces that were secretly . . . how to express it? Secretly delighted? No, that wasn't the word. Superior, perhaps; they would feel superior. They who had never had anything would feel superior to him who had lost everything. Had he himself not felt superior in the old days to those poor wretches who gravitated round him, begging a pair of boots, a cigarette? Had he not felt swollen with pride by all their obsequiousness, all their deference? Stéphane Morani himself would despise Socrates tomorrow, if he were to confess . . .

"They're eating *fêta*, they're eating *pasturna*, they'd devour my heart," he thought, magniloquently but sincerely. He was filled with hate. "Whenever I meet a Greek . . ." Did he not need these phrases to feel that he was alive?

Eternal was the foolish idol he had set up with his own hands.

Madame Prêtre greeted her daughter with glacial coldness, saying nothing of her grief, keeping it buried beneath her shawls. Sylvia would come of age in three months. She would marry the photographer. She would live in the back room behind his studio, and would have her place among the photographs on the wall. She would bear his children. Her portrait would never appear on magazine covers. Never again would she arrive at the Café Céleste in an American car, with all the gossips staring at her enviously. "She's doing well, your daughter, isn't she, Madame Prêtre?" Never again would she hear that. Sylvia had condemned herself. She had fulfilled the expectations of the others concerning her. Madame Prêtre well knew that they were right; but she had wanted to fight it. Her own daughter had condemned herself. Beneath Madame Prêtre's evil-smelling shawls, wrath and humiliation and grief were eternal.

Beside her, Sylvia babbled of her futile and second-rate happiness.

Jean Cadou painted, a scowl knitting his brows, wrinkling his forehead, and Gérard Ducas watched him paint. Eternal and unalloyed is admiration, confidence and the chaste friendship of men. . . .

Stéphane played the piano in his Brasserie Dorée. Bruno sang of life without a care, and of its trifling pleasures. After all, there's no reason to be ashamed of such things. Hasn't a man who is mediocre the right to enjoy his condition?

If nothing more happened, if everything remained in place, then, who knows, life itself would seem to be eternal.

But winter was nibbling its way through this lethargic autumn. . . .

On the one hand there was the autumn, the complacent smiles, the tactful silences, the smothered anxieties, courtesy pure and simple, and everything that forms the outer layer of human life: names, pretexts, functions. And set against all this, there was Martine, alone in her bedroom. Barricaded.

"But she'll lose her job!"

"It's incredible, doesn't she want to see anyone?"

"It's grotesque!"

"It's pathological."

"Do you take up her meals to her?"

"I put the tray down in front of the door."

"What will happen when she runs out of money?"

"Oh, that . . ."

"It's very embarrassing to everyone in the house."

Curiosity to begin with, then blame. Then a growing embarrassment. Questions put to the man held responsible. "Have you tried to see her, you who . . ." The little question barely sprung to life grew big, propagated itself; one question led to another. "To think that we believed . . ." Such a thing is very embarrassing in a house.

The window of Martine's room overlooked some quaint little courtyards. One evening she began to look at them, and decided she would go on looking at them for some time. And now, below her, the house was in a ferment. If they stopped bringing her food, she would obviously have to capitulate. But Madame Prêtre did not refuse to bring her food. Martine had always known she would not refuse.

"It seems she's still on a hunger-strike, your little friend?"

"She's not on a hunger-strike, my dear Louise, she eats her meals."

"She must be completely crazy, isn't she?"

"She's doing this to annoy me, the poor child."

"And it's certainly annoying. They'll end up by thinking you've driven her to despair! You oughtn't to hide yourself like this, Stéphane. If I were in your place, next Monday I'd simply go to their meeting and I'd tell them, 'It's not my fault if a half-crazy girl has fallen in love with me. Let's go on as before.' "

"Yes, but . . ."

"I assure you, something must be done. That girl up there not budging, thinking God knows what. . . . They'll end up by saying that she may have good reason to behave like that, or something. It's embarrassing in a house!"

Embarrassing. They had all spoken the word.

The little court to the left was occupied by a cabinet-maker, and the door of his workshop opened out upon that court. When he turned on a motor, it roared, and the shavings flew. . . . Was someone knocking at her door?

"Martine! I implore you. . . ."

Some children, in the triangular court, were dressing up a cat in bright colours. The animal struggled. The children's mother came to scold them, quite in vain.

"Mademoiselle Fortin! It could be very bad for your health. . . ."

An aeroplane passed in the grey sky. In the summer it had traced the letters of a gigantic advertisement in the sky; this evening it would be impossible, unless the mechanic used black smoke.

"This dodge of yours is ridiculous! For God's sake stop it, and come out!"

In the dawn that was barely beginning, through a yellow fog, lights glowed in the little courtyards. A bicycle was drawn out of a shed and went off towards the invisible street.

"I've brought you some rice and some eggs, Mademoiselle Martine. They cost less than anything else. All the tenants came to my lodge this morning again, talking about you to me. Even that woman asked about you. Well, I suppose you know what you're doing?"

Towards ten o'clock the radios blared out, reinforced by static. It was the housekeeping hour, with dustcloths and mops being shaken out of windows, brooms being wielded, and even, despite the city ordinances, carpets being beaten.

"My dear child, I feel that my age authorizes me . . ."

"Would you like me to bring up some good hot coffee, Mademoiselle Martine? Please realize that I understand you. When I was in Athens, if a fellow didn't keep his promise to me, I . . ."

The autumn was vanishing in decay, the Café Céleste and the whole building were falling into decay, while doors opened upon anxious questioning. And Martine was alone, in her room. . . .

It was with something of surprised shock that Stéphane entered the Café Céleste again, as if he had expected to see it changed. What a ridiculous delusion! To think that he had needed to draw courage from Louise, that without her urging he would not have found the courage to come downstairs for this meeting! Ridiculous. The room was the same, his friends were the same. . . . But within himself that old uneasiness that came from the depths of time was stirring faintly again.

In a corner of the room, the chairs were stacked in an airy pyramid. A dirty towel trailed, forgotten, in the metallic "helmet" at one end of the bar. It was already dark outside, and the white fluorescent sign shone down on the sad, deserted little terrace. The bottles were neatly aligned. The goldfish were tracing straight lines in the green water. And the young girl, and the gilded god, and the mandarins smiled at the silver triangles on their blue blackground. The Café Céleste wore its everyday aspect, and Stéphane felt reassured.

They all came in at once, making more noise than usual, calling out to him with more effusiveness, as if in an effort to break the ice that had frozen between them in the past few weeks. Ducas was very kind, very moved, or seemed to be. Jean Cadou grunted out a welcome. Germaine Lethuit gesticulated nervously, her hands fluttering from white-cuffed sleeves. Bringing up the rear-guard were a rather embarrassed Dr. Fisher, a morose Madame Prêtre, and a very shy Sylvia.

"At last, my dear friend! We were beginning to be worried!"

"We missed our little reunions!"

"Feeling okay, now?"

Stéphane was quite affected by all this tactful understanding. Apparently they were not going to make any embarrassing allusions. What good friends, what excellent friends! He shook hands all round, feeling like hugging them all. Louise was right. One should face things squarely. Particularly since, to anyone with brains, Martine's conduct was absolutely incredible! Incredible, and utterly without logical foundation, moreover; a piece of childishness. But why had that childishness obsessed him for so many days? Already his expression had lightened, his smile had returned, and he sat down feeling that he was surrounded by friends.

"I hope this isn't going to last too long," said Dr. Fisher in a constrained way. "I have some calls to make."

The excuse seemed quite improbable, but Stéphane meekly accepted it. The Doctor must be embarrassed over his outburst of the other day. With good reason, one had to admit! But he must have been drunk. Stéphane promptly banished the awkward memory. If Martine were to show repentance, he would deal with her sulks in the same way.

"What joy, my good friends! Believe me . . ."

But Gérard Ducas, perhaps out of embarrassment, cut him short. "Ladies and gentlemen," he said in the professional manner he was apt to adopt in the exercise of his duties as agent for the co-operative tenants, "before we do anything else we must settle a small practical question. I know that we have assembled here for quite other reasons. . . . I mean to say, that these little matters of a practical nature may seem rather ridiculous, but in short . . . We should discuss the question of having the roof repaired."

Everyone sat down simultaneously, with a great scraping of chairs. Sylvia and Madame Prêtre were not concerned with matters of this sort, so they pretended to fix their eyes on the bar. Socrates misinterpreted their glance and hastened to take down a bottle.

"Can I offer you something to drink?"

Yes, it was the truth, everyone felt relieved and everyone laughed, their cheeks rather flushed, as if with wine, and even Dr. Fisher seemed to relax. Apparently they had all dreaded this moment, but now they found it was like any other, this reunion like all the other reunions of "the Celestials". How gay they all suddenly felt!

"Go ahead, tell us about the roof, Gé-gé?" joked Jean Cadou. And they all burst out laughing, all of them, without reason, even Sylvia, relegated to a corner, like a culprit.

"You are not unaware of the two possible solutions," Ducas began, with that very slight pomposity which he knew to be rather ridiculous ("Victorian", he told himself, for that was his favourite period). "There is the expensive solution, which would have the advantage of . . ."

Germaine Lethuit quickly interrupted him, not in the least conscious of the antiquary's subtle humour. "I don't like to hear this matter treated in an off-hand way," she said warmly. "It's going to cost me personally more than a hundred thousand francs; and I'll not tolerate . . ."

"In monthly payments, don't forget," said Ducas affably. "The Merle company has agreed to special terms . . ."

"You must have put money in the bank, with that foreign tenant of yours," said Jean with a laugh.

Germaine flushed angrily, but one had the feeling that even this indignation cleared the atmosphere, like an electric storm. The tension that reigned was undeniable, and they all chose every means to escape it. Socrates poured out another round of *vin rosé*.

"If you ask me," he said, "I think the other solution, the one that costs less . . . Not that I couldn't afford the other, but . . . Anyway, what's the difference between the two when you come to it?"

There was another general outburst of laughter, which seemed to concentrate the electricity floating in the air.

"But you've had it explained to you two hundred times, Socrates!" yelled Jean Cadou, doubled up with laughter.

Socrates stood on his dignity. "Me, what I say is," he said. "Besides, you don't see the roof, do you? So, if it's not very pretty . . ."

"In short, you're for the less costly roofing?" said the antiquary with the same politeness. "And you, Mademoiselle Lethuit?"

"I think this is all being tossed off too lightly," she said, with a show of stubbornness. "Who knows what kind of people we're dealing with? Thieves, perhaps! Have we thought of consulting other firms?"

"This was done a long time ago, as you must be aware. And we all agreed on this firm."

"That's so. I remember," said Socrates happily.

"Are you for or against the zinc roofing, Mademoiselle?"

"Oh, for it, since you insist," said Germaine.

She had hoped for a longer and more technical discussion, in which she could have showed off her natural authority. But they all seemed to be more conciliatory this evening, more intent on not upsetting an all too evident display of good understanding. That was the impression one might have taken away of the general attitude of the meeting: Ducas was more exquisitely polite than usual, Jean Cadou more jovial, Socrates more ready to laugh at anything and everything, Germaine was smiling in a forced way. . . . It was like witnessing a theatrical rehearsal where the actors had been requested to mime cordiality. In vain Stéphane tried to drive this idea out of his head. It was his own anxiety, he told himself that made him see things in this light. This reunion was just like all the others. But now he began to wonder if the other meetings had not also been stamped with this constraint, this slight exaggeration which struck him today as it would have struck him in a drawing or in a film. . . . A fugitive impression, due to his fatigue, no doubt. He must dismiss it all as idiotic.

"Jean, you're for the zinc roofing, too?"

"I swear it, nothing but the truth. . . ."

"And you, Doctor?"

"Why not, my dear Ducas? I believe we're all in agreement here, aren't we?"

A very slight exaggeration. . . . The Doctor's manner seemed to hint at something unsaid; he had spoken like the villain in a melodrama. How Stéphane would have liked to banish these unwelcome thoughts! They were not even thoughts. He was quite aware that the faint anguish gnawing at the back of his mind was a delusion, that his way of seeing things was a distortion, a veil woven by fatigue and annoyances (yes, that moderate word was wonderfully apt), screening him off from reality. But . . .

"As for myself, I am not opposed. . . . I consider the Merle firm an honest one," Ducas went on, taking pleasure in following the meandering of his own circumlocutions, like a child pushing a pebble ahead and following after. "It's a firm which would not like to skimp on the quality under the pretext of cutting the costs. What's your opinion, Stéphane?"

Stéphane gave a start. This was his cue, he must now play his part in the comedy; he felt a kind of tension in the pit of his stomach that might well be called stage-fright. He had the feeling that his response was being waited for, lain in wait for, that it would have a significance. . . . And like any inexperienced actor he stumbled on the words.

"Er, that is to say . . ." (What silence!) "These material questions are, for me . . . But my wife thinks . . ."

Of course, he had said the words that should not have been said. But the flood of talk that drowned them out was more rapid still, more powerful than his confusion. He would not even be given time to blush.

"So you're for the zinc. . . ."

"You're right, Stéphane. Me, I think slate . . ."

"It's an old prejudice. In town . . ."

Who had spoken, he would not even know. They were laughing, exchanging snatches of remarks, but they did not look him in the face. . . .

"In short," said Gérard Ducas urbanely, "it's unnecessary to put the question to a vote, since we're all agreed. . . . I believe that we may now close this little utilitarian parenthesis and . . ."

"If I may be allowed," said a voice at the end of the room.

They all turned, surprised, towards Madame Prêtre.

"We're all agreed?" she said suavely. "What about Mademoiselle Fortin?"

"We're a majority, and that's all that's needed," said Gérard Ducas curtly.

But the damage had been done. And Sylvia's innocent voice was at once questioning, with touchingly good intentions: "Is Martine ill?"

There was a quite disagreeable moment of silence. The earlier cordiality was broken, undone before their very eyes. They all turned towards Stéphane, staring at him. Oh, not aggressively, but wasn't it up to him to clarify things, to smooth things out? However, since he remained silent, Germaine Lethuit made a loyal effort.

"Really, Madame Prêtre . . ."

But the haste with which the concierge excused herself added to their embarrassment. "Oh, I beg pardon! I shouldn't have said . . . I didn't know . . ."

"You shouldn't have said what, Madame?" asked Gérard Ducas, a note of sharpness in his fluty voice.

"There's no reason," Dr. Fisher began, drumming the table with his fingertips, and leaving his sentence unfinished.

"Mademoiselle Lethuit seemed to mean . . ."

Thus cornered, the social welfare worker defended herself haughtily. "I simply thought, Madame Prêtre, that in an affair concerning the proprietors of the building, you had no voice. And your interruption, let me say, was misplaced, to put it mildly."

"Yes, and anyway," said Socrates, well-meaning as usual, "Mademoiselle Fortin hasn't a very big share in the building. As Monsieur Ducas says, we're in a majority."

This remark fell in an even denser silence, a silence into which one could sink, with the feeling of never emerging again. Besides, each one of them had his own cause for embarrassment. Sylvia and

Socrates were suffering from the simple discomfort of not understanding the language spoken in front of them. The antiquary was
annoyed at finding himself caught in this ridiculous situation; it was
as shocking to him as a slovenly act, a mistake in grammar. Jean
Cadou was suffering from the obscure and universal mistrust that he
was liable to feel, a mistrust that included even himself. Germaine
Lethuit was merely shocked as she would have been at a coarse word
or a piece of obscenity, and she reacted with a fierce wrath which
saved them all. For she was the first to speak, and she spoke with
the voice of a social welfare worker carrying out an investigation
("What, *exactly*, is your husband's income?"), a voice she had never
used at the Café Céleste before, using it now, doubtless, to indicate
that everything she would say should be considered as part of a
different world, a kind of parenthesis which they could close as soon
as they liked, when they would return to their usual atmosphere,
the pleasant, circumspect conversation of the usual meetings.

"Well, now," she said, addressing herself directly to Stéphane,
"since the subject has been brought up, kindly tell us exactly what's
the matter with Martine Fortin?"

"You see . . ." Stéphane began, hesitatingly. They gathered round
him at once, listening with an understanding expression on their
faces, approbation already on their lips, in their hearts, all of them
obviously quite ready to close the parenthesis and forget the whole
thing as if it had never happened. Eternal approbation. . . . "You
see," said Stéphane, "you know as much as I do, you've been as
surprised as I have been by . . ." (He was searching for his words, oh,
how he was searching for them! But this crowd of people around
him, ready to help him, to urge him on. . . . Oh, let the parenthesis
close! Let repose be eternal! And yet all of them had climbed the
stairs to knock at that shut door.) "You've all been as surprised as I
was at the incomprehensible attitude of . . . of Martine. As for
myself, I have been deeply hurt . . . wounded . . . by what this
attitude of hers revealed. . . . I had believed . . ." (Suddenly the
words came more easily, and he began to speak very rapidly, in
his desire to satisfy and convince them.) "I had believed, as you
know, my dear friends, that I had found in her a friend who

would be nothing but a friend, who would not be a woman . . ."

"Yes, yes, I understand," said Gérard Ducas eagerly. "You expected that quite pure, incorporeal affection that all of us seek. . ."

"I thought I had found it. I have told you of this, tried to share my joy with you. I believed I would always have at my side a presence, a comprehension. I now realize that I expected too much."

"We always expect too much," said Dr. Fisher bitterly.

"Doctor! There are women, and I speak as one who knows, who could have been exactly this to a man, and without ever any intrusion of their femininity!" said Germaine warmly.

"Oh, yes. Surely!" murmured Sylvia.

Her mother shrugged. Socrates brought the argument down to earth by affirming in his heavy voice, "Oh, for my part, Monsieur Morani, I could always see that the girl was in love with you."

Stéphane gave an involuntary smile, which he immediately tempered with an air of melancholy. "There are friendships, my dear Socrates, that one might confuse with love."

"Amorous friendship," said Gérard Ducas with a smile. "Lecomte du Noüy put a whole epoch into those words."

The atmosphere had cleared. Stéphane was conscious of it. A wave of warmth flooded him. His face flushed. "It is only too clear that the unhappy girl confused the two things. I found I had to make her understand. . . . Oh, with extreme subtlety. I must add that her attitude was in no way . . . unpleasant. Far from it! Merely, I thought I detected a growing sentiment in her . . . that it was my duty to quell. One never knows to what extremes a person like that may be carried, she is so refined, so sensitive. . . ."

"That's so," said Socrates. "When a woman's in love, watch out! Take me, for instance: the countess . . ."

"Naturally, you had to cut the whole thing short," said Gérard Ducas smugly. (These tragi-comic adventures of the worthy Stéphane Morani! There was really no harm in them. "But why," he wondered, "did I go to knock at the door of the insignificant young creature?")

"I'm sure she'll understand. She's a well adjusted and reasonable girl."

"Poor Martine!" said Sylvia. "Couldn't we do something nice for her?"

"Oh, so *that's* the reason she's locked herself in?" said Madame Prêtre.

"For what other reason could it be?" said Dr. Fisher curtly. "A typical case of frustration. A plain girl, most surely a virgin, falls in love with the first man she meets. It was inevitable."

"I protest!" exclaimed Germaine Lethuit. "Virginity . . ."

"Yes, you exaggerate," muttered Stéphane. "These physiological questions . . ."

"Oh, oh," said Gérard Ducas, with a smile.

Jean shrugged at the controversy.

"Oh yes," said Socrates, "that must be the reason." And he marvelled at his own perspicacity.

Stéphane was entirely happy: once again he was surrounded by approving friends. Martine's withdrawal had been a veritable attempt at blackmail. God knew why he had taken it so seriously. He could now see quite well that it was not tragic. But he was still angry with himself for having been so disturbed. "There's always the physiological part of man," he said, smiling, "but our dear doctor attaches too much importance to it. All the same, there is the human mind, a sense of responsibility controlling and dominating the body." (He was experiencing a kind of intoxication at being surrounded by them again. What in the world had he feared?) "I must say that Martine's attitude has deeply pained me, in fact, to the extent of partially affecting my health. You know how I prize the friendship of all of you, and she had been able to inspire such confidence in me. . . ." (Gérard Ducas nodded his head in approval. Jean Cadou gave him a friendly pat on the shoulder. Germaine Lethuit indicated with a sigh her woman's understanding of these delicate problems. Socrates poured out more wine for him. Sylvia was quite bemused. Only Madame Prêtre and Dr. Fisher gave no outward sign of sympathy, but they said nothing. He was surrounded by friends, they were like a solid armour. What in the world had he feared?) "Oh, I don't hold it against her. I know from experience, alas, what solitude is. There are some natures who cannot fight it, who become confused and embittered."

"That's true," said Germaine. "It's been scientifically established."
(And she thought of Pauline's reproaches: some slight frustration
there.)

"In some cases the results of frustration go to the point of delirium," said Dr. Fisher, with a tinge of irony. (Poor Morani himself
he thought, is an inoffensive crackpot. As he himself had been in his
youth: what else but the insane excitements of adolescence had
driven him, once married, to continue to be preoccupied with
politics? Let's not contradict ourselves, he reflected; I, too, was once
a lunatic.)

They were all with him. Oh, how wonderful to feel, at last,
understood, to see the world approve and acquiesce. He had suffered
so much at feeling himself surrounded with disapproval, Louise's,
Martine's, perhaps even his own. . . . What good these friends were
doing him, how borne up he felt! How stupid to have allowed
himself to be depressed by the disdain of Martine Fortin! He had
been mistaken in her, nothing more. That could happen to anyone.
What had upset him was to have made the mistake in front of these
friends, to have, in a way, called upon them to witness his error.
But since they, too, were ready to admit it . . .

"Delirium, that's a little too much. But a kind of spurious exaltation. . . ."

"That's what fooled you before, my dear fellow!" eagerly
exclaimed Gérard Ducas. "You believed she was acting in the same
good faith that you were, you believed that she returned the friendship you offered, a friendship which might be qualified as romantic,
if you'll pardon the term; but instead she became exalted in earnest,
it was a way of filling the emptiness of her lonely life; but also, she
entertained the hope, which I would like to believe was unconscious,
the hope of . . ." (Why yes! This poor devil Morani was the authentic article, in spite of the old-fashioned side of his nature. It was
stupid to have doubted it for a moment. And it had been still more
idiotic to go and knock at the door of that repulsive little female.)

"Why yes," laughed Jean, "she must have had ideas from the
beginning, and you, poor chap, suspected nothing! Oh, women!

(Poor chap! Even at his age women were trying to hook him! And he didn't suspect a thing. He was exactly Gérard's type, absurd and gullible. Charming types, fundamentally. And that described the little circle: a bit ridiculous, a bit baroque, but well-meaning. It was to this kind of people that he had to show his paintings. Who was it who read his books to his concierge or his servant? Rousseau? Anatole France? He must ask Gérard.)

The little room seemed to expand under the effect of the cordial voices, the kind feelings. "What an impressionable person I am!" Stéphane reflected. But to think that he had gone to knock at that girl's door! And to think he had implored her! While all his friends understood him quite well. . . .

"So she wanted to marry you?" asked Sylvia in her small voice. "Oh, that wasn't nice of her!"

"It's not nice," said Socrates with a sigh, "but it's life." (Monsieur Morani preferred to keep his wife: that was in the natural order of things. A very handsome woman, and a profitable one.)

"Oh, I don't think she went as far as that," Stéphane protested indulgently. "But I must admit that I was very naïve. I am even inclined to wonder if perhaps, from the beginning, there was not an unconscious desire on her part, surely an unconscious desire, to supplant the woman she deemed unworthy . . ."

"Why, that's horrible!" Sylvia exclaimed indignantly. "I think you were all very nice to go and talk to her through the door!"

There was a little laugh, issuing from the silent Madame Prêtre, hidden away in her corner.

Stéphane was their spokesman. Stéphane would answer for them, be answerable for them. Stéphane would exonerate them. They said nothing.

"Pity, my child," said Stéphane gravely. "Pity for a human soul burying itself in solitude, a soul that could have been—I am more optimistic than you are, my friends, perhaps incurably optimistic— a soul that could have walked in beauty."

Sylvia sighed voluptuously. Socrates, more sensitive to the atmosphere than to the words, felt the moment had come to set them up again and he made the rounds of the table.

"To change the subject, old man, I've just begun a big canvas, an objective painting, inspired by music."

"I could wish, all the same, that we might reserve a meeting for the discussion of a burning social problem. . . ."

They were all talking at once, as if they were sharing Stéphane's ingenuous contentment. And Stéphane went on talking, resting one hand on Sylvia's shoulder, the other on Jean's arm. "You two, who are youth itself," he said, "you do understand, don't you, how I could be so excessively credulous? And I cannot keep from hoping, even now, that she may perhaps return to us. . . ."

Sylvia opened her beautiful empty eyes wide. Withdrawn from the group, silent and malevolent, Madame Prêtre resembled more than ever some dark, discarded idol.

"Yes, my child," Stéphane continued, "and yet, God knows how I have suffered these past days. I who had confided all my life to her, shared with her my inmost secrets. . . ."

"Oh come," said Jean with awkward cordiality, "mustn't think of it any more."

"It's hard, my dear Jean, to forget at once, with the ease of youth, such a disappointment." (His face was radiant with the pleasure of having such an attentive audience.) "To think that a girl in whom one has confided utterly can turn against one, and at a moment, besides, when one is already so stricken!"

"At a moment?" murmured Jean.

And all their faces, suddenly grown pale, turned towards him.

The chairs were stacked in a corner, an airy pyramid. In the metallic "helmet" at one end of the bar, still trailed a dirty towel. . . . The gilded god must have smiled.

Madame Prêtre took the floor. "Yes," she said, smiling, "at such a moment, obviously . . ."

They said nothing, as if thunderstruck, and Stéphane hesitated, anxious, feeling the ground suddenly caving in beneath him. But Sylvia was there, guileless instrument that a clever hand had no doubt prepared.

"What do you mean by that?" she asked.

Madame Prêtre carried on. "You mean by that, of course, that

you now know everything, Monsieur Morani? What a shame! You
who were always so good to your wife!"

"Yes . . . I . . . I did my best," Stéphane murmured uncertainly.

"Yes, that's quite right," said Socrates ponderously. "I said to
myself the other day, when I saw you going out with her, that you
are certainly a patient man."

Gérard Ducas averted his eyes. Dr. Fisher smiled in an odd way
and tapped on the table. Jean Cadou shrugged nervously. But
Germaine Lethuit got to her feet. She approached Stéphane with
dignity, looking rather clumsy in her strict tailored suit, but as if
entrusted with a sacred mission.

"Fine, Stéphane, fine!" she said. "I expected no less of you.
You're taking the bull by the . . ." (She stopped in the middle of
the ill-chosen metaphor, although no one, not even Jean Cadou
laughed.) "You are facing up to things, taking them as you should.
And you are going to announce your decision to us, aren't you?
There were some who could doubt you, but not I. I know what
you are going to tell us. I know."

Stéphane was too stupefied to open his mouth in reply. The
antiquary spoke up, assuming a huffy tone.

"My dear lady, I don't know to whom you allude when you
speak of doubts. We were persuaded, as you yourself appeared to
be, that our friend knew nothing of . . . of this misfortune."

"I did not merely appear to be, I was!" said Germaine, flushing
with anger. "You were the one, on the other hand, you and your
friend Jean Cadou who seemed to imply . . ."

"Me?"

"Your memory's not very good," said Jean rather rudely. "It
was Socrates who pretended that Morani knew what was up and
was even pleased with the arrangement."

"But that's not at all what I meant to say!" protested Socrates.
"Besides, you can see very well that . . ."

"Yes, you see very well?" said Dr. Fisher, nonchalantly. "But
I'd like to know what it's got to do with any of you!" (They all
felt the need to make that poor devil face up to his contradictions!
In any case, all that about Morani's high moral standards had never

been taken any too seriously. No reason to put on those tragic faces. True, he himself the other day in the office . . . But he had been in an exhausted condition, overworked, and had needed a shot. Tonight, he'd taken the shot before coming: result, he was calm.)

"It concerns us," said Germaine. (When she was angry, she made one think of a concierge's dog trying to pass itself off as a mastiff.) "It concerns us, because Stéphane wants our advice. Don't you, Stéphane?"

"Why yes, of course. . . ."

"For my part, I'm revolted," said Gérard Ducas, speaking to Stéphane sympathetically. (Morani, the poor fellow, must have learned about it the day before or very recently. It was surely the hateful little Fortin creature who had revealed it to him. What a shock for the poor boy! A bomb in the drawing-room of Queen Victoria! And what would become of him? For after all!)

"Oh yes, it's disgusting," said Socrates placidly. "You can only hope it won't last."

"Last!" exclaimed Germaine furiously. "Why, it shouldn't last one more week, what am I saying, one more day!" (Had she ever allowed Pauline to see her black sheep of a husband again, even for three minutes? No, wickedness should be banished at once, thrown out, far from the quiet atmosphere of the home.) "Stéphane cannot tolerate such a thing."

"It's not a question of . . ." began the one concerned.

But they would not let him get a word in, as if they were anxious over what he might say.

"Oh, no, he cannot tolerate it!" said Sylvia, taking Stéphane's hand in hers.

And Madame Prêtre, again silent, smiled. (Sylvia has not won, but you won't either, she mentally addressed him. Sylvia didn't take advantage of the godsend she had, right in front of her, but I swear you shan't benefit by yours, either.) She smiled, and gritted her teeth.

"Naturally," said Jean Cadou flatly. "We all agree on that point. You must . . ."

"No doubt, no doubt," the bewildered Stéphane managed to say at last. "I must talk to her, I must make her realize that she's gone too far, that . . ."

"Yes, that's right," said Socrates approvingly. "You must tell her that she can't carry on like that with no matter who, giving herself all that notoriety."

"But that's not what we mean at all," chorused Gérard Ducas and Germaine Lethuit.

"All the same, I cannot . . . Her fault is no doubt a passing one, realize that; it's a bit of wildness, in which vanity must have played a part." (Stéphane would never have believed that he would reach the point of pleading for Louise. And what had led him to this? He was not very sure of what was happening.) "She is my wife. Clearly, my duty is to make her see that she has lost status in everybody's eyes. But . . ." (What did they want of him, in short? He surrounded himself in a fog, so as to lose sight of them.) "You see, Louise is not a wicked woman. It's just that she has no idea of the rules of morality. That's all. It's been the torment of my life to try to inculcate in her some notions of morality. And in vain. A Danaïd's task, it must be admitted, if I may dare to present myself in the graceful rôle, for it was like pouring water into a sieve." His awkward pleasantry did not raise a laugh.

"Listen, my dear fellow," Dr. Fisher intervened, "all this is none of our business. Morality, as far as I'm concerned, you know . . . If you like your wife as she is, keep her, and let's say no more about it. But why drag in morality?"

"Doctor!" exclaimed Germaine Lethuit. "How can you . . . when the entire life of our friend . . ."

"Why yes," said Gérard Ducas with perhaps more force than he intended, "how can you imagine that there's any question of love, in the vulgar sense of the word, involved in this matter? Stéphane cannot love that woman, for heaven's sake!"

How they spoke in his name! How positive they were, how sure! And suddenly he saw rising up before him a strange and deformed image which resembled his life, at least the life he had made for himself.

"It would be unthinkable for Stéphane . . ." (It would be un-thinkable for Pauline. After all these years, could doubt in any way trouble a clear sense of duty, a clear conscience? Could it have any effect?)

"If Stéphane hasn't left that woman up to now," said Ducas, "it's because . . ." (How could he have anything but a feeling of horror for her? That viscid, disgusting world of men and women, of love, of . . . It was all horrifying and had neither style nor nobility. But friendship and art, ah, yes. There you had sentiments stripped to the bare bone, nothing hidden. And that rather antiquated virtue, of which Stéphane was the symbol, in which he rejoined the roses of Saint-Jean-le-Vieil. . . .)

"It would be bloody awful," Jean blurted out, catching himself at once, "I mean, pretty lousy, if things continued like this." (They could not allow it. Unthinkable for good old Stéphane, now that he'd lost his blinkers. . . . When he didn't know a thing, okay. But they'd not be able to speak to him any more, they'd have to pretend to . . . something they'd never done. They were sincere. As Stéphane was, too, certainly, and Gérard . . .)

"Well, then, my friends, what do you propose?" Stéphane imprudently asked, with a sigh. "I don't see what . . ."

With the clear voice of the obvious, Germaine Lethuit trumpeted: "Why, you must leave her, of course!"

"I must leave her?" he stammered. It was like hearing Martine again. He did not understand. His friends. . . . He looked at them, one after another, stupefied. Yes, there they were: the devoted Germaine Lethuit, author of the "Ode to Conscientious Objectors", support and torment of her family; the slender antiquary with the graceful gestures, so concerned with respectability; the petite Sylvia, prettier and more infantile than ever; and Madame Prêtre, whom he had never bothered to analyse, although he was aware of her devious efforts to place the girl; and there was Socrates, to whose stories he had always pretended to listen; and Dr. Fisher. . . . Fisher? No, of course, it had been fatigue from overwork, the other day. They were engaged in a discussion, a simple discussion, all he had to do was to speak out, explain himself. He talked. The nuisance of it was that Socrates, with disarmingly good intentions, echoed him, endorsed him, and created a constant embarrassment.

"My responsibilities. . . . Alone, without someone to restrain her, what would become of her? . . . A certain gratitude . . ." said Stéphane.

And Socrates: "Naturally you can't leave her like that. . . . And what would become of you, without anyone to take care of you?"

Stéphane talked. But for the first time his words met with a kind of hostility, not aggressive hostility, but repressed, ashamed, as if they were trying by every means to hide it from themselves. In vain, however, for it oozed from every pore. He talked. They did not hear him, they were listening only to their own thoughts, embarrassed and incredulous for the first time; or had they not always secretly harboured these feelings? The seed had been sown some time ago (by the reading of the journal to begin with, then by the apparently better relations established between the Moranis, but especially by that door Martine had shut upon herself, exactly seventeen days previously, that door which seemed to reject Stéphane and themselves equally), now it had suddenly sprouted and they had become conscious of it. He talked, but what they heard, along with the rumbling voice of Socrates which seemed to echo Stéphane's, was their own voice.

"I don't understand," murmured Sylvia. (Behind her, she felt her mother gloating with triumph, could almost hear her unspoken thoughts. This is the way things go. You see, my poor Sylvia, what life is. You see why you couldn't understand him. Talk, talk, yes, but he stays with his wife. The money, the flat—they're the truth for him.)

"No one is thinking of forcing you to do anything," said Germaine Lethuit in a voice that was becoming sharp. (She had *never* forced anyone, despite what Pauline said. But this was too much. That Stéphane knew about the infamous behaviour of his wife and yet . . . She began to hate the sound of the voice reeling off excuses in which she had once believed. Had she really believed? Yes! She had been sincere! She had always been sincere. . . .)

"Of course, Stéphane is free to do as he likes," said Ducas with some coolness. (Had Dr. Fisher spoken the truth? Was Stéphane still enamoured. . . . No. Then, a question of interest, perhaps? But how sordid all this was! The touching and convenient image he liked to form of their friendship, of this little circle of people, as charming and outmoded as a piece of home-made *petit point* tapestry, was becoming blurred; would he have to look at everything in this crude light?)

"Oh, to hell with it! Let him do what he likes," said Jean sulkily. (Easy to say, but . . . Could they possibly go on meeting and chatting with Morani, behaving as if nothing had happened? At least Gérard would certainly not tolerate such a thing. He who was always so sincere that it was almost ridiculous, he who was so devoted, lugging the paintings to this gallery and that, calling on dealers, trying to get to know the critics. . . . Saying, "I have such a profound admiration for your paintings." . . . No, Gérard would not tolerate such a thing!)

"No one is forcing you, but I must say it would be thought strange . . ."

"Stéphane is free, but from what we know of him, we have a right to expect . . ."

"Use the knife, old man! No half-measures!"

"You're not going to leave her, Monsieur Stéphane?"

The chairs were stacked in a rickety picture-puzzle. The fluorescent light hummed like insects on a summer day. The nenuphars, the gilded god, the mandarins were of no help. The goldfish traced their comings and goings with more geometrical precision than ever, and took no interest in the question.

Stéphane did not understand. No, he did not understand. He seemed to be walking in an impenetrable forest of strange faces. Could it be that he had never before looked at his friends' faces? He defended himself to the best of his ability. "You tell me this today," he hesitantly began, "but for weeks and months you've known my situation, and have never . . ."

This was the supreme blunder. Germaine Lethuit bounded up to exclaim, "That's not true!"

Gérard Ducas used his most mellifluous voice to express his indignation. "No, my dear sir, no. Don't try to impose upon us! The situation has changed. Your wife is having a serious affair; to put it boldly, she is the mistress of a wealthy man. It would be unthinkable . . ."

Madame Prêtre cackled. Unthinkable, indeed. Oh! He intended to benefit by the wealth stolen from Sylvia, did he?

"Yes, Monsieur Stéphane, you see, people might think . . ." (Poor Stéphane, surely he had not realized that. He didn't know what "life" was, either. Sylvia was ready to enlighten him.)

"But really, my dear friends, it's always been . . ." (Oh, the impenetrable forest! Let music be eternal! Who was it that had suddenly struck a false note? Just when they had been getting along so well together!)

Dr. Fisher got to his feet. "Well now, there you are," he said in an unexpectedly ponderous and vengeful voice. "You have what you were looking for. You didn't want to believe me, did you? You hung on to your noble ideas! Yet I warned you. And they are crashing down on your head, now. And a good thing. A good thing! All you have to do now is send these people packing. All you have to do is . . ."

There was a great commotion, with everyone exclaiming. Stéphane was snowed under with words, he was unable to open his mouth in reply.

"Oh, come, you're not going to justify him!"

"You must surely see the necessity . . ."

They were surrounding and harassing him now. Even Madame Prêtre had got up and had come forward with mincing little steps. The Doctor let himself down on his bench. The shot of morphine had been of no great avail. He had been unable to keep back the words that were filling him with bitterness. But still, why did the fellow go on talking, trying to defend himself? All he had done was to provide them with more arguments, and now here they all were flinging themselves at him like a pack of hounds. So, Morani, you didn't feel like going away, you didn't feel like leaving your life, your habits, and why not say it, your wife! You wanted all that, even more than to be cured of your disease. Then why not tell them? What is it that makes a man hang on to his noble and empty ideas, prizing them more than life? Shut up, will you! Stop protesting. Tell them to go to the devil, all of them. You won't? You're still protesting? "Certainly, I no longer love her, but I fear that without me . . ." The word Duty? The word Sacrifice, again. Well then, die, since that's what you want. Let yourself be driven from everything that kept you alive. Die for your theatrical make-believes! As I did not know how to die. And then you will suddenly discover, when they have deprived you of everything, that it was all no use. And to go on living isn't any use either. Was it worth the trouble to hang on, to keep on living in a world of jelly-fish? Oh! Who knows?

The chairs were frenziedly stacked, the scene lit by the fluorescent tube was tumultuous, the smile of the mandarins and the calm of the goldfish were very out of place. The voice that finally made itself heard was the heavy and spuriously jovial voice of Madame Prêtre.

"Come now, Monsieur Morani, you're surely not going to justify the rumours, are you? You can't imagine what they're saying about you in the neighbourhood!"

"You cannot lend yourself to vile rumours!" Gérard Ducas almost shouted, beside himself.

"They'll end up by saying you're making a good thing out of it. . . ."

"Oh, you must leave her, Monsieur Stéphane!"

"Have some guts, old fellow!"

A groan escaped the unhappy man, hemmed in on all sides. Why, oh why had they suddenly pitched into him, why were they demanding this, as if something gave them the right, as if something important to them was at stake? And those faces bent over him, inflamed with a timeless wrath which he seemed to have seen on other faces, in a dream, perhaps. His little idyllic world, already upset by Martine, was now being blown to bits in this savage assault. He wanted to say something but could not. He lacked air, tried to stand up, but had not the strength. He leaned back, gasping, fighting for breath, but no one had pity. They continued to jostle and crowd round him, asking, demanding.

"If I were in your place . . ."

"In your place, I'd . . ."

"In your place . . ."

Yes, they had to see themselves in his place, imagine themselves bravely leaving this house, imagine themselves pure and incorruptible, in order to preserve their peace of mind. For one instant, one sole instant, and without intending to, he had presented them with another image of themselves: that was a sacrilege that nothing could redeem except a human sacrifice. How could they have pity? The mirror had been held up to them, with those simple words, "For weeks and months . . ." No, that could not be true. They could only deny such blindness and complaisance. Their clear consciences demanded it, as did their pure affection and sincere admiration; even Socrates lost a little of the sadness that usually marked his jaundiced face, where a glimmer of hope now flickered. It would be foolish to give up all those things, but folly could exist, it seemed? And Sylvia was already sighing with anticipatory pleasure: it would be so beautiful, so heroic. It would surround her with a pink cloud as she ran errands for the photographer, as she scrimped and scraped for him, denying herself the luxury of new clothes. Madame Prêtre alone attacked with joyless ferocity. For it was Sylvia she was condemning, Sylvia she was driving out. The dazed suffering that could be read on this man's face was Sylvia's suffering. It was life, and Madame Prêtre was the representative of that savage life which takes revenge without pleasure.

They would get him, thought Dr. Fisher. He would not be able to hold out against them. He was bound more surely by his big words and pretty phrases than by real bonds. That is, if he did not die of a heart attack, for his heart was in a bad condition. The Doctor thought of intervening. . . . But why? The fellow had wanted this, had sought it. He had challenged their beliefs. Dr. Fisher in his time, too, had challenged beliefs; and had paid the penalty. Morani would pay. Oh, how furious they all were, and how magnificent they looked in their unwholesome excitement:

they could not do without their cherished ideas. How could they endure their frightful little lives without that flattering screen? He had shattered it unintentionally, the poor devil; he had shown himself as they all were, inside and out. Blood had to flow in order to purify them. Oh, the jelly-fish!

The chairs. . . . The mandarins. . . . The hard and abject light. . . .

"You owe yourself that!"

"It would be so beautiful!"

"Why, we'd not be able to associate with you any more!"

He tried in vain to get up from his chair. He needed some air. . . . Ducas clutched feverishly at his sleeve. Madame Prêtre's hand was pressing upon his shoulder. Jean Cadou was braying right into his ear. And Germaine Lethuit, every time he tried to straighten up, flattened him out with a load of principles. He tried again to free himself, to thrust them aside. It was a nightmare, it was his childish nightmare in which he found himself surrounded by strange faces that were commanding him to account for a secret fault. At least, they might allow him to breathe! But they continued to harass him, in a panic of collective fury which lost all sense of decency.

"We'd not speak to you!"

"So, everything you told us was nothing but a lie?"

"You would be odious if . . ."

And the worthy Socrates himself, infected by the general madness, went so far as to grab Stéphane's arm and give it a shake.

"Can't you see that they're all against you?" he said, with his habitual knack for saying the wrong thing, though for once he wasn't so far off the mark.

All of them against him. As always? He felt again that childish distress against which he had struggled so hard. The Abbé Mourron and his Holy Eucharist, the marriage to Lou and his satisfaction at defying "them", his musical studies which had got him only as far as the Brasserie Dorée, all that had not been enough. They were all against him. Had he not obscurely felt it from the beginning? All against him, his parents, old One-Eye, and Louise, and Martine, and God Himself. Everything had crumbled in his hands. Always this fundamental injustice which in vain he had tried to compensate with words and phrases. To go on struggling, struggling. . . . He inhaled, with a loud and frightful choking sound. He was going to speak. And his eyes fell upon a little face which was not animated with rage, which was not "against him", which was only anxious, woeful, puzzled. Is this life? Sylvia seemed to be asking. Had she been mistaken and had the others been right? Was her mediocre happiness despicable? Was she condemned?

He was vanquished. At last he found the strength to thrust them aside and to go as far as the door (where the placard "Closed Monday" was as usual hanging askew), to open it a little, and to breathe some fresh air. Then he went back towards them and spoke in a voice that was miraculously steady.

"For several days," he said, "I have been considering it, to tell the truth. Your . . . advice has helped me to come to my decision. I shall go away."

He was not equal to the struggle, thought Dr. Fisher. Perhaps he would not have been strong enough, either, to hold his breath in the hideaway? Perhaps he would have called back the men who were already leaving and would have said, grandiloquently, "Kill me there, on the dead body of my wife!"? And that would have been futile, as futile as his departure now would be. As would be the years and years he would spend, a living dead man in a sanatorium (where else could he go, since his wife paid their living expenses?). Oh, why, why had he not had the strength to tell them the facts, to spit on their ideas and to live as he liked? His departure would but add another item to that absurd mythology with which he had poisoned his life. But what about himself, the noble refugee, Dr. Fisher? Had he not played a part in this? Not as brilliant as that of martyr, but on the whole . . .

"I shall go away," Stéphane said. And suddenly they moved aside, not knowing which way to look, their excitement fallen, eager to wash their hands of the whole thing.

Germaine Lethuit was the most unabashed. She was even enjoying a feeling of relaxation, as if after a physical exertion. Once more, virtuous principles had triumphed. Her footsteps as she returned to the villa at Meudon would be firmer than ever. Jean

Cadou shrugged; good, everything was as it had been and should be. No problems. That poor devil of a Morani didn't even realize that he'd been acting like a pimp. Just as Gérard never understood when people joked about their friendship. . . . No, Gérard did not understand.

Gérard Ducas was eager to be gone. The violence of that scene had been almost too much for him. Those screams and exclamations had been most unpleasant. It would take him at least three days to recover. It would be at least three days before the touching and ridiculous image that had stepped out of the calendar would sink back again, once more becoming inanimate; it would take that long for things to recover their mannered charm and their non-existence.

Sylvia was happy. She alone drew near the haggard man. "Oh, Monsieur Stéphane! I knew you'd do it. Mamma could say what she liked. . . ." Tears glittered in her eyes. She, too, had greatly suffered from an incomprehensible injustice. Stéphane was for a moment comforted. "It's magnificent, it's like something in a book. . . ." Tomorrow in her newspaper she would find other causes for sorrow and other tears would fall from her big dark eyes, other useless tears.

And the room emptied. Jean Cadou was the first to disappear, giving Gérard Ducas a discreet signal; then Ducas also vanished, after shaking hands with Stéphane silently, as if in a house visited by death. Dr. Fisher gave him a look, shrugged, and went out. Madame Prêtre had already returned to her lodge, the work of justice having been accomplished. But her wrath and grief were not appeased, and she would not open her door to Sylvia, who wanted to say good night to her before returning, quite exalted, to the photographer's lodging. And Germaine Lethuit spoke of a train to catch and gave him an energetic handshake.

They had gone. The chairs were stacked. The mandarins resumed possession of the room. The goldfish had some serious matters to debate. Socrates and Stéphane were alone.

"Can I offer you a drink?" said Socrates who, when embarrassed, always turned his back and rearranged the bottles. He did not understand why Monsieur Morani had given in. They were all determined, of course, but . . . Socrates forgot that he, too, had entered the fray and had wanted, with all of them, to see Stéphane succumb, heaven only knew why.

"A glass of white wine," said Stéphane weakly.

Life was difficult and mysterious. Why had Monsieur Morani given in? He had a wife who earned money (and after all, what did it matter how she earned it?), he had a flat. . . . Would he really go away and leave all that? Why did they all demand it? All these "whys" tired his brain. The only sure thing was that the house would be more tranquil once Monsieur Morani had left. Socrates poured out the wine in silence, averting his eyes. Unheard-of thing, he had no wish to talk.

Automatically, Stéphane took out his wallet, and no less automatically waited to hear Socrates' ritual objection to being paid. But there was no objection. All of a sudden, Stéphane Morani was a stranger, sitting at a bar in an unfamiliar bistro, and, his gesture completed, the little click of the coin falling upon the zinc was like that of a door being shut.

"Will you be home late, tonight?" he asked Louise.

"I don't know. Why?"

"I'd like to have a talk with you."

"Very well then, I'll be back for dinner."

He had gone downstairs slowly, his heart pained him. He had not met anyone he knew.

Outside, the long-awaited winter was there at last, although it was only the end of October. Sunshine filled that narrow, gaudy passageway, the street; the dry cold gave its peculiar resonance to the air, some women in coats too thin for this weather were putting up their collars, and the smoky railway-station had a comfortable look. It would be so easy to enter the Café Dupont, take off his top coat, relax in the warmth, and have a steaming hot grog, while watching the passersby through the protective glass of the window. He had done this every day for the past eight winters. But not today. Instead, he continued up the boulevard, leaving behind him the reassuring little shops and the little foreign restaurants in the kindly

shadow of the big rumbling railway-station. The boulevard was
swept by a cutting wind, the bright sun was a winter sun, without
warmth. Stéphane forced himself to breathe rhythmically, like a
swimmer cleaving through water, and continued on his way, step
by step. It seemed important to him to accomplish this journey
correctly. At last he reached the Brasserie, where as yet there were
only three or four customers.

Bruno and Marcel were already there, but they did not notice
Stéphane at once, and went on chatting. Perhaps they were talking
about him, in their usual gently mocking way. How strange to find
the Brasserie looking as usual, and Bruno and Marcel just the same.
The room had its usual dusty smell, and Toni was shamelessly
admiring herself in the mirror, smoothing her sweater over her
bountiful breasts. The restaurant looked as it always did in the early
afternoon, with only a few customers morosely staring at the purple
nudes and the lunatic Pierrot. He would have to go into the little
cloakroom, and put on the white jacket marked pompously with
initials. . . . How many times more would he put it on? Oh, the
reassuring laughter of Bruno and Marcel, oh, the tranquil ugliness
of the Brasserie!

"Feeling fit?" Marcel asked with a smile. "We'll have to be in
pretty good form tonight to play for the Americans. Might as well
not count on getting home before six o'clock in the morning.
Seems they've hired an accordionist, as well. To give them old-
fashioned dance-hall music. Crazy idea. Can I take the guitar and
leave the 'cello?"

"They're paying well," said Bruno. "Maybe I'll get to sing
something for them?"

It would be so easy to be there in the Brasserie without anything
having happened. . . . Stéphane had a headache, and he was going
to have to talk to Louise, to make decisions. . . . No, it was impossible.

"How's the baby girl?" he asked Marcel, mechanically.

"Oh, she's superb," said the guitarist proudly. "Superb! I'm
going to buy her a little push-chair with a canopy over it—saw one
today—that's what I'm going to buy with the American dollars we

get paid tonight. Boy, am I going to ram music-hall music down their throats! Those Americans must be insane, to give a party on a canal-barge! Imagine a piano on a canal-barge! And it's going to be a posh affair, much more so than the evening reception we played at in the rue de l'Université."

Stéphane wasn't in the least interested in the extra money, he was too tired. But Bruno and Marcel were apparently crazy to go, and what did it matter if he felt tired, now? He'd go along with them. . . . It's not true, all that business of last night, he told himself, as he had done as a child in the family sitting-room, while old One-Eye sat there staring at his school-report. I'm dreaming. It's not true.

"Ready?" said Bruno, as he did every day. "Since we're going to play tonight, let's not wear ourselves out here. Let's give them the *White Horse Inn* music, and then more of the same."

Stéphane followed Bruno into the little cloakroom behind the orchestra stand. Even this hideous little room with its greasy walls was something he did not want to leave. The very thought made him afraid. After all, he had been very comfortable here at the Brasserie Dorée, had felt sheltered here.

"Marcel has a shine on his baby daughter," said Bruno, "but he also seems to have a shine on one of the customers, did you see?"

Marcel had lingered on in the restaurant and was sitting beside a little blonde in a gooseberry-pink sweater.

"You don't look up to much," Bruno said to Stéphane. "Not feeling well? Hate the idea of tonight?"

Stéphane suddenly wanted to confide in someone.

"Listen, Bruno. I've decided to leave my wife."

"No!" said Bruno, with an amused look. "On account of the girl?"

"Heavens, no. I've told you hundreds of times she was never anything but a friend to me. But my situation is becoming shocking, and so . . ."

He tried to convince himself, tried to boil down the incident to the proportions of a decision he had freely made; yet the faces of his friends had pursued him all night long.

"But you—you mean to say that she . . . I mean, you'll go on working here?"

"Unfortunately, no."

In a way, Bruno's stupefaction was flattering. Already somewhat recovered from the rude blow received the night before, the machine had started functioning again, smothering his anxiety, quickly fabricating a fog, a reassuring fog. . . .

"But how are you going to live?" asked Bruno hesitantly. "And . . . well, I must say I don't understand."

"Good gracious, Bruno, I've always lived on almost nothing, I can live on still less." It was the first time in twenty-four hours that he had heard his own voice with pleasure. "I can even imagine living on charity, if need be, in some hospital or sanatorium."

"But you don't have Social Security," said Bruno. "And even supposing you did, you always said you'd prefer . . ."

"What I'd prefer doesn't enter into it, Bruno. I can't do otherwise." He was beginning really to believe it. He would repeat it soon to Louise. At last, he would surprise her; at last, he would surprise "them". She wasn't expecting this. At last she would be ashamed, would cry, perhaps. And he would remain aloof, dignified, ruthless. Maybe Dr. Fisher could get him into a sanatorium that would be decent enough? Perhaps they'd let him return occasionally to Paris?

"Well, I don't understand you," said Bruno. "If you'd told me it was for that girl . . . There's no accounting for tastes, as they say. But why make such a fuss? You're going to get yourself into a mess."

Stéphane was annoyed. He wanted to forget the happenings of the night before; he was intent, now, on seeing in a pleasant light what was going to happen after his "decision". "After all, Bruno, knowing what I know, I couldn't go on," he said.

"She's been like that for such a long time. . . ."

"But a rich man who keeps her—there's no other word for it!"

"He can afford to," Bruno said crossly. "And you're not obliged to know."

"Oh, after all!"

"Well, Morani, you're free to do as you like. All I can say is, I wouldn't like to be in your shoes. Naturally, we all have to paddle our own canoes, so it's not for me to criticize. But I do think . . ."

"What do you think?" asked Marcel, entering the cloakroom and taking down his white jacket.

"Nothing, nothing." But Bruno's expression remained glum. He had never taken Stéphane altogether seriously. But now what was he to think? Apparently the girl had not been Stéphane's mistress, as he had been convinced she was. He was suddenly overcome with embarrassment, realizing that he should have said something, applauded what Stéphane was doing. But after all, it was idiotic, nothing more could be said. He hurried to take his place on the orchestra stand.

"I can't imagine how I'm going to endure this evening," said Stéphane, as he sat down at the piano. "And on a canal-boat at that. It will be cold. And I'm exhausted from all these emotions."

Bruno said nothing, but stared moodily at the violin he played so badly.

"I say, Bruno, what's wrong?" said Stéphane. Couldn't the little fellow realize that now, more than ever before, Stéphane needed his friendship? Friendship and approval. The Brasserie would be with him to the end; while as for the "Celestials", he preferred to forget them. "Bruno," he insisted.

"Well, what do you expect me to say?" said Bruno. "Naturally, I see your point, but . . ." From now on, even if that "now on" represented only a few weeks, how could he possibly continue to joke with a man who had made such a decision? Stéphane should have waited, should not have announced this until the last minute, thought Bruno. Comradeship, the ritual chaffing, were no longer possible with this martyr. "Well, I'll admit," he said, speaking frankly, "it's sort of embarrassing!"

And Stéphane, once more, despite what had happened the previous night, despite their effect, pronounced again the fatal, the magic words. "But after all, you've always known about it," he said.

Always known? Could Bruno now admit that he had just let Stéphane go on talking, without bothering to believe anything he said? He remembered, now, Stéphane's denials in regard to Martine, but neither he nor Jacquotte had taken them seriously. And now. . . . Of course, Jacquotte would approve of all this: she was all for noble sentiments. And once more she would pester him to marry her. The thought bothered him and Bruno became still more gloomy. "Are we beginning, yes or no?" he asked.

Stéphane, forsaken at his piano, automatically began to play, and Marcel softly accompanied on the guitar. The Brasserie Dorée looked as usual, looked as it always did at three o'clock in the afternoon when the accumulated dust had been shifted about a little and the tables wiped off with a sour-smelling rag. But Stéphane's distress increased as the minutes passed. The morning had seemed like all mornings, so much so that he had doubted his memory of the evening before, and it wasn't until the moment of his departure that he had been able to say the words that condemned him: "I would like to have a talk with you, Louise." In vain he tried to work himself up again, to imagine her surprise and embarrassment. No, she would merely turn away from him as the others had done, as Bruno had done. He had never felt more than a mild and condescending liking for Bruno, but seeing him draw away now, as from a leper, made Stéphane almost weep. He began to relive the scene of the night before. The Brasserie, which had seemed so welcoming and protective, became strange and foreign, like the little Café Céleste. Yet he had thought he had taken root here, had become a fixture in this undistinguished quarter. And now everyone drew away from him. The old, old nightmare which he had carried within him since childhood was stirring in the dim depths of his consciousness and would, perhaps, emerge into view, become a reality. . . .

No, it must not. He played, and Bruno approached the microphone with elephantine grace, to intone an old refrain:

> *Les mains de femme . . .*
> *Je le proclame . . .*

The song over, Stéphane whispered loud enough to be heard: "When do we get paid for tonight? If they're like most

Americans . . ." Pitifully he attempted the bantering tone, but
without success.

"I asked them to pay us as soon as we arrived," said Bruno, still
with the same air of constraint.

And again Stéphane felt that wave of embarrassment that had
suddenly swept over him the night before, again saw those hostile,
flushed faces around him. He recalled the night at the restaurant
with Martine and saw again her desperate, spiteful little face; more
distantly in the past he saw again his wife's face, fixed in that same
morose look of incomprehension that Bruno displayed today. He
had felt nothing but kindness for them all, and they had all rejected
him. The old, old rancour, which he had borne within him was
stirring, threatening to explode.

The restaurant was filling up, time was passing. Stéphane played,
leafed through the stack of sheet-music placed before him. Toni
brought him coffee. He wanted very much to say to her, "Toni,
I'm leaving my wife", to see if she, too, would withdraw from him.
But it wasn't worth the trouble. In imagination he could already see
her respond with a laugh and a wink. He felt the warmth of the
restaurant, saw the pictures in all their ugliness, saw the manager
scowling at an unduly prolonged pause; but these humdrum,
everyday things did not reassure him; instead, they threatened and
judged him, as had the big shabby sitting-room at home and the
little dining-room with its cretonne, where hovered the scent of orris-
root associated with his mother. It was unjust, it was terrible. . . .
The old fear quickened within him. . . .

And time passed. Would it pass as quickly until the day when he
would have to . . . All at once it seemed to Stéphane that he had
always known this moment would come, the moment when
everyone would see him not as he wanted to be seen, the day when
even the places that had known him would no longer receive him.
The day when he himself would . . . The old shame revived in
him, and the wrath that followed it. But what had he done to put
them all against him?

Time passed. Automatically, resentfully, Stéphane continued to
play the piano. It had been years, it seemed to him, since he had

played with any pleasure. Defiantly, he signalled to Marcel, and began his variations on Chopin, but even Chopin betrayed him. He recalled the efforts he had once made, long ago, and how he had enjoyed, both as performer and spectator, his brilliant runs, the precision of his touch. That pleasure had disappeared when he realized at last that he would never play before a concert audience. Was it fair? There, too, something had slipped through his fingers without his knowing exactly when it happened. Could the "joys of music" which he had dinned into Louise's ears be experienced only in public? Or was it simply rancour that had stopped his own ears?

And time passed, until the moment came when Marcel desperately signalled to him, whispering at first, and finally almost shouting: "Your wife! Your wife is in the restaurant!"

There she was, and he was going to have to talk to her. He must talk to her. And no matter how desperately he tried to revive his old antagonism, he now felt nothing but utter weariness, a total inability to imagine why he need say or do anything. He was afraid, he was worn out, and above all, he didn't in the least want to talk to her. It was there again, the old nightmare, of explanation, of judgement, from which he had thought himself totally freed. . . .

The music stopped. The afternoon and his respite had come to an end.

Louise raised her eyes, smiling at him, as if they had made a rendezvous.

"You came here," he said stupidly.

"I thought, since I had nothing to do, that I might as well come here as wait for you at the house."

"Why, of course, my dear, of course. . . ."

He was rather embarrassed at seeing her there in the restaurant to which she had never before come, sitting there so calmly, motioning to the waiter.

"A martini. You, too?"

"Me, too," he said quickly, to get rid of the waiter. After all, he would have been as embarrassed had they met for this talk at home.

They were so unused to talking! But he was tired, terribly tired, and the party that evening would finish him. . . .

And why talk to her? And how? His ears were ringing, his heart thudded in a horrible way. Why, too, did she say nothing? She was waiting, as he was. He wished he might feel something of the anger against her that had sometimes filled him, but she appeared to him now in such a different light! She was wearing a dark tailormade, of a very soft shade of blue, which he had seen her wear only once or twice before. "The way your wife flaunts her luxury!" Martine had remarked. A wave of hatred welled up against that Martine who was at the bottom of all this, who had forced him to be here and on the point of saying things he had no wish to say.

The "regional orchestra" took its place. Louise remained silent, her head reflectively bent over her cocktail glass. The attitude gave her a thinner, more pensive face which, with the lowered eyelids, was devoid of any hardness. God! How powerless he felt, how close to tears, and above all how filled with a strange drowsiness, as if his body itself wanted to avoid the disagreeable scene.

"Listen," he said, forcing an aggressive tone, "I must talk to you. I must!"

"But you *are* talking to me," Louise said gently.

He thought she was making fun of him and felt with pleasure a resurgence of his old grudge against her, but then she raised her eyes, and he read in them an anxiety which again left him paralysed. He summoned to his aid all his past grievances, her incomprehension, her infidelity and her dull resistance to his finest eloquence. "This can't go on," he said, when the regional orchestra, to loud applause, struck up a sparkling piece.

"What?" She had not heard.

"This can't go on," he said, this time too loudly, so that a girl at the next table turned to stare. "This can't go on!"

"I heard, for goodness sake!" she replied rather shortly.

He had expected her to do as she had so often done in the past, to become indignant, exclaim, protest: "If you don't like it, well, you can just . . ." Then he would have found the strength to reply nobly, to show her the frightful life he was going to lead, dragging from hospital to hospital, penniless, ill, driven from pillar to post, the despised captive of the nurses, the victim of a hard-hearted wife. But without a feeling of anger to bolster him up, he hadn't the physical strength to begin a tirade.

"I must . . . I am going away," he said, clumsily. And he took a swallow of the martini, which made him cough.

"Going away where?" she said, not understanding.

He did not have the strength to reply.

"But why? Because . . ."

He shrugged. Could he make it all clear to her, could he tell her about Martine transformed into a Fury, about the others pitching into him, about his life which had fallen apart in his hands? "You can't understand," he said, wanting peace at all costs. How could she understand, when he himself did not understand what had happened?

"I suppose you heard that Henry . . ."

"Do you think I'm as stupid as all that?" he cut in. He was recovering something of his habitual tone.

"No, but I wanted to tell you," she began again, not at all reacting as he had expected. On the contrary, she appeared to be embarrassed. "I mean, you see, he's asked me to live with him," she said.

"I imagined he'd be willing to look after you, otherwise I would not have considered a separation which would leave you alone."

"Alone? Alone!" she scoffed. She was annoyed, and this made her suddenly resemble the everyday Louise, the Louise he knew. "I don't need you to support me, you know."

"I know it all too well, my dear," he said, recovering with some difficulty his usual tone of hurt dignity, the tone he had adopted on the occasion of her first outburst against him, long ago. Yes, that was the tone needed, yes, and those were the words. He would cling to them as to a life-buoy; then matters would go as they should, as he had so often imagined them. For he had imagined this interview; her anger, and then his words, casual, unconcerned, forgiving. What he had not imagined was that the interview might ever actually take place. It was now actually happening, in a café, over cocktails, and he had a strange feeling of emptiness and desolation. "I see that you can find happiness at last—your kind of happiness, at any rate, but since that's what you want, I don't feel that I have the right . . . I've done all I could for you, very badly, no doubt, but I did my best. I wasn't able to give you what you wanted, and now you have it. There's nothing for me to do but to wish you luck."

It was a little short, that speech. He had become entangled, had been unable to find the words he had so long cherished, had failed to give the melancholy smile at the end. He had not been in good form at all, but then . . . He wished she would get up and go, banging the door after her. Had he, however, enough money on him to pay for the drinks?

"So," she said, "this is what you want? You're serious?"

"Do I look as if I were joking, my dear?"

"I mean, you're not just saying all this because you're upset?"

"Why no, I'm not upset," he said wearily. (Oh, to sleep! To forget the spiteful faces, the indifference, and this woman whom he could not even manage to detest!) "Why no, I only want to do what's best for you."

"But, look here, Stéphane, stop and think, for heaven's sake. You are a sick man. . . ." She had not imagined that he would propose this, and yet she had always felt sure that something would happen and that, without having to decide for herself, she would, one day, be there in Henry's house, in Henry's bedroom, since that was her place. However, she had never imagined that Stéphane himself would bring this about, and as a result she was disconcerted, almost angry. Was this just one more of those tricks he liked to play on her, since he was so clever at putting on an act, at playing a kind of hide-and-seek, jumping out at her just when she least expected it, to shower her with reproaches that she scarcely understood? Was he merely laying another trap, as he had often done before? She almost expected him to say in another minute, "Now, confess, you've been unfaithful." Was he laying a trap so he could get the better of her?

"You know," she said with sudden bitterness, "it's always been like this with you. You like to make a fuss. You can't do anything without making a scene. Always the same, always . . ."

She realized that this was probably unjust. He had spoken simply enough, and was even acting calmly. Fundamentally what she was reproaching him for was the entire past, right up to Henry's transformation, of which he knew nothing. Naturally, if he knew about that, he would take advantage of it to put on still more superior airs.

"My dear, I don't believe I've made many scenes, as you say, over what you do. I'm even inclined to believe that few husbands would have behaved with as much moderation." The word "fuss" had hurt him. It was the very word Bruno had used. However, he fully realized that she was trying, no matter how awkwardly, to express in words the thing that had separated them almost from the beginning.

"After all, I don't see why you have to go away," she said crossly. She still suspected him of putting on an act.

"Isn't it what you've wanted?"

"I've never thought about it," she said sincerely.

"You've just admitted that another man has asked you to live with him."

How like him, she thought, to pretend not to want to pronounce Henry's name.

"But I said no."

"You said no?"

He was almost as surprised as she herself had been. Yet surely Lou was not in the habit of lying? "And why, may I ask?"

She did not know what to reply. Henry had said in bewilderment, "Yet you're not one of those dutiful women", and it was true. Stéphane would be alone and ill, but there were so many people alone and ill. Marriage, to her, was far from being a sacred institution: Stéphane had nauseated her with that word "sacred". Even so, it seemed to her that a kind of pact existed, not between herself and him, but between herself and life. She was there, in the rue d'Odessa, in that street, that house, that flat, and she felt it would

be an irresponsible act on her part to make any change in this order
of things. She would have liked to say all this, but could not find the
words. To express what she wanted to say required, it seemed to her,
something tangible, something with weight; or perhaps a graph
would do. She had always taken so little pains to say what she
thought, was so unused to making the effort. "It wasn't my place,"
were the words she finally uttered.

Stéphane lowered his eyes. His look was one of tender grief. He
possessed to a very high degree the childish capacity of letting himself be invaded by the feelings of the moment. For an instant he
forgot his distress, becoming completely preoccupied with the
pleasure of seeing Louise in a new light, a light which might prove
advantageous to him.

"My dear," he said, "you cannot imagine how touched I am by
your scruples! That one gesture, you know, is enough to make me
forget all the painful past. You thought of me alone and ill, and you
rejected the temptation, at least a part of the temptation, and
suddenly, Louise, the cup overflows, atonement has been made."
He took her hand in his. How he was enjoying this sublime moment.
Besides, why leave her?

"I don't understand a word of what you're trying to say,"
she replied peevishly. "Fussing and fuming! Always and for
ever!"

She was defending herself as best she could, as she had always
done, by making herself out to be more gross and dull-witted than
she was, while he went on charting his own intricate course, to her
great irritation.

"Perhaps," he said, "it's still finer in you, my dear, to have that
reaction unconsciously, and you deserve more credit than the more
enlightened. . . ."

The more enlightened! That meant him, no doubt! Always
words, to get nowhere! Nowhere! But Henry was wrong when
he said that the only way to get rid of Stéphane was to kill him.
Henry was going to be quite surprised! She contained her anger,
not flaring up as she usually did and as she felt like doing. . . . It
would be useless, since she would never see him again. The thought

made her feel strangely empty. She might have difficulty in imagining herself leaving Stéphane, but the idea of his leaving her was stupefying. At any rate, this would floor Henry.

"Listen," she said, speaking seriously, and not withdrawing her hand, "you can't do this. Where will you go?"

Stéphane, with displeasure, came down to earth. He had banished from his mind such unpleasant details. "I suppose," he said, "that Dr. Fisher will be able to find a place for me in some sanatorium or other in the provinces."

"But you've told me a hundred times that you didn't want to go to a sanatorium," she said weakly. She still could not banish the suspicion that he would change his mind. Oh, and then wouldn't Henry exult! And all this would just be one more scene to add to the others.

"I suppose I'll get used to it," he said hesitantly.

"But if we sell the flat, surely you'll accept . . ."

"Nothing, Louise, nothing. You must understand that my dignity would forbid . . ."

He noticed that she had said, "you'll accept", as if it were a foregone conclusion. "Of course," he said, "if we get a divorce, I'll take the blame."

"No, not that," she said, recovering her brusqueness, much to his satisfaction. "Why, Stéphane, you've nothing to blame yourself for," she ended, uncertainly.

"I'm to blame for not understanding you, Louise."

He returned to the elegiac tone with pleasure. It dispersed the too precise images and perhaps he obscurely hoped that everything might still dissolve in that fog. She was apparently embarrassed. In former times, she would have shrugged, but now she controlled herself, since he was going to leave her.

"Oh, we didn't get along too badly," she said awkwardly.

"Perhaps . . ." He was still hoping. "There are some things, you see, my dear Lou, that you never understood in me. Ambitions, perhaps very badly realized. You thought me incapable. . . ." He was artlessly twisting the facts, ascribing to her the reproaches he had made to himself. This was his usual method, but she did not flare up, for she had just realized absolutely that she had never believed he was capable of leaving her.

Their glasses were empty. "Would you like another?" he asked. The martini had momentarily alleviated his fatigue. "Two more martinis please," he said to the surprised waiter.

The orchestra stopped playing. The conductor stepped forward. "We now have the pleasure of presenting to our kind audience a promising young singer. Will you acclaim her a star? Her fate is in your hands! We present Annette Vidal!"

"I know them," said Stéphane, "those young hopefuls, singers, dancers. . . . They grab them when they come out of some studio, they pay them next to nothing. As you can imagine, the girls are only too glad of a chance to appear in public! Then, afterwards, nobody's interested in them, and they go back to being an artist's model. That's the kind of performers they have here!"

Louise laughed. She had always preferred a jesting Stéphane to a serious Stéphane. "I say, isn't she awful. She looks like Martine." Then, suddenly struck with an idea: "You're not going to marry Martine, are you?"

She said, "You're not going to!" Still talking as though about foregone conclusions. She had been easily persuaded; she couldn't have refused that man's proposals very firmly.

"How could I marry her even if I wanted to? You're all too well aware that I can't afford to support a wife." (After all, he admitted it.) "And even what income I do have won't continue much longer, for my health is steadily failing. And besides, as you know, Martine was never anything to me but a friend."

"Then you're really going to the hospital?" she said, in a final effort of disbelief.

She seemed to think he was incapable of such a thing. He had an outburst of vanity that was his undoing. "Most certainly!" he said. "I've told you, without wanting to hurt you, that my dignity will no longer permit me to endure this situation in which I seem to benefit by sharing you with someone else."

She said nothing for a moment, drank her martini slowly, set down the empty glass on the table. "I'm sorry. . . ." she said, almost in a whisper. "I'm sorry."

He had the idea that she was going to finish the sentence she had left in mid-air and that in some odd way her words would straighten out everything. But she said nothing more, merely sat there, fumbling with her handbag, as if trying to compose herself.

"I'm sorry too," he said. "I . . ."

If only they could have put into words what lay between them, what separated them today as always, something for which they wanted, for the first time, to tell each other they were not responsible. It seemed so absurd to be there, saying goodbye, when there was no real reason to separate. She had had her faults, obviously, thought Stéphane. But after so many years of marriage! And then, what had those faults to do with his fear and bitterness, or with those nightmare-faces that had surrounded him the night before? What had they to do with old One-Eye, with his parents, with music that had given him no joy? And yet the relationship had seemed clear to him, only yesterday. Had he been mistaken from the beginning? He gave her a look of distress.

Poor Stéphane! she thought. He was going to be so unhappy! Why, why did he do things he didn't want? She had always reproached him for it; why try to pretend to like paintings if you don't like them, why pretend to suffer if you don't suffer, why pretend to be faithful if you don't want to be? She was sure he must have been tempted more than once: he was not without charm, and women still ran after him. (She had had some suspicions on that score years ago, and these had contributed not a little to souring their relationship.) Even his marriage, she was inclined to believe, had been one of those things he had "felt in duty bound" to carry out, without wanting to. Why? She asked herself the question again, but her bitterness had disappeared, because he was really sincere. She had never entirely believed it, she had suspected him of acquiring a pleasant sense of superiority at small cost to himself. Yet this was not so, for if he left her, he would indeed pay the price. She did not feel pity for him, but rather a kind of astonished respect. Had she always been mistaken in him?

"Will you give me your address when you know it?" she asked, still in a whisper.

"What would be the use? You'll be so busy in your new life, with receptions, cocktail parties, and the rest."

She almost laughed aloud at his conventional notions of the life of "the wealthy", so foreign to everything that was really Henry. But why correct him?"

"I would like . . . " she began.

"Louise. . . ."

They hesitated another moment, suddenly appalled at the abyss of explanations that opened before them. They drew back from these. She stood up.

"I'll come for my things tomorrow afternoon," she said, speaking very rapidly, "while you're at work. Naturally you will go on living in the flat until you . . . until you've found something. Madame Prêtre will keep me posted. As for the divorce. . . . I suppose the lawyers will manage. . . ."

"Yes."

Was it, then, as simple as that? They remained facing each other, highly embarrassed.

"Au revoir."

"Au revoir."

They said the same words each noon, each evening. *Till we meet again.* She was gone, leaving on the table some money which the waiter came to take away. Stéphane sat there, motionless.

Outside, she hurried towards the metro. "It's idiotic," she thought, for her eyes were wet, "I didn't really even like him all that much. . ." Suddenly she changed her mind and went towards the taxicab rank. "There's no point in saving pennies now." The cab bore her away, a woman wearing a soft shade of blue, a still beautiful woman, with a puzzled look on her face.

She had really gone. He waited a moment, foolishly, for her to return. But such things don't happen after years of silence. He felt chilled, physically.

Bruno came and sat down at the table with him.

"Well? You've told her?"

"Yes," he replied mechanically, as if from the depths of a dream.

"Good, good. It's your right, isn't it? Now, let's forget it. Are you going home for supper? I'm just having a sandwich here. Want me to order one for you?"

"If you like."

"And a glass of beer?"

"If you like."

He felt shattered, and the warmth of the martinis had left him. He must banish this feeling of absurdity that had invaded him. If his leaving Louise was absurd, then his whole life was absurd. But had he not always been secretly convinced of this? He drank the beer thirstily.

"God only knows," groaned Bruno, "if they'll even give us anything to drink tonight. The last time . . ."

The last time, when they had substituted for a fashionable orchestra which had cancelled the engagement at the last minute, had been at a young girl's coming-out party in an eighteenth-century house with tapestries all over the place. The owners of the house had been highly indignant when, towards midnight, the musicians had asked for a drink during a break in the dancing.

"Naturally, Marcel is hanging round that little blonde again," Bruno went on. "Let's hope he doesn't get tight and disgrace us. On the whole, did things go off pretty well with your wife?" He asked nothing better than to believe they had, and to forget Stéphane's inexplicable behaviour, putting it all down as just one more of his eccentricities.

"On the whole, as you say, yes." Stéphane tried to recapture his usual sarcastic smile, but his trembling lips betrayed him, and he managed it badly.

"It was the best thing to do," said Bruno hurriedly. "When a man and woman don't love each other any more, they should part good friends. For my part, that's what I've always done."

"But it's not . . ." Stéphane began weakly. He would have liked to say, "It's not the same thing," but he hadn't the strength to argue. He had been beaten yesterday, when he had tried to defend himself; he wouldn't try to defend himself any more.

Bruno, however, wanted it to be "the same thing", and went on prodding. "After all, it's been a long time since you've really lived together, hasn't it? Naturally, people get tired . . ."

"But look here, that's not the point. It's a question of dignity. She herself, I believe, felt for a moment what I've tried in vain for so many years to arouse in her."

In the depths of his lassitude, he clung to that real surprise he had read on Louise's face. That, at least, existed. That was a fact. But his words sounded as if spoken in a vacuum, and he tried in vain to find on the little musician's face the warm, sympathetic and comforting affection he had often encountered there.

Bruno's expression indicated nothing more than the stubborn intention to banish all sorrow, all reflection, at any price, and the desire to be rid of this unhappy man. Bruno, too, was rejecting Stéphane. His pity and sympathy went out to the pianist who consoled himself with a girl for the infidelities of his wife; to the talkative old beau whose tirades he let go in one ear and out the other; to the slightly mad but likeable eccentric. For this disturbing individual who left a comfortable job, a cosy flat, and a wife with money, for no conceivable reason, he had no sympathy at all.

They fell silent. The hopeful young singer went on singing. She was being paid five hundred francs a day for a week here. She must think her career was made! Then, there would be another one, a penniless young student, or even a girl of good family—that had happened twice—inanely trilling Gallic ribaldries.

Alone, alone. If he could afford to refuse the fee for the evening performance, how he would have liked to sleep! His back was aching, his legs were heavy as lead, he was breathing with difficulty. But if he refused to play that night, what would Bruno say? Absurd as it might appear, he was now even afraid of good old Bruno, with his ridiculous little moustache, his big dreamy eyes, his hair slicked down with brilliantine. Why? Good old Bruno. . . . Ah, but the night before, hadn't he also naïvely believed in the goodness of his little circle of friends at the Café Céleste?

In an effort to relieve the constriction in his chest, he forced himself to inhale and exhale rhythmically, but the smoky air did not lend itself to this. He tried to think about nothing, to stare at the singer, who, though very young, was much too plump for her tight borrowed dress, whose forehead was covered with beads of sweat (the effort to hold that note was too much), and he pitied her, because he pitied himself. Oh, to sleep! How he would have liked to sleep, to forget the hostility that surrounded him, the decisions he must make. . . . Oh, to sleep!

But already it was time to go. Looming up, as if by a miracle, in the smoke-filled air of the restaurant, the chauffeur sent to fetch them was surveying them with disdain.

"Are you the musicians?"

"We're coming, we're coming," said Bruno eagerly.

They had some difficulty in dislodging Marcel from his table in the corner with his little blonde.

"Oh? Is it time to make the sailors dance?" said Marcel, with a laugh.

It was really something to laugh at, when people rich enough to live in a house of their own went to live on a canal-barge. Did they, Stéphane wondered, also sleep there? Someone was in the car already, a fellow with an accordion who seemed to be drunk.

"He picked me up in the street," said the accordionist, pointing to the chauffeur's back.

"Well," said Bruno, immediately at ease and ready to make friends with the stranger, "we'll take turn about."

Marcel absent-mindedly plucked at his guitar.

The car turned round the Étoile and entered the Avenue de la Grande-Armée. The melancholy street lamps lit an almost empty boulevard; one had the feeling of driving down a country road. "I hope they'll send us back in the car," said Stéphane dismally. They seemed to be going a great distance. He had the impression of being kidnapped, and that this excursion out of the city prefigured, in a way, his own departure.

Without reason, Marcel laughed. "You're lucky, Stéphane," he said, "I'll wager theirs is the only boat in Paris with a piano!"

In the darkness of the night, the illuminated barge seemed weirdly unreal. A lady, who was holding something round and red—it was a lantern—advanced towards them. "Oh, at last!" she exclaimed, speaking in French but with a strong American accent. "I was afraid you'd been in a road accident. Quick, let's have music! No, wait. Here are the envelopes, the agreed fee. By the end of the evening I hope no one will be in a condition to think of such things! Quick, you must have some whisky, to put you in the mood. . . . Yes, yes, you must have a drink. I wanted a good orchestra, a jazz orchestra, but Harold—my husband—said 'It will be more fun with a little French orchestra, and for the accordion, we can pick up some fellow in the street.' But you've brought a guitar! And the thingamagigs for the cha-cha-cha. I wanted a violin and a 'cello, more fun. It doesn't matter. Come in. We've got the drinks ready. Did you actually find the accordionist in the street, Jean?"

The chauffeur indicated, with some hint of disapproval, the man with the accordion.

"Another whisky, for the accordionist!"

"Thank you, Lady, but I have my own," the man of the street replied, very politely, extracting a bottle from his pocket.

The lady with the horsey face gave a laugh. "Your own! That's just wonderful. Let me have a taste?"

The man held out the bottle to her, with some apprehension. The lady, without the least hesitation, took a long pull at it. She was wearing a shimmering green dress, and she was excessively thin. A bearded man, wearing a sailor's striped jersey, came forward.

"Harold darling, here's your little orchestra. But they've brought a guitar, and that's not at all funny!"

"Did I ask for this orchestra, really?" said the gentleman, surveying them vaguely but benevolently.

"Why, for Heaven's sake, Harold, try to remember. . . ."

Stéphane was longing to sit down, even at a piano. Bells seemed to be ringing inside his head. Perhaps, after he had played a little, this would pass off? Mechanically he drank the whisky and stood there holding the empty glass in his hand, while the lady and gentleman went on with their argument as to which of them had

had the idea of bringing the Morani Trio here. They agreed on one
point: it was an absurd idea. Finally they let the musicians go down.

The piano and bar were in a room none too big, but not as small
as Stéphane had feared. The boat had evidently been specially
arranged for this type of festivity. But why did they not dance on
deck? Evidently, the season. The Morani Trio settled themselves to
wait. The host and hostess had remained on deck, where they were
welcoming the first arrivals.

"It's unbelievable!" said Marcel disgustedly. "Just think how
comfortable they could be in a fine big flat, and they choose to
wedge themselves into this musty old house-boat!"

"That's what Americans in France are made for," Bruno chuckled,
"to buy old dugouts like this at the price of swank flats."

"And to hire seedy little orchestras like ours at the price of a good
jazz band," said Stéphane, with an effort. He so wanted everything
to be exactly as usual, for one more night, at least! He must join in
their chaffing and bantering. Tomorrow, after a good sleep, he
would announce to his little circle that he had spoken to Louise.
He would regain—at what a price!—their admiration. Tomorrow,
too, he must leave. . . . But tonight he hadn't the strength to think
of it, even. Bruno had not laughed at his remark. It seemed to him
that Bruno was avoiding meeting his eyes.

The guests came noisily into the little room. "Play now, play!
Music!" called the hostess.

Stéphane resolved to play without even looking at the people
behind him.

"Let's make as much noise as we can," Marcel suggested. The
comparison with a jazz band had cut him to the quick.

He bent to his task, invoking the spirit of Django Reinhardt.
They all made "as much noise" as possible. The piano which
Stéphane's fingers struck had one broken key. It was, he supposed,
a hired piano. He tapped the keys, Marcel plucked his guitar, Bruno
frenetically shook his maracas. How much time passed at this,
Stéphane would have been hard put to say. The whisky, a drink to
which he was unaccustomed, surrounded him in a fog; he welcomed it at first, as a protection but soon it became a nuisance that

was finally painful. Fatigue weighed heavily in his head, circled his eyes, put a stabbing finger between his ribs. Fatigue was there beside him, trying to mix up the notes, confuse the scores. He had to make an enormous effort to strike, with regularity, the right chords. This was work he had accomplished for years without even thinking, these were the songs he had played hundreds of times, but tonight, as if wilfully, they seemed strange to him, strange and supremely difficult. He made so many mistakes that he was overcome with anguish, expecting someone to say, "But this won't do!" and drive him out, as he had been driven out everywhere.

Everywhere. He was alone, shorn of everything—and he tried in vain to find the words that had always comforted him: they eluded him as the notes eluded his fingers. His head was empty. He was no longer conscious of anything but the fatigue which was oppressing and stifling him, getting the better of his heavy limbs, making his tired heart throb with anguish, drawing the blood to his suffering head. The sounds he was making were intolerable, the noise they were making behind him was an insult. What had got into those people to make them carry on like that? As he played, the room had filled with people and the air was soon warm and stuffy. Stéphane turned round with displeasure to survey the noisy guests—and gave a start. Was it a nightmare, was it a mirage due to his dream of the night before, when he had·seen those transformed faces bending over him? The guests were large-headed monsters, human beings with animal heads. . . .

"It's a scream, isn't it?" said Marcel. "These Americans! They don't do anything like other people. Just imagine, they're celebrating carnival in October!"

Stéphane hadn't the strength to laugh. His forehead had broken out with sweat. Though he told himself that those gigantic heads were masks, that at this grotesque entertainment no one knew him or wished him ill, he averted his eyes, in fear, and when a masquerader wearing an enormous bull's head approached, its scarlet tongue thrust out, he shuddered with repulsion. Then the curled hair, the buck teeth, the hilarious face of the hostess appeared as she removed the grotesque papier-maché head.

"Bravo! What nerves you have! Here, have some champagne!" she said, handing them a bottle.

"Will you allow me to sing a number?" asked Bruno, dissatisfied with his modest rôle.

"Why yes, that will be great fun! But first, let's have the accordion," she said, and pulled on the scarlet bull's head again, as the accordion let loose.

Some couples were laughing and embracing. Others were trying to do an Apache dance, swaying their bodies, hands on hips. Still others, with their papier-maché heads half off, were drinking stupendously. The night was mild. Stéphane leaned against the piano, breathing deeply. At last, a little rest! He accepted a small glass of champagne. His chest was as if on fire.

"Swell people these are," said Bruno. "Champagne, and good champagne! Anyone can see they're foreigners!"

"Oh, I don't know," said Marcel, "I once played for a barrister who was celebrating his thirtieth year at the bar, and there was all the whisky and vodka you could drink."

Neither one asked Stéphane how he felt. Bruno did not hand him his vast silk handkerchief to wipe away the sweat, as he usually did. They were paying no attention to him; it was as if they imagined the piano had been playing all by itself.

"Look at that one!" Bruno said. "My eye, he's tight! And it isn't midnight yet!"

"Oh, we're not near the end. This is a shindy that won't end till five o'clock in the morning," Marcel said.

"Do you think they'll send us back in the car?" asked Stéphane. His own voice sounded strange to him and it must have sounded strange to the others for they turned round and looked at him with some anxiety.

"Oh," muttered Bruno, "with this fee, you can well afford a taxi."

The tumult in the room was increasing. Bruno's attitude struck Stéphane as oddly distant. Oh, to be nothing but a musician like the others, mediocre and satisfied. . . . Oh, to be one of those guests, already half drunk and protected by a hideous mask. Oh, to melt

in the crowd, to dissolve. . . . Not yet midnight! And every passing
minute increased his anguish. Yesterday, after the terrible scene,
the thought of his interview with Louise had sustained him: he
had had that to think of all day long. He would say . . . She would
reply . . . He had imagined this scene for so long, without really
believing it would come about, that it had become for him like
some huge stone in his path, hiding from his view whatever lay
beyond. And now that the stone had at last been thrust aside, where
did that deserted and solitary road lead? "I'll pick up my things
tomorrow afternoon," she had said. The flat would be empty
tonight. He would not wake up at the sound of Louise coming in
and banging the door, as she always did. True, she came home so
late, always. He would not have to give her his fee, previously
docked of a small portion. Besides, he'd now need all of it to pay
for his meals in restaurants until . . . "If you like, I could have you
put under the care of the League for Political Refugees," Dr. Fisher
had said one day, "I have quite a lot of influence, there's my
cousin. . . ." Those words "put under the care of" had made a
strange impression on him. The League had a sanatorium. The
League could do this and that. The physician of the League. So
this was what had been hidden behind the stone? Was this the
future?

"Let's go, fellows," said Bruno, enlivened by champagne.
"Let's go. It's our turn. The Panama-Postman song, Stéphane!"

And even before Stéphane had finished the prelude, Bruno
recklessly launched into:

> *Le Facteur . . . de Panama*
> *Savait danser, savait danser*
> *le cha-cha-cha . . .*

The laughter that arose was explosive. It hurt, that immense
roar. Were there echoes of it on the banks of the Seine? No matter,
Stéphane seemed to hear several echoes.

A fan had been turned on, but it blew nothing except stale, warm
and suffocating air. The guests were drinking more and more, and
no one made a move to leave. They created such a commotion that

an orchestra was scarcely needed. From time to time a woman screamed. People were still arriving in the already overcrowded room. "Let's have some fresh air!" cried someone. A porthole was opened but it made little difference.

Stéphane's fingers continued to strike the keys. He was conscious of this and of his fatigue. Behind the stone . . . It was the nightmare of a child, in which masqueraders appeared. . . .

Bruno nudged Marcel. "Get an eye-full of that, will you!"

A duck-headed woman dancing alone in the middle of the room had just pulled off her blouse and flung it into the air, laughing shrilly. Under the grotesque disguise, her bare breasts were revealed, voluminous. Marcel stopped playing; Stéphane turned, crashing out a masterful discord on the piano keys. The hostess hurried up, her mask thrown back, her face alight with fury. "Will you kindly go on playing! You're paid to play, not to stare!"

They began again, off-key. The woman kept on dancing in the middle of the room, her breasts swinging, unreal and at the same time absurdly present under that enormous green duck-head which was almost terrifying. After the first moment of surprise, an applauding circle had formed around her. "Another! Let's have another!" someone shouted.

Women uttering little shrieks, refusing the ready assistance of the men who were trying to unhook their bodices, collapsed in hysterical laughter. Some men danced around the floor, looking for a willing victim.

The Morani Trio came to the end of a piece and it was the accordionist's turn; but the hostess, after vainly trying to revive the slumbering tramp, started to berate the orchestra shrilly. "Don't stop playing! No matter what happens, keep on playing! Play! Play! Play!"

Stéphane had removed his jacket; he now took off his waistcoat, for the heat was intolerable, his whole body was burning hot, even his arms and hands. But he must keep at it, mustn't stop. The keys fled before him and he tried to catch up with them; his thoughts fled before him and he tried to collect them; he had the feeling that he must run without stopping from left to right in order to make his thoughts have any sense. Suddenly a memory loomed here, a face there, and always they were painful memories, enemy faces. "You're not an eagle"—that was old One-Eye. "It's not for people of our class"—that brought up the memory of his desolate parents. "Oh, you aggravate me, you aggravate me!"— and he saw the lovely face of Lou at the age of thirty. "Oh, I was sure of it"—and there was the pale face of Martine, triumphant and desperate. . . . And those people at the Café Céleste yesterday, and everyone, the whole world against him, and now all these masqueraders. . . .

He pounded the keys until his fingers hurt, yet had the sensation of producing no sound. It was a nightmare resembling that of the night before, when he had spoken in vain to hard, shut faces, pitiless, ready in advance to condemn him.

The hostess was wearing her bull's head mask again, but stood nearby, shouting from time to time at the orchestra, in an effort to urge them on: "Keep going, play louder! I'll pay you extra. Louder! Louder!"

Two men came up, interrupting her to draw her into the applauding circle. One of them was disguised as a drunk, and clearly the face beneath the mask could not have been very different; the other was disguised as a good-natured lion. They seized the hostess, the lion taking her by one hand, the drunk by the other, forcing her into a lumbering dance, crushing the poor creature between them. She was soon out of breath. The lion pulled her, the drunk pushed her, as Bruno howled into the microphone, to a maliciously stepped-up rhythm set by Marcel and followed by Stéphane as in a dream

> *Reviens, reviens, reviens-moi, chérie,*
> *C'est l'instant . . .*

Now the drunk seized the skinny hostess by her hips and, to loud applause, flung her upward, where she banged her head hard against the ceiling. The lion caught her awkwardly and tried to encircle her in his arms to dance with him again, but she fought him off furiously, laughing all the time. A man in shorts, wearing the mask of a moustachioed bon viveur and crowned by a silk topper, loomed up from nowhere.

"You're not one of the guests!" screamed the hostess.

In her shrill voice was a note of distress, and Stéphane, despite himself, turned to stare. The bon viveur indignantly clasped her in his arms (she was grotesque, wearing that bull's head), the lion held her, and the drunk tugged at the zippered fastening of the shimmering green dress (from Saks of Fifth Avenue). "No!" she howled in rage, as the dress fell open to the hips.

Her scraggy body, three-quarters naked, brown and flabby, was glimpsed only briefly as she fled through the crowd of dancers, and disappeared, still surmounted by the fiery red head of a bull. . . . A stupendous burst of laughter arose, a delirium of laughter, as other half-naked women appeared, some without bodices, others casting off their long skirts, their breasts bearing red marks from the boning in their discarded dresses, their heavy thighs waggling above high heels; and those heads, those enormous heads that all the guests continued to wear despite the heat and concealing Heaven knew what behind those perpetual and sinister grins. . . . Intoxicated, infatuated with noise, everyone who still preserved a semblance of sobriety came towards the musicians, holding out their glasses, imploring them for more and more noise. The stench of sweating flesh became stronger, the air was constantly harder to breathe, Stéphane felt suffocated, his head swam. That woman being undressed and screaming, those masqueraders with their impassive false faces, those were the enemies relentlessly pursuing him; his enemies who had laughed and cruelly unveiled the skinny nakedness of the woman who had fled from the jeers of the crowd.

Why was he there, at grips with his enemies? He was stifled and crushed by the lack of air and the noise, his strength was used up in the mere act of controlling his hands, his head, he was consumed by the hope that suddenly everything would stop, would hush, would change, and that the obscene nakedness of those bodies would be covered, that the gigantic false heads would become human again. . . . But the heads swelled larger and larger, appeared to be laughing louder and louder; they were crowding in on him, defying him. . . . He tried to cry out to Bruno and Marcel, to make them turn round and come to his aid, but he hadn't sufficient breath to scream and his lips moved to no avail.

Just then a creature with the head of a dog, dressed only in a short pink satin jacket and black slippers, climbed upon the platform, drew near him. . . . He must flee, must flee. . . . In vain he tried to find within himself something with which to defend and protect himself. He was drained of words and phrases. And yesterday his words had only excited the demons. Nothing would protect him now; if the masqueraders wanted, he, too, would find himself naked among the jeering crowd. The fear in his breast grew, fluttered and swelled like a bird beating its wings. And the foul creature was there, quite close, and Marcel and Bruno did not defend him but remained with their backs turned, far removed from him, and the creature was about to place its hand on Stéphane's shoulder, its hand on which glimmered a colourless gem. No! In a final effort that tore his breast, he stood up abruptly, overturning the piano stool. A bottle smashed to the floor. Human bodies pressed against him, but he thrust them aside, staggered, almost fell. . . . With a struggle he managed to climb the steep little stairs to the gangway. Now he would never know the sex of the vile creature of whom he had seen nothing but a fat, naked back.

Outside, he was outside at last. He leaned against a tree on the quay, avidly breathing in the fresh air. He must go home, back to the house, the refuge. That was his sole thought. He must go home. At the end of the quay was a light. How many trees were between him and the light? Perhaps ten, perhaps thirty. But someone might come to look for him, fetch him back. He set himself to walk, counting the trees: one . . . two . . . He was panting, his heart was pounding, but fear urged him on. The house, the refuge. Oh, to shut himself in a room where no one could reach him! Oh, to be where no one could lie in wait for him, spy upon him. Oh, the silence, the protective darkness! He pressed forward, almost at a run. The air seemed cooler. He had left his jacket and waistcoat behind him, down there, but no matter. He would willingly have left his skin down there, to be even more free of that fusty air with

its smell of blood. Yes, that was what had made him run away.
Tonight on the canal-boat, as well as the night before at the Café
Céleste, he had smelt blood. With all the fear there was in him he
had sensed the delirium of the mob and had been afraid of being
its victim. He almost ran. A tree, another tree. It was dark and silent
now. He had been running along this quay for an eternity. But
if he had to run for ever, he would go on until he collapsed.
The refuge, the house, the room, the light. The quay was endless
and his legs were heavy as lead. It was like being in one of those
dreams where, no matter how fast one runs, the very air seems to
stop you and the landscape remains the same. He had never made
such an effort before. Then at last, at the very end of the quay, was
a light which he managed to approach. Beneath it was an open space.
It was a metro station. . . .

At the very moment he placed his burning palm on the cool
stair rail, at that exact moment, the thought returned to him:
the house towards which he was hurrying was no longer his. Tomorrow or within a week, he must leave it. He no longer had a
refuge.

Slowly he went down the stairs, sank into the bowels of the
earth. He held out a ticket, which had miraculously turned up in his
pocket, heard the sharp click of the ticket-collector's punch.

"The first train's just gone through," said a man who was sitting
in the shadows.

The first train. That meant it was morning now. He went through
to the station platform and let himself sink down on a bench. He
felt broken. Far ahead of him, his thoughts unrolled like a tapestry
which had nothing to do with him. He leaned his head against an
automatic weighing-machine and stared vacantly at a poster on the
opposite platform. With difficulty he managed to spell out the
words, letter by letter: it was an advertisement for Bornibus
mustard, in three colours: a brownish red bench beneath the letters
B-O-R-N-I-B-U-S stretched away to infinity. The rails at the bottom
of the black hole stretched away to infinity and vanished in the
vast, sinuous tunnel, deceptively mysterious. . . . Perhaps the
thought was due to his immense fatigue, but it passed through his

mind: could that be the goal which had been hidden from him a short while ago?

Stéphane let himself drift, and found a sort of comfort in his total despair. The noise was far behind him, at any rate, he had left behind him the loud laughter, the shrill screams, the nightmare faces, and the ignoble and good-natured individual who had guessed his fear. . . . In the metro station there were only reassuring noises, the sounds of machinery, the bell ringing, the sliding door that closed by magic, uselessly, for there was no one. He was alone. Only a gentle rumbling disturbed the maternal viscera which sheltered him. No one knew where he was, no one could pursue him now. From time to time, unconsciously, he shuddered. His eyelids closed. Unexpectedly, he found a moment of peace as he imagined the circumvolutions of this subterranean labyrinth of Paris, this vast network of tunnels in a corner of which he was coiled up, protected from everything, isolated from everything. His mind, it seemed to him, was sliding along the rails, circulating freely, making light of difficulties. From time to time, like ghostly impediments, faces loomed up, soon to be effaced, but hideous like those at the masquerade. There was Martine's pale face and her pointing finger repelling him; the face of Ducas, contorted in a snarl; Dr. Fisher's, flushed and darkened with cruel joy; Madame Prêtre's, like an animal, sniffing disgustedly at his fear; Sylvia's, demanding her share of inane exaltation. . . . He thrust them aside and thrust aside the obsessing image of the sexless creature, half naked under the pink silk jacket, and the memory of the creature's little hand, fat, warm, nauseating. Again, again, his mind slid over the rails, faltering at the crossings and junctions, seeking once more some part of that person who had been himself. Here and there he caught a word, a phrase, a gesture. . . . Painfully he tried once more to piece these things together, but the meaning always eluded him and the phantoms always returned. For such and such a word revived an avenging Martine, another brought up the flashing-eyed Louise of former times, and still another called up the terrible faces of the night before, in the midst of which, incongruously, loomed the masquerader in the pink silk jacket. But how could he go on living if he dared not use those words and attitudes that had ruled his life?

He was there, his head leaning against the automatic weighing-machine, his body broken with fatigue, but his mind still struggled against a fascinating and terrible dissolution. The mind still struggled to be Stéphane.

To be Stéphane . . . to find again the words and phrases which had been a bulwark. But the phrases he brought together with enormous effort resuscitated monsters. The mirrors he set up reflected hideous faces. Must he allow the bulwark to collapse, must he open the gates to fear?

Leaning against the automatic weighing-machine, his body shuddered, but he did not feel it. His limbs trembled, but he did not feel them. The reassuring metro station was humming with activity, now; two or three people had sat down farther along on the brown bench. Slowly even his head was reached by that paralysis. The mind continued to defend itself, but with failing strength. Fear had become incarnate in that plump little hand on his shoulder, and gained ground. . . .

And now, despite himself, he was walking down a narrow corridor, at the end of which was a shut door. That corridor might be the hallway of the little house in Signac, or the cool, damp corridor of the nearby school, or the presbytery where the child Stéphane had thought to find a refuge, or perhaps the corridor of the big echoing house with the shabby draperies—might it be the passageway that led into the drawing-room? Or was it the dusty corridor at the town hall, where he and Louise had gone alone? That passageway had opened (if one could call it an opening, since it had led into a misunderstanding as shut and real as a bedroom), into the registrar's office, where civil marriages took place. Or it might be one of the endless corridors of the war (that war when he was a prisoner starving, but free of responsibility, and not too miserable); or could it be the hallway, closer to him in time, that led past Martine's door? And all those doors which had so unjustly refused to open: the revelation that had not come at his First Communion, despite the Abbé Mourron's promise; his marriage, despite the love he had had for Louise; music, despite the world's respect for "the arts". Right down to the last attempt he had made, that of friendship; all those doors, all those refuges had remained shut against him, and between these walls of injustice, where was this corridor leading him, now that he was weak and defenceless?

However, he continued to advance down the corridor, while his body, the body of that thin man in shirt-sleeves, shuddering, leant its head against the automatic weighing-machine, roared at by the passing trains, shaken by shadows, whispered at by phantoms. Down the corridor he went, dragging after him that fatigue which was no longer in his body but in his very mind, so that bones, muscles and nerves weighed ever more heavily, became ever harder to drag along. Would prostration be his final refuge? Would sheer fatigue prevent his reaching the end of the corridor? Already he had gone beyond the fear of this evening, the fright of yesterday; already, in passing, he had recognized the grotesque and stupid pleasure he had derived from a submissive Martine; already, beyond that, he had reached the old hope he had once entertained of wounding Louise, of opening in her resisting soul a wound identical to his own. . . . And the last fear was ready to seize him, that of his childhood—the fear that had neither name nor face and which he must encounter if he continued to advance. . . . Already he had gone beyond music, even, which was too demanding to be a friend; farther, still farther, there was old One-Eye taking his measure, weighing him up and his humiliation alike; and even still farther there was the humble face of his father and a child's revolt against the fear of that man who had bequeathed him nothing but fear. And farther on, much farther still, more painfully embedded in his brain, in his living flesh (so deeply embedded that at the instant the thought grazed it his whole body flinched), there was the anguish of being judged, the consciousness of a nameless weakness, the shame of endorsing the judgement which condemned him, and there was that knot which held body and soul together, that point so tenuous that it would take an infinitely fine needle to penetrate it: the rancour against Him the All-Knowing.

The door had finally opened. The needle at last penetrated the knot. The man remained motionless, suspended, his breathing arrested, his mind motionless like a weight of gold at the end of a thread, so fine and light that the merest breath of air would move it, but which did not move but remained fixed there by some unknown miracle, glimmering faintly in the shadows. The man was naked, powerless; and in that moment of catching his breath, he at last knew what he had always known. He saw himself, judged himself, dissolved into nothingness. Shorn of his protective coverings, flayed alive, his whole being quivered under the stab of annihilation. . . . And the needle sank into the invisible wound; the flesh was sound, what no longer was had never been. Time flowed backward, a white, luminous, palpable flood; wounds had ceased to be, the monsters were no more, dead words and gestures swelled and came to life. The past itself melted into thin air; and revived, justified; time exploded. Quite suddenly level again, the horizon extended in all directions. The future was set down there, the past was set down there, two objects that could be named without fear. He saw them, named them, without knowing whether they were memories or forebodings, saw the mediocre years spent in self-avoidance, saw the mediocre years to come, the grey days, the grey bedrooms, the futile herd of invalids, the inadequate pity, the weary kindness, the gentle scorn. A whole procession of good souls, kind care, paltry pleasures, even . . . He saw those mindless days, saw even the forgetfulness of this unforgettable moment, the oblivion which was there, within reach. One second more he oscillated in a miraculous equilibrium—and oblivion submerged him. He must now, with dizzying speed, turn back towards that man slumped with closed eyes on the bench, who could now only whimper softly, that man whom an ambulance would soon bear away towards a mindless world.

The world around Martine took shape, things fell into place: objects, houses, streets, the city; circles, squares, lines; colours, smells, shapes; and finally men. And Martine was in accord with all this.

"What time is it?" she called to Gisèle.

"Five o'clock!"

One more hour till closing time.

"A jar of strawberry jam, please."

Martine recognized that face. "Why, in a jiffy, Madame Prêtre. Here you are."

"You seem to be in a good humour, at any rate!"

"And why not, Madame Prêtre?"

She liked words, syllables, names, her own name, Martine. "But oh, for closing time!" she said aloud.

"You're in something of a hurry, aren't you, Mademoiselle Fortin?" smiled Gisèle.

"I thought we'd agreed on first names from now on?"

"I'm not used to it yet. What about having supper together?"

"I can't."

"Oh, ho! I see why you're so anxious for closing time."

"Don't be silly," said Martine, but she burst out laughing.

She cast an admiring glance round her. Food was stacked all around, and she was hungry. The cheap perfume that an automatic vapourizer dispensed at regular intervals was called "Pine Forests" and she inhaled the scent avidly. Her eyes feasted on the colours: the blue plastic dustbins, the yellow pails, the mauve nylon underwear, the multicoloured socks for children. She liked to read the labels where the prices were importantly displayed. Her wages would let her buy such and such a garment, and not another. Her taste permitted her to choose one item of food and not another. How good it was to have her place in the world, to be Martine, to earn the money she earned, to live in such a street, such a house. . . . How pleasant the certitude of being in a world devoid of mysteries and secrets! How well organized things were, the seasons, the years, everything that could be measured and named, a world where, from now on, she was in her place, she, too, measured and named, with that young man who was waiting for her in her bed-sitting-room. The impossible sum had been added up, she knew its total. Would there be other numbers, other harmonies, another equilibrium of which the one she was now enjoying was but a rehearsal, an insignificant preview? She would know, one day, perhaps. Or perhaps she would never know, she thought, as she left the Prisunic store, along with many other people.

Without stopping in the bar, where a number of customers were assembled, people of no interest to her, she climbed the stairs.

The young man was waiting for her, yawning, in her room. He had a little moustache and was a Post Office employee with a retirement pension to look forward to.

"I feel like some steak and chips," he said as he kissed her. "Let's eat first, and then go on to the cinema. They're showing an English film at the Miramar."

"Why not? But let's not eat downstairs. Let's go to a real restaurant: I'll pay."

He agreed. He did not mind being invited out at her expense. Martine had casually let him know of the existence of her small capital. He might marry her. That, too, was good. She asked no questions. She would pay the bill, they would go to the cinema and enjoy words and acts of middling quality. She would like those words and gestures, would like being Martine, now that she was free of that man, Stéphane, whose name she had almost forgotten.

The chairs were stacked, the goldfish were circulating in their tank, and the placard "Greek Cuisine" was turned round to "Closed Mondays".

"I think we ought to organize a political club," said Monsieur Levassu firmly. He was the new owner of the Morani flat. "If things are going badly here in France, it's because people do not know their rights!"

Germaine Lethuit beamingly approved. Now, here was a man who understood his responsibilities. If everyone did his duty, all would be well with the world. She herself had always done her duty; let others do the same.

"Politics? You really think so?" asked Gérard Ducas. He considered that the newcomer had assumed quite a lot of importance in the house. Well, after all, perhaps men of action were needed, so as to provide leisure for irresponsible artists. By next year, Monsieur Levassu (who ran a big shoe company), would no doubt be the agent for the co-operative tenants of the house. "Leave it to me, my dear man, I'm used to this sort of thing," he often said. And he had already bought two of Jean's canvases! And, so he said, he knew people who knew nothing about modern art but asked for nothing better than to learn. What a funny face he'd got, this Levassu! Like a massive Breton sideboard, ornamented with hideous little columns. Jean had condescended to laugh at the comparison. One day, when the antiquary had sold enough milk-glass lamps and mahogany chests of drawers, he would retire and they would go to live in Saint-Jean-le-Vieil, among the roses. That, too, would be deliciously picturesque. And Jean would decorate their house which they would buy for a song. Oh, the purity of that artistic retreat!

"Political and . . . pictorial," said Monsieur Levassu, with a laugh. "We'll not neglect art, believe me. People always imagine that tradesmen are savages, but . . ."

"For my part, I'm for politics," Madame Prêtre put it. "We all have the right to know what's going on in this country. We might . . . I don't know what. But I'm sure there are scandals that . . . Oh, politics, there you certainly have something that's none too clean!" It would please her to know the dirty side of politics, to work up indignation, to laugh again. . . . It would please her to put some of her shrewdness to use, some of her wiliness, which were of no use to her since they could no longer be of help to Sylvia. Politics. . . . "There you have something that's none too clean," she repeated, vengefully convinced. And yet, in the old days, she had felt very comfortable in this faulty world. What was the source today of her feeling of discomfort, her new aggressiveness? Surely she was not one to be duped by the sentimentality of a Sylvia, now in a swollen state of expectancy, or deluded by everyone's expressed satisfaction over "Our poor dear Stéphane"—whom none of them would ever go to visit in that sanatorium in the Haute-Savoie; no one had even asked what it was called. She was no dupe and never would be, but she no longer derived the same unadulterated pleasure from her knowledge and experience. The world, for the Madame Prêtres, would never be "clean", but that they suffered on that account was already, perhaps, a kind of redemption.

"A glass of wine, Monsieur Iean?" Socrates feebly proposed. He did not look at all well. "Verging on hysteria", was the mental diagnosis of Dr. Fisher, who was there from habit. There was a new mortgage on the Café Céleste, which Constantine and Dimitrios were devouring by little mouthfuls. One day he would have to go, Socrates reflected, like poor Monsieur Morani, to beg in the streets or to become an employee, working for others. For others! And he would no longer be able to uphold by lies the colossal idol he had erected and which was threatening to crush him. Supreme humiliation? Or supreme deliverance? Who could tell?

Jean had one drink, and then, at Monsieur Levassu's invitation, had another, as an artist should. A good fellow, this Levassu, without problems, and an admirer of Jean's. Good fellow, Gérard. An artist needed admiration, had a right to it. He needed nothing else; as for the problems and the affections of others, their scramble for possessions, let them have it, he wanted none of that. But suppose the artist were not an artist? What then would remain to him, since he had refused all else? In Jean's eyes there appeared that look of stubbornness and melancholy which, for a moment, turned him into a human being.

"It's a scream, that little thing there," said Levassu, speaking as a connoisseur of art. "What god is it? Is it Chinese? I'll bet this little restaurant's hauling in the money."

Dr. Fisher sighed as he watched Levassu's performance. He was just the kind of man who, in another week, would be tapping him on the shoulder, condescendingly, as they all did, forgetting that he, Dr. Fisher, was decorated by the government, backed by the Ministry. . . . It didn't matter, it didn't matter at all. As he had thought before—how many weeks had it been now since Morani went away—all this was quite futile. In any case, Morani would have had to be put in a sanatorium sooner or later. He didn't know it, or didn't want to know it, true. And he had chosen freely? Agreed. All the same, it was all quite futile. "And yet," Dr. Fisher reflected, "I'm the only one here who misses him a little." Then,

replying to the portly Levassu: "No one knows. No one."
No one knew the name of the little gilded god.

It was time for dinner, but Louise had fallen asleep. As always,
her face was hidden in the crook of her arm, and her blue-black
hair, undone, almost covered the bare shoulder. Henry remained
motionless, lying there beside her.

Would she again, tonight, have that look of vague and gentle
astonishment that he did not like to see in her eyes? Would she
again, tonight, knit her dark brows, like a child trying without
pleasure to solve a difficult problem? Or would he succeed, for one
evening, for a week, or even for a few weeks, in defending her, in
saving her? He waited, as he would often wait again. He had sometimes feared old age, the emptiness of days when, his work accomplished, there would remain nothing but to wait for only the Lord
knew what. In that emptiness the voice of Mozart would again have
risen, and would have signified something, perhaps. But now, there
would be no emptiness. He had a job to do, a function in life.
He would save her. He would stay beside her, like a sentinel, for
ever. She would not hear the voice of Mozart.

Night fell in the studio. He did not light the lamp. She was still
sleeping, she might sleep until next morning. No matter. He would
keep watch. For a moment, she turned towards him, uncovering
her face. He expected the worst, expected to hear her murmur:
"Stéphane. . . ." But she only complained softly, in a childlike
voice: ". . . so tired . . ." and went back to sleep in his arms.